# Time's Hammers

## James Sallis

**THE COLLECTED SHORT FICTION OF JAMES SALLIS**

### *Praise for James Sallis*

"It is quite possible that speaking of Jim Sallis in the same tone as Poe and Dostoevski is not overblowing on my part. His early work indicates a mind and a talent of uncommon dimensions... He may well be one of the significant ones."

—HARLAN ELLISON

"James Sallis is one of the best writers in the United States."

—SUE WALKER, EDITOR, NEGATIVE CAPABILITY

"James Sallis's extraordinary fiction is distinguished...honesty and meticulous artistry."

—TWENTIETH CENTURY FICTION WRITERS

## Novels

*The Long-Legged Fly*
*Moth*
*Black Hornet*
*Eye of the Cricket*
*Bluebottle*
*Death Will Have Your Eyes*
*Renderings*

## Stories

*A Few Last Words*
*Limits of the Sensible World*

## Other

*Chester Himes: A Life*
*Difficult Lives*
*Gently into the Land of the Meateaters*
*Ash of Stars: On the Writing of Samuel R. Delany (editor)*
*Saint Glinglin by Raymond Queneau (translator)*
*The Guitar Players*
*Jazz Guitars (editor)*
*The Guitar in Jazz (editor)*

## Forthcoming

*Ghost of a Flea (novel)*
*Sorrow's Kitchen (poems)*
*Black Night's Gonna Catch Me Here: Selected Poems 1968-1998*

## James Sallis

# Time's Hammers

**THE COLLECTED SHORT FICTION OF JAMES SALLIS**

This edition published in 2000 by Toxic, an imprint of
CT Publishing, PO Box 5880, Edgbaston, Birmingham, B16 8JF

A CIP catalogue record for this book is available from the British Library.

ISBN 1 902002-28-8

9 8 7 6 5 4 3 2 1

Typography & Cover Design by DP Fact and Fiction
OCR and scan by Russell Clark

Printed and bound in Great Britain.

# Time's Hammers

THE COLLECTED SHORT FICTION OF JAMES SALLIS

# Acknowledgements

"Jim and Mary G" copyright 1970, first appeared in *Orbit*.

"I Saw Robert Johnson" copyright 1989, first appeared in *Ellery Queen's Mystery Magazine*.

"Vocalities" copyright 1998, first appeared in *Blue Lightning*.

"Others" copyright 1985, first appeared in *The Georgia Review*.

"Pure Reason" copyright 1994, first appeared in *Urbanus*.

"Wolf" copyright 1994, first appeared in *Pacific Review*.

"Dogs in the Nighttime" copyright 1989, first appeared (as "The Incident") in *Ellery Queen's Mystery Magazine*.

"Memory" copyright 1998, first appeared in *Fugue*.

"The Leveller" copyright 1983, first appeared in *Gallery*.

"Joyride" copyright 1988, first appeared in *Ellery Queen's Mystery Magazine*.

"Delta Flight 281" copyright 1974, first appeared in *Alternities*.

"More Light" copyright 1998, first appeared in *New Mystery*.

"And then the dark—" copyright 1970, first appeared in *A Few Last Words*.

"D.C. al FINE" copyright 1982, first appeared (as "The Window") in *Alfred Hitchcock's Mystery Magazine*.

"Blue Lab" copyright 2000, appears here for the first time.

"Blue Devils" copyright 1996, first appeared in *Alfred Hitchcock's Mystery Magazine*.

"Oblations" copyright 2000, appears here for the first time.

"Winner" copyright 1970, first appeared in *A Few Last Words*.

"Shutting Darkness Down" copyright 1998, originally commissioned for and broadcast by BBC radio, subsequently
published in *Louisiana Literature*.

"Dear Floods of Her Hair" copyright 1999, first appeared in *The Magazine of Fantasy & Science Fiction*.

"Moments of Personal Adventure" copyright 1990, first appeared in *Painted Hills* Review.

"Good Men" copyright 1990, first appeared (as "The Need") in *Ellery Queen's Mystery Magazine*.

"Attitude of the Earth Toward Other Bodies" copyright 1989, first appeared in *Full Spectrum*.

"Kazoo" copyright 1967, first appeared in *New Worlds*.

"Bubbles" copyright 1968, first appeared in *New Worlds*.

"The Anxiety in the Eye of the Cricket" copyright 1969, first appeared in *The New SF*.

"Breakfast with Ralph" copyright 1984, first appeared in *Rampike*.

"Intimations" copyright 1980, first appeared in *The Portland Review*.

"Letter to a Young Poet" copyright 1968, first appeared in *Orbit*.

"Faces, Hands" copyright 1970, first appeared in *Nova*.

"The History Makers" copyright 1969, first appeared in *Orbit*.

"Impossible Things Before Breakfast" copyright 1985, first appeared in *Isaac Asimov's SF Magazine*.

"Echo" copyright 1974, first appeared in *The Berserkers*.

"Doucement, S'il Vous Plaît" copyright 1971, first appeared in *Orbit*.

"Front & Centaur" copyright 1970, first appeared in *New Worlds*.

"Changes" copyright 1978, first appeared in *Fantastic*.

"At the Fitting Shop" copyright 1971, first appeared in *Again, Dangerous Visions*.

"Walls of Affection" copyright 1994, first appeared in *The Fractal*.

"The Invasion of Dallas" copyright 1976, first appeared in *Lone Star Universe*.

"Driving" copyright 1984, first appeared in *Pacific Review*.

"A Few Last Words" copyright 1968, first appeared in *Orbit*.

"Powers of Flight" copyright 1993, first appeared in *Amazing*.

"Finger and Flame" copyright 1991, first appeared in *Reed*.

"Potato Tree" copyright 1986, first appeared in *The Magazine of Fantasy & Science Fiction*.

"Need" copyright 1985, first appeared in *Isaac Asimov's Science Fiction Magazine*.

"Old Times" copyright 1998, first appeared in *Realms of Fantasy*.

"Becoming" copyright 1997, first appeared in *South Dakota Review*.

"Dawn Over Doldrums" copyright 1993, first appeared in *Amazing*.

"Ansley's Demons" copyright 1992, first appeared in *The Magazine of Fantasy & Science Fiction*.

*To those first editors*
*who leaned close to listen:*

*Fred Wolven, Damon,*
*Mike Moorcock, Eleanor Bender,*
*Joseph McCrindle, Bob Lewis,*
*Eleanor Sullivan*

# Time's Hammers:
## Volume One

# It's Three O'Clock: Do You Know Where Your Monsters Are?

PERHAPS, as a Chekhov character says of women in *Uncle Vanya*, you can only become friends after the affair is over.

Some thirty years ago, for about ten minutes, I was a full-fledged science fiction writer, published in the magazines and in anthologies of original writing such as *Orbit* and *Again, Dangerous Visions*, soon scooped out of rural Iowa (where I'd given up pretending to be a student, for which I had little knack, in favor of pretending to be a writer, at which I remain passable) to edit *New Worlds*.

I never really left science fiction, but just went on pursuing my own interests, drifting further and further out to sea. I sent postcards back from time to time. I visited.

At any rate, I'm happy to say that we're good friends now, science fiction and myself.

When I paid those visits, folks were always wanting to know where I'd been. But rumors of my silence were greatly exaggerated. I'd been dancing all along—wearing different masks at each ball. Stories, poems and essays showed up regularly in places like the *Georgia Review, American Poetry Review, Pequod, Ellery Queen's Mystery Magazine.* You weren't supposed to *do* that, of course. But I've done it all along. I'd had my first poems for *Ann Arbor Review* and my first stories for the science fiction magazines accepted at the same time; I'd published in *Transatlantic Review* while I was editing *New Worlds*.

So science fiction and I cohabited back then. And when our interests began to diverge, we parted happily. George Effinger may have put it best. "I didn't really resign from science fiction," he said years back. "What happened, I think, was that when the music stopped playing, no one had a chair for me. So I'm just going to go on doing what I do, writing what I write, standing up."

Here I am, then, at three o'clock in the morning, all alone, standing up.

There's long been a peculiar relationship between science fiction and its practitioners, one remarkably documented in the series of informal essays Barry Malzberg collected as *Engines of the Night*. Writers such as Kurt Vonnegut, sensing perilous downdrafts, have taken care to distance themselves from the field. Others believe the constraints of the form integral to its power and appeal, much as one finds imaginative freedom within the strictures of the sonnet or blues, and lobby against importation of values from outside. Some have kept stacks of hats by their typewriters, from time to time taking off the one with the Science Fiction logo and putting on Mystery, Western or Men's Adventure. Science fiction's great originals, meanwhile, people like Philip K. Dick, Jack Vance, Fritz Leiber and Philip José Farmer, have simply gone on about their work, largely ignored, making griffins out of sparrows, doing what they do, standing up.

As I've remarked elsewhere, many of us who began writing in the Sixties during the *New Worlds* era perceived SF as a kind of working man's metaphysical fiction, Borges in stainless steel, Cervantes on the half-shell. It came up in the back of our minds like small hammers insisting that there was another world besides, or beside, this one. We believed that science fiction, speculative fiction, might provide the contemporary mythology, a form that would pull together all the old literatures' themes while at the same time revealing profoundly new ones.

For all its brief life as a genre, Richard Lupoff notes, science fiction has carried out these periodic flirtations with maturity, reaching up and out, sending water over the sides in rolling waves, before relapsing to its usual mishmosh of crude narrative and hackneyed themes. Those who mistook the one-night stand for true love were left waiting at the station.

Writing this, I'm intensely aware that, in speaking of science fiction, what I load onto the truck is almost certainly quite different from the cargo you take off. Most commentators throw all science fiction, fantasy and anything smelling faintly of them into the same bin, babies unseen in the bathwater; there seems little choice. But the genre is now so large and varied and compartmented that the term has ceased to be of much use, like the earlier, once useful term jazz. If we're talking about Kenny G or Eric Dolphy, we're not only saying different things, we're speaking a different language. Likewise, science fiction extends from hordes of heroic-fantasy trilogies at the east border, to the latest Star Trek tie-in on the south, to the furthermost psychic explorations of a J.G. Ballard (there in the northern mists), to the uncategorizable Stanislaw Lem and the innovations of Sturgeon, Bester, Delany, Bill Gibson. Loading the truck, I shove cases of Cordwainer Smith up against Cortazar, stack Landolfi and Lem over there by Lucius Shepard, Howard Waldrop alongside Pynchon. That doesn't clear things up much, I know, but it makes for a hell of a load.

So for convenience's sake, let's agree that we both know what it is we're talking about. Almost certainly we don't, but without that fundamental agreement all communication much beyond the bounds of "Leave my food [or your mother] alone" becomes impossible.

Anyway, there I was, at the station, three o'clock in the morning.

Even back then Tom Disch argued that science fiction was irretrievably an adolescent literature, an argument taken up at length by Norman Spinrad in *Science Fiction and the Real World*. Come to life in the swamp of pulp fiction, the genre never could quite get its feet clear of the mud; like Aristophanes' Socrates, it kept stumbling into potholes while gazing at stars. Disch, Malzberg, Spinrad—and yes, Lem, who's taken science fiction most severely to task—would agree that there's something perverse, something epicene or niggardly at its center, which forever confounds science fiction, racking its promise with commercialism and mere cleverness, carrying the coals of received wisdom to the Newcastle of wonder, holding out offers to expand our consciousness through travel yet giving back, when we send in money, only the same old postcards.

"The doors have been thrown open to start on a great quest," in Michel Butor's words, "and we discover we are still walking round and round the house."

When I began reading it, SF was outlaw literature, with absolutely no literary cachet whatsoever—no cachet period. Only brainy, odd children read the stuff, and there remained something smarmy and illicit about it; a part of the pleasure was my sense of transgression. We science fiction readers thought about things, knew things, worried over things, others did not.

Looking back on the writers I have most admired, too, what I find in common among many of them is a similar maverick status. When everyone else stood, they sat. So I skipped without out a thought, wholly by instinct, past much of the approved canon and settled on the like of *Tristram Shandy*, Machado de

Assis, Chandler, Boris Vian, *Miss Lonelyhearts*, Marek Hlasko, Queneau, John Collier, Blaise Cendrars. I sought edge literature, yes, but also people *writing* at the edge, writers not so much lighting out for the territory as dragging the territory back with them farting and belching and smelling unmistakably ripe to civilization.

One of science fiction's or the fantastic's great strengths is its ability, like poetry, to throw into sharp relief the world about us: to make it new again, large again; to wipe out our assumptions, automatic responses, certitudes. Now, this is precisely what any good literature does—what Lionel Trilling called its "adversary intent." As for how this stuff works, Vian put it best in the avant-propos to his still-astonishing *L'Ecume des jours*:

> *Its so-called method consists essentially of projecting reality, under favorable circumstances, on to an irregularly tilting and consequently distorting frame of reference.*

Thirty-four years of stories here, then, in this volume. Not all of them by any means, but a goodly portion. Plucked from science fiction magazines like *F&SF* and *Amazing Stories*, excavated from anthologies like *Orbit* and *Full Spectrum*, rediscovered in uncategorizable venues like *New Worlds* and *The Edge*, saved from drowning in literary magazines like *The Georgia Review* and *South Dakota Review*, discovered hiding in the upstairs closets of *Alfred Hitchcock's, Gallery, Ellery Queen's*, one of them even written on commission for the BBC.

Obviously no one is safe.

*James Sallis*
*Phoenix, April 1999*

# Attitude of the Earth Toward Other Bodies

*B*ECAUSE SHE IS GONE.

Each morning, still, he rises at five and puts on coffee. For an hour he studies—languages, usually—then takes the wireless terminal into the kitchen and with breakfast (grapefruit, one piece of wheat toast, a single scrambled egg or bowl of oatmeal) reviews news aspects of the project. All these are habits acquired in college and never given up. He showers then, dresses, and stands for a moment at the door, his apartment still and quiet as the sky.

He arrives, as always, before the others. "Good morning, Doctor," the guard says to him. He inserts his card into the slot, places his palm briefly against the glass plate. He goes through the door and repeats the clearance routine at another door, then down a long, narrow corridor. Here he says simply, "Good morning, Margaret."

"Good morning, John." The door opens for him. "I hope you slept well."

"Not very."

"Then I am sorry, John." A polite pause. "Where will we start this morning?"

"Program Aussie for a sweep of sector A-456/F, I think. Logarithm tables, continuous transmission."

"Duration?"

"Until redirected. And at whatever power levels we've been using in that sector."

All is quiet for a moment until Margaret says, "It is done. Transmission is beginning. You wish Granada to continue broadcasting geometrical theorems?"

"Yes, though maybe we could boost levels a little. Paris is still sending out the Brandenburgs. Leave her on that. But let's switch Nevsky over to something new."

After a moment Margaret says, "Yes?"

"I don't know—poetry, maybe."

"What poetry did you have in mind, John?"

"Milton maybe? Or Shakespeare, Dante—Pushkin?"

"Might I suggest Rilke?"

"Yes, Rilke by all means. The *Elegies*. Of course."

Margaret's voice fills the room:

> *Who, if I cried, would hear me among the angelic*
> *orders? And even if one of them suddenly*
> *pressed me against his heart, I should fade in the*
> *strength of his stronger existence.*

And he thinks how cruel it is now, though often before it had filled his days with joy, that Margaret should have *her* voice.

"Leave all the others on current transmissions."

"Yes, John. Will there be something else?"

"Anything unusual incoming?"

"Some interesting variable emissions from Dresden's sector. A possible new black hole in Paris's."

"You've notified astronomy, of course."

"Yes."

"Okay, just run off some copy for me and I'll have a look. The rest of the morning's your own."

Daisywheels begin spitting out thickly printed sheets of numbers and symbols.

"You'll call me, John, if there's anything else?"

"Certainly, Margaret. Thank you."

"It is my pleasure, John. *Au revoir.*"

And he is alone in the lab, without even her voice now. He looks up through hanging plants and the skylight to a bright day with no cloud in sight. There should be rain, he thinks, torrents of rain: *il pleure dans mon coeur comme il pleut dans la ville.* Then he bends over the serrated sheets, peering into them as one looks into a friend's face and knows instantly, without analysis, his thoughts and mood, entering into them as one exists in one's language, beyond particulates or grammar. The emissions from C-389/G-B were indeed most interesting, but (alas) still random.

Random as two people coming together in a sea of others. Random as the chances (they were, after all, so different) they'd fall in love.

She was a musician, working as a secretary to try and make ends meet. For two hours each day after work she practiced oboe. Most of the remaining time she bicycled or read, usually in the bathtub or curled up against the bed's headboard with a glass of wine close to hand. She had a mane of thick brown hair, a narrow waist, and worked at her desk in shirtsleeves, arms alarmingly soft and bare. From her first day she'd always smiled at him.

He watched her for a time, aware of her presence halfway across the building even as he worked, and finally began speaking to her, mostly in the stairwells or halls at first, a couple of times in the lunch line. Then they started coming across one another more often. One day she asked if he'd had lunch yet (he had) and the next day they went together. On the stairs he asked her to dinner. She sat cross-legged in the car with her feet tucked under and slid her hand, at the restaurant, up inside and around his arm. That night, Sunday, he could not sleep and went to the lab at three in the morning. Monday night she went back with him to his apartment. It was her birthday. Neither of them was at work on Tuesday.

They were both so wary, so afraid of being hurt, and yet they seemed unable to stop themselves, to control, whatever its source, the attraction they felt. Verbally, they circled one another like dancers: But what if it happened that...I couldn't stand it if...I don't want any more surprises. They were two moons circling that central attraction, trying desperately not to collide, knowing they would. Once Margaret spoke to him four times before he surfaced from his thoughts of her to respond. Later there would be an interfering sister, not a villainess, nothing is that simple, that easy, just a sister concerned, a sister afraid things were going too fast, suspicious (as well she might be) of his intentions. But none of it mattered.

Her name was Kim. She'd been through two awful marriages and much abused by the men in her life; she had difficulty believing that a man could be kind to her, could be giving, could truly care. She did not recognize that there was anything within her a man would be drawn to. She kept asking him Why me? And he truly did not know. Perhaps her sister was right; perhaps he only wanted her, wanted her youth, her beauty, her obeisance.

Perhaps he was just afraid to be alone any longer under this sky pressing down on him.

And so he said, I will not lie to you. I want to be with you.

If the time comes that I want to back away, I will tell you so.

You don't want to?

No. No, I don't. You must know that.

I thought you did, maybe. I was afraid.

He runs his hand up her spine, along the soft line of her arm. She leans her head against his chest. *To be so wanted.*

You should be getting home, he says.

Yes.

But they do not move. Carlights wash over them, the guard's flashlight washes over them, they are flooded in moonlight. And still she holds him close against her. From the heave of her chest he realizes she is crying. He asks if she is all right. Yes, she says, I'm fine, but this will all change, you know. It has to, she says. Someday we won't have it anymore. He looks down at the pale coarse skin of her hands and knows he has come too far now ever to be safe again.

He stands at the door of his apartment as though he'd just entered, trying to imagine how another, seeing this for the first time, how *she*, would perceive it. It has character, of course; it's a bit out of the ordinary. And comfortable, like the corduroy coat he wears most days. In fact the apartment is a fairly precise graph of his inmost life. His solitude, his passion for knowledge, the kenning of order and intuition so important to his work—all are there; there in the orderly stacks of books where Chomsky is sandwiched by Tolstoy and Tom Paine, in the bathroom where the medicine cabinet is stuffed with index cards, in the kitchen where he keeps most of the computer and electronic equipment, even in the series of small rugs thrown about seemingly at random over the carpets. He decides that he would like the person who lived here. He would trust this person, somehow.

Listen to this, she tells him one night as they sit side by side reading, hands locking from time to time and (from time to time) reaching for wineglasses. It is by Flaubert, she says, then reads it aloud: *Human language is like a cracked kettle on which we beat out tunes for bears to dance to, when all the time we are longing to move the stars to pity.*

"That is for us, John," she says. "That was written for us, for the two of us alone."

He moves a hand towards her face and she bows her head to touch it. From far off they hear sirens, the sounds of traffic and slamming doors, the whine of wind, a babble of unintelligible voices.

Everything depends upon our interpretation of the noise surrounding us and the silence at our centers.

By the late-middle twentieth century (and he found this as beautiful as a kite looping into May sky, as the order in a closed system of numbers or the sudden flight of birds) science had advanced sufficiently that it ceased being merely descriptive—that is, narrative—and became almost lyrical. There is, after all, not much distance between William James's insight that reality is relative and multiple, that the human mind (and therefore the world) is a fluid shimmering of consciousness, and Schrödinger's cat. Science had become Wallace Steven's blue guitar, a fecund reservoir of our attempts to understand, to contrive order. Trying to explain the world to me, Camus wrote, you are reduced to poetry. Perhaps he was right.

Language was at the base of both, of course, of everything finally, the limits of our language the limits of our world. And Chomsky believed that all the world's languages shared certain abstract rules and principles, not because these were implicit, particularly rational, or historical, but because they had been programmed into human minds by the information carried in DNA. HE hoped in studying the most formal of these universals, rules and how those rules determine the structure of sentences—in short, basic grammar—to map the mind's self-limits. For grammar is a highly sophisticated information system, admitting messages, screening out noise.

Every day he sat surrounded by noise, tape upon tape of noise, noise turned into simple, fluctuating graphs on the screens about him, noise as rows of binary figures on huge sheets of spindled paper, noise analyzed for him in several ways (only some of which he understood) by Margaret, searching for a single incontrovertible instance of *grammar*, for algorithms that would (he knew) leap from the noise surrounding them.

What he did not know, was what he would do when that happened; he had no doubt that it would. His life *would* in many ways be over then, his great work, the work for which he'd programmed himself so long, done, done at age thirty-six, or forty-nine, or fifty-three. He could spend his remaining years studying languages, he supposed. Or music.

He brought the brandy glass close to him and looked at the world upside-down within it, a tree, a black car, the house across the street. Remembered how on their first night together they had shared a glass of brandy and in the morning, after she was gone, he stood staring at traces of her lipstick on the glass's rim. Remembering how she'd left a note saying she couldn't talk to him now or she wouldn't be able to do it, then had phoned, and finally met him, because he had to understand, goddamn it, he just *had* to understand.

In quantum theory nothing is real unless it is observed. Or as Einstein held, It is the theory which decides what we can observe.

And so he watches her walk away from him into a stream of people sweeping toward the subway entrance. And in the morning he returns to Margaret, to his graphs, his paper, his noise.

But now, in a circle of light and the ever-present, distant din that is the city's pulse, he reads about the male spadefoot toad. For a year or more he waits buried beneath the parched surface of the Arizona desert, and when the rainstorm he awaits at last arrives, plunges into daylight, racing to the nearest pool of water and sending out frantic calls to females. If he does not mate on the first night, he may never mate at all; by morning the water will be dwindling, and his life with it.

Because he wanted, just one more time, to be in love.

Gradually he realizes that he is awake. A sense of loss in the dreamworld receding from him; the brightness of the moon in his window; a murmur of wind. The phone rings again. His mouth is painfully dry. He tastes far back in his throat last night's Scotch.

"John? I rang earlier, just once, to allow you to awake a bit more naturally...Are you there?"

*Her* voice, as though continuing the dream.

He grunts.

"Barleycorn again, John? Are you all right?"

He grunts a second time.

"There is incoming you will want to see, now. Emissions from a new sector. They are diverse, unaccountable, and do not appear random."

He is instantly alert.

"Thank you, Margaret. I'll be right in. Please notify Security I'm on my way."

"I've already done so."

He glances at the clock beside him (2:59 A.M.) and downs a quart of orange juice while dressing and washing up. He glances in the mirror on his way out and sees a rumpled youngish man with round glasses and serious, downturned mouth, hunched over as though always in a hurry, as though bent about some central pain deep within him or slowly closing in upon himself. This fleeting image stays with him.

The night is clear, each star bright and perfect as a new idea. There is no traffic, no one else about. He is alone in the world. And for the nine minutes it takes him to reach the lab he is a part of the earth, and yet escapes its pull, its final possession, enters into sky, as only the night walker, sheathed in solitude, ever does—something like Rilke's "angels," he imagines, though transitory. He remembers Creeley saying that it's only in the relationships men manage that they live at all, thinks of Goethe's "emptiness above us," of the first poem he can remember ever reading, Walter de la Mare's "The Listener."

A guard stands just inside the outer doors and unlocks them for him. He feeds his card into the terminal, places his palm against the glass: actions he no longer thinks about. Then through another door, past the second terminal, into the corridor. Hall lights come on as he advances, are shut off behind him.

"Thank you, Margaret."

"You are welcome. I hope that I've not disturbed you unnecessarily. Copy is on your desk. I will wait."

He goes into the lab and stands for a while at the window, looking out at the light-choked horizons of the city, at the dark above riddled with stars. Finally, knowing he is only delaying, he goes to the desk and looks closely at several of the thickly printed sheets. He senses that Margaret is about to speak.

"No," he says. "It is nothing. I thought, for a moment…But no."

"Then I am sorry, John."

"It's all right. My dreams were not good ones. I'd as soon be awake."

"That is not what I meant."

"I understand. Good night, Margaret."

Then, later, dawn not yet rosy-fingered but definitely poking about in the sky: "Margaret?"

"Yes, John."

"I want an override accessing me to all transmissions."

"There is no facility for such access."

"But it can be done?"

He sits watching incoming noise waver and change on the screens about him until (and it is by then full dawn) Margaret says, "It is done."

"Thank you."

"Is there anything else?"

"No, not now."

"I will wait, then."

"Margaret…"

After a moment: "Yes?"

"Nothing…I will talk to you later."

"Yes, John. I will wait."

He rolls his chair towards the console. For a long time he sits there motionless, considering, sorting through phrase after phrase, seeking the precise algorithms, the barest grammar, of his pain. Light blossoms about him like a wound.

With two fingers he types out *I loved her, and she is gone,* then a transmission code and Enter/Commit.

He waits. Day marches on outside, noise builds. A telephone rings somewhere. Graphs quiver and shimmer about him. Soon there will be an answer. Soon he will hear the click of daisywheels starting up and his work will be done.

# Kazoo

WALKING DOWN THE STREET on my way to see The Leech, I'm attacked by this guy who jumps out of the alley shouting *Hai! Hai! Feefifofum!* (you know: bloodcurdling) over and over, cutting air with the sides of his bands. He says *Hai!* again, then *Watch out, man! I'm gonna lay you open!* He's still assaulting the air, battering it too.

*My,* I think, *an alley cat.* Then I stand off and kind of watch this little dance he's doing. Dispassionately in front, you see, but I get to admiring it. I mean, he's cutting some great steps, beating hell out of the air. I snap my fingers for him, clap a little.

*You watch out, man!* he says. *You get cute, I'm gonna hurt you bad, put you through that wall there.* Then he goes back to his *Hai!* and *Feefifofum!* He's standing off about three yards from me, jumping around, chopping his hands back and forth, looking mean, a real hardankle. He's about five foot and looks like he might have modeled for Dylan Thomas' bit about the "bunched monkey coming."

By this time there's quite a crowd piling up. They're all standing around clapping, snapping their fingers, digging the action. Some guy in like black heads in to sell *Watchtowers* and this Morton pops up and starts passing around stone tablets and pillows of salt. There's a spade out on the edge

29

of the crowd, he's picking pockets, got three arms. Deep Fat Friar passes by, frowns, goes on down the street flogging himself with a vinyl flyswatter. And there's this cop on the fringe giving out with a mantra of dispersal. *Ibishuma, go go; Ibishuma, go* go (don't think he had it quite right, you know?).

One guy pulls out a set of plastic spoons and commences to make them go clackety-clack, clackety-clack between his thumb and great toe. Another guy has a kazoo. Someone else is trying to get them to do Melancholy Baby. *Take your clothes off and be adancin' bare,* this smartass yells out of the back of the crowd. He *is* kinda hairy, this guy.

*Come on, Ralph,* he shouts at me. *Come on, man, we're gonna tangle. Hai! Feefifofum!* But you can tell he likes it, the attention I mean, because he goes up on his toes and pirouettes.

I stand there looking at him, frowning a little, dispassionate again. I mean, I'm getting kind of tired of the bit by now. Some guy comes by about then with a monkey on his back, grinding at a nutchopper. Another one's hunkered-down on the corner to demonstrate his Vegamatic; his buddy's scraping bananas. And there's this like arthritic wobbling down the sidewalk with a Dixie cup, begging green-stamps.

*Hai! Hai! Hing!* (that last one way up in the nose).

He stops and drops his hands, looks down at the concrete, shuffles his feet. *Aw come on Ralph…* Then he's *Hai!*-ing and *Feefifofum!*-ing again, going at it like mad, jumping around like a spastic toad.

And by this time I'm beginning to get *real* tired. I mean, I put up with his bag through here but now I'm gonna be late to see The Leech, so I—and let this be a lesson to all of you—I move in for the kill. I've been watching Captain Conqueroo on the morning tube, you see, and I'm like eager to try this thing out. So when this guy sees me coming and charges in like a rhinoceros or something, I just step ever so casually to one side and with a sudden blur of motion I get him with the Triple-Reverse Elbow Block, lay it right on him. He folds up like a letter that's getting put in an envelope that's too small for it and he falls down in like slow motion. His tongue's hanging out and a fly's walking up it toward his teeth.

*Name's not Ralph,* I tell him. Then I stand there humming along with the spoons and kazoo till he can breathe again. Which doesn't take him over twenty minutes or so—we'd only got through Black Snake Rag, Mountain Morning Moan, and part of America the Beautiful (raga form).

Anyhow, he starts coming back from violet toward the pinkish end of the spectrum, and he looks up at me and he says, *Aw gee, Algernon. Look, give me a chance. Sorry I bugged you.* Saying that reminds him of something and he stops long enough to spit out the fly. *Wasn't my idea,* he goes on. *Nothing personal against you, guy told me to do it...Bartholomew?*

I shake my head. I kick him a little. *Who.*

*Guy just came up to me at the bus stop, told me you were on your way to the bank, don't know who he was. Said if I beat you up I could have the money and if I didn't he'd send his parakeet out to get me...Chauncey?*

I kick him again. *Big guy? Southerner? Hair looked like a helmet? Scar where his nose should be, cigar stuck in it?*

*Yeah...Look, you wouldn't be Rumplestiltskin by any chance?*

*Sorry.* I tell him that as I'm kicking him.

*Didn't think so.*

I reach down to help him up, since he's obviously going to need help. *That'd be Savannah Rolla, a friend of mine,* I tell him. Savvy's a film-maker and I know he and a poet-type by the name of Round John Virgin are hassling with a love epic called *Bloodpies*—in which the symbols of the mudcake, the blood bath, the cow patty, and innocent youth find their existential union—so I look around for the cameras. But I can't spot them.

*I'm on my way to the blood bank,* I tell the guy. *He's got a funny sense of humor, Savannah does. Do anything for a friend, though.* And since his hand's in mine anyway since I'm helping him up, I shake it.

*Ferdinand Turnip,* I introduce myself—*Ferdinand. My wife is a Bella, name's Donna.*

*Percival Potato,* he says, and gives me this big grin like he's busting open. *Mad to greet you.* He's giving me the eye, so I take it and put it in my wallet right next to the finger someone gave me the day before.

We talk a while, have lunch together in the laundromat, then it's time for me to split. We notice the band's still going at it and Percy cops a garbage can and heads over to blow some congadrum with them. I walk a mile, catch a camel, and rush to the blood bank. I realize I've left all my beaver pelts at home again, so I take off one of my socks (the red one) and give it to the driver. He blows his nose on it, thanks me, and puts it in his lapel.

At the blood bank Dr. Acid, who's the head, tells me The Leech is dead from overeating. Dr. Acid has three friends: Grass, who's rooting around in the drawers; Roach, who looks like a leftover; and Big H, who rides a horse—Joint has the bends and is taking the day off. They're all eating popcorn balls and scraping bits of The Leech off the wall, putting the pieces in a picnic basket that has a place for bottles of wine too. They ask me to stay for a potluck dinner, but I say no. I cop some old commercials with them for a while, then I dive out of the window and swim to my studio. Someone's dumped Jello in the water, and it's pretty tough going. The crocs are up tight today, but the piranha seem placid enough.

At the studio, reverently, I apply the 65th coat to my *Soft Thing*—four more to go. I got the idea from Roy Biv, a friend of mine. Each layer of paint is a step up the spectrum, a solid color. I have carefully calculated the weight of my paint, canvas, medium. The last brush stroke of the 69th coat, and my painting will fall through the floor. It will be a masterpiece of aesthetic subtlety.

By the time I've drunk all the turpentine and finished burning the brushes, it's willy-nilly time to dine. But the lemmings are bad in the hall so I'm late catching my swan and I have to wait on top of the TV antenna for over an hour. Then by the time I get home, the vampires are out. They wave as I pass. Everyone knows you can't get blood from a Turnip—and anyway, they're all saps.

I go in and Donna comes up and kisses me and puts her arm around me and tells me she doesn't love me anymore. I look out the window. Sure enough, the world's stopped going 'round.

So I go in the john and find my kazoo and I play for a long time.

# Bubbles

*D*—, WHERE ARE YOU NOW?
I've searched for you down in the cove, by the little sandstone temple that the Greek built when his daughter married, where a wild cat lives, all butter and ginger; in the Soho pubs and Hampstead house parties; down by the docks where the air smells of banana, oil floats out on the water (Ophelia's gowns), and spiders crept across the top of my black shoes that stood like open graves on the whitewashed boards.

Once, I asked after you at the small café on the bridge by Paddington Station and a man in the corner, overhearing, paused with a forkful of soft dry cheese in front of his mouth (his forefinger nicotine-stained halfway down between the joints) and spoke across the room through already-parted lips: "Kilroy, you say? Ah yes, he was here. Remember him well; almost like my own son, he was. Yes, he was here"— then delivered the fork and chewed: a mouthful of crumbling custard. On the brown table beside him sat his teeth, poundnotes clenched between them, a pink moneyclip in the morning sun.

("Love, hate, indifference," you used to say in your flamboyant way, "they can work wonders, miracles. If you have belief. And—flamboyantly, extravagantly—I believed. In you. And now have only this, all this guilt, that bangs away inside me.")

Outside the café now, four men point in four directions and step backwards until they come together. A delivery boy in white pedals along the bridge and stops before me, returning undelivered another of the cables by which I have tried to reach you:

> Yesterday the cows came
> home stop Bailey expected
> later today stop Where
> are you stop

On the opposite wall of the bridge someone has spray-painted *Kilroy the savior*. "Is it true, sir?" the delivery boy asks. "Can he really do all they say he can?" I go over and scrape the white letters off into an envelope, marking it *near Paddington Station, 4 Jan, 6 AM*. Does this mean he has left the city? A lorry comes by, killing the delivery boy, who has tried to follow me across the street.

And so I go walking down Westbourne Grove where teddy bears hang by their ears on the clotheslines, where marzipan elephants lounge in the palms of children and American Indians camp in the dustbins, their salty, tee-pee smoke spiraling up between the Queen Anne houses. Leaning against one of the spear fences, a flop-hatted old man blows his nose into a tiny rag of flannel then holds it out away from his eyes, looking to see what he's brought up, like a fisher, from the deeps. "Hey, got a sixpence?"—and his huge nostrils hang there in front of my face like two black holes in the morning. As always, walking—its regularity, the rhythm of it—brings me to another kind of rhythm; I always end up singing or, in busier parts of the city, humming quietly to myself. So now as I walk (hopefully toward you) over the gobbets of paint and the heelspores of crushed orange chalk, past the walls and fences painted with six-foot flowers and diminutive Chinese dragons, past the bakeshops with their pastel facades, I'm singing softly to myself *Jesus wants me for a sunbeam.*

Who would have thought it. When we squatted together in piles of dust behind the books upstairs, sharing the last disposable yellow paper robe (luckily a 44, so it fitted us perfectly) and nibbling at the cake of vanilla seaweed we found in a drawer when we took the flat? That you should leave, and months later the realization of what had happened would come so suddenly upon me, and with such force, that I would sit for days without moving or speaking, until friends came at last and carried me away. That finally, obsessed with the depth of my guilt and loss, I should come searching for you, asking everywhere, sending these messages out ahead of me (cables, phonecalls, bits of paper thrown out the window to passers-by), out from my tiny room in Clapham Common, and following these signs across all of London: chalk on brick walls, letters sprayed from cans, empty chocolate wrappers which could be yours.

On the street in front of a fish shop two children are killing one another with wooden swords while all the silver-bubble fisheyes watch them calmly and dogs sit across the street quietly looking on. Farther down, where wind has rattled windows, a burglar alarm clangs. In this amazing new stillness a young man enters a nearby dentist's office ("Half a pint, sir? Three bob, please; just put this over your face") and emerges giggling. The window is filled with old dental tools, toppling in lines off the velvet-covered shelves and looking like instruments for exquisite torture: the relics of orbicular inquisitions.

In Notting Hill Gate (I wonder if you remember this) the buildings catch the wind and lay it like a ribbon down along the pavement; it swirls about my ankles, clinging, resilient, as I tramp through. Three one-man bands glare at one another from the corners of an intersection, waiting for the light. The flowerseller's black Alsatian is wearing a chain of daisies at its neck; it can catch pennies on its tongue. Remembering the old man's nostrils on Westbourne Grove, I make for the tube station—then bump bump bump (down the funny stairs from the tipitittitop). One wall is covered with telephone numbers; vast 69's scratched into the cement with belt-buckles or penknives; a poem in red shoe polish:

> *During the raids*
> *the lost plane*
> *reported*
> *the war over*
> *the pilot missing*

On the other, in a tiny elegant script, is penciled: *When Kilroy returns.* I stop and with people staring over my shoulder scrape the minute gray flakes off into an envelope.

The third level is deserted. I stand alone by the track, hearing the far-off rumble of trains and the dim, flat voices that float after me, tangling together, down the corridors behind. I turn to look down the rails and when I turn back, a cleaning machine is rushing toward me, its tiny mechanical arm erect out in front like a bull's horn. Quickly I step back against the wall, into the leering two-dimensional arms of a Chinese prostitute. *"Look out! Mind!"* the little machine shouts—penny-sized speaker rattling, distorting under the load—then pulls to a stop just past me and comes slowly backwards.

"Who," it asks (the arm quivering), "are you," (the arm stabbing out toward me). "I" (bending back on itself to point, dead center, at itself from above) "am The Machine. *Look out for The Machine!"* A pause "I'll get you, you know; going to take your place, replace you, do away with your sort." (The arm stabs out again, almost to my knee.) "And about time, too. So *look out!* I'm giving you fair warning now!"

It starts away; then stops, purrs a moment and returns, the little treads lugging sadly backwards.

"What are you doing here!" it demands. "Let me see your passport! Would you like your shoes shined. They need it. I have some nice red polish."

I back away from the arm.

"Kilroy," I say quickly. "Have you seen him; has he been here?"

"Kilroy! You know Kilroy! Yes, he was here!" The little machine pauses, waving its arm thoughtfully. "*He* listened to me. We used to sit here for hours, talking over philosophical problems—mostly ethics, I remember. That was before he went away." The arm droops. "A good man. Sometimes, thinking about a man like that, it almost makes me want to forgive you for everything. Almost." The arm suddenly springs back to life, full of excitement. "Do you know where he is!"

"I'm afraid not. I'm trying to find him."

The arm wilts again. "The only one who ever had enough sense, enough compassion, to listen. *He* knew I was right…"

"When I do, I'll let you know, and tell him that you asked

after him." I turn and start back up the corridors, but the little machine shoots around in front of me.

"Just a moment," it says. "I'm supposed to give you a riddle, you know, before I can let you go." It sits for several minutes, the tiny arm flopping and waving, in deep thought. "But I can't think of one just now. Would you like to hear me clap my hand. I suppose it's all right for you to pass, since you know Kilroy. But I should have something done about those shoes if I were you."

I walk up the tunnel. Behind me the little cleaner shouts: "You don't have much time left, you know. *Watch out for The Machines!*"—and goes zooming away down the concrete beside the tracks. The last syllable had blurred, rattling like a cough; apparently the speaker had finally been too much strained, and the diaphragm had cracked.

I climb back up past all the posters of girls in yellow swimwear and the ticket machines into the crowds. It's five now, and the streets are full of dogs. As I walk past a row of phonebooths outside a Wimpy Bar, one of the phones rings. I beat the others there and pick it up:

"Yes?"

"We've found him." Outside, it's raining; this booth contains me perfectly, with the water breaking on the gray glass, destroying the world outside.

"Where?"

"There's been an accident. Mercy Hospital. He's asking for you. Hurry." The rain is washing cigarette butts up under the door and into the booth. On a minicab sign someone has written on the cab's window: *He slept here.* Not bothering this time to collect the sign, I ring for a cab.

At the hospital I'm greeted by a nurse in layers of diaphanous white that slide over one another, with pink somewhere underneath. She's painted black rims around her eyes, and has a pink-white mouth.

"This way, hurry. He's been asking for you. It may be all that's keeping him alive, making him hold on."

We go down white tile halls where everyone else walks near the walls; the center is new and clean. Then into a room full of soft murmurs and liquid sounds. Five surgeons squat in one corner talking together quietly. A nurse kneels by the bedside crying. Outside the window four young girls stand still and straight, and sing.

He lies on the bed under a clear plastic tent, with the sheets pulled up to his chin. All around him the air is filled with tubes and small, pumping engines. Fluids run bubbling through the tubes; go slowly down, and more quickly up, along them. It's as though his blood system, lymph system—all the delicate soft machinery of his body—has been brought out into the world, redirected through glass and plastic. He is larger than the rest of us. (I remember the long months I lay still and dazed, recovering from the loss of your leaving. Perhaps it was here that I lay. My guilt sustains me.)

When the nurse folds back a flap in the tent he opens his eyes, and I hear the soughing of the pumps more distinctly.

"You...came." When he speaks, the fluids run faster in the tubes, gurgling in time with his voice. Bubbles forming, bursting, passing slowly, like fisheyes, along the tubes.

"I...told them...you would." His eyes are gray, pupil and iris barely distinguishable from the rest. It occurs to me now that he can see nothing; I could be anyone; it wouldn't matter. (And how you smiled and brought coffee and talked to me quietly. Your face was always so different, so changed, in the dark.)

"I…knew you…would." There is a gentle hissing as the nurse opens the oxygen valve a degree wider. (The way I stood at the window, watching, not yet understanding. Afterwards, the room seemed…larger. I was aware of the space between things.)

"Bless…you."

Fluids jumped in the tube *(bubble bubble bubble:* the rhythm of a laugh) and now are still, as the pumps shut off. There is only the hiss of oxygen coming into the tent, out into the room. One huge bubble hangs motionless at the bend of a tube, watching.

"Is he dead?"

The nurse goes over to speak with the doctors. They listen carefully, tilting their heads toward her, and nod. The nurse returns:

"Yes."

So I go into the hall and stand there looking out at the polished green grass and flowers in the hospital lawn. A vine which has climbed the building is now blossoming, scattering leaves down into the yard. It looks like the veins in a hand. Flowers climb along it toward the roofs.

"I'm sorry…" She comes up behind me.

"You needn't be. It wasn't him."

"Then who? Your guilt—"

"I don't know." I turn to face her. The pink-white lipstick is smudged at one corner of her mouth. Should I tell her? How much she resembles his wife; that this may have made it easier for him, near the end? "I don't know who he was. I've never seen him before." I start down the hall and she comes after me.

"Please. Just a moment. This." She holds out a large manila envelope: bulky, jangling. "His personal effects, what he had in his pockets. I wonder...could you take them? Please." I take the envelope from her and leave. Hardly anyone in the halls now. The sun is slanting in through the window, moving out across the tiles. When I turn my head to look back at the vine, it almost blinds me. But the flowers are spilling up over the edge of the roof.

Later, on the street, I open the envelope and spread the things out on top of a low wall. It contains: thirty-nine ha'pennies, two sixpences marked EM in red ink, a child's gyroscope top, and a number of small white envelopes containing bits of paint and graphite, each with a place and date scrawled on the outside.

Farther along the wall in black chalk: *We shall be reborn.* Conceivably. But I've used all my envelopes. The only unsealed one I have is the one with the dead man's things—so I scrape the chalk off into that and mark it *Mercy.* (Tomorrow I will have to return to the phone-booth.) And go walking softly down the street toward home. With a song in my mouth.

Like eyelids, all the windows are open, rolled up on their cords.

And night blooms over the heads of the buildings.

# The Anxiety in the Eyes
## of the Cricket

AFTERWARDS, they sat together on the terrace patio smoking.

Behind them on the steel slab, the house, with its forty rooms separate as the chambers of a nautilus, stood like something grown up out of the hill. The steel extended several yards down into the gray ash-like soil, steel scaffolding still farther, to the baserock. Behind the house, for more than a mile, the ground was pitted into a bare colorless canyon, scooped out and pushed forward to form this hill.

Jerry had just come from the East, with his arm torn loose from the socket and one eye half-closed on itself. Passage was difficult these days. He had come on impulse; felt the pull one morning and responded to it as he had so many times before. In China now, and certain portions of India, at least one small part of the economy would be finding itself empty and crippled.

"How is it there now?"—his friend had asked as he smoothed on the salves, wheeled the square white machines, tables, glass chambers across the floor in the bare white room, pulling Jerry's body, wrecked by disease, malnutrition and damage, back into a single organism. For Jerry, accustomed to the tonal languages of the East and its strange inverted thinking, the rough, assonant rhythms of his friend's speech, its somehow Parnassian starkness, were oddly disturbing: a disorientation which was to continue, in fact to grow ever more persistent. English, which had become the French of the last century, then a kind of mirror-image Mandarin—sparse and subtle in its rhythms but yielding great resonance, a quality first noted by mid-century mystery writers and exploited by certain American poets—was now atrophying, dying in upon itself. Words tumbled readily off the tongue, too readily, in brief economical strings like a kind of verbal semaphore, and increasingly had relevance only to themselves—poets, Jerry knew from personal experience, were having a hard time of it. Simultaneously, the tone-rich Chinese language was bursting open, becoming rich and resonant in substance as well, coming more to resemble the evocative, implicit poetry of its written form, now in turn increasingly linear and stylized. What was the precise relationship of language to society, of spoken to written language? English, with its truncated bursts of energy; the flow of Mandarin. Did entropy in one predict, or establish, entropy in the other? Which way did the influence flow? Jerry wondered.

"Better," he had answered his friend.

"You have a perverse love for ambiguity, Jerry. Better than before, or better than here?" He selected a scalpel from the tray and moved behind Jerry with it. The shoulder was anaesthetized, but Jerry could feel the warm blood running down his ribs.

In answer, he had simply grinned.

Now two Drambuies sat on the red enamel deck-table between them and the taste of the thick, sweet liqueur was still in Jerry's mouth. Another glass, a tumbler, was partly filled with cigarettes of strong black tobacco—perique, Jerry thought, from the smell—wrapped in meerschaum papers. His friend held one of these, hand cupped against his ear and elbow on the chair arm, violet smoke pouring out around his bleached white hair. He was dressed in black silk pajamas, and Jerry wore a similar pair; his own Western clothes had been spattered and torn when he arrived. Near the center of the table, almost touching the pole which suspended a Union Jack umbrella out over them, sat a wineglass left out overnight. It was half full. A delicate crust of ice skimmed the deep red surface and, thinner still, ran up the side of the glass along which, yesterday afternoon, Jerry had sipped the wine. Its gold stem was as thin as a flower stalk, the glass itself as large as a man's cupped hands, the base formed of three long, twisted gold tendrils, like roots or the foot of a bird. Jerry, newly aware of color, sat staring for some time at the form all this took, then reached out and shifted the glasses. His right arm and shoulder, the damaged ones, were in the sun, and ached slightly. No use—just another form. The umbrella's gold-braid fringe was still. There was no wind, no movement.

Far below, a small private boat slid through the black water, lugging a makeshift barge—actually more a raft—behind it on a single thick cable. There were still those who cared. The barge was filled with the bodies of the suicides, stacked randomly crisscross on the flat deck like matches in an ashtray. Miles away down the river, where the boat was headed, the flames showed dim in the sun. Jerry imagined for a moment that he could hear the popping of flame within flame as it reached out and ran across the bodies, choosing eyeballs which would explode into gray sizzling mush, lips which would burst and let out fresh pink meat, soft swollen testicles. The chaos, he knew, was apparent. An illusion.

The real problem was over-organization, entropy, the seeming confusion only the final struggle against its imposition. Fact and metaphysics were, finally, the same thing.

Looking back to the barge he thought of Gericault, and only then noticed the words stenciled in bright red letters across the boat's prow: *The Medusa*. Irony or humor? He wondered. Was it form or quality that separated them—if, indeed, the distinction could exist anymore, if any could. A defense, he supposed, but what sort of man—

"It's a question of guilt." Michael snapped the cigarette away from him and it tumbled through its own smoke out into space, down along the cliff and into the water, to collect with the refuse and bodies which floated several feet out from each bank.

Jerry shrugged. "For some." A knife stabbed into the socket of his shoulder and twisted, then quickly withdrew, leaving behind a dull throb. He lifted his Drambuie and looked across the rim to the city far below beyond the water. The city was completely still; nothing moved inside it. "You?"

"Perhaps..."

"You told them the city would kill them. You predicted that much." Jerry found it difficult to look at his friend. Difficult, too, to speak in the old language: he had no right here, he didn't belong. Not any longer. He was intruding.

"I predicted everything. Save for the end..."

"They struck first."

"And the city is dying. Like the rest." He took another cigarette from the tumbler. The remaining ones toppled, like jackstraws, into a new pattern. "But do they know? If they knew..." His hand stopped in mid-wave and fell back onto the chair—too much effort. And no reward. It didn't matter. It was too late.

He struck a match and for a moment Jerry shrank back in his chair, then overcame the reflex. But when Michael pushed the tumbler toward him, he shook his head violently.

Jerry said, "They might do something?"

His friend sat smoking, staring out across the water. Finally he spoke, only his lips moving.

"The boats. From the States. They are coming in at the rate of ten, twelve a day now. The holds are full, the decks as well. The bodies are stiff as boards. They say the crews have learned to walk across them without noticing they're there. Or what they are. As though they *were* boards. Southampton is packed with them, miles out to sea, the Pool of London filled months ago."

"And you began it? By telling them—"

"Jerry. That was after I came here, after all this was built. You should understand. You've been here a week now." (That morning as they lay side by side in bed, exhausted, Michael had said, "Jerry, you are the most religious person I know. I'm in awe of that, it frightens me.")

"And tomorrow I leave."

Michael looked up at the sky. It was choked with smoke from the burning bodies, smoke that hung motionless in dense, shapeless clouds, like clots of blood. "Where will you go?"

Jerry paused. "Into the city. I'd like to borrow your boat." Suddenly he caught the smell of cabbage from the gardens beside the house. There were a dozen varieties—it was one of the few things which would grow from the soil now— and the smells of each mingled together, though Jerry felt, if he wanted, he could separate every one, like picking out individual strands of seaweed. A small plot of artificial flowers stood beside the cabbage, their bright red and yellow heads lost to the sheer mass of greenery. "I have a family there."

Michael said nothing for several moments, then looked down at the river; away from the smoke. The boat was almost out of sight; only the barge showed. "You never mentioned that before. You knew—"

"That it would be against your principles? Yes, but I care more for you than for your principles. I haven't seen them for years. But now..."

"You're amused, Jerry? That I hold to my own morality, even in all this?" He sipped at his Drambuie, then suddenly threw the glass away from him out over the cliff. The liquid spilled, spinning in a flat disc and, while the glass plunged downward, seeming to hesitate before it followed, breaking into a loose shower. "No. Of course you're not. I had the boat destroyed. Burned. I'm sorry."

"I'll find a way."

Michael looked at Jerry, opened his mouth, then shut it again and turned away.

"A wife," Jerry said. "And a son." It might be reassuring, it might help him, if his friend wept. The separation, whatever, would not be an easy one.

Michael nodded quietly. He reached up to the monogrammed pocket and took out a boiled egg, already peeled, put it on his palm then returned to the pocket and brought out a small silver spoon between his first two fingers. The spoon dangled loosely between them; the hands were pale, bloated white, the fingers perfectly straight, joints hardly creased at all. He knew from experience that offering one to Jerry would be a futile gesture. But a gesture these days, however futile....He looked across the table at his friend and Jerry shook his head. His hair was short now, shorter than Michael had ever seen it. He had arrived with hair filthy and tangled; repairing him, grooming him, Michael had no choice but to cut it. He remembered how Jerry had sat staring into the mirror, very still, watching the fine, tangled black strands fall onto his shoulders and tumble down across his chest and arms as his friend moved behind him, manipulating the scissors.

Michael lived on eggs (difficult as they were to obtain) and Drambuie, but had been unable to discover what kept Jerry going. He had never seen him eat. Anything. It seemed to him that Jerry grew thinner every day, and there had been, these past few days, a weakness in his movements—a weakness Michael had first noticed in bed, and one all the more remarkable for its contrast to Jerry's strong, deep voice. What strength he had left seemed to have gathered in that voice, and in his hands, and even here there was a quality of stillness.

Michael lifted the egg in his palm and looked at it against the smoke-swaddled air. So simple, symmetrical. Egg and hand were barely distinguishable. His friend's voice came across the table to him, soft now, and low.

"It's not the effect, but the *fact*, that one finds intolerable."

Michael made no response. Neither of them moved, looking out across the water toward the city.

"They are there. Inexorable, ineffable, intolerable."

"If such things as facts exist…?"

"The absence of fact, in effects, *becomes* fact."

"Yes. I suppose…" What had he begun to say? It was lost, whatever. He shook his head and looked back at the egg. "Don't try to help me, Jerry." He stabbed the spoon into the egg and a plug of white flew off into the air, landing just past the patio and throwing up a fine cloud of ashy dust. Jerry watched as he scooped out a daub of dull yellow on the tip of the tiny spade the size of a fingernail and lifted it to his mouth. A pink tongue met it, rolled back into the mouth. Jerry wondered idly how the egg would taste on top of Drambuie. He lifted his own glass, empty now, and a drop of the thick liqueur which had gathered back to the bottom slid slowly down it to his tongue. The egg was smashed into dry fragments now on his friend's open hand.

Jerry looked toward the garden. He found himself unable to watch the eating. For the first time he noticed a sign there, a handpainted square on a short stick, almost lost in the rolling folds of cabbage: *Keep ceaseless watch for* COLORADO BEETLES. *They can destroy our potato crops.* He remembered seeing the same sign, years ago, printed then and neatly designed, in every London post office. When he turned back, two more private boats were moving slowly down the water, pulling cluttered barges. A body toppled off one and fell into the wake, drifting, slower still, toward the base of the cliff below.

It was getting dark. Michael had finished the egg and now wiped his palm on his leg, smearing the bits which were left into the dark silk pajamas. He looked down at the barges.

"A question of guilt: is it real? Can it ever be real? Or is it just a word, something conjured up, manufactured, to hide something else we're afraid to face?" He walked to the edge of the patio steel and looked down. (Associations, Jerry thought. I can't stop making associations, not even me. It's the place, I have no right to be here. Mallarmé said that poetry was made from words, not ideas. And Goethe said that whereas an idea was one thing, a word could always be found to replace it. Associations. I can't stop them.) "As you say, a fact....Truth."

Ten feet out from the base of the artificial cliff, the body, propelled by the lazy euphoric wash of boat and barge, collided with the outermost of the bobbing refuse, disrupting it. Finally it came to rest alongside another body, this one gray and bloated from long exposure to the water, and there was only the slight synchronized rippling of movement among the whole. Final remnants of the boats' passage.

"No. A fact."

He turned back to Jerry and smiled. There was a gentle wind from downriver, where the bodies were burning. The umbrella fringe leaned into it, the cabbage swayed all together, its complex leaves rippling lightly backwards, backwards, backwards again. Jerry suddenly remembered something from Wallace Stevens—"All of our ideas come from the natural world: trees=umbrellas." Was that true. It occurred to him that this was important; he would have to face it. Later. When there was more time.

"To bed now, Jerry?"

"But—"

After a moment he got up and followed his friend, obsessed with the almost imperceptible gray smear on his pajamas. His eyes fastened to it. He thought of his own brown hands: the fingers long and thin, sagging in between the joints, the joints themselves crooked, irregular, the end ones bending back on themselves. Associations. He looked at the cabbage, the sign. He looked back at the smear of egg on Michael's pajamas. He thought of his marriage.

Later that night he woke alone in bed. Michael was standing naked at the window, looking out, with a cigarette in his hand. There was a bright erratic light outside. The radio was on low, Glen Campbell singing, *Gentle on My Mind.*

Michael seemed to know instantly that he was awake.

"Jerry. Come to the window."

Jerry slid across the black silk sheets. Were they actually damp or was it simply the absence of a body there, the coldness, which gave that illusion? The door, at least, was warm. Jerry went across the room and stood beside his friend. Yet when he looked out he felt alone; the sense of Michael as a person faded from him and he knew somehow that it would now be always like this.

The city was burning.

The fires were steady, slow, borne in every building, every house, every street: there was no violence to them, and Jerry, watching, felt a strange sense of peacefulness. Even at this distance, climbing slowly, quietly toward the top of the city, the flames showed on their faces. The black water was full of fire. Only there, in reflection, did the flames become violent.

Without turning from the window Jerry said, "Put that out." Michael stared at him for a moment, then dropped the cigarette and ground it into the carpet with his bare foot.

They stood watching silently. Neither of them moved. It was a single fire now, and as it rose, smoke fluttering upwards, the cloud of black settled down onto the city. They could hear the crackling, explosions, the steady rumble of buildings tumbling back into themselves, pushing the flames higher through the empty corridors.

"They knew," Jerry said finally.

When Michael spoke, his voice was like the click of a revolver rolling onto the next chamber, a beetle shutting its wing case.

"You'll still—"

"Tomorrow," Jerry said. "When the fires have died down."

The fire's light showed on the bodies and refuse against the far bank, making each thing a different object, something apart from the rest. People stood on the bank and looked down into the water. They stood completely still.

"Your wife and son?"

Jerry nodded, and the flames were in his hair. Several minutes passed. Rubble began to fall into the water, pushing the bodies and refuse out away from the bank. They began to drift slowly across the river toward the cliff. Still no one moved. There was no energy left for them. They stood with their heads down, staring into the water, the rubble, refuse, bodies, the reflected flames. Finally, very quietly beside him, Michael broke the silence.

"We'll go together. My boat—"

Jerry cut him off, nodding again, then walked away from him through the doors and onto the patio, where he sat down at the edge of the steel. Michael would know enough not to follow.

He sat there all night, alone, watching the city burn.

# Breakfast with Ralph

*A*T BREAKFAST KATIE drops a piece of egg on the floor. One of the younger roaches catches it on the bounce and wheels off towards a closet. Buttered biscuit in one hand, coffee in the other, Mr. Dosey swivels in his chair and plants a foot (size 13, orange sneakers) in its way.

"Just a minute," he says. "Hold on there. How are we ever going to live on this earth in harmony as a single be-ing, etcetera, etcetera—all that stuff in the Charter; you know it as well as I do—if you can't even mind your manners?"

"I'm sorry, sir," the cockroach says. "Might I please have this stray bit of egg?"

"Well of course you may, my young friend," Mr. Dosey says. "And how's the family, if I might ask?"

"*Well*, sir, I'm pleased to say. Except for Paulie, that is."

"Still sickly, is he?"

"Yes, sir."

"Sorry to hear it. But then, I suppose there's nothing for it but time."

"I suppose not, sir. That's what old Doc Branson says, at any rate."

Outside, Conestogas creak past on their way to a new world. Milkcarts take the corner on two wheels, bottles ring-ing together like chimes, rattling like scrap metal. A toothless old man hawks papers from the curb. *Amelia Earhart Lands at La Guardia*, one of the headlines reads.

"The boy really *is* sorry, sir," a new arrival says. "It's so difficult to bring them up right, these days. *You* try raising eighty-three children. And I'm a lawyer: successful, well-paid (by *our* standards, of course), secure. I don't know *how* others manage. My nephew, for instance. A mere nineteen kids and he still can't hack it. Makes you wonder what it 's all coming to."

"O yes," Katie says. "At school we study the economics. It is good. Things go badly and will go worse."

Something of an *idiot savant*, Katie has problems with the four languages she speaks, all of them somehow sounding pretty much the same when she speaks them, relics of a weekend spent beside the short-wave radio at her uncle's. Neither is she very well coordinated. A second piece of egg drops to the floor. Everyone ignores it. Four of the roaches are working up a barbershop-quartet version of *My Old Kentucky Home*.

"Free enterprise, this may not be the answer," Katie says, "the ultimate answer, I mean. Perhaps it is that we must, so to speak, think in different categories, no?"

And soon all are gathered around the table for a lively discussion of political means and ends. That the roaches are somewhat more conservative is almost certainly explained by their having (racially, at any rate) been around so much longer. A kind of adaptive ultimate, they've not evolved physically in thousands of years on the principle that if something's not broken, don't fix it.

"The one I worry about most, though," the older roach says after a while, "is Gary George. Fancies himself a poet. Always scribbling on napkins and things. Free bus rides for poets in Guatemala, of course, but what *else* is there?"

"Alcoholism, suicide, despair," Mr. Dosey's wife, the children's mother, Dee, says. "Random sex with writing students. Strange enthusiasms for suspect literatures. Terrible mood swings. Resentment. Fury. Silence."

"Really?" Mr. Dosey says.

"All that?" the roach (whose name, he later explains, is Ralph) says.

"And more." Dee gets up and pours more coffee for all.

"Plato banished poets from his republic," Paulie says.

"In the old days, Presidents Nixon and Reagan required the CIA to maintain lists of practicing poets alongside those of potential and manifest subversives. Youngish men in gray suits and short haircuts regularly attended poetry readings. Sometimes they were the only ones there."

This again from Dee, who goes on to recite, proud that she does not sing-song it, *The Raven*. Then *The Bells* and a pound or two of Edna St. Vincent Millay. I shall die but that is all that I shall do for death, Life must go on I forget just why, Wine from these grapes, etcetera.

"I had no idea you loved poetry so," Mr. Dosey says to his wife.

"As a child I spent a great deal of time alone," Dee says. "I dreamed. I wondered. Words, for me, were new worlds. By nine or so most nights my parents had passed out in their bedroom; they drank. The younger kids were all asleep. For an hour or two I would own the whole world."

"*We'll* someday own the world, my father says." One of the youngest of the roaches. "We must only be patient."

"That may well be the case—"

"The world is the case,' according to Wittgenstein," Katie says.

"—and I hope you'll be kinder to it, less apart from it, than my own kind has been."

"Aren't we all morbid for such a beautiful early morning," Dee says.

"Gotta be a pony here somewhere," one child says, and the others laugh, knowing Dee so well.

"I thought after breakfast we 'd have a nice stroll down to the museum," Dee goes on. "Perhaps on our way back we might stop off at the library. You *will* come along, won't you?" she says to the roaches.

"Well, of course I'd have to ask my wife—"

"Please, Daddy, please, can't we?"

"—but yes, I believe we'd like that. And you'll take tea with us afterwards, of course."

"Of course," Dee says.

"'Civilization is two men sitting over tea as the world falls apart,'" Katie says.

"Not two men," Mr. Dosey corrects her. "Man and roach together. It makes a difference."

Outside, unaccountably, Conestogas begin circling the house. Milkbottles crash against its sides. Wind ferries in the warcries of Indians, aberrant children or enraged economists.

"It's a strange world, my friend," Mr. Dosey says.

"And a tasty one," Ralph answers, finishing off the eggs.

# Intimations

$S$OMETIMES THE CHILD, who has no name, bangs the tin can (for water) along the bars of its cage.

She has not been in the room, near the room, for months now.

Each morning before he goes to work he snaps on the leash and takes it for a walk. Raising a leg, it waters fireplugs, trees, automobile tires.

In some ways the child is very bright.

Though he tried, at first, they do not talk of the child anymore.

He feeds it at five each day in the little bowl with the Disney characters on it, table scraps and rich red meat. It hunkers in the corner of the cage, the far corner (to which it always carries the bowl), and shoves the food into its mouth with tiny hands. This lasts two minutes.

Its hands are dexterous.

Sometimes at night he goes in and talks to it. Business, that is what he knows, that is what he speaks of. The events of his day, the latest Dow-Jones, the new management position in the Midwest.

It lies on its side on the floor of the cage, looking out at him with wide, uncomprehending eyes.

But there is a spark of intelligence deep within them.

His own IQ has tested out at, variously, 121, 136, and 156; he does not know hers, but it must be high. (Often, he suspects she is more intelligent than he.) She has an M.F.A. They have built a studio onto the house. She spends most of her time there. It has a daybed.

He wonders at these times if the child knows who he is. Why he is there.

He suspects it does.

One night it reached out to him as he talked. Its hand struck the bars of the cage. It made sounds.

I—no longer can I accept the burden (I had thought it freedom) of an impersonal "he"—stand in the park at 12th Street and Forest Lane. While around me on this Monday morning range children retarding their journey to school and young girls (or so they seem) with bright cheeks pushing prams.

The air is clear and fresh, some freak of wind or other direction having borne away our accustomed weekend smog. Sunlight rests almost palpably on every surface.

And the child paces the leash. No longer does it pull against it, run to the end, or ferry side to side; this has not happened for some time now.

I stop, and the child stops.

Above our heads in a willow tree (I know this because the bronze plaque on the trunk names it), an adult bird—male? Female?—injects half-digested worms (insects?) into the gaping beaks of fledglings. Far off to the right, a plane appears to be plummeting through the blaze of morning and into the river.

I whistle softly and the child turns from its study of the dragonfly buzzing its face. Eyes like spots of tarnish move to my own.

I walk forward and unsnap the leash, coiling it about my wrist. I suppose I wonder (I must) if I know what I am doing. Or why.

(The eyes descend momentarily, return to mine.)

And walk away from this.

Glancing back at the end of the walkstrip (yes, Lot; yes, Orpheus—see: even now I try to distance the real event with allusion, dead things) to find the child trailing behind me.

I lift my arms. Wave them wildly; stamp my feet on the pavement.

The child skitters away a few steps and ranges back.

And so—save me, that it should come to this; that I should have to confess it—I raised a foot upon which at that moment resided an Italian slipper of softest glove leather, and directed it towards the child's small, strange body. It struck him in the ribs; he fell.

Again and again I struck out at him and still he made no move. Six times. Until, on seven, his hand clawed at the grass beneath him. Eight, nine, he was to his knees, ten, his feet, running, eleven, going, gone.

Far horizons released the last captive strands of day.

And as he ran into it, I saw that he limped.

Into the room where I've never been, I move carefully. To see will these objects, forms accept me.

Light falls through orange glass and lays the head of a Renaissance lady dimly on the covers and green cushions of the daybed before me. In the corner beyond, stacks of newspapers and journals ascend, Babel-like, towards the ceiling. A huge ashtray supports a single smoldering cigarette.

On an easel by the window is a painting in progress. The

background of park, grass, swings is well defined, the closer slide less so. On the slide a formless something courses towards the ground.

She is standing by the painting and, with but a brief glance at my face, passes beside me and into the hall. We do not speak. I follow.

Even before the door to his room, words do not pass between us, though perhaps at this point I nod once and quietly (I do not remember).

Silently, she swings the door out, steps inside, shuts it.

Now she sits in the far corner of the cage, looking out at me.

I think there is a smile on her face and as her hand moves towards the tin can, I realize she is thirsty.

# Letter to a Young Poet

*D*EAR JAMES HENRY,
This morning your letter, posted from Earth over two years ago, at last reached me, having from all indications passed through the most devious of odysseys: at one point, someone had put the original envelope (battered and confused with stampings and re-addressings) into another, addressed it by hand, and paid the additional postage. You wonder what word suits the clerk who salvaged your letter from the computer dumps and took it upon himself to do this. Efficiency? Devotion? Largesse? Gentilesse?

At any rate, by the time it finally reached me here, the new envelope was as badly in need of repair as your own. I can't imagine the delay; I shouldn't think I'd be so hard a man to find. I move around a lot, true, but always within certain well-defined borders. Like Earth birds that never stray past a mile from their birth tree, I live my life in parentheses....I suppose it's just that no one especially bothers to keep track.

For your kind words I can only say: thank you. Which is not enough, never enough, but what else is there? (Sometimes, as with our mysterious and gracious postal patron, even that is impossible.) It makes me happy to learn that my poems have brought you pleasure. If they've given you something else as well, which you say they have, I am yet happier. You have expressed your joy at my sculpture. That also makes me happy. Thank you.

In brief answer to your questions, I am now living in Juhlz on Topfthar, the northernmost part of the Vegan Combine, though I don't know how much longer I shall be here. Political bickering breeds annoying restrictions and begins to throw off a deafening racket—and after four years the Juhlzson winter is at last creeping in (I'm sitting out on my patio now; I can see it far off in the hills). The two together, I'm afraid I can't withstand.

The hours of my day hardly vary. I rise to a breakfast of bread and wine, pass the day fiddling at my books. I rarely write, sculpt even less, the preparation is so difficult…. Night is a time for music and talking in Juhlz cafés, which are like no others. (The casual asymmetry of Juhlzson architecture always confounds the Terran eye. The people are like the buildings, off-center, beautiful. You never know what to expect.) I have taken up a local instrument—the thulinda, a kind of aeolian harp or perhaps dulcimer, fitted to a mouthpiece—and have got, I am told, passably good. I play for them and they teach me their songs.

(The sky's just grown gray cumulus beards and a voice like a bass siren. It should snow, but won't. My paper flaps and flutters against the table. Darkness begins to seep around the edges. This is dusk on Juhlz, my favorite time of day.)

As to your other questions, I was born on Earth: my first memories are of black, occluded skies and unbearable temperatures, and my parents fitting filters to my face when, rarely, we went outside (my poem, Eve Mourning).

My father was a microbiologist. Soon after I was born, he

became a Voyager; I remember him hardly at all, and his
hands mostly, at that. My mother, as you probably know
since one of my publishers made a thing of it quite against
my wishes, was Vegan, a ship's companion, a woman whose
gentle voice and quiet hands could do more than any medic
to soothe a hurt, salve a scar. They met during a Voyage my
father took in place of a friend—his first—and were together
always after that. One of my early sculptures, Flange Cou-
pling, was realized as a memorial to my parents. I don't know
if you've seen it. The last I heard, it was in a private collection on Rigel-7. But that was years and years ago.

My early life was spent in comfort, in my grandparents'
home on Vega and other times in crèches on Earth. When I
was seven, my parents were killed in Exploration; shortly
after, I was sent to the Academy at Ginh, where I passed my
next twelve years and for which the Union provided funds
and counsel. My *Letters Home,* which I've come in past years
to misdoubt, was an attempt to commemorate that time, at
least to invest it with private worth.

I don't know what command you have of Vegan history;
I suppose when I was a young man I cared nothing for history of any sort. But these were the years of the Quasitots,
who supposed themselves a political group and spent their
time and talents in metaphorical remonstrance against the
mercenary trends of Vegan-Outworld affairs. (If I am telling you things you already know, please forgive me, but
what looms large on my horizon may be unseen from yours;
I have no way of knowing.)

In one of the "Letters" I quoted Naevius, an early Roman
poet (my interest in Latin being perhaps the sole solid tie I
have with my father's world)...."Q. Tell me, how was your
great commonwealth lost so quickly? A. We were overrun

by a new lot of orators, a bunch of silly youngsters." I believe we thought that fitted us. We answered their declarations and old speeches with avant-garde aesthetics; we thought we would be the "silly youngsters" who'd usher in a new order. I suppose, vaguely, we believed that artists should inherit the universe.

One of my friends at the Academy took to composing symphonies of odor, the foulest odors he could find and produce, dedicating each work to the two governments. Another created an artificial flower which would wilt if touched; yet another gathered dung and baked it into likenesses of the Heads of State. My own contribution (half-hearted at best, I suppose) was the sculpting of single grains of sand, using the tools of my father, then scattering my invisible beauty in handfuls wherever I walked.

I'm not certain any longer what we really thought we were accomplishing. In our own words we were reacting, we were speaking out, we were being ourselves, we were caring. At any rate, this activity channeled our energies, made us work, made us think, let us live off of each other's various frenzies. It taught some of us, a few, that words and gestures get nothing done. Maybe somewhere, somehow, it accomplished something larger; I don't know. (I understand, by the way, that microsculpture is quite the thing in the academies today.) Such, anyway, was the temper and tempo of my youth.

When I was twenty, I left Ginh with my degrees and came to live in a small room up four flights of stairs here on Juhlz (my poem, *Crown of Juhlz*). I worked for a while as a tutor, then held a position at the old Empire Library, but came very soon to realize that I was unable to fit myself to a job of any sort.

I fled to Farthay, where I wrote my first novel and married. She was a young, small thing with joy in her heart and light in her eyes, a Vegan. Two years with me, and without the comfort of a child, was all she could bear. She left. It was best for both of us. We had already spent too much of our separate selves.

The rest of my life (I am 84) has been spent in forming and breaking idle patterns. I travel a lot, settle for short periods, move on (your letter retraced, and made me remember, many years of my life). What money I have comes through the kindness of friends; and from other, distant friends who buy my books.

My books: you ask after them. Thank you. Well, there's *Letters Home,* which I've already mentioned and which you've probably read. Quite against my own preferences and wishes, it has proved my most popular book; I've been told that it's taught in literature and sociology classes round about the Union.

There are the novels: *Day Breaks; Pergamum* (a sort of eulogy for my marriage); *A Throw of the Dice; Fugue* and *Imposition;* one or two others I'd just as soon not admit to.

Essays: *Pillow Saint; Halfway Houses; Arcadias; Avatars and Auguries.* Two volumes of letters between the Vegan poet Arndto and myself, concerning mostly Out-world poetry, entitled *Rosebushes* and *Illuminations.*

A collection of short stories, three volumes, *Instants of Desertion.*

And of course, the poems...*Overtures and Paradiddles; Misericords; Poems; Negatives; Abyssinia; Poems* again; *Printed Circuits; Assassins of Polish.* Some while back, I received a check with a letter informing me that a *Collected Poems* was to be issued through Union Press. I can't recall just how long ago that was, and can't know how long the message took to find me, so I don't know whether the book is available.

And coming at last to the poems you've sent, what am I to say? All critical intent is beyond me, I fear. I've been constantly bemused and confounded by what critics have found to praise and damn in my own work: I was aware neither that I had "narrowly ordered my sensibilities" nor that I "struck out boldly into the perilous waters that lie between a poetry of device and the poetry of apocalypse" (which another renders as aiming between "a poem of sentiment and one of structure"). Give me always the Common Reader, the sensitive ignorance.

("The perilous waters"...had I known there was danger of drowning, I might never have begun to write.)

You want Authority; I can give you none. Let me instead look up at these winter-blurred hills and say this: the poems you've sent, and which I return with this letter—they are not unique, but they speak of something which may come, something which may become yours alone. Perhaps you have it now. But two years is a very short time.

They are direct, compact, all the flourishes are beneath the surface—things greatly to be praised in a young writer. In one line you are content to give shape, in another you pause and form; always something comes easy, to the ear, the eye, the tongue, the mind, the heart. Also to be admired.

You evidently achieve control with little struggle, effective structure with somewhat more difficulty (precision and accuracy are often separate things). But you have patience, and this will come. Your diction draws crisp, sharp lines around a poem, while imagery and resonance make what is contained soft and yielding. This is at least a proper direction. And I think you are right to work from the outside in, the way you seem to do.

Two years ago, when you wrote the letter, you were looking for an older, wiser, gentler voice than your own. I am sorry that I have been so long in admitting that I cannot provide it. Perhaps you've already found one, in some academy, some café. Or perhaps you no longer need it; edges have a way of wearing off. Peace, calm—but what I can give you is closer to a stillness.

I was quite moved by the Betelgeuse mood poems in particular: I should say that. I envy you these poems. Because of a late-developing nervous disorder, a clash in my mixed parentage, I am confined pretty much to Vega. I've not been outside the Combine since the day I came here. Something in the specific light complements my affliction, and I can go on in good health. But I believe I shall have to return to dark Earth before I die, that at least, in spite of all.

It occurs to me that you obviously know about writing, and I think you must have known the worth of your poems, so I can only assume that you are really asking about living. And I have one thing to say, a quiet thing: Ally yourself to causes and people, and you'll leave bits of yourself behind every step you take; keep it all, and you'll choke on it. The choice is every man's, for himself.

The day is wearing down, burning near its end. Lights have gone on then off again in the houses around me. Everyone is feeling alone.

So as darkness and winter move in, hand in hand, let me wish you the best of luck in your ambitions, apologize again for the delay, and bring to a close this letter, longer than any letter has a right to be.

And in closing, please accept again my thanks for your

kind words. They are given so easily, yet mean so much, always.

Night now. Juhlzson birds have come off the lakes and out of forests, and are throbbing softly around me. The moons are sailing in and out of clouds. In a moment I shall move off the patio into the house. In a moment.

Yours,
Samthar Smith

# Faces, Hands

## KETTLE OF STARS

*A* LOT OF Couriers are from academic backgrounds, everything from literature to energy mechanics, the idea being that intellectual hardening of the arteries is less likely to occur if you watch what you eat and keep the blood flowing. You have to stay flexible: one loose word, one unguarded reaction, and you've not only lost respect and a job, you've probably thrown an entire world out of sympathy with Earth. In those days a Courier was a kind of bargainlot diplomat/prime minister/officeboy, and we were playing most of it by ear; we hadn't been in Union long enough to set standards. So when they started the Service they took us out of the classrooms, out of the lines that stood waiting for diplomas—because we were supposed to know things like unity being the other side of a coin called variety. Knowledge, they assumed, breeds tolerance. Or at least caution.

Dr. Desai (Comparative Cultural) used to lean out over the podium he carried between classrooms to proclaim: "All the institutions, the actions, the outrages and distinctions of an era find their equivalent in any other era." He said it with all the conviction of a politician making the rounds before General Conscript, his small face bobbing up and down to emphasize every word. I took my degree at Arktech under Desai, and in my three years there I must have heard him say that a hundred times: everything else he—or any other instructor—said, built back up to it like so many stairsteps. A zikkurat: climb any side, you get to the top. Some early member of the Service must have had Dr. Desai too. They had the same thing in mind.

For me it was June, on a day like yellow crystal. I was sitting in an outdoor café across from the campus with my degree rolled up in a pocket, cup half full of punjil, myself brimful of insouciance. It was a quiet day, with the wind pushing about several low blue clouds. I was looking across at the towers and grass of the Academy, thinking about ambition—what was it like to have it? I had no desire to teach: I couldn't get past Desai's sentence. And for similar reasons I was reluctant to continue my studies. An object at rest stays at rest, and I was very much at rest.

Distractedly, I had been watching a small man in Vegan clothes work his way down along the street, stopping to peer into each shop in turn. When finally he reached the café he looked around, saw me in the corner and began smiling. I barely had time to stand before he was at the table, hand stuck out, briefcase already opening.

Like Desai, he was a little man, forehead and chin jutting back from a protruding nose.

"Hello, Lant," he said. "I was told I could probably find you over here." He sat down across from me. He had small red eyes, like a rabbit's "Let me introduce myself: Golfanth Stein. S-t-e-i-n: stain. I wonder if you've heard the Council's organizing a new branch." I hadn't. "Now that we're in Union there's a certain problem in representation, you know. Much to be done, embassies to establish, ambassador work. So we're beginning the Courier Service. Your degree in anthropology, for instance..."

He bought me a drink and I signed his papers.

Ten years...Ten years out of school, ten years spent climbing the webwork of diplomatic service—and I found it all coming back to me there on Alsfort, as I sat in the wayroom of the Court.

There was a strike in effect; some of you will remember it. A forced-landing had come down too hard, too fast, and the Wagon had snapped the padbrace like a twig, toppling a half-acre of leadsub over onto the firesquads. So the Court workers were striking for subsurface landings, for Pits. My inbound had been the last. They were being turned away to Flaghold now, the next-door (half a million miles away) neighbor, an emergency port.

And if you sat in a Court and sweated at what was going on a Jump-week behind you on Earth and two ahead of you, on Altar; if you cursed and tried to bribe the crews; if you sent endless notes to both ends of the line you were knotted on; or if perhaps you are a history student specializing in the Wars...you'll remember the strike. Otherwise, probably not. Alsfort isn't exactly a backyard—more like an oasis.

Two days, and I'd given up insisting, inquiring, begging. I'd even given up the notes.

So I sat in the wayroom drinking the local (and distant) relative of beer. The pouch was locked into my coat pocket and I was keeping my left arm against it. I spent the first day there worrying what might happen on Altar without that pouch, then I gave it up the way I'd given up trying to surmount the strike, to curtail my immobility and its likely disastrous consequences. I just sat and drank "beer" and punjil and watched the people.

There was a short, wiry man of Jewish blood, Earth or Vegan, who limped from a twisted back, as though all his life he'd been watching over his shoulder. He drank tea saturated with grape sugar at ten and four and took his meals as the clock instructed: noon, six. He wore skirts, and a corduroy skullcap he never removed.

There was a couple, definitely Vegan. The woman was old (though only in profile), dressed in Outworld furs and wearing a single jewel against her emphatic and no doubt plastic bosom—a different jewel each time I saw them. Her companion was young, beautiful and asthenic, always precisely dressed in a fine tight suit, and quite often scribbling in a notebook he carried. They came irregularly and drank Earth brandy. By the third day too much sameness had taken its toll: she sat with her face screwed into jealousy as he smiled and wrote in his book. When she spoke, there were quiet, gulping rhythms in her voice, and her only answer was the boy's beautiful smile and, once, a hand that held hers tightly——too tightly—on the table. He waited in the halls while she paid; she kept her face down, an older face now; they went away.

A Glaucon, a man I knew from Leic, but his ruby robes signaled pilgrimage and forbade us to speak. I watched him at his evening coffees. A recent convert, he was not at all the craftsmanlike politician I had come to know in those months spent on his world, in his home. He had been quick, loud; now he plodded, and his voice followed softly in the distance, muttering at prayer.

And there were others, many others....

A Plethgan couple with a Vorsh baby, evidently returning home from the Agencies at Llarth. They came to the wayroom just once, to ask about Vorshgan for the child, and were told there was none. The mother was already pale with fear, the father raging and helpless; the baby screamed and was turning blue. They went out talking quietly to themselves under the child's cries. I never saw them again.

A Llyrch woman, alone and wearing only a formal shawl. it was brown, showing midcaste. A single green stripe and a small silver star proclaimed that her husband was dead; that he died in honor, in a duel on Highker, away from home. Once she turned in her seat and the shawl fell partly open, exposing, beneath her hairless head, exorcised breasts and the carvings in her belly. She took nothing but water, and little of that.

And there was a man who came to the wayroom as often as I and sat as long, sipping a pale violet liquid from a crystal cup, reading or simply sitting, hands together, staring at the wall and moving his lips softly. He was short, with a quick smile and white teeth, hair gathered with ribbons to one side of his head. I wondered what he was drinking. He carried it in a flask to match the cup; you could smell it across the room, a light scent, pale as its color, subtle as perfume. Outworld, probably: he flattened his vowels, was precisely polite; there were remnants of a drawl. Urban, from the way he carried himself, the polished edge of gestures. His mien and clothes were adopted from the Vegans, but that was common enough to be useless in reading origin, and might have been assumed solely for this trip. Vegan influence was virtually ubiquitous then, before the Wars. I generally traveled in Vegan clothes myself, even used the language. Most of us did. it was the best way to move about without being noticed.

The Outworlds, though. I was fairly sure of that....

Lying out along the fringe of trade routes, they were in a unique position to Union civilization. Quite early they had developed a more or less static society, little touched by new influences spreading outward from Vega: by the time ripples had run that far, they were pretty weak. There was little communication other than political, little enough culture exchange that it didn't matter. The Outworld societies had gone so far and stopped; then, as static cultures will, become abstracted, involuted—picking out parts and making them wholes. Decadence, they used to call it.

Then the Vegans came up with the Drive, the second one, Overspace. And suddenly the Outworlds were no longer so Out, though they kept the name. The rest of us weren't long in discovering the furth's fur, shelby and punjil, which for a while threatened to usurp the ancient hierarchy of coffee and alcohol on Earth with its double function as both stimulant and depressant. Under this new deluge of ships and hands (giving, taking) the Outworlds were at last touched. They were, in fact, virtually struck in the face. And the Outworlds, suddenly, were in transition.

But there's always an Orpheus, always those who look back. Under the swing of transition now, decadence had come to full flower. Amid the passing of old artifice, old extravagance, dandyism had sprung up as a last burst of heroism, a protest against the changing moods.

And there was much about the man I watched—the way his plain clothes hung, something about his hair and the subtly padded chest, his inviolable personality and sexlessness; books held up off the table, away from his eyes—that smacked of dandyism. It's the sort of thing a Courier learns to look for.

There were others, fleeting and constant. Single; coupled;

even one Medusa-like Gafrt symb in which I counted five distinct bodies, idly wondering how many others had been already assimilated. But these I've mentioned are the ones I still think about, recalling their faces, the hollow forms hands made in air, their voices filling those forms. The ones I felt, somehow, I knew. These—and one other....

Rhea.

Without her Alsfort wouldn't be for me the vivid memory it is. It would be a jumbled, distorted horror of disappointment, failure, confusing faces. A time when I sat still and the world walked past me and bashed its head into the wall.

Rhea.

I saw her once, the last day. For a handful of minutes we touched lives across a table. I doubt she remembers. For her now, there will have been so *many* faces. I doubt she remembers.

It was mid-afternoon of my fourth day on Alsfort. The strike was beginning to run down; that morning, perhaps from boredom, the workers had volunteered a bit of light, routine work away from the Wagons, just to keep the Court from clogging up beyond all hope. I watched them unpack, adjust, and test a new booster. One of the men climbed into it and with a hop went sailing out across the pads, flailing his arms violently. Minutes later, he came walking back across the gray expanse, limping and grinning. He went up to the engineer and began talking quietly, shaking his head and gesturing toward one of the leg extensions. They vanished together, still talking, into the tool shop, hauling the booster between them.

I had gone from lunch at the Mart to coffee from the lobby servicors. Settling into a corner I watched the people wander about the arcade—colors, forms, faces blurred by distance; grouping and dissolving, aimless abstract patterns. Going back to my room had been a bad experience: too quiet, too inviting of thought.

The landscape of Alsfort…

You can see it from the rim in the top levels—though *see* is inappropriate. *Study* would be better: an exercise in optical monotony. Brown and gray begin at the base of the Court and blend to various tones of baldness, blankness. Brown and gray, rocks and sand—it all merges into itself. Undefined. You walk out on the floating radial arms, trying to get closer, to make it resolve at least to lines. But it simply lies there. Brown, gray, amorphous.

So, after the briefest of battles, I wound up back in the wayroom. There was a booth just off-center, provided with console-adjustment seats and a trick mirror. Sitting there, you had the private tables in front of you; quick-service counters behind. You could watch the tables and, by tilting your head and squinting, dimly see what went on behind you, at the counters. Through the door you could watch people wandering the corridors. I had spent most of my four days in that booth, washing down surrogate-tablets with beer and punjil. Mostly Energine: sleep was impossible, or at least the silent hours of lying to wait for sleep. And somehow the thought of food depressed me almost as much. I tried to eat, ordering huge meals and leaving them untouched. By the fourth day my thoughts were a bit scrambled and I was beginning, mildly, to hallucinate.

The waiter was bringing me a drink when she came in. I was watching the mirror, hardly aware of his presence. Behind me, a man was talking to a companion who flickered in and out of sight; I was trying to decide whether this was the man's hallucination or my own. The waiter put my drink down with one hand, not watching, and knocked it against the curb. Startled, I felt the cold on my hands. I turned my head and saw what he was looking at....

Rhea.

She was standing in the doorway with the white floor behind her, blue light swelling in around her body. *Poised* was the word that came to me: she might fly at the first sudden motion.

She was...delicate. That was the second impression. A thing made of thinnest glass; too fine, too small, too perfect. Maybe five feet. Thin. You felt you could take her in your palm: she was that fine, that light. That fragile.

Tiny cameo feathers covered her body—scarlet, blue, sungold. And when light struck them they shimmered, threw off others, eyefuls of color. They thinned down her limbs and grew richer in tone; her face and hands were bare, white. And above the small carved face were other feathers: dark blue plumes, almost black, that brushed on her shoulders as she walked—swayed and danced.

Her head darted on air to survey the room. Seeing my eyes on her she smiled, then started through the tables. She moved like leaves in wind, hands fluttered at her sides, fingers long and narrow as blades of grass. Feathers swayed with her, against her, spilling chromatic fire.

And suddenly karma or the drugs or just my loneliness—whatever it was—had me by the shoulders and was tugging, pulling.

I came to myself, the room forming out of confusion, settling into a square fullness. I was standing there away from the booth, I was saying, "Could I buy you a drink?" My hand almost...almost at her shoulder. The bones there delicate as a bird's breast.

She stood looking back past me, then up at my face; into my eyes, and smiled again. Her own eyes were light orange beneath thin hard lids that blinked steadily, sliding over the eyes and back up, swirled with colors like the inside of sea-shells.

"Yes, thank you," in Vegan. "it would be very nice. Of you." She sang the words. Softly. I doubt that anyone but myself heard them.

I looked back at the Outworlder. He had been watching; now he frowned and returned to his book.

"I was tired. Of the room," she said, rustling into the booth. "I said. To him. I could not stay there, some time ago, much longer. I would like to come, here. And see the people."

"Him?"

"My...escort? Karl. That the room was. Not pretty, it made me sad. The bare walls, your walls are such...solid. There is something sad about bare walls. Our own are hammered from bright metals, thin and, open. Covered with reliefs. The forms of, growing things. I should not have to. Stay, in the room?"

"No. You shouldn't." I moved my hand to activate the dampers. All sound outside the booth sank to a dull, low murmur like the sea far off, while motion continued, bringing as it always did a strange sense of isolation and unreality.

I ordered punjil. The waiter left and returned with a tall cone of bright green fluid, which he decanted off into two small round glasses. His lips moved but the dampers blocked the sound; getting no response, he went away.

"I'm Lant."

"Rhea," she said. "You are, Vegan?"

"Earth."

"You work. Here."

"No. Coming through, held up by the strike. You?"

She sipped the punjil. "It is, for me, the same. You are a, crewman? On one of the ships then."

"No. I'm with a travel bureau. Moving around as much as I can, keeping an eye out for new ports, new contracts." Later, somehow, I regretted the lies, that came so easily. "On my way Out. I think there might be some good connections out there."

"I've heard the cities are. Very beautiful."

"This is my first time Out in ten years." That part, at least, was true; I had gone Out on one of my first assignments. "They were beautiful, breathtaking, even then. And they've done a lot in the last few years, virtually rebuilt whole worlds. The largest eclecticism the Union's known——they've borrowed from practically every culture in *and* out of Union...They're even building in crystals now. They say the cities look like glass blossoms, like flowers grown out of the ground. That there is nothing else like them."

"I saw a picture of Ginh, a painting, once. Like a man had made it in his hand and put it, into the trees. A lot of trees, all kinds. And sculpture, mosaics. In, the buildings. The trees were, beautiful. But so was. The city."

"We've all been more or less living off Outworld creativity for years now."

"A beautiful thing. It can take much...use?"

I supposed so, and we sat quietly as she watched the people, her eyes still and solemn, her head tilted. I felt if I spoke I would be intruding, and it was she who finally said: "The people. They are, beautiful also."

"Where are you from, Rhea?" I asked after watching her a while. She turned back to me.

"Byzantium." She set her eyes to the ceiling and warbled her delight at the name. "It is from, an old poem. The linguist aboard the Wagon. The first Wagon. He was, something of a poet. Our cities took, his fancy, he remembered this poem. He too was. Of Earth."

"I'm afraid I don't know the poem."

"It is, much. Old. Cities they are hammered of gold and set, in the land. All is. Beautiful there, and timeless. The poem has become for us. A song, one of our songs."

"And is your world like that? A refuge?"

"Perhaps. It was."

"Why did you leave?"

"I am going, to Ginh. To...work." She moved gently, looked around. I noticed again the tension in her face and hands, so unlike the easy grace of her body.

"You have a job there."

"Yes. I—" The mood passed. Her feathers rustled as she laughed: "Guess."

I declined.

"I sing." She trilled an example. Then stopped, smiling. We ordered new drinks, selecting one by name—a name she delighted in, repeating it over and over in different keys. It turned out to be a liqueur, light on the tongue, pulpy and sweet.

She leaned across the table and whispered, "It is. Nice." Her breath smelled like new-cut grass, like caramel and sea-breeze. Long plumes swept the tabletop and whispered there too. "Like the other, was."

"What do you sing, Rhea?"

"Old songs, our old songs. Of warriors. Lovers. I change the names, to theirs."

"How long will you be on Ginh?"

"Always."

You have been there before, then? No.

You have a family there? No.

You love Byzantium, you were happy there? Yes.

Then why...?

"I am...bought. By one of the Academies. I am taken there. To sing, for them. And to be, looked at." She seemed not at all sad.

"You will miss Byzantium?"

"Yes. Much."

I cleared my throat. "Slavery is against Regulations. You—"

"It is. By my own, my will."

A long pause...

I see.

"My race is. Dying. We have no techknowledgy, we are not, inUnion. Byzantium can not longer, support us. The money, they give for me. It feeds us for many years. It too buys machines. The machines will keep us. A part of us, alive."

She drew her knees up into a bower of arms and dropped her head, making the booth a nest. After a moment she lifted her face out from the feathers. She trilled, then talked.

"When I was a child, Byzantium was, quiet and still. Life it was easy. We sang our songs, made our nests, that is enough. For a lifetime, all our lives, lifetimes. That is enough. Now it is not longer easy."

"Perhaps it seemed that way. *Because* you were a child."

An arm hovered over the table. A hand came down to perch on the little round glass. "We took from her, Byzantium, she asked nothing. Our songs, our love. Not more. Our fires, to keep her, warm. The sky the earth it was. In, our homes."

"But you grew up."

"Yes and Byzantium, much old, she grows. Old-more than my Parent. Once it sang, with us. Now its voice broke, too went away. The souls left, the trees. Our homes. The rivers it swelled with sorrow, too burst. It fell, fruits from, the trees, too they were. Already dead. The moons grow red, red like the eye. Of a much old man."

"You tell it like a poem."

"It is, one of our songs. The last poem of, RoNan. He died before it was. Finished."

"Of a broken heart."

She laughed. Gently. "At the hands of, his sons. For to resist coalition. He spoke out in his songs, against the visitors. He thought, it was right, Byzantium to die. It should not be made to go on to live; living. He wanted the visitors, to leave us."

"The visitors…Outworld?"

She nodded. The plumes danced, so deep a blue. So deep.

"They came and to take our fruits, too our trees. They could make them to grow again-new on Ginh. They took our singers. They…bought, our cities, our unused nests. Then they to say, With these can you to build a new world. RoNan did not want, a new world, it would be much wrong, to Byzantium."

"And no one listened."

"They listened. Much of, them. The younger ones to not, who wanted too a life, a life of their own, a world for it. They learned, about the machines. They go much to Ginh and learned in, the Academies, there, they came back, to us. To build their new, world. Took it of the machines, like too bottomless boxes."

"Ginh. They went to Ginh…."

"Yes, where I am. Going. I am with our cities, too our trees on Ginh, in a museum, there. I sing. For the people. They to come. To look at us, to listen, to me."

The ceiling speaker cleared its throat. I looked up. Nothing more.

"He must have been a strong man," I said. "To stand up so strongly for what he believed was right. To hold to it so dearly. A difficult thing to do, these days."

"The decision was not his. He had, no choice. He was, what he believed. He could not go against it."

"And so were the others, the younger ones, and they couldn't either."

"That is, the sad part."

Someone blew into the speakers.

"You knew him, you believe what he said?"

"Does it matter? He was. My father."

And we were assaulted by sound:

*ATTENTION PLEASE, ATTENTION PLEASE. THE CHELTA, UNION SHIP GEE-FORTY-SEVEN, BOUND OUT, IS NOW ON PAD AND WILL LIFT IN ONE HOUR STANDARD. PASSENGERS PLEASE REPORT AT ONCE TO UNDERWAY F. UNDERWAY F.*

So the strike was over, the workers would get their Pits. A pause then, some mumbled words, a shuffling of papers:

*WILL CAPTAIN I-PRANH PLEASE REPORT TO THE TOWERMAIN. CAPTAIN I-PRANH TO THE TOWERMAIN. THE REVISED CHARTS HAVE BEEN COMPLETED.*

And the first announcement began again.

Rhea uncurled and looked up, then back past me, as if remembering something.

Her face turned up as he approached.

"Hello, Karl," she sang. "This is, Lant." My Outworld dandy. I reached over and opened the dampers.

He bowed and smiled softly. "Pleased, Lant" Then added: "Earth, isn't it?"—seeing through my Vegan veneer as easily as he'd made out her words through the dampers. His own voice was low and full, serene. "Always pleased to meet a Terran. So few of you get out this far. But I'm afraid I'll have to be rude and take Rhea away now. That was the call for our ship. Excuse us, please."

He put out a white hand, bowing again, and she took it, standing. Feathers rustled: a sound I would always remember.

"Thank you for talking to Rhea, Lant. I'm sure it was a great pleasure for her."

"For me."

A final bow and he turned toward the door. She stood there a moment, watching me, feathers lifting as she breathed.

"Thank you for, the drinks Lant. And for…to listen." She smiled. "You are going, Out. You will be on this ship. Perhaps I will. See you, on the ship."

She wouldn't, of course.

And she went away.

Most of the rest you know.

I Jumped the next day for Altar, where I got down on my callused knees and went through my bag of time-honored politician tricks. Money bandaged the wounds of insult, outrage was salved by a new trade agreement. The Altarians would withdraw troops from Mersy: the wars were stayed.

But not stopped. The Altarians kept their sores and when, several weeks later, one of our writers published a satirical poem attacking Altar for its "weasel colonialism, that works like a vine," the wound festered open. The poet refused to apologize. He was imprisoned and properly disgraced, but the damage was done.

War erupted. Which you don't need to be told: look out your window and see the scars.

War flashed across the skies, burst inside homes. Which doesn't matter: look in your mirror for the marks that tell, the signs that stay.

I don't have to tell you that the Vegans, victims of too much sharing and always our friends, sided with us. That they were too close to the Altar allies. That they were surrounded and virtually destroyed before our ships could make the Jump.

I don't have to tell you that we're still picking up the pieces. Look out your window, look in your mirror.

That we have the bones of Union and we're trying to fatten them up again....

I was one of the sideways casualties of war. One of the face-saving (for them) disgraces (for me). I believe I would have left anyway, I might have. Because there's something I have to say. And here I can say it, and be heard.

The Union gives a lot. But it takes a lot too. And I'm not sure any more that what it takes, what it shoves aside, is replaceable. Maybe some things *are* unique. I know one thing is.

Which is what I tell my students.

I sit here every day and look out at all these faces. And I

wonder, Will this one be a Courier, or that one in the front row, or the one in back—the girl who swings her leg, the kid who brings sandwiches to class in his briefcase? Will they be the disciples of Earth's ascendance?

I wonder.

And I tell them that a society feeds off its people. That the larger it is, the more it consumes. That you never know what effect your words will have a hundred million miles away.

You never know. But you try. You try to know, you try to balance things out on your own scales. Utility; the best for the most; compromise and surrender. Your smallest weights are a million, a billion, people.

But I tell them something else to go with that.

I tell them...

That there may be nothing new under the sun. But there *are* new suns, and new faces under them. Looking up, looking down...

The faces are what matter.

## THE FLOORS OF HIS HEART

*T*HE LITTLE ANIMAL went racing up the side of its cage, made a leap to the top, climbed upside-down halfway out—then dropped back onto the floor. It did this over and over, steadily tumbling, becoming each time wilder, more frantic. The last time, it lay still on its back in the litter, panting.

And she was lovely below him, beside him, above him. Was lovely in dark, lovely in shadow, lovely in the glaring door as she fingered the bathroom's light....

(She is sitting on the bed, legs crossed, one elbow cocked

on a knee, holding a ruby fang that bites again, again into the dark around her. The window is a black hole punched in the room, and for a moment now when she lifts her arm, light slants in and falls across her belly, sparkling on semen like dew in dark grass; one breast moves against the moving arm.

Light comes again, goes again. It strikes one side of her tilted face and falls away, shadows the other. She looks down, looks up, the small motion goes along her body, her side moves against yours. There are two paths of glowing where light touched her skin, here on her belly, here on the side of her face, a dull glowing orange. Already it is fading.

Her cigarette drops through the window like a burning insect, drops into darkness. It's this kind of darkness: it can fill a room.)

She came back and sat on the edge of the bed. The light was off, her skin glowing softly orange all over, darker orange for month-old bruises on her breasts and hips. "Strong. He hadn't been with a woman for three years," she had said when he touched one of the bruises. "A real man." He had beaten her severely, then left twice what was necessary.

She struck a match and the spurt of light spiderwebbed the dirty, peeling wall.

"You're really from Earth...." (Silence breaking, making sounds. The little animal moving slowly now in his cage.)

"Naturalized. During the Wars."

"Oh. I see." She was thinking about ruin, the way it started, the roads it took. Her skin was losing its glow. "Where were you born?"

"Here. Vega." (She turned to look at him.)

"In Thule." (She waited.)

"West Sector."

She turned back to the window. "I see."

"I was signed Out. It was a Vegan ship, we were getting the declaration broadcast when communication from Vega stopped. Captain turned us around but before we hit Drive, Earth told us it was too late. We went on into Drive and stayed in till we could find out what happened—Altar had ships jumping in and out all along the rim, grabbing whatever they could, blasting the rest—a big Wagon like *The Tide* was no match for what they had. We came out near Earth. Captain's decision, and I don't envy his having to make it. Anyway, the ship was consigned and the Captain pledged to Earth. Most of us went along, enlisted. There wasn't much to come back to."

The room was quiet then with the sound of her breathing, the rustle of the animal in its litter. Light from outside crept across the floor, touching her leg on the bed with its palm. She sucked at the cigarette and its fire glowed against her face, against the window.

"You're not Terran. I thought you were."

"I'm sorry. I'm sorry I didn't tell you. I didn't realize—"

"It doesn't matter."

"But I didn't mean to—"

"It doesn't matter." She smiled. "Really."

He lay watching her face above him, a quiet face, still. And the room itself was quiet again, was gray, was graying, was dark....

And later: her hand on his shoulder, her lips lightly against his and his eyes opening, something warm for his hand.

"I made coffee. You'll have to drink it black."

He stared at the cup, breathed steam and came more awake. The cup was blue ceramic, rounded, shaped into an owl's head. The eyes extended out at the edges to form handles. "You shouldn't have. Coffee's hard to get, I know, you sh—"

"I wanted to. You gave me cigarettes, I gave you coffee." She tore her cigarette in two, threw the smoking half-inch out the window, dropped the rest into the cage. Her fingers glowed orange where the cigarette had been.

"Thank you. For the coffee," he said. Then: "You're beautiful."

She smiled. "You don't have to say that."

"I wanted to."

And she laughed, at that.

He got up and walked to the cage, his hands wrapped around the mug. The little animal was leaning down on its front legs, hindquarters up, paws calmly working at the cigarette. It had carefully slit the paper and was removing the tiny lumps of charcoal from the filter one at a time, putting them in its mouth.

"Charcoal," she said. "There's charcoal in the filter, I just remembered. He likes it."

Having finished eating, the little animal rolled the remaining paper into a ball, carried it to one corner and deposited it there. Then it returned to the front of the cage and sat licking at the orange fur that tufted out around its paws.

"What is it?" he asked after a while. The charcoal pellets were still in its mouth. After sucking at them for several moments, it began to grind them between its teeth.

"A Veltdan."

"Vegan?"

She nodded.

"I've never seen one."

"There aren't many left—none around the cities. Dying

out. They're from Larne Valley."

He thought a moment, remembered: "The telepaths!" The colony of misanthropic sensitives.

"Yes. That's where the colony is. I was born there, came to Kahlu after the Wars. Not much left, even that far out. The colony was wiped out."

"Are you—"

She shook her head. "My mother. Mostly I was born without their physical deformity or their talents, though I guess I got a *little* of both." She came up to the cage, thumped her fingers against the side. "The telepathy...some of it filtered down. I'm an empathist, of sorts." She grinned. "Makes me good at my work."

She walked to the bed and lit another cigarette. An insect came in through the window, skittered around the room hitting the ceiling again and again, finally found the window and flew back out. It was neon, electric blue.

"Veltdans are supposed to be the deadliest things in the universe. Four inches from nose to tail, altogether seven pounds—and you can put them up against any animal you want to, any size, any weight."

He took his hand off the cage and put it back around the mug. The Veltdan was over on its back in the litter, rolling from side to side, square snout making arcs. Watching this prim, almost exquisite little animal, he found it difficult to accept what she was saying; to put the two facts together.

"It registers external emotion. Whatever made the telepaths got into the Veltdan too—as much as they can handle with their brain. You get something coming at it with a mind full of hate and killing, the Veltdan takes it all and turns it back on the attacker—goes into a frenzy, swarms all over it, knows what the attacker is going to do next. It's small but it's fast, it has sharp claws and teeth. While the attacker is getting filled back up with its own hate and fury, the Veltdan is tearing it to pieces. They say two of them fighting each other is really something to see, it just goes on and on."

He looked down at the little orange-cerulean animal. "Why should they fight one another?"

"Because that's what they like best to eat: each other."

He grimaced and walked to the window. A shuttleship was lifting. Its light flashed against his face.

Every day just past noon, flat clouds gather like lily pads in the sky, float together, rain hops off to pound on the ground. For an hour the rain comes down, washing the haze of orange from the air, and for that hour people come together in cafés and Catches, group there talking. And waiting.

They were sitting in an outdoor Catch, drinking coffee. Minutes before, clattering and thumping, a canvas roof had been rolled out over them. Around them now the crowd moved and talked. Rain slammed down, slapped like applause on the canvas roof.

"This is where the artists come," she said, pointing to a corner of the Catch where several young people were grouped around a small table. Two of them—a young man with his head shaved and a girl with long ochre hair—were bent forward out over the table, talking excitedly. The others were listening closely, offering occasional comments. When this happened the young man would tilt his head away from the speaker and watch him closely; the girl would look down at the floor, a distant expression on her face. Then when the speaker had finished they would look at one another and somehow, silently, they would decide: one of them would reply. Cups, saucers, crumpled sheets of paper were piled on the table. One of the girls was sketching. Rain sprinkled and splattered on the backs of those nearest the outside.

"The one talking, that's Dave," she went on. "A ceramist, and some say he's the best in Union. I have a few of his pots at home. Early stuff, functional. He used to do a lot of owls; everything he threw had an owl in it. Now he's on olms. Salamanders. They're transparent, live in caves. If you take one out into the sun it burns. Turns black and dies." She lit one of the cigarettes he'd given her. "They all come here every afternoon. Some work at night, some just wait for the next afternoon. I have a lot of their work," She seemed quite proud of that.

"You like art quite a lot, then?"

"No." She grinned, apologizing. "I don't even understand most of it. But I seem to feel it—what they think, their appreciation. And I like them, the people. They always need money, too."

She sat quietly for a moment, smoking, watching the group of young people.

"It's a tradition, coming here. This Catch was built where the *Old Union* was before the Wars; Samthar Smith always came here when he was on Vega. It's called *Pergamum* now."

"'All Pergamum is covered with thorn bushes; even its ruins have perished.' The epigraph for his novel, *Pergamum*. The eulogy he wrote for his marriage."

"Yes." She stared out at the rain. "I love that book." Then she looked back at him. "Dave tells me they've taken the name as a symbol. The ruin of the old, the growth of a new art."

A disturbance near the center of the Catch caught his attention. Holding a glass of punjil, a fat middle-aged man was struggling to his feet while the others at his table tried to get him to sit back down. He brushed aside their hands and remarks, came swaying and grinning across the floor. Hallway across, he turned around and went back to put his drink on the table, spilling it as he did so.

"Hi," he said, approaching the table, then belched. "Thought I'd come over and say that—Hi, I mean. C'n always spot a fellow Terran." Another belch. "William Beck Mann, representing United Union Travel, glad to meet you." He leaned on the table with one hand, shoved the other out across it. "Coming in from Ginh, stuck on this goddamn dead rock while the com'pny ship gets its charts revised or somethin'. Nothing going on here at all, eh. You heading home too?"

Others in the Catch, Vegans, were staring toward their table in distaste.

"No...I don't know. Maybe."

"Mind if I sit 'own?" Which he did, swiveling on the tabled hand, plopping into the chair.

"No, I don't mind. But we're about to leave."

"I see." He looked at the girl for the first time and grinned. His teeth were yellow. "Guess you got plans. Well. That case, s'pose I'll get on back." The fat man hauled himself out of the chair and went back toward his own table. Two of the young people were leaving and he tried to walk between them, knocking the girl against a table. Hatred flared in the boy's face and a knife suddenly appeared in his hand.

"No, Terri, don't," the girl said. "He's drunk, he can't help himself."

The boy reached and pulled her to him. Then, just as suddenly as it had come, the hatred vanished from his face. He smiled squarely into the man's face (the knife, too, had vanished) and spat at him. He and the girl went on out of the Catch, holding hands. The fat man goggled after them, reeling out obscenities till someone from his table came and took him back.

"You know which part I like best?" she said after a while. "In *Pergamum?*" She turned from the rain and looked at him. "The part where the girl pours coffee and says, 'This is the universe.' Then she holds up two rocks of sugar and says, 'And this is us, the two of us.' She drops the sugar in the coffee and it starts dissolving, you can't see it any more...."

"Yes, I know. They say it really happened, that Smith heard of it from one of his friends and later used it in *Pergamum.* I wonder if the friend felt honored?"

"I would have. He was a great man."

"He was also a very lonely man."

Disheartedly, they began to argue over whether Smith should be called a Terran or Vegan poet. She seemed strangely affected by the previous trouble, and his heart was just not in the discussion. Smith had been born on Earth, had adopted Vega as his home, for many years....

She had difficulty lighting her next cigarette. The rain was over and the winds were rising now.

A shuttleship was lifting.

Against the darkness, bands of pearl spread in layers and deepened, swelling into rainbow colors. They flashed on his face. When he turned from the window, her skin was glowing rich orange.

"Will you stay here? Have you come home now?"

"I don't know. That's why I came. To find out."

"It would be nice. If you stayed." She fed the Veltdan

another filter; it was making muted, moaning sounds. "That's one of Dave's cups," she said. "He also built the cage for me."

Everything was quiet for a long while.

Finally he said: "Do you remember how *Pergamum* ends?"

"'Wherever we are content, that is our country.'"

He nodded. "That's what I have to decide. Where I'm content, where my country is." He put the cup on the cage. "We keep talking about Samthar Smith...."

"An Earthman who became Vegan, as you're a Vegan who became Terran."

He turned to look at her. The orange glow was fading. He nodded again. "He finally found contentment. On Juhlz."

"And you?"

He shrugged. The Veltdan was grinding the tiny bits of charcoal between its teeth. It sounded like someone walking over seashells far away.

"There's an insect. On Earth," he said. "It dies when you pick it up. From the heat in your hand." He walked toward the bathroom.

A moment later: "The switch isn't working."

"There's a power ration. This area's cut off for several hours, another gets to use the power. The peak periods are shifted about."

He came back and stared sadly at her.

"You don't know how ridiculous that is, do you? You don't realize. There's enough power on my ship—one goddamn ship!—to give Vega electricity for years. You don't see how absurd that is, do you? You just accept it." He picked up the cup. The Veltdan was carrying its rolled-up paper toward the corner of the cage.

Suddenly he threw the cup across the room. It struck the

wall and shattered; one eye-handle slid back across the floor and lay at his feet, staring up at him.

"I'm sorry," he said.

"It doesn't matter. I can get another from Dave. An olm, one of his olms."

"I'll leave you money."

"It doesn't matter." She bent and began picking up the shards. "Besides, I have others. Would you like more coffee? Now?"

"No...thank you." He walked back to the window and stood there for several minutes, staring out. He could hear the Veltdan pacing in its cage.

"You know," he said finally, "I feel free now. Because of you, and all this. I feel free, content. I can go on."

When she spoke, her voice was very quiet. "Then you're not staying."

He paused. "No."

Then: "Thank you, thank you very much. I'll leave money...for the cup."

She turned away from him, and spoke very softly again. "It doesn't matter." The Veltdan depended from the top of the cage. "I knew you would, from the first. You never believed you would stay. I could tell," She sighed. "The empathy."

He took the blue shards out of her hands and put them in the empty waste-bucket. Then he put money on the cage and left.

Pearl spread outward and shelled the sky.

She stood at the window watching. The colors deepened, flared to a rainbow. Her skin glowed orange under the colors; the cigarette in her hand gleamed weakly.

Behind her the little Veltdan sat very still in its cage and blinked at the light.

# The History Makers

*I*N THE MORNING (he wasn't sure which morning) he
began the letter....

Dear Jim,

The last time I saw you, you advised against my coming
here. You were quite insistent, and I don't believe the perfectly awful 3-2 beer we were drinking was wholly
responsible for said adamance. You virtually begged me not
to come. And I suppose you must have felt somewhat duty-
bound to sway me away. That since it was yourself who
introduced me to the Ephemera, you'd incurred some sort
of liability for my Fate. That you would be accountable.

I remember you said a man couldn't keep his sanity here;
that his mind would be whirled in a hundred directions at
once, and he would ravel to loose ends—that he would
crimp and crumble, swell and burst, along with this world.
And you held that there was nothing of value here. But the
government and I, for our separate reasons, disagreed.

And can I refute you now by saying that I've found peace,
or purpose, or insight? No, of course not, not in or with
this letter. For all my whilom grandiloquence, and accustomed to it as you are, such an effort would be fatuous and

absurd. What I *can* do: I can show you this world in what is possibly the only way we can ever know it, I can show you where it brims over to touch my own edges. I can let you look out my window.

The Blue Twin. That was…three years ago? Close to that. ("Time is merely a device to keep everything from happening at once." Isn't that wonderful? I found it in one of the magazines I brought out with me, in a review of some artist's work about which I remember only the name of one painting: A Romantic Longing to Be Scientific.) Three years…I miss Earth, dark Earth. I miss Vega.

(I remember that you were shortly to be reassigned to Ginh, and wonder if this letter will find you there among the towers.)

The Blue Twin, which we always insisted was the best bar in the Combine at least, probably the Union (and did I ever tell you that bars are the emblem of our civilization? A place to lean back in, to put your feet up; a place of silences and lurching conversations: still center, hub for a whirling universe. And pardon my euphuism, please).

And the two of us sitting there, talking of careers and things. Quietly, with the color-clustered walls of sky-bright Vega around us and the massive turning shut out. You dissuading. And bits of my land slaking into the sea. Talking, taking time to talk.

My work had soured, yours burgeoned, I envied you (though we always pretended it was the other way around). All my faces had run together like cheap water-color. My classes had come to be for me nothing but abstract patterns, forming, breaking, reforming—while the faces around you were becoming distinct, defining themselves, giving you ways to go.

I envied you. So I took this sabbatical: "to do a book." And the sabbatical became an extended leave of absence, and that became a dismissal. And no book.

Things fall apart, the center cannot hold....Talking about dissent and resolution, the ways of change, things falling by the way and no Samaritan—and you mentioning something you'd seen in one of the Courier bulletins that crossed your desk: which was my introduction to it all, to Ephemera. (Ephemera. It was one of those pale poetic jokes, the sort that gave us Byzantium and Eldorado and Limbo and all the others, names for out-Union planets, for distant places. You wonder what kind of man is responsible.)

How many weeks then of reading, of requesting information, of clotted first drafts? How long before the night I collapsed into my bed and sat up again with the line "Hold hard these ancient minutes in a cuckoo's month" on my lips—days, weeks? It seemed years. Time, for me, had broken down. And I came to Ephemera....

The Ephemera. My window looks out now on one of their major cities, towered and splendid, the one I've come to call Siva. It is middle season, which means they are expanding: yesterday the city was miles away, a dark line on the horizon; tomorrow it will draw even closer and I'll have to move my squatter's-hut back out of the way. The next day it will swell toward me again, then in the afternoon retreat—and the collapse will have begun. By the next morning I'll be able to see nothing of Siva, and the hut will have to be relocated, shuttled back in for the final moments.

They live in a separate time-plane from ours—is that too abrupt? I don't know another way to say it, or how I should prepare for saying it. Or even if it makes sense. They are but vaguely aware of my presence, and I can study them only with the extensive aid of machines, some I brought with me, a few I was able to requisition later (the government always hopes, always holds on to a chance for new resources). And all I've learned comes down to that one strange phrase. A separate time-plane.

When I first came here, I was constantly blundering into the edges of their city, or being blundered into by them; I was constantly making hasty retreats back into what I started calling the Deadlands. It took my first year just to plot the course of the cities. I've gotten little further.

It's a simple thing, once you have the key: the cities develop in dependence to the seasons. The problem comes with Ephemera's orbit, which is wildly eccentric (I'm tempted to say erratic), and with her queer climate. Seasons flash by, repeat themselves with subtle differences, linger and rush—all in apparent confusion. It takes a while to sort it all out in your mind, to resolve a year into particulars.

And now I've watched this city with its thousand names surge and subside a thousand times. I've watched its cycles repeat my charts, and I've thrown away the charts and been satisfied to call it Siva. All my social theories, my notes, my scribble-occluded papers, I've had to put away; I became a scientist, then simply an observer. Watching Siva.

It's always striking and beautiful. A few huts appear and before you can breathe a village is standing there. The huts sprawl out across the landscape and the whole thing begins to ripple with the changes that are going on, something as though the city were boiling. This visual undulation continues; the edges of the village move out away from it, catch the rippling, extend further: a continuous process. The farther from center, the faster it moves. There's a time you recognize it as a town, a time when the undulation slows and almost stops—then, minutes later, endogeny begins again and its growth accelerates fantastically. It sprawls, it rises, it solidifies.

(A few days ago while I was watching, I got up to put some music—it was Bach—on the recorder. Then I came back and sat down. I must have become absorbed in the music, because later when the tape cut off, I looked up and the city was almost upon me. I keep thinking that someday I won't move back, that I'll be taken into the city, it will sprout and explode around me.)

Siva builds and swells, explodes upward, outward, blankets the landscape. Then, toward the end of the cycle, a strange peace inhabits it: a pause, a silence. Like Joshua's stopping the sun.

And then: what? I can't know what goes on in the city at these times. From photographs (rather incredible photographs) and inspection of the "ruins," I've gathered that something like this must occur: some psychic shakedown hits the people in full stride; most of them go catto, fold themselves into insensible knots—while the rest turn against the city and destroy it. Each time, it happens. Each time, I'm unable to discover the respective groups or even the overall reason. And each time, destruction is absolute. The momentary stasis breaks, and the city falls away. No wall or relic is left standing; even the rubble is somehow consumed. It happens so quickly the cameras can't follow it; and I walk about for hours afterward, trying to read something in the scarred ground...."All Pergamum is covered with thorn bushes; even its ruins have perished."

Three years. Amusing and frightening to think of all I've seen in that time, more than any other man. And what have

I learned? One thing perhaps, one clear thing, and this by accident, poking about the "ruins." I found one of their devices for measuring time, which had inexplicably survived the relapse, a sort of recomplicated sundial—and I guessed from it that this race reckons time from conclusions rather than beginnings. (I leave it to you to decide whether this is a philosophical or psychological insight.) That is, their day—or year, or century, or whatever they might have termed it—seems to have been delimited by the sun's declension rather than its rise; and I assume this scheme, this perspective, would have become generalized (or itself simply expressed an already prevailing attitude). There's a part of the mechanism—a curious device, either rectifier or drive control, possibly both—that seems to work by the flux of the wind, I suppose bringing some sort of complex precision into their measurements: a kind of Aeolian clock.

And since that last sentence there's been a long pause. As I sat here and tried to think: what can I say now....Hours ago, when I began this letter, I had some vague, instinctive notion of things I wanted to tell you. Now it's all fallen back out of reach again, and all I have for you and for myself are these pages of phatic gesturing: Look. See. That, and the first piece of an epiphany, an old song from the early years of Darkearth: "Time, time is winding up again."

And so I sit here and look out my window, watching this city build and fall. I stare at their clock, which no longer functions, and have no use for my own. I am backed to the sea, and tomorrow Siva will spread and extend out onto these waters. I'm left with the decision, the ancient decision: shall I move?

I put on my music—my Bach, my Mozart, my Telemann—and I beat out its rhythms on chrome tiles. For a while I lose myself in it, for a while I break out of the gather and issue of time….

And outside now, the sky fills with color like a bowl of strung ribbons, the ribbons fall, night billows about me. Twelve times I've begun this letter over a space of months, and each time faltered. Now at last, like the day, I've run through to a stammering end. I've filled hours and pages. Yet all I have to offer you is this: this record of my disability. Which I send with enduring love.

> Your brother,
> John

In the evening he finished the letter and set it aside and felt the drag of the sea against his chest.

He sat at the empty table he used for a desk, looking up at the opposite wall. On it, two reproductions and a mirror, forming a caret: mirror at the angle, below and left The Persistence of Memory, one of Monet's Notre Dame paintings across from that. Glass bolted in place, stiff paper tacked up—time arrested, time suspended, time recorded in passing. And about them depended the banks of shelves and instrumentation which covered the hut's walls like lines and symbols ranked on a page.

He rose, making a portrait of the mirror, seeing: this moment. Behind that, three years. Behind that, a lifetime. And behind that, nothing.

(Take for heraldry this image: the palimpsest, imperfectly erased.)

He ambled about his room, staring at the strange, three-dimensional objects which surrounded him, not understanding. He picked up the Ephemera chronometer, turned it over in his hands, put it back. Then (four steps) he stood by the tapedeck. Making sound, shaping sound.

(All of this, all so...vivid, so clearly defined. Clear and sharp like an abstraction of plane intersecting plane, angle and obtrusion...hard, sharp on a flat ground.)

Bach churned out of the speakers, rose in volume as he spun controls, rose again till bass boomed and the walls rattled.

And then he was walking on the bare gray ground outside his hut....

(Feet killing quiet. No: because the silence hums like a live wire, sings like a thrown knife. Rather, my feet tick on the sands. Passing now a flat rock stood on its feet, leaning against the sky. A poem remembered...Time passes, you say. No. We go; time stays....And on Rhea there are a thousand vast molelike creatures burrowing away forever in heart-darkness, consuming a world.)

He stopped and stood on the beach in the baritone darkness, with the pale red sea ahead and the timed floodlights burning behind him. Three yards off, a fish broke water and sank back into a target of ripples.

Looked up. Four stars ticked in the sky, an orange moon shuttled up among them.

Looked down. The city, Siva, swept toward him. (A simple truth. What denies time, dies. And that which accepts it, which places itself in time, lives again. Emblem of palimpsests. Vision of this palimpsest city. Saturn devouring his children.)

The Bach came to his ears then, urgent, exultant. The night was basso profundo, the moon boxed in stars. He sat watching a beetle scuttle across the sand, pushing a pebble before it, deep red on gray.

Later he looked up and the music was over. He turned and saw Siva at his penumbra's edge, turned back to still water.

Turned back to silence...

Then the lights went off behind him and he was left alone with the fall and the surge of the sea.

# Impossible Things Before Breakfast

*E*ACH MORNING my cat Ahab returns from nightly wan-
derings to tell me all he has seen. It does not go well,
Ahab says. Plague and pestilence have followed close upon
the heels of initial destruction. Ahab has seen groups of men
and packs of dogs fighting over abandoned bodies. Near
the center of what was once town these bodies are piled
high within a compound of barbed wire, and are burned
daily.

For some time I believed that Ahab made up these stories
to amuse me, aware of how bored I grew with his daily reports; I am still not completely certain. Details change from
day to day, waver as though windblown, but his descriptive powers are so profound that surely he *has* to have seen
what he recounts; surely he cannot be *that* creative.

After he has gone and Motherdear brings breakfast and
bath, I lie here thinking what it was like before. I am supposed to study during this time, but I cannot imagine why.
What could I possibly do with knowledge? And in the world
Ahab brings me, what use could study ever be—or anything
else?

Actually I remember very little from before. I imagine that
I can feel myself pulling against a swing's ropes and lifting
my feet to see blue squares of sky approaching, receding,

returning. I think I may recall sometimes the feel of sunlight and wind on bare legs, on my face, the sound of words blossoming in my mouth, Father's hands on my hips.

All this was in a different world, of course. And as with Ahab's tales, I may be conjuring it all up, spinning these stories on memory's loom with thin air in place of flax.

*Flax* was in my vocabulary lesson yesterday.

I am almost fourteen. Motherdear brings me books from the library about fourteen-year-olds who spend all week worrying over who'll ask them to the Saturday dance and whether Sally or Billy still likes them. After dinner Motherdear turns me onto my side and the TV to a sitcom. As soon as she is gone I use my chin to switch to evening news. Central America simmers on the back burners while, pushed to the front, the Middle East boils over. Soviets and the CIA take turns overrunning smaller, neighboring nations. There's no one alive who can understand why there has to be so much hatred and pain in the world. Perhaps there's really no one alive even to try anymore. But again, as with Ahab's stories and my memories, I've no way of knowing what, if any, of all this is true. Is the human race's hatred, greed and fear about to bring it to wipe itself off the face of the earth like a spreading spill, and everything else with it? Maybe that is what should, must, happen. But all this, this news, could be, like the sitcoms, just another form of entertainment, only something to distract us, something to divert attention from private, unbearable despair.

Sometimes at night, after Motherdear retires, I am able to switch the TV back on and watch the adult-entertainment channel. It's about then also that Ahab wakes from his daylong nappings, dark pearls on a string. He always comes to see me before leaving, peering curiously at what takes place on the screen, much as I watch the news, I think, then vaulting onto the sill by the open window (open always for fresh air) and, muscles bunching under his sleek coat, into the night.

Days ago when Ahab returned there was a cricket in the room and I'd been unable to sleep for many hours, its chirring like an electric current in the darkness. Ahab listened for a moment and went directly to where the cricket hid in a corner beneath the bureau, but somehow understood that I did not wish it harmed. Emerging from beneath the bureau he brought it to show me (black as himself, and just as alive), then dropped it onto the grass outside the window. He told me of bodies burst open like melons, of others wearing black disguises of ants and carrion birds.

Breakfast has been only oatmeal or other cereal with dried fruit added for weeks now, sometimes with watery milk, once with even a small cup of cocoa. It is all there is, Motherdear says, and it is good for you. I eat what I can of it. The skin of Motherdear's arms has turned hard and transparent; they are two yellow candles, hands flicking about at their ends like pale flames. I have noticed that she has difficulty lifting even a part of me from the bed as she straightens it and bathes me each morning now. Every day she comes to my room a little later.

Sometimes I imagine that I remember (though of course I could not possibly do so) the afternoon this world began ending. Maybe it's just another story Ahab has told me. I hear the doctor outside telling Motherdear (though she wasn't then, not yet, Motherdear) that "the most we can hope for's a quad." "A what?" she says. "A quadriplegic." Then a brief pause. "That's my daughter, young man," Motherdear says. "That's my ten-year-old daughter in there." Father cannot keep his eyes away from my bare breasts. I see Billy Devin, the one who dared me to jump, huddled into a corner by shelves. He must have been one of the first to die.

And that was the end of before. For a time friends came to visit, even Billy and some of the teachers, but no one comes anymore. Even Motherdear doesn't want to come.

How can people so uncaring, so taken with their own needs, with their tiny plots and lives, people inured or oblivious to others' pain and terrible loneliness, possibly expect to survive?

Ahab comes late this morning: Motherdear is already here. "Ahab?" she says. "A cat? But you *have* no cat, dear. We had to get rid of the cat, surely you remember. The doctors insisted."

Very well. But Motherdear will not be back tomorrow.

And soon there will be none other than Ahab and myself, no one but us to begin the new world. In the mornings he will bring me food and news (insects, at least, will survive, they say) and in the long nights lie beside me, his cruel, soft paw against my quickening thigh.

# Echo

*T*HE DOOR SWINGS SHUT and locks. Light comes from a caged bulb overhead; it is dim. The walls are gray.

"Hello, Lauris."

After a long pause: "Say hello, Lauris."

The young man's eyes flicker to the doctor, back to you. Fear is running down the inside of them like rain on a window. He wraps his arms around himself and pushes back against the wall. He is very thin. His eyes slide to the corners of the room and back. There is danger everywhere.

The doctor steps forward, closer to him.

"Lauris. What is today's date?"

"The...fourteenth."

"Of?"

"May."

"Do you know where you are? Where are you?"

"In...the hospital. A hospital."

"What kind of hospital, Lauris?"

"...A mental hospital."

"Do you know why you're here?"

"Yes."

"And who I am?"

"Yes, sir."

The doctor pauses and glances at you. He walks across

the tile floor and puts his hand on the young man's shoulder. The young man looks down at it as though this is the first time he has ever seen a hand; he is trying to imagine its use.

"Lauris, can you tell me what this means? 'People in glass houses shouldn't throw stones.'"

He looks up into the doctor's face. "Yes, sir: 'Let he who is...without sin...cast the first stone.'"

"Very good." The doctor pats the young man's shoulder and moves back across the room. "I think he'll talk to you now. Will you talk to Mr. Vandiver, Lauris?"

"Yes, sir...I'll try."

"Call me Bill, Lauris," you say.

"Yes, sir."

Outside, the sun is just now pushing up above the trees. It would be best in the morning, the doctor had said when you called for the interview; they're all more responsive, more in control, in the morning. A group of patients crosses a patch of grass outside the window, an attendant at each end of the line. The one in front has a volleyball under his arm. All of them have their heads down.

"Do you know why I'm here, Lauris?"

Several moments pass, and the patients are out of sight now.

"I want to write an article about you. About people like you. So that other people can understand."

He is still silent; you look to the doctor for assistance. He smiles.

"Sometimes Lauris doesn't want to talk. Lauris, you have to talk to Mr. Vandiver."

"...Have to?"

"We want you to. It's important to us—to you, too."

118

"I...the room..."

"You have to ignore those feelings, Lauris; I've told you that. You have to learn to live with them, function despite them. Would you feel better if Tom were here?" Turning to face you "Tom is one of the attendants, the person Lauris is most responsive to."

"Doctor, I—" He shakes his head violently. "I'll try, I really...will." He rubs his eyes with the back of his hand; there are jagged scars across the wrist. ("He came to us after his third attempt at suicide. I think you'll find him satisfactory for the interview: he's more in touch than the others. But then, he's still quite young.") He stares at his hand and says, "My hand doesn't know what to do."

"Don't talk crazy, Lauris."

"But you're both watching it."

"No, Lauris."

He puts his hand in his lap and covers it with the other. He stares at the floor. "I know, Doctor Ball," he says. "I know you're not. I...I can't help it."

"Lauris?"

"Yes, sir?"

"I've asked the doctor to let me talk to you so that I can tell people your story. So that they can understand what it's like."

He looks up at you. His eyes are empty now, dull like old pennies.

"You don't believe that, do you? You don't believe anyone can know what it's like. And maybe you're right. But we can *try* to know, we can *try* to understand. If you will help us."

He turns to look out the window and in that instant, goes away from you. ("He'll be 'clear' when you see him, though he will seem distracted and inattentive. Try to remember that he's not always like that; those are his good times. Others, he is totally out of control, not even conscious of what he does. And he knows what's happening to him. He can feel himself inching over the edge, losing control and consciousness. He's terrified—all the time. Whatever he does, he's working through that terror; it's like a fog all around him.")

The doctor, finally: "Lauris?"

"Yes, sir?" He still has not turned his head. He seems to be watching something beyond the window, but nothing is there.

"Mr. Vandiver wants you to tell him how it feels."

"It feels...like I'm dying. All the time...like I'm dying." He looks up at the doctor as though he should know this. He tilts his head, listening. "They say I'm not supposed to talk to him."

"Why?"

"Because...because he doesn't understand. They say he'll hurt me."

"*You* say, Lauris. You know I won't let him hurt you; I won't let anyone hurt you. But you must talk to him."

The doctor looks at you and you say, "When did you first realize you had this, Lauris?"

His eyes move about the room, searching for support, relief.

"Ever since...since I can remember. I remember being a kid, a little kid, and...afraid. I didn't know what it was, then. I...I would scream. I scream sometimes now, I think. I can't remember."

"I see. But when did you first know it for what it is?"

He shakes his head again, tentatively. His mouth moves

several times, shaping words, before he speaks.

"I was...eight or nine. My teachers saw...there was something...different...about me. I had some...tests. Then they...explained it to me."

"And you were twelve when you were sent to a hospital for the first time?"

"Yes...yes, sir. My parents, they...sent me."

"And this is your tenth commitment."

"Yes, sir. I...I live here now...I guess."

The doctor frowns and clears his throat. Lauris is moving his eyes slowly across the floor, as though counting individual tiles. You think of him now, for the first time, as a boy.

"Lauris, are you receiving?" the doctor asks.

The boy faintly nods.

"I thought so." The doctor turns to you. "He seems to be peaking again. He spent most of the last week in wet sheets; it shouldn't be happening again so soon."

"Perhaps the stress of the interview—"

The doctor crosses the room and moves his hand across the space directly before the boy's eyes. There is no response.

"It's no use now, Mr. Vandiver. He's out of touch again. I'm afraid we'll have to terminate the interview."

"'Receiving,' you said. He was actually reading my thoughts?"

The doctor purses his mouth and frowns again. "Not thoughts, Mr. Vandiver—feelings. I was under the impression that you understood that. Feelings, you see, are illogical, confused, destructive. Right now he's picking up on several hundred people. He's taking all that on himself, with no way to get rid of it or shut it off. And you see the result."

"It's not quite the way we thought it would be, is it?" you

say. The boy is shaking, his entire body, as though he is being pulled in many directions at once. Which, you suppose, is the truth of the thing. "How many are there like him?"

"In our facility, twenty-three."

"And what will become of him now?"

"He'll be put in a padded room, and in restraint when he becomes violent; we can't allow him to injure himself. Perhaps he'll come back to us, perhaps not; we never know. He'll be given injections of Thorazine—in some cases it helps psychotics think more clearly—and, if all else fails, electroshock."

"I didn't think anyone used electroshock anymore."

"What would you have us do? We feel we have to try everything, anything that might help. Our approach here is reality oriented. We—"

He stops because the boy has stood and walked closer to you. For a moment his eyes come alive. He says, "Will you come again to see me, Mr. Vandiver?" And now the eyes blank out again. They are blue and still.

"I'm afraid I must insist we leave; he could become violent at any moment."

So hard to believe those lost eyes violent. But you turn and move toward the door, and for the first time something flickers behind the doctor's professional mien.

"Don't let it get to you, what he just said. It takes some getting used to. He's a good kid; everyone likes him." He moves his hands for a moment, reaching for words, and says again, as though he can think of nothing else, "It takes some getting used to."

Now the door closes behind you, and something else closes within you. The hall is brightly lit; you blink in the sudden light. The hall is empty.

"Then there's nothing anyone can do."

"Nothing *more,* Mr. Vandiver."

Inside, you hear a scream.

# Doucement, S'il Vous Plaît

*T*HEY'RE FORWARDING ME on to Versailles now. At least
I think it's Versailles. I watched the postman's lips as he
readdressed me, concentrated on the stammering pressure
of the pen as it darted across my face—the *a*'s and *e*'s, unaccountably, in small capitals, the rest properly in lower
case—and tried to ignore, to block out, *faire taire*, the dragging accompaniment from the side of his hand. And I think
the word he printed, with his felt-tip pen, was *Versailles*. I
felt the four strokes of the *V* and *l*'s quite distinctly; they
were rapid, hard. That I am being forwarded is certain, for
I saw the stamp descending like a dark sky and was able to
read quickly, and backwards through the smear of ink before it moved away, leaving my eyes blotched with black,
the words *prière de faire*. And if the next were *renvoyer*,
there would have been no need for the postman's pen, for
the additional letters among which I was able to discern
only (I think) the single word *Versailles*; a simple circling,
an arrow, should have been sufficient to send me on my
way back to 1, Petherton Court, Tiverton Road. It must
have been, then, *suivre*. So at least, for another day, another few weeks, perhaps my abiding fear—that I bear no
return address and will end among the dead letters—this
fear is allayed.

I am dropped from a box into a hot canvas bag. The smell of paste and ink, of dry saliva and, somewhere deep inside us, perfume. Apparently, while sleeping I have gone astray and been returned—to travel to some scrawled new address, to be set aside for inspection and at least referred back—to the post office collection box. It was the shock of falling through the slot onto hard edges and sharp corners, no doubt, which awakened me. The other letters will have nothing to do with me; they sense difference. And their language is unfamiliar now. Something guttural, that might be German. My questions go unanswered. Deep in the canvas (the perfume?) I can hear a British accent, a soft weeping, but am unable to make out the words.

I wait in a cold hall, propped against the frosted mirror of an ancient oak wardrobe near the door, for a week before someone finally scribbles *Not at this address* in a cramped, small hand, afterwards retracing several of the letters and scoring beneath them, four heavy lines which feel at first like rips then like deep bruises, and drops me in the corner mailbox on his way somewhere. The mailbox is round. British.

Why do they move about so much? How are they able; where does she get the money? And is there the faintest remain of a familiar perfume in this box....

I am being forwarded again. I have no idea where.

It is Christmas, I think, and I am lost in the deluge of mail. Crushed with parcels, shuffled like a card but never dealt. High in my solitary forgotten pigeonhole now, I observe the functioning of our postal service. It never before occurred to me how astounding, what an efficient, essential instrument of society, this service is. Or the complex problems dealt with each day as little more, actually, than part of the routine. I watch with fascination. Perhaps this is the work I was meant for.

I was a writer. More and more, my attention centered about the mail: my correspondence, the possible arrival of checks or hopeful word from my agents, rejected manuscripts that must be sent back out at once, copies of my books or magazines containing some small piece of mine, perhaps a foreign translation of something I'd done long ago and almost forgotten, packets of books about which publishers hoped I would be inclined to say something complimentary, a note of praise from some editor of a non-paying quarterly. The post was delivered twice daily, nine in the morning and just after noon. I would sit on the steps in the hall with a cup of tea, or the worst times, days I was definitely expecting something, with a drink, waiting. My wife and I got into shameful screaming fights over this, and once I struck one of the children who raced out of the flat before me and grabbed the mail from the postman's hands. (I always waited, looking away, until he had deposited it in the box and left the building; then forced myself to walk slowly to it, whistling, and to every appearance completely uninterested. I believed that somehow this outward display of unconcern would influence what was there.) After we left the States and came to live in London, things became much worse; my expectations more desperate. And while my wife was conscientious about collecting it from the box, that having done, mail lost all importance to her, as though for some reason she could not accept it as a real thing, part of the daily discourse of our lives. Forced to be away from the flat during the time of delivery, I would return to look hopelessly into the empty box, and then to spend untold minutes searching the flat—for she could never remember just what she had done with it. Often I would find an important letter leaning against a dirty cup among stacked lunch dishes, forgotten. Others would finally appear in my oldest son's wastebasket, the stamps having just been torn away for his collection. Generally, considerable portions of the message were torn away as well.

Faces bend down and leer at me where I lean in the boxes. Shade light from the small window with their hands so they can see my diagonal cutting through the stream of fluorescent light from behind. Breath frosts the glass. Finally I'm removed between two fingers, crushed with others in a gloved hand. The thumb of the glove is empty and flops against us.

Later a man stands over me. All the others have been opened. They are lying, torn and empty, at one side of this table, and he is turning me over and over again in one hand, mumbling to himself, a pink plastic letter opener in the other hand that I see periodically, rising jerkily toward me as though by its own will, then retreating again from sight. Minutes pass, and the next time the hand appears, the letter opener has been replaced by a pen; then a rapid scribbling. He puts me down, goes away. From beside me, among torn bodies, comes the scent of familiar perfume. It is fading.

It would seem that I am in Poland. Or perhaps Yugoslavia.

I always wanted to travel. Jane and I would lie for hours in bed with carlights sliding in sheets across the walls and ceiling and talk of all the places we should go—making plan after plan and abandoning each in turn, as some consideration of my work intervened. Departures were postponed time and again, applications for visas were canceled, passports expired. Jane collected a sizable library of travel guides, two cardboard boxes full of travel folders. She became well known in the lounges of airports, ticket agents, foreign consuls. Soon she read nothing else, thought of nothing else.

"How were the children today?"

"They were in Hawaii."

Other places.

They're forwarding me on to Rhodes now. Ailleurs. Gdzieś. I have no idea where. And my sole, my only consolation, is that somewhere, at the end of all this, somewhere my wife and family wait to receive me. I imagine how they will discover me one morning on the floor by the door, beneath the mail slot—perhaps they will have heard the outside door, the brass lid swing shut as I'm pushed through, even the sound I make striking and sliding out onto tile or wood, a few inches—and how then they will prop me up lovingly on the table between them; between, perhaps, the cornflakes and Billy's strained fruit.

# Front & Centaur

S O THEY WENT TO LONDON and they got a flat to-gether on Portobello Road and they wrote.

Down in the street dogs shoved their snouts into tin-cans, scraping them along the pavement; babies waited for mothers outside the shops in prams; the pubs burned brilliantly. One of them had observed: "My urine steams in British bathrooms!" Also, they had discovered that plugs of linoleum would appease the electricity meter.

Dave Dunder was the tall one, the thin one with a voice like vanilla pudding, and he wrote westerns. Bill Blitzen was short, with legs like two huge bolognas, eyes that jumped on you if you came too close, and a burning red bush of a beard; he turned out true confessions, four a week, and ghostwrote poetry (by a machine he had invented) on the side. Seeing them at opposite ends of a bench in Regents Park, a man would automatically tilt his head to one side, trying to get the world back to a level. When they walked together, Dunder leaned out over Blitzen from behind, sheltering him from sun and rain. They wore two halves of a six-foot muffler, ripped in two by Dunder one evening in "a moment of excessive charity." And they were in love with the same girl.

Tonight, after their customary mutual reading from the

*Ulysses* nighttown sequence, they had boiled up the day's left-over coffee and gone to work at their desks, which faced one another across the length of the room. A stein of soupy coffee steamed on each desk. With the flat they had inherited an electric heater. It had two filaments, one of which Blitzen had removed, extending it on wires across the room and hanging it from the ceiling directly before his face.

It was in the general order of things that Blitzen would sit down, ringed by sweets and smoking apparatus and small jugs of beer, and set immediately to work. For the next several hours, until he was through for the night, his typewriter would cluck away furiously, steadily, one hand now and again snaking out to light a cigarette on the heater—while Dunder would be ripping sheets off his pad, balling them up and throwing them toward the corner; jerkily spurting and halting toward the end of a story; rewriting, trying to find some pattern in it all, revising and banging away angrily at his desktop.

So Dave had fallen to work tonight, laboring, like a man constipated for weeks, at the final revision of a short-short, and was soon lost to the ordered confusion of pages, inserts, scribbling and deletion. An hour later, suddenly noticing the silence at the other end of the room, he looked up. There was a walrus sitting in Bill's chair, smoking a meerschaum pipe.

"I say," he said. "You're looking rather odd tonight, Blitzen."

The walrus glanced up, then looked back down at his work. "You should talk," it said. "That's the silliest red nose I've ever seen—and I've seen a few in my time." Then, almost as an afterthought: "Now is the time, you know." At these words, Dave's desk became a hippopotamus and went galloping off toward the bathroom. The floor creaked threateningly.

Dave sat for a moment staring at the little circles on the linoleum where the desklegs had been. As he watched, they suddenly started moving and scuttled off into a dark corner. He uncrossed his leg and his hoof clattered on the floor.

"Now that *is* strange," he said. "Blitzen, do you think you could take a minute off? I really think we should talk this over." Having finished its pipe, the walrus was methodically going through all the drawers, eating every scrap of paper it could find. There was a small but growing pile of paperclips on the desk before it.

"Now is the time," the walrus said again. It bent its head and its tusk scraped along the desk, scattering paperclips: one pinged into the wastebasket. Minnesota was never like this.

"Yes, it would appear to be, wouldn't it?"

The papers were turning into doves, which flapped away from the walrus and out the window. Dunder ducked to avoid one and caught a glimpse of print on its wing as it went wheeling frantically past him. A moment later it came back to the window with an olive leaf in its beak.

"But I really think we should put our heads together and give this a bit of thought. What are we going to eat, for example? I'll wager there's not a bale of hay in the house...Is that right: hay?" As he said this, the rug began to grow. "And what will Berenice say if she comes and finds us like this?" The rug was now three feet tall, a thick field of grass. Not far away, Dunder could make out his beaded belt lying like a snake across the top of the greenery, sunning itself. The rug rustled with the movement of many small things scurrying to safety. He jumped to his feet just as his own chair went hopping off into it; for several seconds he could see its back, bobbing up and down—then the grass was too high.

Dunder stood poking gently at the grass with his antlers, trying to decide what to do. What was needed was organization, some careful thought, a system. They could cope.

And with a *pop*, flowers began growing off the wallpaper, small bunches of orchids, slowly drooping towards the floor under the weight of their heads as the stems lengthened like spaghetti. Feathers from the pillows had gathered in cloudy masses high in the room, and when they parted for a moment, Dunder saw things like waterbugs skimming across the surface of the blue ceiling.

He heard a snuffling at the base of the kitchen door; a rather foreboding growl issued from the bedroom. And then the walrus came crashing through the grass and yellow blossoms, muttering to itself: "Berenice...I don't know what we saw in her in the first place. She's awfully *thin*, you know." It looked up, saw Dunder standing there, and went running, terrified, back into the growth. After a bit, Dunder could hear it far away, gamboling in bucolic splendor. Then there was a mighty *splash*—

And a knock at the door. It was getting dark; Dunder's nose began to glow like an electric cherry.

And another knock.

And another knock.

And another knock.

"Go away," a voice gurgled from across the room.

A key rattled in the lock and the door opened. Berenice stood there naked, clothes and the makings for a late tea under her arm. Her hair was done up in a honeycomb and a silver disk hung against her chest, like the moon sighted between two hills.

"Cut it out, fellows," she said.

"Glug. Glug."

"Now is the time," Dunder told her. That was all he could think to say. Minnesota had certainly never been like this.

"What does this *mean*?" she asked, coming a few steps into the room. "Are you trying to get rid of me? Don't you think you owe me an explanation at least? You don't want me to come around to see you anymore."

"Oh, no," Dunder said. "It's just—"

"That's what always happens. They always do this, it always turns out like this in the end."

"Go away," the walrus bellowed from deep in the weeds.

"See? See? God knows I try to make them love me; it's not my fault. I do everything I can—"

"Now is the time." Dunder. He was rapidly running out of words.

"—and in the end it's always like this, this always happens."

Far away, they could hear the walrus dancing a softshoe and singing *America the Beautiful*.

"I'm pregnant, you know....We used to be so happy. Damn you. Want accretion, the James-Lange theory of emotion. I thought you would *amount* to something. What happened to us? Epithesis, existentialism. I love you."

It was beginning to rain. "It's raining, deer," she said, then giggled horribly. They huddled together in the fireplace, warm and talking quietly, watching the rain come down outside. "What will become of little William David now? That's what I decided to call him, see." Together they nibbled at chocolate biscuits. She fed him, offering each biscuit on her open hand after taking a few bites, and he chewed them daintily. He ran his tongue along the soft skin at the base of her thumb. She thought it was the walrus' dance which had brought on the rain. "Or do you think David William sounds better?"

There was a polite cough at the door: Dunder and Berenice turned together. A handsome young unicorn stood outside in a shaft of sunlight, tossing its head so that the mane swirled down around its horn.

"Come live with me and be my love," it said.

Dunder was aware of the walrus standing behind him, peering furtively out from the bushes. "Minnesota was never like this," it whispered.

Berenice stood and with one last look at Dunder, a look full of scorn and contempt, walked to the unicorn and leapt onto its great ridged back. "*Americans!*" she said.

The unicorn nodded and swung its tail to brush away a fly that had settled on her bare bottom, in the dimple at the top of her left buttock. They turned and rode off together down the hall toward Cheshire....

And nothing's been the same since.

# Changes

"*You will not find me. Get this sad certainty firmly into your head.*"

—Jean Cocteau

*I* SHOULD LIKE very much to begin this account by writing "When I was a child," then go on to catalogue the discoveries and anxieties of, say, an average childhood in Brighton, or Hoave. This has forever seemed to me the most honest, the most direct mode of autobiographical narration; even Master Copperfield could do no better. Furthermore, it would seem that after sixty-some years I should be entitled to so small a favor. But the truth is, of course, that I never *was* a child: I was born when I was twenty years old and I was walking across the university campus at the time.

Curiously, the arrival of consciousness was some delayed, and I reeled for several minutes beneath the sudden impact of simple, pure perception: color and motion. I am told that I dropped to my knees then fell prostrate into a nearby flowerbed, and that my eyes closed. It is generally agreed that I assumed the classic fetal position, though none of the witnesses can be certain on this point. At any rate, a student strolling back into his rooms from a class in elementary calculus was the first to come upon me. By his own testimony he stood for a moment indecisively, then walked over to ask if he might be of some assistance. It was at this very moment that consciousness beset me, and I began to wail.

The university professors were quick to take me in. Together they fed and clothed me, saw to my every need: during the days their wives would fondle me and push me in oversize prams through the park. Articles concerning my education and development appeared in every leading learned journal. Educators, psychologists and sociologists made hegiras from all about this world I was gradually coming to know, till at last it was impossible for me to leave the guarded campus grounds; such was my fame. I was given a room at the university. Domestic servants were also provided and a call to the Board of Regents on my private phones would, at any late hour, produce whatever—anything—I might desire. As my education continued.

At the age of "4" I destroyed the chemical laboratory and burned the phys ed building to the ground. At "5" I killed the Dean of Arts and Sciences and successfully breached three out of the four women's dormitories. The women were subsequently expelled.

But I can recite the Canterbury Tales in the original, complete with variants, and the same with all Shakespeare. I can conjugate Latin verbs without conscious thought while working the *London Times* crossword. I can even tell you where a staff vacancy exists in seventeenth century drama, and the manner in which Mrs. Bonfiglioni passes her time while the good professor is leading undergraduates down some tricky path of *The Faerie Queen.*

In America I became an artist and took a studio on Eighth Street. Commissioned to provide for the Audubon Society a statue, to be set in cement outside their national offices, I conceived a project in which the statue of a robin, ten feet high, would be composed of a substance impervious to weather and general attrition but highly sensitive to the droppings of our city's pigeons: as the pigeons frolicked on and about the statue, decorating it again and again with their droppings, the statue would slowly deteriorate, a kind of living, ever-changing sculpture. Put in place, it was an instant success, and a continual source of temptation for the community's youngsters.

For a time I was supported by women. One would feed me each night; another would replace buttons on my clothes; yet another would crouch beside me at the championship marble tournaments, cheering. I attempted to express my gratitude, feebly, with flowers and lines of verse, typing up three copies of each poem and dedicating one to each of the kind, glad ladies. (It was the least I could do.) To one, on her birthday, I sent a dozen yellow roses. The roses wilted in three days, then I replaced, while she was away from the house, a single flower; it stood among the others, a lonely, bright exemplum of hope. And for more than a month I secretly replaced this rose again and again, while she marveled and brought friends around to see it, this amazing reminder.

I arrived in Buffalo without money, family, or friends. The only jobs available were doughnut cooking, computer programming and bounty hunting, and since cripples bought only five dollars a head, I turned by attention to children, bagging thirty-three—all of them boys and a full two-thirds of them infants or babies—before I took my just rewards and departed with them to Canada where I applied for a position executing draft dodgers for the United States government.

Shortly after my misadventures in Yucatan I got a job at the New Orleans morgue, filing dead letters and performing the occasional autopsy. Working alongside me were Zipporah Grosche, who had the largest collection of perfumed letters in existence, and Clarence Culbreath, whose belts came in formfitting plastic cases and who had worked the past summer on the road gangs in order to buy his mother, who blind, a color TV. There was also a cute little thing in a miniskirt whose name was, I believe, Edward. While working at the morgue I surpassed all previous records by resurrecting three hundred and eighteen letters. At the time I was wearing my hair long, the sides brushed back over my ears and the top flopped back over on itself like an omelet. It was very difficult work—grueling, as they say—and each night in the solitude of my own room I wept for the poor lost things which were in my care, but without it I could never have made a successful career in politics. I saw trouble brewing when I grew so popular that 74.8% of the letters reaching my office were addressed to me personally: a scant few months after this began. I was dismissed by the authorities and made my way to Salt Lake City where I began voice lessons.

At about this time there developed a sort of game which I played every morning. Getting out of bed, with eyes still closed I tried to decide, by touch alone, where I was: then, should I find myself in my own apartment, I would try to decide, again by touch, who the woman with me might be.

If I failed at this I would ask her name, but never remained long enough to hear the answer—for immediately upon speaking I would dive from the room and flee with whatever clothing happened to hand. For some time then, I would walk in Central Park—wearing perhaps an overcoat or a miniskirt—until I summoned enough courage to call my landlady. Good Mrs. Deal would put a drinking glass against the common wall and listen. When she had announced that sound had ceased, and after several calls on my part, I could generally return home safely.

I fell in love. (This was my religious period, just before I wrote my best-selling sci-fi novel *It Came from out of Town*. She was a *petite chose* and French major from Georgia, with rings on all her fingers and little happy smiles sitting in her eyes getting fat; her hair was drawn to one side, where, shouting for help, it cascaded back over one shoulder. We ate fried clams together at Howard Johnson's and visited the snake house at the St. Louis zoo, among other things. I was wearing my hair short and heavy workmen's boots. We both wore liederhosen, in which we hid matching copies of *The Prophet*, Scientology bulletins and leaflet proclaiming New York "A Summer Festival." I lost her to a wrangler down in Dallas on the way to Amarillo. She met him at a MacDonald's while I was washing out a few things at a nearby laundromat and I never saw her again, though for a month she telegraphed greetings every morning at five o'clock. (The delivery boy and I grew close; many mornings he stayed to breakfast with me, dissolving with his good cheer, the bright, hot pearl of hurt.) It is difficult, as she once remarked, to say no to the world champion bulldogger.

In the District of Columbia I was stricken with social con-
science and, purchasing a wig and shaving my legs, marched
with the women against the Washington monument. After
demanding that the monument be sheathed in a huge pink
condom we moved on to Newport, Grand Rapids and San
Francisco. By day I marched and by night I studied
cosmetology in a beautician's school and sculpture in a college of continuing education, studies which several months
later resulted in my being appointed hair-dresser to Mount
Rushmore.

Once, having played for two seasons on a Boston pro foot-
ball team, I experienced a nervous breakdown, grew unable
to remember the plays, and was interned in a revolutionary
new psychiatric hospital in Hartford, Conn., to which I was
driven in the team's bus. It was unlike the hospitals I'd previously known in East Orange and Westchester. There was
no occupational therapy, no baseball playing, not even the
enjoyable bouts of bingo and square dancing with joyful
schizophrenics in the name of recreation. Instead, the nurses
wore nothing below the waist and attended small vegetable
patches outside the dormitories where we slept in ham-
mocks and dogtents pitched anew each night. The sole
therapy was simple and direct: upon internment each patient was given a guitar and when he learned to play it, was
discharged. Doctors roved the halls at night with cassette
recorders, occasionally making trades.

Finally, in late 197—, I was apprehended and returned to
Europe, where I settled back at the University and insti-
tuted a program of American Studies. These several months,

bored with my classes, I have had much time to think over the events of the past, which thoughts have led to my setting down these incidents by way of notes for my memoirs; meanwhile I busy myself with trying out for amateur plays, serving as second on the rowing team and , having no taste for Spenser, with Mrs. Bonfiglioni.

She of the grand imagination and large thighs, O!

# At the Fitting Shop

C AN I HELP YOU SIR; you seem to have lost your way? Why yes, thank you, I'm looking for the plumbing shop.

Certainly, sir. That would be, let's see, department fifteen-bee. Up this aisle, turn right, right again at Canned Goods, left and keep bearing left around Magazines till you get to Needlework, go through Hobbies and Crafts and take the corridor down through Exotic Foods, then aisle eighty-three-and you're there. Simple. You might want to pick up a compass at Sporting Goods—that's on your way, swing back right just past Suspenders, big stuffed bear, you'll know it when you're there. Makes things a little easier...You *do* have a map?

Uh yes. Yes, thank you very much.

Matson.

I beg your pardon?

Matson: my name. My card. Give me a ring if you need any further help. Number's down there, use one of the house phones.

Thank you very much.

No thanks necessary, son, it's my job.

Ah, pardon me. Is this the plumbing shop—down there?

Ha. Sorry, kid, you're in the wrong wing. Up that way.

Garden Tools—next floor up. You can take the escalator at Stamp Redemption, elevator at Cosmetics, or walk up just past Archery. Me, I'd prefer the walk—takes you right smack through Tupperware, that'll put a smile on your face.

Sir...Sir? Could you tell me, is this how I get to Garden Tools?

Afraid not, Sonny. You're way off course. Look, you go down there and ask that guy in the pink shirt. He'll show you the way to Power Tools and from there you're okay, got a straight shot. Sure thing.

Ah...Sporting Goods? Can you tell me which way to go— right, or left?

Well, I'll tell you. You could take that right down into Tall-n-Slim, then come back around Canned Goods Imported till you get to Stationery and pull another right there. Or you could follow that left fork there on to Belts and Neckties, work your way over toward Lavatories and go down on the Autolift. But if *I* were you, I'd go back along this aisle till I got to Stamp Redemption, then I'd make straight for Lay-Away and cut across Carpets-and-Draperies to Complaints. That's the quickest way to get to Hardware, from here anyhow.

Hardware? That's what I want to ask for, then—fifteen-bee?

You bet.

Sorry, but you gave me a fright. You the new helper?

Ah, no. I'm looking for Hardware. Fifteen-bee.

I see...well, you're in the basement, you know.

No, I didn't.

Well, you are.

146

I see. Could you tell me how to get to Hardware, then?

That'd be fifteen-bee, right?

Yes sir.

Well son, I'm not sure; haven't been up there for months myself. Since last Christmas as a matter of fact. Had to go up for some shopping then, though. Waited till late at night 'fore I'd go up. Near as I can recall…you got a map?

Yes sir.

Let's have a look then…yeah, that's it. Look, somehow you gotta get back up to Coffeepots-n-Cannisters—that's on Level Four about halfway down Aisle twenty-eight-cee, next to Lingerie, see? You can find that by yourself now, can't you, just look for the nekid women. I mean, you can get there with the map?

Well, I *think* so.

Good boy! Sure you can, that's the spirit. I reckon you'll make out okay; you've got lots of spunk for a youngster, and that's what it takes.

Yes sir. Thank you very much, you've been very helpful.

Don't thank me, son—you'd do the same for me. We gotta help each other out, don't we. I mean, what else is there? Man can't help a guy that's in a jam, what else matters?

Won't you take a seat, son? You look a little tired. Here, this one, with the pink arms. Gives you a good view. Notice how the indirect lighting sparkles on all the chrome fittings—it took four engineers and two interior decorators ten weeks to get that effect. You really do look tired, you know. Shouldn't push yourself that way; there'll be time enough for that when you're older. Take care of yourself, enjoy your youth while you've still got it.

I'm sorry, thank you. I had some trouble getting here.

No wonder, either: that's last week's map you've got there.

O. But this *is* Hardware?

Right!

Department fifteen-bee?

You bet!

Where they sell the penises?

Sure thing!

Finally...

Ah, you'll pardon my asking, son, but you do have a certificate? From your parents, I mean, testifying to your age—and of course notes from your teacher and minister. I'm sorry: rabbi. The law requires it, you see, and...ah yes, that's right, everything seems to be in order. Now. Just what style did you have in mind?

Well, I really hadn't given it much thought. I don't know a great deal about all this, I'm afraid. Uh, what would *you* recommend?

Well sir. Of course it's difficult to form an *accurate* judgment without knowing the person, I mean *really* knowing him, if you get my meaning. That is to say, the *essential* him— all the little qualities and quirks that make up his whole, his personality. But judging from your *apparent* physique, and from certain mannerisms which I've noted already, I would go so far as to suggest that one of our *Sassafras Tangles* would not be *too* terribly amiss. And it *is* one of our more *popular* models, quite a *serviceable* style...a hunch, of course—but intuition is often to be relied upon, especially when it comes of long experience, familiarity with the product. The shape of the face and buttocks is a particularly useful indication. And the hand of course.

I see. Uh, would it be too forward of me to ask a more, uh, *personal* recommendation?

Ahhhh. Of course, I understand. Well, *personally* I go for the *Polish Sausage*—quite stylish, never out of vogue, the upkeep isn't as demanding as some. Also, formally, I find it compelling: a certain purity of line, simplicity, an essential *honesty*. The floor manager would swear by the *Mushroom Arrow*, though, and that's one of the best recommendations you can get—I mean, from a man who really knows his trade, knows what is available. The *Arrow* particularly fits the jauntier, dashing sort, I feel.

Uh, could I, do you suppose...

*Certainly* sir!

Yes...that *is* very nice.

We have one of the finest fitters in the trade. It is exquisite, isn't it? Truly exquisite. A man feels proud, with a product like that, the result of a totally *committed* craftsman. Exquisite.

It certainly is. A *Polish Sausage*...

Shall I measure you for one then, sir?

Well, I'm not quite sure, I mean I haven't seen any others. Do you suppose I could see a few modeled? Perhaps that would help in the final decision?

Why certainly, sir. *Keiris:* the models!

You are most kind.

A fine choice, sir. The *Mandrake Special*, in red, with full attachments. Possibly the best-tooled model we make, and we make the best in the business. Each one finished by hand—an absolute *triumph* of craftsmanship. No: of *Art!*

I believe that I'll be very happy with it.

Yes sir, you'll be *most* happy with it. I can personally assure you of that. You'll find it quite durable, and with care it will bring you many years—even a lifetime!—of pleasure.

Simply return it once a month for adjustment; and should anything go wrong—the least malfunction—we will repair it free of charge or, in more serious cases, replace it entirely. Just like a Zippo.

Zippo?

A cigarette lighter, sir. Like our *Mandrake Special,* the best available.

Ah. I'm too young to smoke, you know. Though perhaps I'll take it up now...

Yes sir, that might be nice. Well, I believe that's everything, then. You'll find lubricant, spare screws and washers—also instructions relating to cleaning, maintenance, minor repairs and adjustments—in the complimentary kit that comes along with the *Mandrake Special.* And the usual instructions on how to use it to full advantage, of course. Your parents will be billed to the sum of five dollars and eighty-seven cents; and if you don't mind, sir, I'd like to add that I think they'll be very proud of your choice, very proud indeed.

I hope so. Thank you very much, again, for your advice. You've been *most* helpful.

My job, sir. More than a job: my duty. *Keiris!* My assistant will show you out, sir: he knows a shortcut. And I believe you will be passing Wine Cellar and Smoke Shop on your way, should you like to stop in there for a quick purchase or two before we close.

Yes, perhaps I will.

It's been a pleasure to serve you, sir.

Yes, thank you. I believe you have made me a very happy man this afternoon.

I hope so, sir. We do our best.

# Walls of Affection

*S*ETTING HIS DRINK on the table, he caught the barest flash of motion in the corner of his eye and looked instinctively away from his book. *Ignore it*, he thought, but a moment later was looking back. It came slowly around the curve of the glass then and through a hole in one of the ice cubes, a skyblue fish the size of a pea.

The first time this happened, three weeks back, he'd been in a restaurant, their favorite, with Paula, trying yet again to work things out. Past months had not gone well, replete with weeklong quarrels, shuddering silences, withholdings. Finally she had moved into a separate apartment close by. Before, there had always been tacit agreement to go on, and gentle conciliations that lasted hours, days, even weeks. This time they both sensed there would be no such thing, and after half an hour of dodging conversation, Paula told him (surprised herself to be saying it: she had not intended to) that it was over.

He'd looked dramatically into the depths of his drink and said, "I don't believe it."

"I'm sorry, Stan. It isn't what I wanted either."

"There's a tadpole in my martini." he went on, then looked up. "Did you get one, too? Maybe they're out of olives?"

"This isn't funny, Stan. You have to be serious about some things."

In response he put the glass on the table between them and together they watched the small blue fish submerged in clear depths, swimming in slow circles.

"It's beautiful," his wife said.

He had himself been half-submerged in a new book, a comic novel about a man who falls in love every Monday and is inevitably alone again by Thursday, and to forestall the pain of Paula's absence he dove ever deeper, finishing the book in just over two weeks. He had a drink with his agent to deliver the manuscript and found another fish. He didn't mention it to Carl and left the drink untouched, ordering coffee instead.

Now, at ten at night, he was reading *Candide*, something he did every few months, and watching a small blue fish come 'round and 'round again in the glass beside him.

He thought of carousel music; of moons circling planets, day and night caught in that looping; of seasons and years cradled in the swing of worlds 'round stars. And because Paula was gone, because he was thinking far too much, remembering too much, because even Voltaire could not bear him away, and because a small blue fish circled endlessly in the glass alongside, he felt walls closing in on him.

They had lived together what seemed a long time here. Nothing failed to bear her impression. Even the mirrors remembered her: her body stepping before them wet from showers, face leaning close in the mornings for makeup. Their bed somehow recalled her form and drew him towards it. Pillows and sheets still smelled of her.

At twelve he threw a sportscoat over sweatshirt and jeans and walked two blocks to Bennigan's. Loud characterless music and lots of smoke, dreams on sleeves, and hope smoldering down towards early, lonely hours. He took a seat at the bar, ordered beer, smiled at the woman on the barstool beside him. She was thirtyish, blonde, knee wrapped over knee with a quiet show of heavy thigh.

She was having Black Russians. He bought her one. She was smoking. He lit her cigarette with bar matches.

Her name was Linda; she taught history in high school. A month ago her boyfriend failed to come home one night after work and a couple of days later phoned to say he needed time, he couldn't make the commitments she wanted just now. She didn't know what to do. She loved him so much. She tried just to go on. There were awkward, ago-nizing phonecalls they both regretted. Nights he'd come over and leave after they'd made love. Nights like this one and three before, when he didn't come, or call, at all.

"I've forgotten how to be alone," she said. "It scares me."

"You don't have to be."

"I just want someone who cares. Even if it's just for an hour, just for the night. I can't be this alone anymore."

"I understand."

And after he told her something of his own story she said, "I think you do."

At his apartment, ghosts of Paula whispered, and *her* form gave way in the mirror to Linda's. He reached across her body and switched the radio from country to classical. Lay with his head cradled on her shoulder, hand gently at her waist.

After a while in blundering dark he said, "Thank you," and she said, "Thank *you*."

He got up and brought wine, glasses, from the tiny kitchen. A bottle long held in reserve.

She sat in his bed with the sheet at her waist and reached towards him, breast swinging freely. He poured wine as

dawn was starting up outside. They held their glasses together in a toast. Within them, small blue fish swam towards
one another, swam towards the glass walls of their ever-sepa-
rate worlds.

# The Invasion of Dallas

*T*HERE ARE 129,596 TRAFFIC SIGNS IN THE CITY.
There are also other signs.
Most are gentle things: Drive Friendly, Stop, Yield.
But some are deadly.

•

Man is a social animal?
So the first reports stated, and so, on the surface, it seems.
They travel in pairs, aggregate in groups.
But each (it can not help realize, though it does not yet understand) is forever locked within its own skull.

•

THE LONELINESS.

•

As a man enters the body of a strange woman the first time, so the alien enters this new social order.

•

In its spaceship that looks like a '73 Datsun pickup, the alien explores the city. The cloverleaves, the freeways, the baskets that scoop up quarters. The traffic signs.
Later it explores a woman's body in much the same way. Here, too, it discovers, and in what led to this, there are traffic signs.
The language, it understands. But this *other* semantics, it does not, can not.

It can see no difference, for instance, between the sprawling proud city and this woman's body.

•

The woman is driving down Turtle Creek Blvd. to a bar called The Stoneleigh P.

It is a Friday night.

The woman tells the alien about the three parties she is attending the next night, with whom it does not know.

This awakens in it, strange feelings it has not experienced before.

Sitting in The Stoneleigh P, it looks around, as the woman talks, at all the different—different!—faces, bodies, gestures. The semantics of a disorder which carries within it an implicit order it can not conceive.

It wonders if it has come too late, if the city has been already infiltrated, If some of these others are not actually, like itself, aliens.

Three weeks have passed.

•

The concept of self-regeneration preoccupies the alien. It can grow a new hand, leg, organ. A thing it shares, or so it thinks, with certain lower species here.

For the first time it occurs to it that there may exist, deeper things which can *not* be replaced.

•

Where is it? what is it doing here?

The gratuitous semaphores which mean so much, the lineaments and cross-hatching of this new "reality."

It fills notebooks.

It is to survey this city; the books contain notes on anthropology, psychology, sociology, defense.

There are other things it is supposed to do as well. (Increasingly, the notes concern the woman.)

•

THE LONELINESS.

•

The woman.

It chose her house at random, as it chose its features, build. Knocked on the woman's back door.

Jim, she said. We weren't expecting you this early.

The woman believes the alien is her divorced husband. "He" will stay with her over Christmas, on the couch in the den (male humans pick her up at the front door); after that, she finds "him" an apartment a few blocks away, to which she never comes.

The alien moves in, parking the spaceship on the street outside.

At times the woman will hug "him" (as though she does not want to let go) and kiss "him" on the cheek, say, I enjoy being with you.

One night it is sitting alone in the apartment, drinking and working at its notes.

The phone rings.

Can you keep the child Saturday night, the woman says. There's a party I want to go to.

The alien pauses.

Sure, it says.

What were you thinking.

Things, it says.

Better left unsaid, the woman says.

Two minutes later, she calls back,

Listen. You don't mind my going out do you, you don't think it's wrong.

No of course not.

I mean I don't want to feel guilty. I don't want to be disappointed. Or you either. You don't expect to have a relationship with me do you. I have a lot of people I go out with.

It is becoming more confused each day. Sex, it can not conceive; no such thing exists on its world. Yet it knows, both from research and observation, that this is, on *this* world, a primary motive force, it, the potential of it, floats like a fog about every human action. Or so it seems, as the alien tries to comprehend.

And these strange new feelings inside it? when it is with the woman, talking to the woman, away from the woman. what are they?

Even that peculiar, seemingly useless appendage carries within it further questions, problems. It is puzzled, perplexed: still another semantics in its rise and fall, to be interpreted.

And how to interpret the woman's ambivalence. The contradictions, chiaroscuro, of her actions, words.

It does not understand.

It is not aware that the human form it has taken, from the time it approached the woman, is gathering itself into it.

It does not realize the simple, overwhelming *power* of this form.

Not strength. Power.

●

It finds alcohol (nothing like this exists on its world) an interesting, alluring experience.

It sits alone at night in its apartment and drinks.

It ponders the relationship of this activity with that of sex and of and of another human thing it can not understand, death.

There are definite, definitive connections.

It understands that alcohol is an open door, a means of escape.

It does *not* understand what it is trying to escape from.

Its true self,

Its human form.

●

Another time, the alien returns the child and a male human is at the woman's house. The male human has wanted to meet "him" for some time. (The woman's husband is a writer; the male human wants to be.)

The alien and the male human talk. The woman asks the alien to stay for dinner. The alien and the male human talk further.

It becomes obvious that the male human is spending the night.

A half-gallon of wine disappears.

The alien leaves at ten.

It awakes in the night from a dream of the woman (this, dreaming, is, again, something it knows nothing of) and the appendage is spurting thick white fluid against the bedsheets.

Perhaps this is when it begins to understand.

●

The alien writes in one of the notebooks,

The woman's hips are broad, inviting; the torso above, fragile, delicate; the legs muscular, substantial.

And then,

Her breasts are small.

●

She calls.

(Patter.)

The alien says, We need to talk.

About what.

You and me.

I told you that several days ago.

The alien invites her to go with it to a nearby city. (She has said she would like to go there.) It says, We can go together. You do what you want, see your friends, I do what I'm going there for.

(Patter.)

What, she says. You're suddenly subdued.

How do you react to rejection. It hates telephones. (There are no telephones on its world.) And words—so inadequate, yet all these people have.

I'm not rejecting you. We could drive down together, it would be fun. I'm just saying.

(Patter.)

Well, any time you want. Tonight, tomorrow. But what do we have to talk about.

The why did you say we needed to talk last night.

I just don't want to feel guilty. I mean I know what you want, what I'm going to do.

And that, the alien supposes, ends it. The door is closed. What to talk about indeed.

Nothing, it would seem.

It does not understand this woman, the confusion.

Is it hers,

Its own.

The jagged ruins of this particular, privileged semantics rise into the afternoon sky.

The alien sits looking at the dead phone, attempting to analyze the "emotions" it is now experiencing.

A physiological semantics in its own right—

But: something more.

●

A woman flees Neiman Marcus screaming,
A monster! There's a monster in there!
And so (though I escape) I am discovered.
And so the missiles are swung towards my world,
Missiles that will strike many years from now.
Computers consulted (logic), steel making its way through
void (poetry).
Buttons pushed.
And even in this, semantics of sexuality.
The woman is twelve blocks away.
My world is (or will be—what difference?) in ruins.
Dead.

●

THE LONELINESS.

# Driving

THE SIGNS BEGAN a few light years out:

> YOU ARE APPROACHING THE END OF THE UNIVERSE
> DRIVE CAREFULLY
> LAST CHANCE FOR GAS FOOD PHONE LODGING
> CURB YOUR DOG

I had a Harry Partch sonata on the cassette player, I remember, and it seemed to be slowing appreciably as I approached, but with Partch it's hard to tell. Then I came around a sharp corner and saw what looked like a dirty shower curtain hanging there in the air, obliterating everything behind.

As I drove through I saw other signs:

> YOU ARE LEAVING THE UNIVERSE
> WE HOPE THAT YOUR STAY HAS BEEN A PLEASANT
> ONE AND THAT YOU WILL VISIT US
> AGAIN SOMETIME

Just below that was a smaller sign:

### DO NOT LITTER

There was a slight tingle, a *frisson,* as I passed through, nothing more. The sun shone brightly. I pulled to the side of the road for a moment and sat with the engine idling. Fields of tract houses stretched away from the road on either side, each with a small cedar fence, bank of lime-green steel garbage cans and rusted-out VW. There was no sign anywhere of shops, restaurants, filling stations. I began to wish I'd paid more notice to the "last chance" signs; my fuel gauge was pegging pretty close to *E.*

As I sat there a truck pulled up alongside me. It was ancient. The bumpers, fenders and door were made of sheets of galvanized metal welded together at odd angles and then to the truck's body with no effort to camouflage the seams, which looked like raggedly healed knife wounds.

"Reckon you might be needing gas." An old man canted towards me in the truck's cab as though against a heavy wind, his left hand still hanging on to the wheel, his chin barely reaching above the truck's window. His beard appeared to be crusted solid with tobacco and food drippings.

I nodded.

"Thought so."

I waited, but that seemed to be all he had to say. I shut the engine off. Then after a while he said, "People don't take much to driving 'round these parts,'" and cackled with sudden laughter. Before I could reply he was climbing down out of his truck. He walked around to the back and stood there squinting into the distance. "Reckon it'll be along any time now," he said. Then he walked to the front of the truck and did the same thing. I noticed that he limped badly, favoring his right leg, on which he wore a cowboy boot.

The other foot was in an old-fashioned, high-topped tennis shoe, a piece of twine tied around it near the toe.

"Excuse me," I said, "but you did mention gas."

He looked at me closely. "Things take time and time takes things." He looked away.

Just then a far corner of the community detached itself and began rolling towards us. As it came closer I saw that it was a fully equipped service station. In the center of an expanse of cement, in a small hut like a tollbooth, sat the attendant. When it pulled up before us I started the engine and drove onto the lot, stopping by one of the pumps. I sat there.

"Self serve," the old man said. And as I got out and began filling the tank, he went over to the hut. The attendant broke a piece of gum in two and passed one half through the tiny front window. They talked together in low tones, gesturing vaguely towards the community, their voices occasionally rolling into soft laughter.

"No charge, son," the attendant said when I approached. He had a well-trained handlebar moustache and full, red lips. "Where you headed?"

"Just driving, I guess."

"Right. Driving." He nodded a couple of times, solemnly. "You drive careful now. Don't be getting in a hurry. Things take time and time takes things."

I thanked both him and the old man and pulled out of the station. In the rearview mirror I watched the station start its glide back towards the houses, then passed around a curve.

The road was absolutely level. Its wide shoulders quickly tapered to a narrow band of bare ground at either side, and beyond that there were only two seas of grass and, far off, twin gray horizons that grass spilled into.

I had just settled back into the seat for a long, relaxed drive and was spinning the radio dial to find some music (nothing but static) when I came over a hill and braked to a stop: with no warning, the road abruptly ended. I got out and stood on a small gray island in the middle of a green sea. No sign of other roads. The grass seemed uniformly six inches tall. There was a slight, unhurried wind.

After a while I turned and drove back towards the town. I was certain (but I may be wrong) that it took me far longer to return. I circled the town four times without finding any way to enter, or any sign of the service station, and finally pulled over and stopped the engine. Sooner or later...

I came awake with a start and realized that the old man had pulled his truck up behind me and was standing by my window. Though the sun was in the same place it had been before, I felt rested.

"You all right, young man?"

"Fine, thanks." I gestured back the way I'd come. "The road ends up there."

"Sure does. Don't need a road. No one ever goes that way."

"I did."

"Well, you tried, anyhow." He glanced off into the distance. "I expect you been trying to find a way into town, too."

I nodded.

"Town's closed. Can't nobody get in. Like to keep to themselves, those folks."

"But you—"

"Closed to me too. Old Zed at the gas station, he just keeps me up on the gossip sometimes."

"But if you don't live there, what are you doing here?"

He peered closely at me. "Why, I drive, son. Same as you do."

He walked back and got in his truck, then pulled up beside me and leaned over, just as he had the first time I saw him.

"Reckon you might try going that way," he said, nodding towards one of the narrow roads to the right. "That would be a good way to start."

"Start where?" I said.

"Driving, son. Just driving: that's all." He lifted a hand. "Be seeing you."

And I knew that he would.

I drove down the, road he'd pointed out and after a while came across a hitchhiker, a small wiry fellow wearing a *yarmulke*. He got in, nodding thanks, and sat beside me quietly for some time. The road began to widen.

"Been here long?"

I shook my head. "You?"

"Forever." He looked out over the expanse of bright green grass. "How shall a man find his way?"

Beats me. I shrugged and turned on the radio. Clarinets and rippling dulcimers: *klezmer* music.

"That's good," he said. "Leave it on."

The road stretched out before us to the horizon, pulling us on. We picked up speed. Far off I thought I could make out boulders, clouds.

# A Few Last Words

What is the silence
*a. As though it had a right to more*
—W. S. Merwin

AGAIN:
He was eating stained glass and vomiting rainbows. He looked up and there was the clock moving toward him, grinning, arms raised in a shout of triumph over its head. The clock advanced; he smelled decay; he was strangled to death by the hands of time....He was in a red room. The hands of the clock knocked knocked knocked without entering....And changed again. The hours had faces, worse than the hands. He choked it was all so quiet only the ticking the faces were coming closer closer he gagged screamed once and—

Sat on the edge of the bed. The hall clock was ticking loudly, a sound like dried peas dropping into a pail. This was the third night.

The pumpkin-color moon dangled deep in the third quadrant of the cross-paned window. Periodically clouds would touch the surface and partly fill with color, keeping it whole. Dust and streaks on the window, a tiny bubble of air, blurred its landscape; yellow drapes beside it took on a new hue.

He had watched it for hours (must have been hours). Its only motion was a kind of visual dopplering. It sped out into serene depths, skipped back in a rush to paste itself against the backside of the glass, looking like a spot of wax. Apogee to perigee to apogee, and no pause between. Rapid vacillation, losing his eyes in intermediate distances, making him blink and squint, glimmering in the pale overcast. And other than that it hadn't moved. Abscissa +, ordinate +. Stasis.

This was the third night.

His wife stirred faintly and reached to touch his pillow, eyelids fluttering. Hoover quickly put out his hand and laid it across her fingers. Visibly, she settled back into blankets. In the hall, the clock ticked like a leaking faucet. The moon was in its pelagic phase, going out.

The third night of the dreams. The third night that lying in bed he was overcome by: Presence. In the dark it would grow around him, crowding his eyes open, bunching his breath, constricting—at last driving him from the bed, the room. He would pace the rugs and floors, turn back and away again on the stairs, wondering. He would drink liquor, then coffee, unsure which effect he wanted, uneasy at conclusions—certain only of this sense of cramping, of imposition. In the dark he was ambushed, inhabited, attacked again from within.

His wife turned in bed, whispering against sheets, taking her fingers away.

Hoover lifted his head to the dresser, chinoiserie chair, sculpt lamé valet, to glazed chintz that hid the second, curiously small window. A simple room, sparse, clean, a room with no waste of motion. And a familiar room, intimate and informal as the back of his hand, yet his eyes moving through it now encountered a strangeness, a distortion. He cast his vision about the room, tracing the strangeness back to its source at the window: to pale plastic light that slipped in there and took his furniture away into distances. It occurred to him that he was annoyed by this intrusion, this elusive division of himself from his things. He watched the moon and it stared back, unblinking.

Hoover fixed his chin between his fists, propped elbows on knees, and became a sculpture. His face turned again to see the window, head rolling in his hands, ball-in-socket.

A cave, he thought: that was the effect. Gloom, and moonlight sinking through cracks: pitch and glimmer. A skiagraphy of the near and foreign. Quarantine and communion, solitude and confederation. A cave, shaped in this strange light.

And bruising the light's influence, he walked to the chair and stared down at the suit he'd draped over one arm—looked at the hall clock—ten minutes ago. It was happening faster now....

The suit was pale, stale-olive green and it shined in a stronger light. The coat barely concealed the jutting, saddle-like bones of his hips; his wrists dangled helplessly away from the sleeve ends like bones out of a drumstick—and Cass hated it. Regardless of fit, though, it *felt* right: he was comfortable in it, was himself.

He took the coat from the chair, held it a minute, and put it back. Somehow, tonight, it seemed inappropriate, like the man-shaped valet that no one used. As with the room, the furniture, it had been taken away from him.

He turned and shuffled across the rug to search through the crow-black corner closet behind the creaking, always-open door, discovering a western shirt with a yoke of roses across its breast and trying it on, then jeans, belting them tightly, and boots. The clothes were loose, looser than he remembered, but they felt good, felt right.

Stepping full into light at the door, he shattered strangeness, and looking back saw that the moon was now cockeyed in the corner of the pane.

Ticking of a clock, sound of feet down stairs.

He assassinated death with the cold steel rush of his breathing....

The night was pellucid, a crystal of blackness; hermetic with darkness. He moved within a hollow black crystal and up there was another, an orange separate crystal, bubble in a bubble....And quiet, so quiet so still, only the ticking of his feet, the whisper of breath. He pocketed his hands and wished for the coat he'd left behind.

Hoover turned onto the walk, heels clacking (another death: to silence).

A sepulchral feeling, he thought, to the thin wash of light overlaying this abyss of street. A counterpoint, castrati and bass. Peel away the light and you: Plunge. Downward. Forever.

Another thought....you can tell a lot by the way a person listens to silence.

(Sunday. It was evening all day. Over late coffee and oranges, the old words begin again. The speech too much used, and no doors from this logic of love. We go together like rain and melancholy, blue and morning....)

At the corner, turn; and on down this new abyss. Breath pedaling, stabbing into the air like a silent cough, feet killing quiet—

*I am intruding.*

*Darkness is avenging itself on my back.*

(And I, guilty realist, dabbler at verses, saying: There is no sign for isolation but a broken spring, no image for time but a ticking heart, nothing for death hut stillness....)

Light glinted off bare windows. Most of the houses were marooned now in a moat of grass and ascending weed. Driveways and porches and garages all open and empty, dumbly grinning.

(Evening all day. World out the window like a painting slowly turning under glass in a dusty frame. Rain in the sky, but shy about falling. The words: they peak at ten, pace by noon, run out to the end of their taut line....)

The shells have names, had them. Martin, Heslep, Rose. Walking past them now, he remembered times they were lit up like pumpkins, orange-yellow light pouring richly out the windows; cars, cycle-strewn yards, newspapers on steps. The casual intimacy of a person inside looking out, waving.

(And I remember your hair among leaves, your body in breaking dew, moonlight that slipped through trees and windows to put its palm against your face, your waist; bright and shadow fighting there....)

Darkness. It moves aside to let you pass. Closes, impassable, behind you.

(Four times: you came to bed, got up, came back to bed. You turned three times, you threw the pillows off the bed. Michael, never born, who had two months to live, was stirring in you and stirring you awake.

Your hair was on the bed like golden threads. The moon had pushed your face up into the window and hidden your hands in shadow. You were yellow, yellow on the linen bed; and opened your eyes.

—If I weren't afraid, I could leave and never look back.
You say that, sitting in a hollow of bed, knees tucked to
your flanneled breasts, arms around yourself.

—Would you follow, would you call me back?

I watch your steps track down the walk to the black, inviting street. And later, when I open the door, you're there,
grinning, coming back; coming back to make coffee and wait
for morning. And another night, another day, saved from
whatever it is that threatens at these times....)

Hoover looked at the streetlight shelled in rainbow and it
was ahead, above, behind, remembered. Darkness shoul-
dered itself back in around him. Snow hung in the air,
waiting to fall. The dead houses regarded him as he passed,
still, unspeaking.

(October, time of winds and high doubt. It comes around
us like the shutting of a light: the same thing is happening
to others. And the people are going away, the time has come
for going away....It all boils up in a man, and overflows.
His birthright of freedom, it's the freedom to be left alone,
that's what he wants most, just to be left alone, just to draw
circles around himself and shut the world out. Every man's
an island, why deny it, why tread water. So people let go....)

Hoover picked the moving shape out of the alley and was
down in a crouch, whistling, almost before the dog saw him.
It raised its nose from the ground and walked bashfully toward him, sideways, tail banging at a drum, whining.

"Folks leave you, fella?" A brown shepherd with a heavy
silver-studded collar; he didn't bother to look at the jangling nametags. "Take you home with me then, okay?" The
shepherd whimpered its agreement. Hoover rummaging in
his pockets.

"Sorry, fella, nothing to give you." Showing empty hands,

which the dog filled with licks and nuzzles, snuffling.

"Bribery, eh. Sorry, still no food." He stroked his hand into the dog's pelt, found warmth underneath. It sat looking up at him, waiting, expecting, its tail swishing across pavement.

When he erected himself to full height, the dog jumped away and crouched low, ready to run. Hoover walked toward it and put out a hand to its broad, ridged head.

"It's okay, fellow. Tell you what. Come along with me to see a friend, then I'll take you right home and see about getting you something to eat. Think you can wait?"

They punctured the night together, down the walk, heels clacking, claws ticking. Hoover kept his hand on the dog's head as they walked. The nametags threw bells out into the silence.

"Or maybe he'll have something for you there, come to think of it."

Click, clack, click. Staccato tattooed on the ponderous night. The sky is still ambiguous.

(Remembering a night we sat talking, drinking half-cups of coffee as we watched stars sprinkle and throb and fade, then saw dawn all blood and whispered thunder. I remember how your eyes were, pink like shrimp, pink like the sky when it caught the first slanting rays and held them to its chest. And as morning opened around us we were talking of Thoreau and men who sailed the soul, of ways and reasons to change, the old orders, and of why things break up. Outside our window it was growing between them, people were letting go, were wanting their Waldens, their Innisfrees, their Arcadias, they were falling away from the town like leaves, like scaling paint, by twos, by ones. Even in our house, our hearts, it moves between us. Between us.

We feel it turning, feel it touching. But we care, we love, we can't let go....)

Hoover drew up short, listening. The shepherd beside him cocked its ears, trembled happily.

It happens like this...

A drone, far off. Closer. Becomes an engine. Then a swelling of light blocks away. Then a rush and churning and soon two lashing white eyes. Loudest, chased by a dog. A roar and past, racing. A thrown thing. Neil's car....and silence again.

And minutes later, the shepherd's body went limp and its head fell back onto his lap. Hoover took it in his arms and walked out of the road, its head rolling softly along the outside of his elbow. In the streetlight his face glistened where the dog had licked it.

Crossing the walk, kicking open a gate that wind had shut, Hoover surrendered his burden into the lawn. Ten steps away he looked back and saw that the dog's body was hidden in deep grass, secret as any Easter egg.

Three hundred and some-odd steps. Two turns. Five places where cement has split its seams, heaved up, and grass is growing in the cracks. Pacing this map...

(The sea grew tired one day of swinging in harness, ticking in its box of beach. One spark in the flannel sea, possessed of fury, gathering slime like a seeded pearl, thinks of legs and comes onto a rock, lies there in the sun drying. It seeps, it slushes, it creeps, it crawls; it bakes to hardness and walks....All to the end: that I am walking on two feet down this corridor of black steel and my hand is turning like a key at this found door....)

The door collapse-returned. He looked around. A single

light cut into the café through a porthole of glass in the kitchen door; powdery twilight caught in the mirror. In the dim alley before him, neon signs circled and fell, rose and blinked across their boxes like tiny traffic signals. Profound, ponderous grayness, like the very stuff of thought....

Decision failed him; he had turned to go when he heard the door and saw light swell.

"Dr. Hoover..."

He turned back.

"Didn't know for sure you were still around." Nervously. "About the last ones, I guess."

Hoover nodded. "Any food, Doug?"

"Just coffee, sorry. Coffee's on, though. Made a pot for myself, plenty left." He stepped behind the counter and knocked the corner off a cube of stacked cups, burn scars on his hands rippling in mirror-bemused light.

"Sugar, cream?" Sliding the cup onto crisp pink formica.

Hoover waved them both off. "Black's the best way."

"Yeah...No one been in here for a week or more. I ain't bothered to keep the stuff out like I ought to."

Hoover sat down by the cup, noticing that Doug had moved back away from the counter. "Like you say, I guess. Last ones."

Doug scratched at his stomach where it depended out over the apron. Large hands going into pockets, rumpling the starched white.

"Reckon I *could* get you a sandwich. Or some toast—then it don't matter if the bread's a little stale."

"Coffee's fine. Don't bother."

"You sure? Wouldn't be any trouble."

Hoover smiled and shook his head. "Forget it, just coffee. But thanks anyway."

Doug looked down at the cup. "Don't mind, I'll have one with you." His penciled monobrow flexed at the middle, pointed down. It was like the one-stroke bird that children are taught to draw; the upper part of a stylized heart. "Get my cup." Over his shoulder: "Be right back."

Light rose as the kitchen door opened; died back down, leaving Hoover alone. He turned his eyes to buff-flecked white tiles; let them carry his attention across the floor, swiveling his chair to keep up. Light picked out tiny blades of gleam on the gold bands that edged formica-and-naugahyde. A few pygmy neons hopscotched high on the walls. The booths were empty as shells, humming with shadow; above them (showing against homogenized paint, rich yellow, creamy tan; sprinkled among windows) were small dark shapes he knew as free-painted anchors.

(All this shut in a small café, sculpt in shades of gray. Change one letter, you have cave again....)

Doug came back (light reached, retreated), poured steaming coffee. He squeezed around the end of the counter and sat two seats away.

"Neil left today."

"Yeah, I saw him up the street on the way here."

"So that's whose car it was. Wasn't sure, heard it going by. Going like a bat out of hell from the sound." He drank, made a face. "Too hot. Wonder what kept him? Said he was going to take off this morning." He blew across the mouth of his cup, as though he might be trying to whistle, instead breathing vapor. He tried another taste. "Will came through, you know...."

Hoover's own cup was sweating, oils were sliding over the surface. It was a tan cup; the lip was chipped. They weren't looking at each other.

"That big cabin up on the cape. His grandfather built it for a place to get away and do his writing, way the hell away from everything. Now it's his."

"I know. My sister called me up last week to say goodbye, told me about it, they thought it was coming through. Wonder when *she's* leaving?"

Doug looked up sharply, then dropped his head. "Thought you knew. She left about three, four days ago." Doug belched, lightly.

"Oh. I guess she went up early to get things ready, he'll meet her there. You know women."

"Yeah. Yeah, that's probably it." He went for more coffee, poured for them both. "Coffee's the last thing I need."

"You too."

"Yeah—lot worse for some, though. Been over a week for me, lost about twenty pounds. Catnap some...Thing you wonder about is, where'd they find a lawyer? For the papers and all. Didn't, maybe, guess it don't make much difference anymore, stuff like that. Anyhow, they're gone."

(And the wall's a wedge. Shove it between two people and they come apart, like all the rest....)

Hoover shrugged his shoulders, putting an elbow on the counter and steepling fingers against his forehead.

"Almost brought a friend, Doug...."

The big man straightened in his chair. His mouth made "Friend?" sit on his lips unspoken.

"But he was indisposed, disposed, at the last minute."

Doug was staring at him strangely.

"A dog. Neil hit it. I was going to see if I could talk you out of some food for it."

"Oh! Yeah, there's some stuff, meat and all I'm just gonna have to throw out anyway. What isn't spoiled already's getting that way fast. Didn't know there were dogs still around, though? Whose is it?"

"There aren't now. I hadn't seen it before. *Was* it: it's dead." Extinct.

"Oh. Yeah, Neil *was* going pretty fast. Dog probably wandered in from someplace else anyway, looking for food after they left him." Gazing into the bottom of his cup, Doug swirled what coffee was left against the grounds, making new patterns, like tiny cinders after a rain. "Always been a cat man myself. Couldn't keep one, though, haven't since I was a kid. Sarah's asthma, you know."

"You do have to be careful. Used to have hay fever myself, fall come around I couldn't breathe. Took an allergy test and they cleared it up."

"Yeah, we tried that. Tried about everything. You oughta see our income tax for the last few years, reads like a medical directory. Sarah got so many holes poked in her, the asthma should have leaked right out. Wasn't any of it seemed to help, though."

"How's Sarah doing? Haven't seen her for quite a while. She's usually running around in here helping you, shooing you back to the kitchen, making you change your apron, talking to customers. Brightens the place up a lot."

Doug tilted the cup to drain an extra ounce of cold coffee off the grounds.

"Not much business lately," he said. "Boy I had working for me just kind of up and left three-four months ago and I never got around to looking for help, no need of it, specially now."

"She's well, though? Doing okay."

Doug put his cup down, rattling it against the saucer.

"Yeah, she's okay. She—" He stood and made his way

around the counter. "She went away a while. To get some rest." He dipped under the counter and came up with a huge stainless steel bowl. "Think I'll make another pot. This one's getting stale. Better anyhow if you use the stuff regularly, easier on it, works better—like getting a car out on the road to clean her out."

He started working at the urn, opening valves, sloshing dark coffee down into the bowl. Hoover watched Doug's reflection in the shady mirror and a dimmer image of himself lying out across the smooth formica.

So Doug's wife had gone away too; Sarah had gone to get some rest....Hoover remembered a song he'd heard at one of the faculty parties: Went to see my Sally Gray, Went to see my Sally Gray, Went to see my Sally Gray, Said my Sally's gone away—only this time Sally Gray had taken everybody else with her....

Doug was chuckling at the urn.

"You know I gotta make twenty cups just to get two for us, I mean that's the least this monster here'll handle. Ask him for forty-fifty cups, he'll give it to you in a minute. But you ask him for two, just two little cups of coffee, and he'll blow his stack, or a gasket or something." He went back to clanging at the urn. "Reckon you can handle ten of 'em?" He started fixing the filter, folding it in half twice, tearing off a tiny piece at one corner. "Hell, there ain't enough people left in town to drink twenty cups of coffee if I was giving it away and they was dying of thirst. Or anywhere around here."

He bowed the filter into a cone between his hands, climbed a chair to install it, then came down and drew a glass of water, putting it in front of Hoover.

"That's for while you wait."

"I need to be going anyway, Doug. Have to get some sleep sooner or later."

Doug reached and retrieved Hoover's cup, staring at the sludge settling against the bottom. "One last cup."

"All right. One more."

One for the road...

Doug bent and rinsed the cup, then got another from the stack and put it on the counter. He stood looking at the clean empty cup, wiping his hands against the apron. He lit a cigarette, nodding to himself, and the glowing red tip echoed one of the skipping neon signs on the wall behind him. He put the package on the counter and smiled, softly.

"You know, you could've sat right here and watched the whole thing happening. I mean, at first there'd be the usual group, but they were...nervous. You know: jumpy. They'd sort of scatter themselves out and every now and then the talk would die down and there'd be this quiet, like everybody was listening for something, waiting for something. Then a lot of them stopped coming, and the rest would sit all around the room, talking across to each other, then just sitting there quiet for a long time by themselves. Wasn't long before the regulars didn't come anymore—and you knew what was going on, you knew they were draining out of town like someone had pulled the plug.

"That was when the others started showing up. They'd come in with funny looks on their faces, all anxious to talk. And when you tried to talk to 'em, they'd be looking behind you and around the room and every once in a while they'd get up and go look out the window. And then they'd leave and you'd never see them again."

Hoover sat with his legs cocked back, toes on the floor, regarding the glass of water (the bubbles had nearly vanished). He nodded: he knew, he understood.

"For a while I got some of the ones that were coming through. I'd be in the back and I'd hear the door and come out, and there'd be this guy standing there, shuffling his feet, looking at the floor. He'd pay and take his coffee over in the corner, then the next time I looked around, he'd be gone—lot of them would just take it with them, to go. Then even that stopped."

(The people: they drip, trickle, run, pour, flood from the cities. They don't look back. And the ones who stay, try to fight it—they feel it growing in them worse than before. Turning in them, touching them, and they care they love they can't let go. But the harder they fight, the worse it is, like going down in quicksand, and the wall's a wedge: shove it between two people and they come apart, like all the rest, like all the rest of the world....)

Doug found something on the counter to watch.

"One time during the War, the ship I was on went down on the other side and a sub picked us up. I still remember how it felt, being in that sub, all the people packed in like sardines, stuffed into spaces between controls and motors. You'd think it would be full of noise, movement. But there was something about being under all that water, being closed in, something about the light —anyway, something that made you feel alone, made you want to whisper. I'd just sit in it and listen. Feel. And pretty soon I'd start wanting them all to really go away, to leave me alone...."

Doug stood looking for a moment out one of the small round windows past Hoover's shoulder.

"Yeah. Yeah, that's the way it is all right." Then his eyes switched back to Hoover's cup. "I better go get that coffee, just take it a minute to perk."

He picked up his cup and walked down the counter toward the kitchen, running his hand along the formica. The door swung back in, wobbled, stopped (light had reached, retreated).

Hoover felt suddenly hollow; empty; squeezed. He looked around. The room was a cave again.

Out in the kitchen, Doug moved among his stainless steel and aluminum. Hoover heard him banging pots on pans, opening doors, sliding things on shelves out of his way. Then the texture of sound changed, sank to quiet, became a silence that stretched and stretched. And seconds later, broke: the back door creaked open and shut with a hiss of air along its spring, clicking shut.

(So now the quicksand's got Doug too, for all his fighting. Now he's gone with the rest, gone with Sally Gray....)

Outside in the alley angling along and behind the café, Doug's Harley Davidson pumped and caught, coughed a couple of times and whined away, one cylinder banging.

Hoover sat looking at the abandoned cup as silence came in to fill his ears. Then he heard the buzzing of electric wires.

*The last grasping and their fingers had slipped.*

*The wedge was driven in, and they'd come apart....*

He stood, digging for a dime and finding he'd forgotten to fill his pockets, then walked to the register and punched a key. "No Sale" came up under the glass. There were two nickels and some pennies.

He fed the coins in (ping! ping!), dialed, and waited. The phone rang twice and something came on, breathing into the wires.

"Cass?"

Breathing.

Again: "Cass?" Louder.

Breathing.

"Cass, is that you?"

Silence.

"Who is this? Please. Cass?"

A small, quiet voice. "I'm afraid you have the wrong number."

A click and buzzing…

After a while, he reached up and flipped out the change tray. As the lid slid away, a tarnished gray eye showed there: someone had left a dime behind.

Nine rings. Cass' voice in the lifted phone. Sleepy; low and smooth; pâté, ready for spreading.

"Cass?"

"Is that you, Bob? Where are you?"

"Doug's place. Be right home." The space of breath. "Honey…"

"Yes?"

"Get your bags packed, we're leaving tonight."

"Leaving?" She was coming awake. "Where—"

"I don't know. South maybe, climate's better. But maybe that's what everyone will think—anyway, we'll decide. Just get your things ready, just what you absolutely have to have. We can always pick up things we need in towns. There's a big box in the bottom of the utility closet, some of my stuff, some tools and so on I got together a while back. Put that with the rest—there's some room left in it you can use. I'll be right home. Everything else we'll need is already in the car."

"Bob…"

"Just do it Cass. Please. I'll be right back, to help."

"Bob, are you sure—"

"Yes."

She paused. "I'll be ready."

He hung up and walked into the kitchen, came out again with a ten-pound sack of coffee under one arm. He started over the tiles toward the door, then turned back and picked up the cigarettes lying on the counter. He stood by the door, looking back down the dim alley: stood at the mouth of the cave, looking into distances (he'd seen a stereopticon once; it was much the same effect).

The tiny neons skipped and blinked dumbly in their boxes; the kitchen light glared against the window, fell softly along the mirror. Shadows came in to fill the café; sat at tables, slumped in booths, stood awry on the floor; watching, waiting. At the end of the counter, the blank tan cup silently surrendered.

He turned and switched the knob. Went through the door. Shut it behind him. The click of the lock ran away into the still air and died; he was locked into silence....

Cautiously he assaulted the street's independence, heels ticking parameters for the darkness, the motive, the town. The sky hung low above his head.

(I walk alone. Alone. Men don't run in packs, but they run....Death at the wheel expects his spin. Dark seeps in around the edges, winds rise in the caves of our Aeolian skulls, five fingers reach to take winter into our hearts, the winter of all our hearts)

And they came now in the darkness, they loomed and squatted about him, all the furnished tombs: this dim garden of rock and wood.

(Bars of silence. Score: four bars of silence, end on the seventh. See how they show on my white shirt among the roses. Bars and barristers of silence)

The quick blue spurt of a struck match. A cigarette flames,

then glows, moving down the street into darkness.

(There is no sign for isolation but a broken spring, no image for time but a ticking heart, nothing for death but stillness...and the wall, the wedge, is splitting deeper but we'll hold, for a while we'll hold on, you and I)

He stood still in the stillness that flowed around him and listened to the hum of insects calling through the black flannel. As if in answer, clouds came lower.

(At the mouth of caves, turning. We can't see out far, in deep, but the time has come for going away the time has come for becoming....At the mouth of caves, turning, and time now to enter the calm, the old orders. At the mouth of caves. Turning)

He walked on and his heels talked and the night came in to hush him.

He shouted out into the dark, screamed once out into silence—and it entered his heart.

He passed a pearl-gray streetlight, passed a graveyard lawn.

("Sudden and swift and light as that the ties gave, and we learned of finalities besides the grave." Is this how it feels, the instant of desertion—a vague epiphany of epochal stillness, primal quiet?)

Around him, scarcely sounding his echo, stood the shells of houses, like trees awaiting the return of dryads who had lost their way.

(The instant of desertion, the instance of silence)

The cigarette arced into the street and fell there, glowing blankly.

He bent his head and began to hurry.

And with a flourish, the snows began.

# Powers of Flight

*A* S HE STEPS AWAY from the shop door, he begins to rise into air, his feet at first scuffing at pavement, then he is above it, clear, floating now over the heads of fireplugs, children, streetlamps, feeling the ground, with something like a long sigh, give up its claim. There is a light breeze and he drifts gently towards the shipyard, the strip of crab houses, checkerboards of docked pleasure boats. Faces turn up to him. I am falling, he thinks, upwards; I am falling into freedom.

"Maybe it's just," Sheila says, "not meant to be." She peers up from a column of figures atop which she has been picturing a diminutive man reposing nude, looking out at her. "Maybe I'll just never be loved, never find the right man out there."

"You could have mine," Jeffrey says, "If I *had* one, that is."

"You and Brian aren't together anymore?"

"Barbells to Beethoven, all gone. Empty room in the flat, black hole for a heart."

"I'm so sorry, Jeff."

"That's what *he* said—right before he hooked our CD player with a little finger and hauled it out to Larry's VW."

"Perhaps you're right, dear," Sheila's father says, turning

from the window where he's just watched her latest young man (Blair, he thinks; they all have these odd names nowadays) float away in a wash of pigeons and seagulls. "Or perhaps," because he knows how much this means to her, "it's just that you've been trying too hard. You should concentrate on your career. Watched pots and all that, you know."

"But I haven't been trying at all Papa. If there's anything I *don't* want, it's all this pain, this having to be around someone all the time, always wondering how *he* feels, what will become of the two of us. Having my life torn up all the time like a road under repair. I hid in my apartment for five months once, remember? Came to work, went home, locked the door. Then one day it was so gorgeous that I thought, I'll just hurry this trash out to the dumpster, no harm in that. So standing there with cans and paper towels falling out of tears in the plastic bags, and a week or more of old newspapers skewing out from under my arms, I met Stephen."

Whom Mr. Taylor had last seen, he was fairly sure, outside the fifteenth floor of Campbell Center, tiny multiple images of him reflected in the building's mirrored surfaces as he rose into a blinding dazzle of sunlight.

"Where'd you have lunch?" he had asked Sheila when she returned to the shop.

"Le Chardonnay."

"The one in Campbell Center?"

"I don't think there *is* another one."

"Eat alone?"

"Well…"

Stephen was followed close on the heels by Claude, then by David, Seth, Ramon. Mr. Taylor began to look up at the sky with dread. He took new interest in reports from traffic helicopters.

His own wife, Sheila's mother, vanished early one March. Snow crept towards them through weeks of sun-drenched weather and finally sprang, and when it was gone (though podlike shells of it hung on for days in dark places), so was Elizabeth. After that, life for Mr. Taylor became largely people and things taken from him. He sometimes feels that Sheila is all he really has left: what his life has come down to.

"Papa, I'll always be here to take care of you, just as Momma asked," Sheila would say as a child. She doesn't say that anymore. And when he goes for dinner to her tiny apartment, she listens again to the stories she's heard so often before and tells him hers (many of them, though he doesn't know this, invented), but her eyes reach out towards the city and its lights, the dwelling darkness, sequestered horizons. This is something they never speak of.

She and Jeffrey, however, often speak of such things. The heart opens like a flower, one will say, and the other continue: and closes again like a damaged fist.

So it is that Jeffrey knows something Mr. Taylor does not. For several weeks now, Sheila has been deeply involved, not with one man, but two. The first, Blaine, whom she met standing in line at her bank, this afternoon has floated off into the sky like a child's balloon. The second's name—he runs a specialty bike shop in one of the northside malls and lives in a garage apartment choked with art deco—is Ian.

"I love him so much, Jeffrey," Sheila says now. "Ian, I mean. There's almost a...a physical *pain* to it, I love him so much."

At which point Jeffrey begins to look rather more interested in what she is saying.

"But poor Blaine. He knows there's someone else, despite all I said. You could tell it from his eyes, from the way he almost touched me, then at the last moment drew back. Do you think I'll ever see him again, Jeffrey?"

"Hard to say," Jeffrey, who has watched from another window the spurned lover's ascent, says. "Sometimes it is possible, *enfin*, to become friends again."

"Oh, Jeff, I hope so."

There's a fall of customers then, and for almost an hour the three of them are diverted from the narrow streets of their own lives onto the boulevards of commerce.

"*Well*," Mr. Taylor says when the customers are gone. "That seems *quite* enough for one day's work. I vote we shut it down and have a few drinks together by way of celebration. Seconds?"

Jeffrey raises one arm, looking at his watch on the other. Two-fifty. He wonders what Brian's doing. And what *he'll* do for the rest of the day, leaving this early.

"Oh, Papa, how wonderful!"

They decide on Schopenhauer's and gather their various coats and jackets, hats, parcels, bags. With two fingers Jeffrey forklifts a thatch of hair half an inch to the right to cover an isthmus of bald scalp.

They walk out into an afternoon of empty streets and wind. Coming towards them on the opposite sidewalk, muffler blowing out like twin exhausts, is a man whom Jeffrey knows, instantly, must be Ian. He is dressed in a gray corduroy suit and brown wool porkpie hat and, seeing them emerge from the shop, starts walking faster.

"So this is where you hide." He reaches for the hand she tucks quickly away in a pocket.

"Papa," Sheila says. "Papa, this is Ian Whatley."

"Whatley," her father says.

"Mr. Taylor. I am pleased." He offers the forsaken hand, which is this time, somewhat hesitantly, accepted.

"And Jeffrey."

They also shake hands.

"We've been, sort of, seeing one another, Papa."

"Seeing one another," Mr. Taylor says.

"Quite a lot, actually, Papa."

"I love your daughter, sir. I did want to come and tell you that."

Sheila turns from her father to look at Ian and sees that he has grown taller: she must now, as never before, look up at him. She turns back, then back again to Ian, beginning to understand in some instinctive way that needs no words.

Wind comes up strongly just then, like waves heaving up against a ship, and very quietly Sheila says, "I'm sorry, Papa," as he begins to rise, slowly at first, then ever faster, into the sky. Leaning out ahead of the wind with feet trailing behind, almost reclining, he moves out of sight through the downtown skyline.

"I love you too," she tells Ian as her father joins the horizon.

# Finger and Flame

*S*O SHE LEFT and he was dead for a while and then, very slowly, he was alive again.

At the studio everything turned into her: expressionist landscapes, still-life, abstracts. The he met Flame.

She was wearing a green T-shirt and green shorts. She had a small shopping basket full of avocados. Beneath the T-shirt her breasts, tapering, full, were themselves like avocados. She had long hair tied at the back, a shy smile, worried eyes.

I am in love, her said to himself, and to her: Will you have coffee with me?

No, she said. Then, catching the disappointment in his face: I don't drink coffee, I meant to say. But tea would be nice. There's a shop I like not far away.

Vaguely oriental music, scented candles, woodgrain plastic chairs, two other people. She stowed the avocados behind her, against the wall, and settled back. They ordered tea and a tray of sweetcakes.

I'm Flame, she said.

Finger.

Is this place okay?

It's fine. I like it. I'm not into crowds.

I don't know you, do I? I mean, I didn't meet you at a party or anything like that.

No.

Well, I wasn't sure. I get pretty wasted sometimes. People'll come up to me and talk like we're friends and I don't know them from water. You'd be surprised.

Will you come home with me, Flame?

Wow. She touched her left breast with her right hand, gently. Can we have our tea and stuff first, you think?

Not really home—the studio. I do have an apartment, but I haven't been there in weeks.

Is it close? The studio?

A couple of blocks. An old gas station I bid for and refurbished. No one else wanted it.

You married or anything?

Nothing.

And you're, what, an artist?

Yes.

Like a painter?

Mainly.

Wow. Right hand to left breast again, less gently. Here's the goods. I'll pour. Cream?

Please.

You paint strange stuff?

Sometimes.

Who's your favorite artist?

Matisse, most days. Sometimes Rothko. What do *you* do, Flame?

Lots of things.

In the realm of awkward beginnings, it was right up there. But all told, there was, too, a kind of grace.

One of the things I do best, she went on, is make other people happy. Are *you* happy, Finger?

On his studio daybed that night she opened her legs and

urged his head into place between them. Tension gathered in trembling limbs as her hips strained against him and she said, Please, Please. And finally O my God, as she came.

And Flame, that simply, was his life.

Everything he did, everything he thought, was for her, to redeem her sorrow, to protect her, to make her less unhappy, to give her fear and sadness a voice, to keep her.

She moved in the next day. He'd never felt this way about anyone else, never would again. (He was right about that.) They began slowly to map one another's contours, the coastlines they'd have to drift along, their overlapping catalogs of need, of debility.

She told him how as a child she'd put the frogs she caught in cardboard boxes, carefully drawing in furniture and doorways, and find them dead there the next morning.

He told her about the first time he heard Mahler.

She told him about her first husband at age sixteen, the way she fled her parents' house and sister, how strong his hands were and how tender some nights, that first year.

He told her about Pam in London. How they'd work together for hours at opposite ends of the studio and fall together finally, exhausted, unable to continue work, on the raw wood floor spattered with paint, and afterwards sleep there. Have tea together in the morning and both go back home.

Then she left me, Finger told Flame. Just didn't show up one day and wouldn't answer when I called. That's what women do, Flame. They leave me.

I'm different, she said. None of the others loved you the way I do.

Long after she was asleep he lay watching the ceiling. Lights slid across it. A spider crossed it obliquely, reminding him of geometrical theorems. They'd been together six weeks.

Flame, he said, very quietly, then louder: Flame. She lay on her stomach. He put his hand on the back of her leg. He loved her so much. Flame, he said. I want to tell you something.

Hmmm.

She turned towards him, threw an arm and leg across him. Grazed back into her dreams.

Something I've never told anyone, he said. There's this trick I can do.

On the nightstand her cigarettes moved closer to her, and one nudged out of the pack. Her mauve Bic lighter came alive with flame.

It doesn't amount to much, he said. One of those things you have inside you, like good manners, or grammar, that the world doesn't care about. No one else knows.

She slept on. And, eventually, he too (keeping watch for the spider, thinking of right and isosceles triangles, recalling their first days together, her body in moonlight) slept.

At the studio that morning he stretched a new canvas and fell to painting with an abandon, an *otherness*, he'd not known for a long time. By twelve he had a finished work, something wholly unlike anything he'd done before, undeniably important and powerful. Such *feeling* to it, so much fear, and strength.

It was all intuition. And that intuition spilled over: he returned home half-expecting what he found there.

Hi, she said. She was sitting on the bed with grocery bags beside her. The bags were full of her things. He could feel the spaces left behind, the hollows in drawers and closet. I was wrong, Finger, she said: I'm not different. I wanted to be, but I'm just like the others. I'm sorry.

Why, he said.

I don't know.

Okay.

So, sudden and swift and light as that, there was no Flame.

He stood looking at the door for a long time. Then he walked through the apartment again and again, looking (he supposed) for scraps and tatters, for something as substantial as his memories, his pain. Against the back wall of the closet he found her pink tennis shoes—all that was left of her. He stood for a long time watching them. Very slowly, first the left one, then the right, they began walking towards him.

# *Potato Tree*

"WE'VE FOUND the problem," Dr. Morgan told me. After a moment I said, "Yes?"

"Basically," he said, "you're crazy as batshit."

He was right, of course, but at ninety dollars an hour I had expected more. I waited. That seemed to be it.

"I see. Well. Is there anything you can do?"

"Oh, yes, a number of things. There are several quite interesting drugs on the market. Years of psychiatry—that might be fun. Shock, megavitamin therapy, behavioral training. Probably a lot of others. I'd have to look it all up."

He swiveled his chair to watch a traffic helicopter swing by outside the window. From his new position he said, "Of course, none of them will help any. You're crazy as batshit and basically you're just going to have to live with it, accept it. Here, I wrote it down for you."

He swiveled back and handed me an index card upon which was printed in large block letters: C A B S. Below, in a painstaking tiny script, were an asterisk and the words "crazy as batshit."

"It shouldn't really be any great bother. I mean, you'll be able to keep on going to dentists, reading cereal boxes, having regular bowel movements, humming old songs—all the important stuff. Just a little bit of an interpretative dysfunction, that's all. You just won't ever know if things are as they seem to you; they could be *quite* different."

He wet a finger and wiped at a smudge on the desktop.

"I, for instance, could well be a wig-maker. A canoeist. We may at this moment be the sole attendants of a missile silo in Kansas. Do you play bridge?"

"No."

"Good. Hate that damned game."

He swiveled again to look out the window.

"Is there anything else you can tell me?" I said after a while. "Any advice, recommendations?"

"Only this," he said. "Go with it, ride it. Enjoy it." He turned back to me. "Most of us live in a much duller world than yours, you know." There was something very like envy in the poor man's voice.

"Thank you, Doctor," I said, rising from my chair and looking for the last time at his wall of diplomas. "You've been a great help."

"It's nothing." He removed his glasses, breathed against them, fumbled in pockets for a handkerchief. "Give me a call now and again to let me know how you're getting along." He looked back at the smudge through clean glasses.

"I'll do that."

I walked a few steps to the door. There was no knob, only a hand protruding from the wood which clasped my own in a handshake. I pulled against it, opening the door.

"Don't forget your diagnosis," the doctor said behind me. I turned. The index card dropped to the floor and scuttled towards me.

* * *

The world looked not at all different, unchanged by my ill-ness as it had been by my former health, in short, uncaring. The first elevator was full—all of them wearing the doctor's face, perhaps patients of his—and I waited. Eventually I made it down to the plaza and sat on one of the benches under a potato tree. Some of the hospital patients were hav-ing a wheelchair race on the grounds, pursued by grim-faced, limping nurses.

"May I join you for just a moment?"

I looked up into a face of great and radiant beauty, though pale. She collapsed onto the bench beside me.

"Are you all right?"

"Fine. Just give me a moment, I'll be okay. Please."

I spent the moment looking at the oxblood gleam of her boots, at the tug and thrust of sweater, into the depths of her gray eyes. Never had I felt more alone; my loneliness entered me like a bullet.

"Well. I proved they were wrong, at least," she said.

"I'm sorry?"

"The doctors...Listen, forgive me. I don't want to inflict you with my troubles. You must have plenty of your own."

"Not really. I'm crazy, you see: nothing can touch me."

I took out the index card and showed it to her. A potato fell to the ground at our feet. The index card leapt onto it and began to feed.

"How wonderful, to have an *interesting* disease. All *I* have's cancer."

"What kind?"

"The worst kind, of course, but it's still pretty dull."

I put out my hand and she held it, just as the door had earlier. We sat together looking out over the grounds as a light snow began to fall. Beside us the potato tree thrust into the sky as though *it* were a hand intent on tearing out that white down, intent upon opening it. The patients had turned on their nurses and were chasing them about the grounds, laughing joyously as they crunched bones with the wheelchairs. Children sat watching.

"How long do you have?" I said finally.

"Not long. They said I wouldn't even get out of the building, it was so bad."

"*How* long?"

She looked at her watch.

"Ten minutes," she said, floating into my arms.

# Need

*H*E WASN'T SURE EXACTLY when he had first noticed the child, but several miles outside Milford, glancing up at the rearview mirror, he saw her there in the backseat and realized that she had been there, an unremarked presence, for some time. Yet he is certain they had no child along when they checked into the Fountain Bay last night. He tries to remember pulling out of the parking lot this morning, looking in the mirror as he would always do. He thinks maybe she was there then. But he's still not sure.

The girl is reading a hardbound book with a green cover. There seem to be (in the mirror it's difficult to tell) dancing bears on the cover, a family of them perhaps.

"Good book?" he says after a while.

"It's okay, Dad."

"What's it about?"

"I told you yesterday. A daughter who vanishes without a trace."

"Do they find her?"

"I don't know. I haven't finished it yet, silly."

"I bet they do."

Beside him Rosemary's needles continue their minute orbits around one another. Whatever she is knitting now is green also.

"Always reading, that one," she says.

"You want to stop for breakfast yet?"

"Not unless you do."

"Well, let's go on another hour or so, then."

"Fine. We could stop at that truckstop just this side of Helena where we stopped last year."

"Sounds good. I'd forgotten about it."

Beneath bare trees the grass remains green. There are scattered small pools shallow as mirrors from last night's rain. From the radio come strains of a waltz.

Once, waking from nightmares of loneliness (he no longer knew how long it had been, or cared), he found Rosemary beside him, as though she had always been there.

They pass through a crossroads with a crumbling onetime gas station (tin softdrink signs still cling to its sides), Mac's Home Cooking 24 Hrs., a small wood church set up on pylons, a feed store. There is a mile or so of fence then, thick posts with single boards nailed obliquely between them, like mirror-image N's.

The girl puts her book down for a while and sleeps, curled into one corner of the seat. Rosemary pulls out an entire row and starts it again. He can hear the needles faintly clacking together.

They stop at a Union 76 for breakfast not too long after. The girl (Rosemary has started calling her Cynthia) does not want anything.

"Never eats anything, that one," Rosemary says.

There is not much traffic, and early in the afternoon a fleet of bright-colored balloons passes over. Behind them clouds gather as though towed into place by the balloons. At one point they follow a truck piled with sugarcane for several miles. Then they drive through a pounding rain back into sunlight. When they stop again to eat (and again Cynthia wants nothing) it is almost dark; the moon is like a round hole punched through the darkness.

They leave and drive into that darkness. There is more traffic now, as they near the city. He spins the dial between classical, country, jazz and rock, unable to decide. Billboards at the side of the road advertise topless bars, car dealers, restaurants and motels, Jesus, museums, snake farms. Cynthia wakes and asks, "Are we almost there, Dad?"

"Almost, honey," he says.

Beside him Rosemary winds in her yarn, tucks the needles away. "Try this on, Cyn," she says. He watches in the rearview mirror as his daughter pulls on the green sweater that fits her perfectly. For the first time he realizes that it is cold.

The traffic gets heavier. It comes from far away, tiny points of light like ideas. Then they come closer, and as they come, cars and trucks take shape around them.

# Old Times

THE MAN IN FRONT of you in line says, "I don't suppose you could tell me if a crash is scheduled?"

You turn to shrug apologetically, impotently, at those behind you in line. Some harsh faces there. You quickly turn back.

He's thirtyish, well dressed in a middle-America sort of way, crumply brown slacks and sportcoat, crisp white shirt with yellow knit tie, hair a close-clipped tangle of curls. There's a newspaper folded in one side coat pocket. An oversize flight bag lies crumpled on its side like a discarded boot beside him.

Smiling, the ticket clerk looks up at him and says, "You know I can't give out that information. Sorry, Paul." It's quite a smile, something she has a talent for.

New statistics scroll onto the board above her head.

FLIGHT INTERRUPTIONS DOWN BY 28%
FATALITIES TO DATE THIS MONTH...923
LOWEST FARES—ALL FOR YOU

He glances briefly about, aware at last of the growing disrest here behind him.

"Hey, it's *me*, Gladys. The guy who taught you how to

overbook, take double breaks—all the important stuff."

Her smile never wavers.

"I remember you, Paul."

"We used to be like *that*."

"Before you went to a competitor."

"Gladys. Western offered me almost twice the money, better hours, perks. What else could I do? What would *you* have done?"

Above her head, with the rest of the board remaining the same, FATALITIES shifts unremarked to 1180.

"Anyone understands, it has to be you. I'd have been right here punching buttons the rest of my life. With Western at least I had a chance to get out—thought I had, anyway."

"It didn't work out for you, then."

"No. No, I'm sorry to say it didn't, not this time. But I'm on my way to an interview in Chicago, and this one, I've got a good feeling about."

She hands the envelope, tickets tucked safely away inside, boarding pass stapled to the outside, across the counter.

"Thank you for flying Allied," she says. "Next, please."

The man turns fleetingly and smiles at you, at this potential mob back there. Rip his heart out. So hard to get a break in this world. He turns back.

"Gladys," he says, "please. I haven't worked in almost a year. Now—finally—I have an interview. And I have a chance. But I need your help. For the old times?"

She looks at him, then down at her VDT. Walks fingers over her keyboard as FATALITIES blinks away at 1180. She looks over the rabbit she's pulled out of this electronic hat.

"You're confirmed straight through to Chicago, Mr. Paulson."

Thanking her, he reaches for her hand but she doesn't

extend it. His own hovers there by the stack of luggage labels and credit-card applications. Finally he withdraws it.

"I won't forget this," he says. "I owe you, Gladys."

He shrugs into his oversize shoulderbag and starts off towards the gate. There is a milling already at its mouth. We could all still make it.

"Friend of yours?" the ticket agent next to Gladys says.

"Sort of. Paul trained me. I had a crush on him like you wouldn't believe but he never so much as noticed me. I cried for weeks."

"Before that competitor got him."

"Yeah." She laughs. "The competitor. A blonde. Of course, we were all a lot younger then."

"Some things stay with you."

"Some things do."

She turns back and says, "Can I help you, sir?"

You hold out your ticket, but for a moment she goes on staring into space, a tight smile on her lips, and doesn't reach for it. You wonder if you really want to go to Chicago today.

# Becoming

*F*OLLOWING MANY TESTS and much consultation among themselves, the doctors inform me that, slowly, inexorably, my body is turning to stone. Sheaves of computer printouts clutched in their hands, they show me X-rays, tracing of various internal pressures and electrical measurements, thick plastic sheets of CAT-scan records with multiple images of brain, liver, digestive system, heart. They tell me they can pinpoint where it began: *here* (a gentle finger taps at one of these icons of self), but cannot say why. It is, at any rate, progressive. And though they can't be certain, of course, since no one to the best or their knowledge has seen this before, the prognosis seems poor. They do not know how long the process will take. But we—myself, my family, friends—must not despair. There has been already much discussion among top specialists as to appropriate treatment regimens. The process could even reverse itself. This sometimes happens. And there is always hope from new research. They do not explain why anyone should be engaged in research on an illness, a condition, never before seen.

Because there is nothing else to be done, I am released from the hospital. In a lime-green glassy cage of an office a young lady all in white, pleated skirt, sleeveless T-shirt, white shadow on her eyes, guides me through what we still call paperwork, though of course no paper is involved. (Now even I am using the words *of course* reflexively. I've contracted this from the doctors.) In parting, the young lady passes me an appointment card. Several weeks' worth of follow-up visits are listed. White-sheathed lips smile and say good-bye, Dr. Bloom.

The doctors' conglomerate offices occupy a fashionably antique building, rambling and oddly shapeless, perhaps once a railway station or post office. In its cavernous lobby, near the outermost of half a dozen noodle stands and yogurt bars, there's even a callbooth, the first I can recall having seen in years. It appears still to be functional.

I punch in my PIC and stand for several moments before the screen as it prompts me, blinking:

PLEASE ENTER LINECODE

In a corner of the lobby, two steel doors like huge leaves open upward, outward, and sink to the floor. Two men and a barge loaded with boxes ascend operatically from the canals bellow. A part of my mind registers that barge and boxes alike are of the so-called organic alloy, banana byproducts and recycled plastic, of which increasingly everything in our world, clothing, containers, furniture, seems constructed.

PLEASE ENTER LINECODE OR CANCEL REQUEST

No one knew I was coming here. I have no idea who I might want to call, or what their linecode would be, if indeed they had one. Even less, what I would say, should I actually manage to place a call and get through.

IF YOU WISH TO REINSTITUTE, PLEASE ENTER PIC NOW

Three blips, and the screen washes. A blue-green photo of fields and misted mountains constructs itself slowly, piece-meal, in the prompt's place. Years of this image have burned away part of the screen; the highest mountaintop and a portion of cloud beyond it fail to materialize.

Leaving the building, I walk along the river. Business complexes like Colony South may be our closest equivalent to feudal land. For thousands of years humankind built, first its villages, then its ports and cities, alongside water. Now, *ex nihilo*, we create bodies of water wherever we erect our buildings, rivers and lakes and lagoons that have no name. Colony South's office buildings, upscale restaurants, health clubs and luxury apartments sit along miles of serpentine river and canals whose banks are paved with tile and stone. Couples sit on scroll-like benches at waterside or stroll beneath the low stone arches of bridges and walkovers. Boats of every sort, flat ferries, maintenance and security outboards, rentable two-man paddlewheelers and canoes, make their way along the river and canals in the shadows of the buildings.

When I tire at last of walking, I take to one of the ferries. There's a pilot with throttle and joystick seated in front, a helmsman with wheel at back, a row of seats along either side. Half the seats are occupied. Across from me sit a young man and woman. They are ten years old perhaps. Both go on staring straight ahead as the books in their laps speak to one another.

*There was a spider who more than anything in the world wanted* to see London, about which he'd heard so much.

Yes, and one day, saying to himself Why not, I may never have this chance again, he stowed away on a milk wagon.

Alfred his name was. It had been his father's name, too.

Soon, before he knew it, he was far, far away from everything he knew.

But he was not afraid.

Oh, no. And years later, he would remember the man who helped him.

Pigeons strut and peck on the paved banks, and squirrels chatter in trees overhead. The water's an astonishingly deep blue, the sky above not blue at all but instead a kind of whitish-gray, shot through with contrails, banners of industrial waste, clouds that seem never to change or move.

At river's edge, outside Hotel Evropa, I catch a cab. The driver doesn't know my part of the city, and I have to direct him onto the loop, to exit just inside the third beltway, and crosstown. Something gamelan-like, like programmed wind chimes, plays loudly on his tape machine. He turns the volume down.

"You have lived here long?"

All my life, I tell him, yes.

"It is for me two years now. A fine city." He looks about. "Fine. At first, just as I did in," and he names a country I make no sense of, "I piloted boats. Now I pilot this fine car. This is better."

Half a mile from my building we pull up, immobile, as a parade of Watchmen in full regalia, tunics, boots and berets, all black, goes by. My driver with a deep sigh at last shuts off his engine. Fast behind the Watch comes the usual second line of street folk, stray kids, vandals and petty criminals.

The computer says how good it is to have me back as I enter.

## 38 CALLS

Then:

**26** COMPUTER-GENERATED
ELIMINATE?
TALLY?

"Eliminate."

**9** AWAIT TRIAGE
TALLY?

"Please."

**3** PERSONAL
**4** PROFESSIONAL
**2** UNCERTAIN
RUN?

"Hold."

I make a cup of maté at the corner sink. The cup is one I picked up in Mexico on a field trip years ago. Grad school? Must have been. Fired ceramic, but utterly hollow in the centimeter-and-a-half between outer and inner walls. The cup weighs less than plastic and feels as fragile as an eggshell. It's outlasted aluminum cookpots, jeans, four notebook computers and every relationship I've had.

I bring my cup and maté back across the room. There are three others, but the only chair I ever sit in is the one by the console. Across from it (the room is narrow) stands a low bookcase. Books are stacked rather than placed, on their sides in double rows. Still, I know where each one is.

"Go."

RUNNING...

A voice I don't recognize starts up.

"I apologize for calling you at home Dr. Bloom, but..."

A student, then. Unable to make class this week, she tells me, though she fails to say what class, because of family illness. Marcie Desai. So it would be the graduate seminar, late Greek history.

I try to match a face to the voice and name, at first come up only with something vague around the eyes, a perpetually unfocused look. Then Marcie Desai's face reconstructs itself in my memory. Green eyes, with hazel flecks. Hair she almost certainly once spent hours each day trying to tame and now simply cuts short. A bright student, very bright. Hard, sure edge to her speech, what she says, the way she says it; and at the same time this subtext of deference in her gestures, motion. Accustomed not so much to being turned away as, instinctively, self-protectively, to turning away herself, everything in her life, major decisions to simple daily tasks, only degrees of departure.

END MESSAGE
FILE? DELETE?

"Delete."

CONTINUE?

218

"Please."

RUNNING...

The next two messages arrived online. In the screen's upper left corner an icon appears, a running stick-man, as the first message scrolls up.

RECEIVED YOURS OF THE 14TH, SORRY, 18TH (MUST REMEMBER TO LOOK AT THE CALENDAR PERIODICALLY), RE CONTEMPORARY (CONTEMP(T)?) MARXIST INTERPRETATIONS OF THE GREEK CITY-STATE. CERTAINLY THE ENTIRE GROANING, CLANKING MECHANISM OF THAT MARVELOUS ATHENIAN FREEDOM, ITS DEMOCRATIC TOLERANCE, SOCIAL WELFARE AND CIVIC ACHIEVEMENT, THE ACCOMPLISHMENTS OF ITS PHILOSOPHY AND ARTS, WERE MADE POSSIBLE ONLY BY SLAVERY AND THE SO-CALLED NAVAL FUNDS, I.E., EXTRACTION OF PROTECTION MONEY (LEST BIG BAD BEAR PERSIA GOBBLE THEM UP) FROM OTHER GREEK STATES. NO ARGUMENT THERE. BUT I WONDER IF FINALLY THIS ISN'T JUST ANOTHER FACE FOR OUR OWN OLDEST BUGBEAR, WHAT WE HAVE TO CONTINUALLY REMIND NOT ONLY OUR OWN STUDENTS OF, BUT ALSO OURSELVES, CARLYLE'S SIMPLE TRUTH: THAT MOST HISTORY DESCRIBES NOT HOW LIFE WAS LIVED, BUT HOW IT WAS INTERRUPTED——BY INVASION, WARFARE, PLAGUE OR FAMINE, RIOT, DISEASE, STRIFE. DURING ALL OF WHICH, NONETHELESS, CROPS WENT ON BEING RAISED, HOMES SMOKEHOUSES AND OUTHOUSES GOT BUILT, MARRIAGES WERE ENTERED INTO, HUSBANDS AND FATHERS DISAPPEARED, FURNITURE WAS PASSED DOWN, BAD BOOKS WRITTEN.

I read this as the larger part of my mind still thinks of Marcie Desai. The set of her features, the softness of her eyes. Memory itself (I think) is a kind of stone. Nudging into place the moments and monuments, the interruptions and departures, that become our lives.

How despairingly Romans sought the secret, that simple, easy grace of Greek statuary. A kind of pure thought coaxed from stone. Stone that like the earth itself bears weight: stone that *is* earth, of earth, ejected from earth yet still weighty with it. Stone we pile above our graves, stone from which we learn to construct fences, stone we come to write upon.

"...I was so afraid then," I hear.

We're down to the last of the messages.

"Stop."

The stick-man icon stands still, blinking.

MESSAGE 7

REPEAT? DELETE?

"Repeat please."

"John? There's no reason you should remember me. I'm sure you don't, and I don't even know why I'm calling you now, or why you've come to mind after all these years. Jean? Jean Patrick? We had Dr. Davis' medieval history course together our first year at Tulane. I was so afraid then. Twelve years in a Catholic girl's school, then that. It was like falling out of a boat and watching the boat pull away. I kept writing down everything Dr. Davis had said in class and getting C's. You asked me out for coffee after class one day, and it got to be a regular thing. You were someone I could talk to. Look, this is ridiculous, I feel like an idiot of some sort, calling you after, what?, almost thirty years? But if by some weird chance you do remember me, or if you'd just like to talk for a while, give me a call, okay? Bye!"

Her linecode and PIC come up onscreen.

END MESSAGES

FILE? DELETE?

"File last voice message. New folder: *Jean*. Print out online re Greek city-states. Delete others."

CREATING FOLDER JEAN...

DONE

PRINTOUT GREEK CITY-STATE

SEARCH IN PROGRESS...

PRINTING...

?CONFIRM DELETE?

"Confirmed."

WORKING...

One of the first messages was from Laura. We've been seeing one another for almost a year now, quiet, rather stylized evenings for the most part, dinners out, theater and concerts, playing the pair among her peers or my own. Undoubtedly, at some level we care for one another. But once alone we have little to say; are careful in fact, in a tiptoeing sort of way, to avoid any conversational doors or paths left open.

I brew another cup of maté and, returning to the chair, place a call to Laura. I tell her computer what has happened:

my pain and growing dysfunction, today's visit to the doctors, their diagnosis.

I'll be away from the apartment, I say, and will call back later.

Sipping tea, I gaze out my window. The sky has settled through deepening layers of gray to the color of ripe plums. Odd patches, catching the city's lights, glow like dull neon.

I place a call to Jean and say that yes of course I remember her (I don't) and that yes I'd love to see her (would I?). Maybe we could have lunch together. I'm free most days. Whatever is convenient for her.

I look up again then, into the crosshatch of branches moving gently, fingers reading the Braille of cloud, wind, dark sky.

From far away, in that other world, the computer tells me I have a call.

As I watch, the branches slow.

As I watch, they stop.

# Dawn Over Doldrums

*S*ITTING FOR COFFEE, he glances back briefly at the doorway with its improvised deadbolt, chain, deadfall bar. She thinks how the sound of unfastenings has replaced a cock's crow as harbinger of morning for them here, and wonders what Keats might have done with that. She thinks of the boundless symbolism in everything, how the simplest objects and actions are replete with meaning, with resonance: hasp embracing flange, the bar's leap of faith into concavity. Everything connects. Once a poet's wife and ruined by it, she puts coffee down and leans into him, arm resting across, pressing on, his shoulder, as her hand lightly grazes his chest.

"How did you sleep?"

"Fairly well," she tells him. "The first part, anyway."

"I was restless?"

She nods. Remembers an old poem of David's: All night the beast beat about its room as I lay forgetting you. As usual, David had thought he was writing fantasy—what he lived—and would never know how right he was, how prophetic, all those years ago.

Everything connects.

Now this man's hand still shakes, and she reaches out to steady it. What they drink is a distillate from one of the mancuspia's holding-glands, not coffee at all; but as with many things here, they have kept the familiar words.

"Sorry," he says now. Never apologizing for what happens at night (this silence, tacitly, is understood), but, in effect, for needing her now, for this small weakness.

You're simply *away*, he told her once, early on, when some of the others were still with them. Then you come back: walk into an apartment that looks just like your own but where someone else lives. You don't know what has changed, and there's nothing you can take for granted now. Your body fails to do what you expect. You watch your own hand reach out into the world without your willing it.

She gets up and pours more coffee. His hand is steadier now. "Hungry?"

"Can we wait?"

"Of course."

She moves closer to him, against him, and his arm goes up over her head (she ducks, readjusts) and behind, to her shoulder. One breast nudges at his palm. She moves until that hand is filled.

Deep in the evening, shortly after the bolts and locks have fallen, winds begin to gather on the far horizon and blow in across the dry swampland she's taken to calling the Doldrums. It's a silent wind, seen in gentle displacements of grass, felt (but only at its peak) against the face, and for her this wind has become the voice of the mancuspia.

One morning long ago she had looked up the word *keening*, simply because the mancuspia's brimful, silent faces brought that word to mind. The computer told her: A lamentation for the dead uttered in a loud wailing voice, or sometimes in a wordless cry. Yes.

They'd known something of the mancuspia's adaptive gifts from initial reports, of course. The animals could live on almost anything, or (more to the point of what this world offered) on virtually nothing. Only when supplies were exhausted and early survivors scrabbled for basics did they begin noticing what a true wonder the mancuspia was. For if the mancuspia could live on virtually nothing, they discovered, another species could live off the mancuspia.

The mancuspia had come among them during their first days here, appearing outside the squat-huts one afternoon without fanfare or prologue. After first fearing, then largely ignoring them, the team tried to domesticate them, taking one of the knobby, shapeless animals into the huts where it promptly died, as though to tell them: I will not be kept. More from curiosity and boredom than any other motive, Marc Gavruski, the team biologist and medic, dissected the creature—an autopsy, they eventually took to calling it. And what he discovered was a machine of exquisite precision. From the rubble and scant, equivocal vegetation of this place, from sunlight and that silent wind and whispers far beyond hearing in the twists and turns of its genetic makeup, the mancuspia urged forth the very basics of life, nutrients, water, essential minerals, all of which it stored away in glands easily accessible.

Since that time, they have not seen a mancuspia die. Of course, the individuals are indistinguishable one from another, and they assume (since numbers are constant) that periodically one of the animals must wander off to its end to be replaced by another, though they have never witnessed young or any evidence of same.

She must know more about the mancuspia than anyone else now, she supposes; must know them better. The work of caring for them, initially shared with others—and now almost the only work remaining—fell to her by degrees, at first because she enjoyed its variance from her mapping and geographical duties and because the mancuspia readily accepted her presence, then because, increasingly, there was no one else to involve him- or herself with quotidian concerns. Now Eric spends his days hoarded scrivenerlike among the indecipherable artifacts of a long-defunct alien culture. And as the group's number declined, as their reliance on the mancuspia redoubled, there seemed always to be more work. The mancuspia would no longer graze; soil and vegetation perforce were brought to them. Their exiguous waste products (since almost everything was somehow used, converted) had to be carried off.

Because it is mindless work, though, it is welcome. And maybe, just maybe (she thinks), there is some extreme, innate truth to woman as nurturer, tenuous threads tacking them still to the race's long traditions and history, echoes of whispers in the bright, cluttered spirals of their genes.

Deep in the evening she sits looking out over the Doldrums and feels the wind against her face like a lover's hand. Hears behind her the rattle and drumming of locks, bolts, chains, doors.

They found Diane one afternoon in the galley, laid out on a long stainless-steel table as though for possible reassembly. Someone—Nyugen, possibly—had gone in to fetch tea and cakes and come back out blanched, gesturing, unable to speak. They were halfway into their fifth month on the world they'd begun calling Catarrh.

Most of her midsection was gone, torn away, scooped out and tossed in gobbets against walls and floor. Her own hand had been forced, up to the wrist, into her mouth, tearing it at both corners into a clown's mouth, rupturing the mandible so that it hung down like a necklace. The fingers of the other hand were neatly severed and laid out in an asterisk at the table's bottom left corner. Bowels, ravelled out like yarn, were a heavy, glistening mound on the floor nearby. An eyeball peered from what remained of her vagina.

They had not known what to do with the body, finally tucking it in a sealed bag meant for geological specimens and depositing it on a rock ledge outside the huts. None of them could bring him- or herself (though this was protocol) to commit Diane's body to the Deconstructor. In all of them, perhaps, was some vague notion of taking her body home, back to its own planet, for burial.

After a while there was quite a stack of bags on that ledge.

One day (for those, days, had become as indistinguishable as the mancuspia) Evelyn took the Mini out, scooped up the bags in its jaws and hauled them away, out of sight.

A week or so later, she went after them and brought them back.

More than anything else, he had to *understand*.

To understand this world, at first: sitting before the computer sifting in blocks of seemingly unrelated information, driving headlong (he hoped) for syncretism—much as, ten years old, he had built, on his first computer, a working model of the solar system.

Next he tried to understand what was happening to them here, logging each drift of personality, each storm or withdrawal in those early days, plotting these against every imaginable variable: weather conditions (though there scarcely *was* weather), changing diet and metabolism, declensions of the planet itself, a bevy of biological and psychological tests. What he derived was as intricate, compelling and ultimately useless as that early solar-system model.

Anything was bearable, if only it was understood. But he could not understand a world; and, finally, he could not understand anything of what was happening to them here. None of them could.

So, finally, he came to the Boroch.

They were a race, or species, long extinct, and so little of them remained that surely in short order (he thought) he would know all about the Boroch there was to know. And perhaps, now, he did.

Of a material nature, aside from a handful of scattered small artifacts, there wasn't much. Some concave objects of an extremely hard substance which absorbed all light, ranging in size from that of the ball of a man's thumb to roughly that of a newborn's skull. (Bowls? Or containers of another sort, perhaps. Body decorations. Religious vestments or utensils. Or for that matter—just as easily—a set of measuring spoons.) A few narrow, vertical slabs resembling nothing so much as the gravestones one sees in history books, each of these inscribed with what might be language—or simply attritions of time and weather.

And that was pretty much it. No libraries, no great government repositories, record-houses or munitions dumps, no museums. No buildings at all, in fact, save one. If, indeed, it *was* one. For it might as easily be (and this had become maddening for him) some inscrutable monument or artwork; a train station, vending machine, aquarium.

Five sides, irregular yet still somehow fitting together in a welter of bends and all but imperceptible curves, the whole of the structure perhaps eight feet at its greatest height, five at its lowest, and ten or twelve feet in circumference. It was mostly the color of the drab, surrounding ground itself, save midday when, for a brief moment, light angled down, caught in it somehow and, pale yellow, spread across its surface, gone then as abruptly as it came. No discernible doors or other egress. But set in each side (each of them, he thought, at a different level) were semi-transparent sections, at times virtually opaque, other times limpid as pool water.

Windows of a sort? Screens?

Periodically mancuspia came to the structure, sat by it unmoving for a few moments or as long as a day, then went on about whatever business they might have, to all appearances wholly unaffected by their tryst.

At first he and Evelyn spent much of their free time observing the mancuspia at this sentry. Drawing close, they would themselves peer by the hour into those watery sections and occasionally see, or believe they saw, vague motions, like movement sensed just outside sight's orbit yet never there when the eye turns to it.

In a notebook whose cover is ringed with layers of overlapping blurred rings, memories of half-drunk cups of coffee in a riot of Venn diagrams, he has copied out, among sketches of artifacts, half-remembered fragments of conversation and markers for the dead (*Jules Yasner; 5-28?*), something from a book he'd read in the drawl of their first weeks when each day, each hour, stretched endlessly to the horizon. Imbedded in a discussion of some French writer he'd never read, or indeed, so much as heard of—in a book like many another, taken up utterly at random—the passage meant little to him at the time, but later, unaccountably, drew him back.

*Rarely do the monuments erected by a culture in its aspirations to eternity betray the forces that propel individuals toward destruction as the affirmative willingness to lose things, meaning, and even self.*

He was remembering that passage when one night, as they stood by the structure, he suddenly said, without thought:

"It was suicide."

And knew he was right.

"Racial suicide. The Boroch simply chose, at last, not to go on. I don't know how I know that, I have nothing to support it—but I know."

"And the mancuspia?"

He paused.

"The mancuspia...have been waiting."

There were five of them. Five of the fourteen who came.

"We should call it the Doldrums," Eric said, looking out across the dry swampland. Of late they'd taken to renaming things. "The land where nothing continues to happen."

"Enough is happening in here to fill a dozen lands," O'Carolan said. "What does Control say now?"

"What does Control always say?" Solomon stood beside Eric, also looking out. "Run some tests, set up new safety standards, keep us informed, we'll get back to you."

"If this goes on..."

"And we have no reason to believe it will do otherwise."

"...there won't be any *you* to get back to."

They were all silent a moment.

"It can't be a virus, then."

"Nothing we can detect, at least."

"Or any physical mutation."

"And why only the men?"

"We're a bit closer to beasts to begin with, no?"

"There *are* genetic differences, whether or not it's politically correct to say so, dear."

It was the last of their strategy conferences, brain-storming sessions which had become, in their futility and repetitiveness, little more than ritual.

Lin Fu brought green tea for them all in the tiny enameled cups he'd packed so carefully among his personal belongings. They had been his grandfather's and father's before him.

"Ceremony is important at such times," Lin Fu said in his quiet voice.

"Especially when there's not a thing else."

That night O'Carolan was killed, and they would hear his brash, bold voice no more.

Some weeks later, Lin Fu. They found him among his shattered cups.

Then Solomon.

Until there were only the two of them.

"What are you doing?" she had asked Eric the afternoon of the day she found Solomon. He stood by one of the storeroom doors, beside him a cart scattered with small tools, chains, metal fixtures.

"Making my bed," he told her.

She remembers a story by Gogol, how the texture of the protagonist's world begins to unravel. One morning on the street he observes two dogs conversing quite civilly; before long he's come to believe he's the King of Spain and dates his journal entries "April 43rd, 2000" or "86th Martober, between day and night."

Poetry is nothing, David had always said, if it's not possibility.

(The possibility of fantasies at once crueler than truth and more comforting. The blur of words becoming action; action, words. The possibility of protracted, unaccountable absences and sudden rearrivals. Of other, distant, forfeited lives.)

On this world where, employed for their comforting familiarity, gently humorous and wayward as orphans, words seldom mean what they say—Catarrh, Deconstructor, the Doldrums—she does not know any more what is real, or greatly care. That wind at night is real; it must be. The heave and metallic leaf-rattle of lock and chain, that piercing aloneness, the sadness in his eyes (or in her own, perceiving it) come morning. Though she knows, she grants, she allows, she accepts, that date and time, day or night, have little meaning for her now.

She is not altogether surprised then when, one night in the crowded hours before dawn, she looks up to see him there. Not *him*, really, but what he becomes, something she has never before seen. Behind him, locks lie open and unavailing. Has he sprung them? Or has she somehow forgotten, neglected, to fasten them securely?

"I love you, Eric," she says.

He starts towards her. Not *him*, she reminds herself; that is not Eric, cannot be Eric, behind those eyes. And for a moment she thinks she sees, she almost sees, the mancuspia's pale, indistinguishable forms there between them in the near-dark. They stand unmoving, as before the structure.

A blink, and they are gone.

Another blink and Eric staggers, comes to a stop, folds

slowly, head onto chest, chest onto knees, knees down, onto the floor.

"You didn't lock the storeroom," he said hours later.

She poured coffee, or whatever it was, for them both.

"I don't know," she said. "I've sat here wondering, waiting for you to surface. I *thought* I had locked it. But it's possible, at some level, that I left things open intentionally. That I wanted you to escape, or—"

"It doesn't matter."

"The *or* matters."

"No. It doesn't."

He reached across the table and put his hand atop hers.

"The mancuspia will not let us die, Evelyn. I understand that now."

He smiled.

"They and the Boroch must have lived in a near-perfect symbiosis. The Boroch had no factories, no food-processing plants, no centers of government because they had no use for them; the mancuspia provided everything they needed. And when the Boroch decided, collectively, to end, the mancuspia chose *not* to. We're their answer, their means for going on. All along we thought we were using the mancuspia—and they've been using us."

"But what of all that's happened here?"

"It had nothing to do with the mancuspia. For all they knew, that was the way we had always lived. But now they know it's not. They stopped me last night. They won't let it happen again. We're too important to them, they've waited too long."

After a while she said, "More coffee?" and he nodded. It was fully light outside, and they sat in the squat-hut looking out at the stack of bags on the ledge, sinking into history and memory, getting ready, like the mancuspia before them, to go on.

# Ansley's Demons

SOMEHOW, INSTINCTIVELY, he knew not to open his eyes, knew that it would end if he did. The touch of those lips lightly and so familiar against his own—and when, again instinctively, he reached up and around, his hand remembered the long curve of her back. For it *was* her: he did not question that.

And somehow she moved within him as well as upon him. Though he felt nothing beneath it, though he did not will this, one hand, then the other, rose into air above him and cupped themselves where breasts would be.

"Ansley," he said.

Outside his window a tidelike wind tugged momentarily at the edge of the house. Across the room close to the floor, a light breeze scuttled, lifting a page of the newspaper lying there, briefly disturbing the leaves of a plant she'd given him on a birthday—hers, not his.

*Shhhh*, the wind told him.

That was a Monday, and she was gone almost as soon as he realized she was there with him. Tears spilled down the side of his face onto ears and pillow, and his penis throbbed, half-erect, above him. For a moment then, wind howled, and it was like the howling of his own bereft soul.

She returned on Thursday, but left almost as soon. He lay for a long time afterward watching lights from cars outside fall across the ceiling; lay probing at his memories as one unpacks luggage, small and much-used things on top and in odd corners, more substantial belongings farther down; then turned and found her again in his sleep.

Sunday she stayed, even afterward, as he settled back breathless and limp onto the bedding. He stretched out his arm, and memory, or the moment, was so strong that he imagined he almost felt her shoulder in the palm of his hand.

"How...?" he said.

There was no wind. Or only the small one of her breath in his ear where she lay against him.

That December, it was unseasonably, impossibly warm, closer to Mississippi Delta autumns than to any Massachusetts winter he'd ever known. Even the birds seemed confused. They'd wheel off into a morning sky in great sweeping waves and disappear, then late the same day be back, chittering and thrashing about, in their accustomed trees.

Those same mornings he fell into the habit of passing his time at a park across town, an oblong block of halfhearted shrubs and bright yellow benches perched at city's edge over a twin abyss of suburb and barrio. He'd sit there watching children dash towards school, their parents plummet to the shopping malls and office complexes where they worked, and he'd think about ambition: what was it like to have it? A phrase he'd picked up somewhere in his reading, *wandering to find direction,* rolled about in his head like a barrel broken loose in the ship's hold. But he didn't want direction. If anyone had asked (though no one did, of course), he would have answered that he didn't want anything.

A woman of twenty or so with long black hair and round glasses, black sweater, yellow tennis shoes, was there some days, and gradually they began to nod, to acknowledge one another. Usually she carried a book, other times a bag filled with papers and composition books. Like himself, she was always alone.

The birds had a fondness for cheese popcorn, and often he stopped at a party-goods store on the way to the park to buy a bag. One morning he looked up from the cluster at his feet (sparrows, wrens, lackluster blue-green pigeons shunning a single albino one) to see her on the opposite bench. Her head came up from her book just then, too, and she smiled. After a moment he walked over and sat beside her. Most of the flock of birds followed.

"Want to help feed them?" He held out the bag.

"Well, actually," she said, "I keep coming here hoping they might feed me."

"And have they?"

She closed the book on one finger and held it against her leg.

"We don't always know right away. Other things, we *do* know, from the first."

He reached over and pivoted the book: *The Surrealist Moment*.

"You're an artist?"

"Art historian. Final refuge for those who love it and can't do it. I tried. Perspective might as well have been Greek, colors swam away from me. But all my life, ever since I can remember, I loved history, too. I read history textbooks the way other kids did comics, starting when I was only nine or ten. I think at one time I may have known everything there was to know about the antebellum South. Then I discovered Matisse, Bonnard, Delvaux...."

"And you teach—I've seen you with papers."

She nodded. "Art appreciation at the community college. Part-time and substitute at the university. That's the best I could find. Oh, and I do occasional reviews for the *Telegram*."

"I may have seen your name, then."

"If so, you'd probably remember it. I never, ever, felt like an Ann, or a Barbara, which were the names my parents gave me. So when I went off to school, I made up a name I *did* like, and had everyone call me that. I've been Ansley ever since. Ansley Devereaux."

"French?"

"Cajun, yes. From a little town nearer Baton Rouge than any other place you've ever heard of, where half the store signs were in English, half in French, and all were misspelled."

"You're a long way from home, Ansley."

"Aren't we all."

"Yeah. Yeah, I guess we are."

He scattered the rest of the popcorn and watched the birds scatter with it. They came back to his feet and waited awhile, then, one by one, flew away.

"Would you like to get some coffee?" he asked.

"That would be good." She put the book away and slipped her arm though the purse's shoulder strap. "But what I'd really like is to spend the afternoon with you."

A bird dropped from one of the trees, shot by just over their heads and wheeled away again, pursued by another. Ansley looked down at the caterpillar the bird had dropped in her lap. It moved tentatively, just the front of it, exploring this new, sudden environment.

"See?" she said.

That there was great evil in the world, evil requiring only the smallest sliphole, an opening, he had never doubted; in their second year together, a piece of that evil detached itself and walked beside them.

After a flurry of short-term jobs, he'd gone to work for the paper, floating steadily upwards from writing bridal news to handling department rewrites to doing layout for the lifestyles section. She had helped at first, on that, but both soon realized that he had the greater knack for it; had, in fact, something of a gift.

About April she began a long siege of illness: initially nausea and cramps which they thought (with a strange mixture of alarm and elation) meant she was pregnant; then a series of colds and respiratory infections leading to hospitalization for pneumonia; and above it all, hovering there, an inexorable weakness, her ever-increasing sense of malaise, helplessness, surrender.

Then just as suddenly and fiercely as they had begun, the symptoms subsided—only to return six weeks later.

Again the hospital, where, after days of blood tests, special procedures in closet-sized rooms, a rain of lengthy, incomprehensible explanations and acronyms (CT, ABG, MRI), they had a name for the evil that had attached itself to them.

Lupus.

She woke that night near dawn. He felt her presence and turned from the window where he sat watching cars climb across the city's concrete horizons. They were on the eighth floor of a building called Hope Memorial.

"How do you feel?"

"Not so good. You get any sleep?"

"A little."

"I told you you should go on home."

"Home is wherever you are."

"You know," she said, "you've always had a habit of saying the right thing, even when you made a fool of yourself."

"But one of my endearing traits."

"Oh yeah? You got a list of the others?"

"I'll get back to you."

"Right."

He walked over and sat beside her on the narrow bed, took her hand in his. In coming months, siege after siege, hospitalization after hospitalization, he would watch flesh fade from that hand as he held it, watch it withdraw imperceptibly until the hand was little more than a glove of parchment draped over bone.

She turned toward him and the gown fell away from her breast. He resisted an impulse to put his other hand there. Dawn pried at the horizon. Time has the best gig going, he thought: it passes so successfully, whatever goes on in our lives.

"I always knew something was wrong," she said, "even as a child. I never spoke about it, I was afraid that somehow the words might make it more real, I guess, but I knew. I was different."

In coming months they would speak of many things they had not before, and most they had. Ice, then birds attempting a nest, appeared in the windows of rooms they occupied. Toward the end, too weak perhaps, her failing energies focused on passage (or on holding it off from her), she spoke hardly at all.

Near another dawn, he woke to his name on her breath,

uncertain in that still, blue room whether she had actually spoken or he had imagined it. Her breath was the barest pulse and all light was gone behind her eyes, but as he leaned above her, his name formed again on her lips and balanced on a brief column of air.

"This is forever," she told him then. "I hope you know that."

*All that is best of dark and light*, he'd think often in the following months. Then, inevitably: Fuck you, Byron, and the simpering romantic horse you rode in on. For the territory in which he found himself could be understood (if at all) only by a Poe, a Baudelaire.

She came to him that first time—somehow, instinctively, he knew not to open his eyes, knew that it would end if he did, knew it was her—almost six months afterward, when grief had shrunk to a hot black pearl deep inside and, it seemed, might pass.

She came that Monday, then Thursday, Sunday, another Monday. Then, for a week or more, every night—and, as suddenly, was gone. He waited, tumescent at the merest hush of wind, thinking each moment that the creak and sway of wires outside his window in the wind might become more.

His grief, his loss, had seemed unendurable, and then, with her second departure, *was*.

Eventually friends came to the apartment and found him there, all but speechless, in a litter of fast-food cartons, discarded clothing and offal. They took him to Hope Memorial where one hour a day of group therapy and sixteen hours of Jeannie, Hazel, Lucy and the Munsters pulled him back into focus.

His pain, he thought then, was a river gone underground.

But time blunts even the sharpest teeth. Slowly, the days he stalked with forms, going about them woodenly and at some distance—rising at six, ceremonial shower, conventional breakfast, hard, steady work, good dinner—began to take on substance, and feelings filtered in through the curtains. At dinner one night with the friends who had helped him, an hour or so into the meal, he suddenly realized that he had become again participant and not observer; that for some time now he had been enjoying himself. It was a revelation.

Anne, he met a few nights later, she leaving La Madeleine, he entering, their coats brushing against one another, leather on leather, among close-set tables. Whenever there's a collision, even with no damage done, you're supposed to exchange numbers, he told her. And called her the next day for lunch (which she couldn't make) then for dinner (which she could, barely, in the space before a scheduled concert with friends at which she never arrived).

Conversation embraced childhoods, work, the dew, popcorn and carrots, the inexhaustible process by which we become our parents.

They had coffee at a downtown diner at one in the morning, sandwiches at a highway truck stop at six. Leaden, indigestible doughnuts and more coffee at ten.

After that, they began spending all their free time together, each day retracing those same improvised routes to the interior, to the heart of their new content and continent.

Things moved slowly through hour-long back rubs, languorous walks taking in most of the city, encyclopedias of talk. She had been "mostly alone" for two years or more, they were so different after all, she was afraid. What surprised *him*, what astonished him one Tuesday morning when it tumbled into his head, something he'd known for some time, known from the first and never acknowledged, was that he was *not* afraid.

Sometimes that old despair licked at him in odd moments and sent chills stamping up his spine; he saw himself again in that solitary room, surrounded by sacks of half-eaten food and his own waste. But more often he looked away from that—to mornings and years where he and Anne sat together over coffee and Sunday papers at La Madeleine, where they walked along the gentle curve of a river as evening shelled the sky, or sat side by side in a circle of light with wind and the dark amoan outside.

He rarely thought of Ansley now, until one night he looked up and, for a moment, saw her face there above him. But then it was Anne's again, framed in a fall of red hair, familiar, endearing, constant.

Afterward he tried, in his mind, to bring back that face, and could not. One eye, a foothill of cheek and lip, would come into focus, then (when he moved on to retrieve some other portion) blur, dissolve, flow away. His mind lunged back into their time together, his and Ansley's—that slow, early awakening, the easy accommodations as they grew to know one another and respond at levels words could not penetrate, the twilight thickening between them in all those faceless rooms—then, with a massive thrust of will, he shut that door forever.

Memory, he thought, is a demon, promising to bring us respite and ease for what we have lost even as it carries away in its stumpy arms what little we have held on to.

That night she, Anne, tells him: I've thought about you all day. I've had this feeling, this sense, that something is wrong.

The question trembles between them and expires. They've lit a candle, and its pale light washes erratically over them and into the room's corners.

It's nothing, he says. Memories. Ghosts.

Briefly her face moves down to him, then back into the darkness above, where she arches her back and begins to move, very slowly and without words, at levels words cannot penetrate, upon him.

Somehow, instinctively, he knows they are not alone. And though he does not move, something moves within him. He watches as, without volition, his hands rise, not to her breasts, Anne's, but to her neck, where they whiten. He watches her face there, like a flower's, the surprise, the growing shock and struggle, the sudden stillness. And on his lips in that speechless room he finds the word *forever.*

# Time's Hammers:
## Volume Two

# Forward, Bravely,
# into the Anthills

*T*HIRTY-FOUR years of stories.

What comes back to me for the most part are a lot of early mornings. I know some of these stories were written during the day, they had to be, but whenever I think back it's always three in the morning and I'm sitting at a table or makeshift desk somewhere in a circle of light. With the world buzzing against my window, maybe, and I'm thinking "Sure glad I got the screens up in time." Or listening to the world's feet clomping around on the porch, wondering should I go look and see what's out there.

The other thing that comes back to me is the astonishing number of places these stories were written. London, some of them, in a bedsitter with gauzy curtains like bandage slapped against the sky and stairways narrow as ladders. Some of the earliest in rural Iowa, looking out over cornfields and the houses of Mennonite neighbors. A second-floor studio apartment in the East Village whose downstairs vestibule was a favorite sleeping spot for the neighborhood's homeless. Damon's and Kate's house in Milford that I rented along with Tom Disch and where we could never be sure just how many visitors might be tucked away in upper rooms. An apartment in Boston that you reached by climbing up, always up, from the streetcar tracks, bank upon bank of cement steps, Azteclike; I lived there when my first book came out. Various apartments in New Orleans whose cockroaches, I swear, moved along with me en masse. A converted garage in Texas where I watched women deliver their children to daycare across the street as I sat to begin writing in the morning and watched the kids get retrieved (this was the summer I wrote *The Long-Legged Fly* in a month, much of what would become *Renderings*, and at least two dozen new stories, plus assorted poems, essays and reviews) as I continued on into the night.

Short stories were always what I loved most, always what I intended to write. I'd take "The Man Who Lost the Sea" or Gogol's "The Nose" over any number of earnest *Bildungsromans* and tales of crumbling marriages; I found it hard to believe (and still do) that any novel could say more about political repression, the human soul and the sources of art than Cortazar's six-page "Graffiti." Having sold my first story, written in a week, for the awesome amount of $300 (this was in 1966), I assumed I would just go on doing this, failing to take into account that, first, I might not be able to write a story every week and, second, that one or two of them might not sell for such splendid sums. In fact, as the market began collapsing a few years later, my checks dwindled steadily, to $100, to $36.25, to $10. Till finally I was out there strutting my stuff on the corner, the literary equivalent of Storyville mattress women. Boxes slowly filled with the complimentary copies of magazines that were often my only pay and followed me from apartment to apartment, city to city, over time squashing down like well-used cushions or old boots.

But I'm not going to write here about trying to make a living as a short-story writer. That all too soon would have one part of my audience laughing uproariously and the other, a very small part, weeping.

Short-story writing. The lemonade stands of literature.

I had started off publishing, as I said, in science fiction magazines and anthologies. Later, in large part due to a wonderful lady named Eleanor Sullivan whom, alas, I was never to meet, I began publishing as well in mystery magazines. Meanwhile, not content with this simple, pure obscurity, I pushed ever onward to new frontiers, heeling my mule all alone over the ridge (for no Indian guide would accompany me; bearers threw down their loads and fled shouting Bwana, Bwana not go there!) towards literary magazines with baker's-dozen circulations that were seen chiefly, in many cases solely, by other contributors.

Yes, I did wonder sometimes, as I stuffed another perfectly innocent envelope with return postage, or tore one open to find my manuscript bearing the hoofprint of the paper clip that clasped a form rejection to its bosom, whether this was not a silly thing for a 33-year old (or 43-year-old, or 53-year-old) supposedly professional writer to be doing. But I just went on doing it, like some out-of-control, perpetual-motion existentialist making his leap into faith, nostrils pinched shut with finger and thumb, again and again, on permanent replay. Headin' em up, movin' em out.

Years ago I wrote a piece for American Pen suggesting that, abandoned by mainstream publishing, our literature—even then we'd begun to miss it, you see, and to go looking for it—had fled to the literary magazines. They were like those remote islands in science fiction upon which prehistoric life has survived into the present. I truly believed that. Some years later I again wrote on the subject, saying that now I didn't know *where* our literature had gone. That I had looked and couldn't find it. That if anyone had seen it recently, they should call; I'd pay for information, photos, confirmed sightings. I put its face on milk cartons.

Well, as it happens, a lot of our literature was sidling its way over towards mystery and crime writing. The situation was similar to what had obtained with paperback originals in the Fifties, when writers like Jim Thompson and David Goodis could pursue their demons, turning out these highly original, intensely personal novels, yet still make their livings as professional writers. Science fiction in the Sixties, when I began writing it, was just then unfolding (soon the airlocks would slam shut again) and had much the same sense of practical freedom about it. Michel Butor said of science fiction that anticipation had created a language by which in principle we could examine anything. Damned if we couldn't—and didn't! But now writers like Jerome Charyn, K.C. Constantine, Jim Burke, Daniel Woodrell and Walter Mosley were discovering that mystery and crime fiction would let them write the kind of books they wanted, personal books, literary books if you will, and still have an audience.

I'm a little slow, but eventually I figure things out. I'd made my way to Chandler and Hammett while in London, and once back in the States, in short order, to Chester Himes, Rex Stout, Ross Macdonald. In my flat off Portobello Road, gauzy curtains slapping at sky through the open window but never making contact, I had written an odd story, all threat and paranoia, titled "And then the dark—." I followed it with one titled "Winner," then over the years with others: "Blue Devils" and "D.C. al FINE" (which oddly enough earned substantial sums upon broadcast over Italian radio) for Cathleen Jordan at Hitchcock's; "I Saw Robert Johnson,"

"Dogs in the Nighttime," "Joyride" and "Good Men" all for Eleanor at Ellery Queen's; most recently, "Vocalities" for John Harvey and "Shutting Darkness Down" for BBC radio.

Somewhere in there, too, begun as a short story, completed as a novel, came *The Long-Legged Fly*. Then others buzzing at the screens. By which time I could pass in most company. I had become, almost without noticing it, bilingual.

Or had begun talking in tongues, perhaps—perspective is everything.

But listen. Savages, barbarians, creep towards you from without and within, savages at every border, every edge, just outside the light. They look like you, they have learned to speak like you. Soon none of us will be able to tell them apart. But we, your writers, can help you. We can defend you. We've always aspired, you see, to be outlaws, hired guns, eternal outsiders, long riders. We've always intended to be dangerous.

Please.

*James Sallis*
*Phoenix, April 1999*

# Jim and Mary G

GETTING HIS LITTLE COAT down off the hook, then his arms into it, not easy because he's so excited and he always turns the wrong way anyhow. And all the time he's looking up at you with those blue eyes. We go park Papa, he says. We go see gulls. Straining for the door. The gulls are a favorite; he discovered them on the boat coming across and can't understand, he keeps looking for them in the park.

Wrap the muffler around his neck. Yellow, white. (Notice how white the skin is there, how the veins show through.) They call them scarves here don't they. Stockingcap—he pulls it down over his eyes, going Haha. He hasn't learned to laugh yet. Red mittens. Now move the zipper up and he's packed away. The coat's green corduroy, with black elastic at the neck and cuffs and a round hood that goes down over the cap. It's November. In England. Thinking, The last time I'll do this. Is there still snow on the ground, I didn't look this morning.

Take his hand and go on out of the flat. Letting go at the door because it takes two hands to work the latch, Mary rattling dishes in the kitchen. (Good-bye, she says very softly as you shut the door.) He goes around you and beats you to the front door, waits there with his nose on the glass. The hall is full of white light. Go on down it to him. The milk's come, two bottles, with the *Guardian* leaning between them. Move the mat so we can open the door, We go park Papa, we seegulls. Frosty foggy air coming in. Back for galoshes, all the little brass-tongue buckles? No the snow's gone. Just some dirty slush. Careful. Down the steps.

Crunching down the sidewalk ahead of you, disappointed because there's no snow but looking back, Haha. We go park? The sky is flat and white as a sheet of paper. Way off, a flock of birds goes whirling across it, circling inside themselves—black dots, like iron filings with a magnet under the paper. The block opposite is lined with trees. What kind? The leaves are all rippling together. It looks like green foil. Down the walk.

Asking, Why is everything so still. Why aren't there any cars. Or a mailtruck. Or milkcart, gliding along with bottles jangling. Where is everyone. It's ten in the morning, where is everyone.

But there is a car just around the corner, stuck on ice at the side of the road where it parked last night with the wheels spinning Whrrrrr. Smile, you understand a man's problems. And walk the other way. His mitten keeps coming off in your hand. Haha.

She had broken down only once, at breakfast.

The same as every morning, the child had waked them. Standing in his bed in the next room and bouncing up and down till the springs were banging against the frame. Then he climbed out and came to their door, peeking around the frame, finally doing his tiptoe shyly across the floor in his white wool nightshirt. Up to their bed, where they pretended to be still asleep. Brekpust, Brekpust, he would say, poking at them and tugging the covers, at last climbing onto the bed to bounce up and down between them until they rolled over: Hello. Morninggg. He is proud of his *g*'s. Then, Mary almost broke down, remembering what today was, what they had decided the night before.

She turned her face toward the window (they hadn't been able to afford curtains yet) and he heard her breathe deeply several times. But a moment later she was up—out of bed in her quilted robe and heading for the kitchen, with the child behind her.

He reached and got a cigarette off the trunk they were using as a night table. It had a small wood lamp, a bra, some single cigarettes and a jarlid full of ashes and filters on it. Smoking, listening to water running, pans clatter, cupboards and drawers. Then the sounds stopped and he heard them together in the bathroom: the tap ran for a while, then the toilet flushed and he heard the child's pleased exclamations. They went back into the kitchen and the sounds resumed. Grease crackling, the child chattering about how good he had been. The fridge door opened and shut, opened again, Mary said something. He was trying to help.

He got out of bed and began dressing. How strange that she'd forgotten to take him to the bathroom first thing, she'd never done that before. Helpinggg, from the kitchen by way of explanation, as he walked to the bureau. It was square and ugly, with that shininess peculiar to cheap furniture, and it had been in the flat when they moved in, the only thing left behind. He opened a drawer and took out a shirt. All his shirts were white. Why, she had once asked him, years ago. He didn't know, then or now.

He went into the kitchen with the sweater over his head. "Mail?" Through the wool. Neither of them looked around, so he pulled it the rest of the way on, reaching down inside to tug the shirtcollar out. Then the sleeves.

"A letter from my parents. They're worried they haven't heard from us, they hope we're all right. Daddy's feeling better, why don't we write them."

The child was dragging his highchair across the floor from the corner. Long ago they had decided he should take care of as many of his own needs as he could—a sense of responsibility, Mary had said—but this morning Jim helped him carry the chair to the table, slid the tray off, lifted him into it and pushed the chair up to the table. When he looked up, Mary turned quickly away, back to the stove.

Eggs, herring, toast and ham. "I thought it would be nice," Mary said. "To have a good breakfast." And that was the time she broke down.

The child had started scooping the food up in his fingers, so she got up again and went across the kitchen to get his spoon. It was heavy silver, with an ivory *K* set into the handle, and it had been her own. She turned and came back across the tile, holding the little spoon in front of her and staring at it. Moma cryinggg, the child said. Moma cryinggg. She ran out of the room. The child turned in his chair to watch her go, then turned back and went on eating with the spoon. The plastic padding squeaked as the child moved inside it. The chair was metal, the padding white with large blue asterisks all over it. They had bought it at a Woolworth's. Twelve and six. Like the bureau, it somehow fit the flat.

A few minutes later Mary came back, poured coffee for both of them and sat down across from him.

"It's best this way," she said. "He won't have to suffer. It's the only answer."

He nodded, staring into the coffee. Then took off his glasses and cleaned them on his shirttail. The child was stirring the eggs and herring together in his bowl. Holding the spoon like a chisel in his hand and going round and round the edge of the bowl.

"Jim…"

He looked up. She seemed to him, then, very tired, very weak.

"We could take him to one of those places. Where they…take care of them…for you."

He shook his head, violently. "No, we've already discussed that, Mary. He wouldn't understand. It will be easier, my way. If I do it myself."

She went to the window and stood there watching it. It filled most of one wall. It was frosted over.

"How would you like to go for a walk after breakfast," he asked the child. He immediately shoved the bowl away and said, "Bafroom first?"

"You or me?" Mary said from the window.

Finally: "You."

He sat alone in the kitchen, thinking. Taps ran, the toilet flushed, he came out full of pride. "We go park," he said. "We go see gulls."

"Maybe." It was this, the lie, which came back to him later; this was what he remembered most vividly. He got up and walked into the hall with the child following him and put his coat on. "Where's his other muffler?"

"In the bureau drawer. The top one."

He got it, then began looking for the stockingcap and mittens. Walking through the rooms, opening drawers. There aren't any seagulls in London. When she brought the cap and mittens to him there was a hole in the top of the cap and he went off looking for the other one. Walking through rooms, again and again into the child's own.

"For God's sake go on," she finally said. "Please stop. O damn Jim, go on." And she turned and ran back into the kitchen.

Soon he heard her moving about. Clearing the table, running water, opening and shutting things. Silverware clicking.

"We go park?"

He began to dress the child. Getting his little coat down off the hook. Wrapping his neck in the muffler. There aren't any seagulls in London. Stockingcap, Haha.

Thinking, This is the last time I'll ever do this.

Now bump, bump, bump. Down the funny stairs.

When he returned, Mary was lying on the bed, still in the quilted robe, watching the ceiling. It seemed very dark, very cold in the room. He sat down beside her in his coat and put his hand on her arm. Cars moved past the window. The people upstairs had their radio on.

"Why did you move the bureau?" he asked after a while.

Without moving her head she looked down toward the foot of the bed. "After you left I was lying here and I noticed a traffic light or something like that out on the street was reflected in it. It was blinking on and off, I must have watched it for an hour. We've been here for weeks and I never saw that before. But once I did, I had to move it."

"You shouldn't be doing heavy work like that."

For a long while she was still, and when she finally moved, it was just to turn her head and look silently into his face.

He nodded, once, very slowly.

"It didn't…"

No.

She smiled, sadly, and still in his coat, he lay down beside her in the small bed. She seemed younger now, rested, herself again. There was warmth in her hand when she took his own and put them together on her stomach.

They lay quietly through the afternoon. Ice was re-forming on the streets; outside, they could hear wheels spinning, engines racing. The hall door opened, there was a jangle of milkbottles, the door closed. Then everything was quiet. The trees across the street drooped under the weight of the ice.

There was a sound in the flat. Very low and steady, like a ticking. He listened for hours before he realized it was the drip of a faucet in the bathroom.

Outside, slowly, obscuring the trees, the night came. And with it, snow. They lay together in the darkness, looking out the frosted window. Occasionally, lights moved across it.

"We'll get rid of his things tomorrow," she said after a while.

# I Saw Robert Johnson

*L*ET ME EXPLAIN.

I'm an insomniac, you see. Not the kind that has trouble getting to sleep, because three minutes after my head's down, I'm out, but the kind that has trouble staying so: at two or half-past three I'm up and wide-eyed, prowling around the efficiency like a werewolf.

So it was particularly surprising to wake this morning and discover that it was already light outside—that I had slept the night through for the first time in many years. I lay listening to birds sing, the slam of doors across the street, a weather report from my neighbor's radio.

I turned on my side and something leaf-light fell onto my lower lip. I touched it with a finger and the finger came away with a brownish smudge. I rubbed a palm against my cheek and that too was reddish-brown. It was blood, old blood. I swung out of bed then and stood in front of the mirror on the closet door nearby. My entire face was covered with it. Like the facials women get, like makeup base, like warpaint or a mask. There were spatters elsewhere, on my chest, legs and feet, but mostly it was on my face. And a long line tracing the descent of breastbone to pudenda. My hands, apparently, had been washed clean.

Perhaps a few words concerning where I live now, and how I came to be here.

My wife, tolerant, compassionate being that she was, had finally told me to get it together or get out, and so I had, taking a garage apartment within walking distance of both my old house (for tradition's sake) and the university (which had an outstanding collection of old blues records). Across the street is a daycare center, and each morning I sit by the window watching shapely young women deliver their children, opera glasses which have known the soaring Valkyries and shared Carmen's pitiable death now focused on bouncing bosoms, long legs in high heels, waggling buttocks. At a distance, every woman is erotic.

So many people fear being alone. But if you cannot be alone, you cannot know who you are. Listen: this culture conspires to make such essential solitude impossible. Perhaps it fears the individual; certainly the individual has reason to fear *it*.

This place is a dump, one in which the blues records checked out from the school's library seem quite at home. Turning off the lights at night I can hear the roaches begin their peregrinations. Dragging their spurred feet across Bessie Smith's "Empty Bed Blues," or mounting the minute summits of Lonnie Johnson's "Careless Love." I have cleaned and cleaned without result. The odor of mildew and carbon monoxide clings to every corner and crevice; spiders and crane-flies perch like dull thoughts on the walls.

There were on my body no cuts, no wounds to explain all this blood. And I had no memory of the night, only a vague remembrance of dreaming: trees with the face of my wife, grass mowed down that spoke in the voice of my daughter, a parliament of fowls done up in tight skirts and unbuttoned shirtwaists.

The women had begun dropping off children, and I stood

at the window nude, my face blood-smeared, wondering what would happen if they should see me. But they did not. Always first the blonde with the pastel sweatsuits and tiny waist. Then the beautiful Latin girl with straight, crow-black hair almost to her knees, always in skirt and jacket. Then the one with impossibly long legs; the pony-tailed red-head who always looked so unhappy; the woman with short brown hair who was always still putting on makeup in the rearview mirror as she pulled away. I know them all, and could not step away from the window until the morning rituals were done. The prettiest of them all, though, a tiny Vietnamese woman, perfectly formed, did not come today.

I brewed a pot of tea and sat at the desk staring out into the yard and drinking tea slowly, cup after cup. The power-ful winds of past days had at last blown themselves out and only a mild breeze remained of them. After a time I realized that the lizard I'd been watching run here and there was actually chasing birds; it would wait in the grass until birds settled, then dash towards them, rippling silver in the sun-light, until they flushed and flew away. The lizard did this again and again. I have no idea why.

I will not turn on the radio, I thought. There will be hor-rible news. There is always horrible news. A tractor-trailer has plunged from an embankment, crushing a bus filled with schoolchildren. A man without food for a week has killed and eaten his neighbor's dog. A woman and daugh-ter living in a house nearby were killed during the night, cut to pieces in their beds. A young Vietnamese was found dead at her apartment early this morning by a friend, mur-dered. That sort of thing. I will sit here and drink tea, at ease with the world, and then I will call them.

But there was no answer, as you know.

I had not realized so much time had passed, but soon (or so it seemed) the women began picking up their children and I still sat as I had that morning. Watching through the opera glasses as the blonde woman's buttocks and breasts swung freely under the turquoise fabric, I began suddenly to tremble. When they were all gone, I got up and put on some Ma Rainey, stood looking at myself again in the mirror. I tried to imagine what it was like to be black in the Thirties, the rage and hatred you were always having to shove back down inside, shut away again and again, until it finally bubbled to the surface in the blues. In the terrible ache that's become all I can feel now. I put on some Son House, remembering the blonde woman moving underneath her clothes, a rhythm like the earth's itself, like the rise and fall of Son House's moan, like a lizard in the grass. I played the records one after another, some of them twice, and by then it was dark. The drapes closed over my face in the glass, watching.

I drew a hot bath and lay in it for a long time, adding hot water now and again by turning the tap on with my toes. Then I splashed water onto my face and the blood began to come away, swirling out into the water like rust. Yes, *rust*. I sat in the tub and watched it spin off into the drain.

After that I stood staring at the closed drapes. Behind them I could see all those women moving around still, their breasts and hands brushing against the back of the drapes. I could see gin-soaked Bessie Smith bleeding to death on a Mississippi highway. I saw Robert Johnson huddled in a corner, his back to me, singing about his hellhound.

# Vocalities

*T*ONIGHT, WELL, TONIGHT there won't be any music. I'm sorry. I know a lot of you are just getting in from work, looking forward to a few hours of fine old jazz, the real thing, and where else are you going to hear that on the radio these days, before going to bed. The rest of you don't or can't sleep much anymore, you're the ones who keep watch while others do. And maybe you've come to rely on me in some small way, my voice and this music out here, staying with you, making the world seem a little less, what's the word I'm looking for, impersonal.

I mean, some of us have gotten to know each other, haven't we? You call up to request Sarah Vaughan, Joe Williams, Lady Day, we talk a while. And the next time you call, likely as not I'll know your voice, remember what music you like best.

I don't mind telling you, that's helped me get through a few bad nights. You too, I hope. Part of what all this, a show like this, is about. Not to mention the music itself.

But tonight's different. I'm sorry.

Without music, life would be a mistake. Nietzsche said that.

I guess maybe that could mean tonight's a mistake?

They say Mozart had music coming to him all the time —

while dining with friends, pulling down Costanza's corset, shooting billiards, drinking wine—the music went on through it all, through everything, sounding perfectly in his head. Like a door that was always open, with this wind of music blowing through from somewhere else. All he had to do whenever he wanted to was stop, sit down, write out what he heard.

Remember Murray Abraham playing Salieri in the movie they made about Mozart, *Amadeus*? They're rolling Salieri through the halls of the insane asylum there at the end. "I absolve you. I absolve you all."

Most of you know, I've been doing this show a long time now, ten to three every night, seven days a week. I get home about four, I'm still wired, it's going to be hours before I can even think about getting to sleep. Martha, that's my wife? she's been in bed since a little after I left, and she'll be getting up for work about the time I'm going down. I used to spend the time watching old movies. *Citizen Kane*, *The Big Clock*, *Casablanca*. Then a few years into it, I figured I'd seen all the good ones, most of them several times. Did I mention *Philadelphia Story*? They don't make many good ones anymore, a few. And movies, even the really good ones, aren't like music. Movies wear out on you.

None of you know Martha, of course, and she never listens to the show, so she doesn't know anything at all about you. Sometimes lately it feels like I'm living two separate lives. Like those stories you hear, some guy had a family in Detroit, another one in San Diego, owned two homes, had kids, and neither life had anything to do with the other. So I have this one life, where I sit here playing music or talking to you, with most of the city shut down around us. And then there's this other one, where I eat meals, take Martha out for Italian when I can, pay bills and worry about them, cut the legs off old jeans to make shorts, pull up bedspreads at the top and tuck them in at the bottom. And neither life has anything at all to do with the other.

Any of you remember that story by Hemingway, "A Clean Well-Lit Place," something like that? I read it back in high school. My father who art in nada, hallowed be thy nada, and so on. I was fifteen, sixteen, I thought that said it all. I don't know. Maybe in a way it does. I guess Hemingway must have thought so when he pulled his favorite shotgun down off the wall and stuck it in his mouth to kiss it good-bye.

Kind of scary how much of my life I've spent right here in this chair, when I think about it. Some of the most important parts, anyway, parts I remember best. You think on it long enough, everything comes down to parts. Of course, I'm just a voice to You Out There. None of you have any idea what it looks like in here, where the voice comes from. Where it lives. Okay. It's well-lit—for a circle about three feet all around me anyway. Clean, well, that's another thing.

Kind of a *non*place, now that I think about it, somehow exempt from the world. Floats like a lily pad, always the same, while underneath, everything else goes on changing.

I've got two big steel desks, big enough you could park cars on them, pushed up together to make an L. Equipment's on one of the desks and pretty well covers it, turntables, CD players, mike and all that. Other one has the log, a ledger where I have to write down what goes on, what music I play, the times. Most people don't know we have to keep records like that. Second desk's also got what folks in the business call the trades, *Billboard* and so on, on it, and a stack of memos from station managers that I've been watching grow all these years, has to be six, seven inches high by now. Which is about how many station managers we've had in the same period, six or seven.

The chair, the very same chair all these years, all of us taking turns in it, is green plastic, with padding torn away at the arms and worn away at the back and bursts of thick cotton stuffing like fusilli hanging from the seat. It's on rollers that work part-time. It's our history.

There's nobody else here, never is. Not like on TV where the talk-show host and his producer or engineer are always signaling to each other like a couple of fools through the glass. There's an engineer all right, but he's in a separate building, a Quonset hut kind of thing out by the interstate, with a broadcast tower that looks like a skinny oil derrick above it and a Denny's next door.

So I'm all alone here.

Except for you, of course.

Martha never did understand fine music. Couldn't see the point somehow. It just goes on and *on*, doesn't it? she'd say when I put on Brahms or Mahler. And jazz made her nervous. Said she could never tell where it was going. Which is kind of the point, of course. But sometimes you see it's just not going to do you any good to go on talking, and you give up.

Look, here's something else: there aren't going to be any PSA's, that's public service announcements, any giveaway tickets or news updates off the wire tonight, either. Who knows, maybe we should even have a few minutes of silence later on. One of the big problems these days is how small the world's become. We've stuffed it full of things — information, facts, theories, buildings, people, cars. And now we think *everything* has to be filled, every moment, every newspaper or magazine, every moment of free time, every broadcast hour, every conversation. Till it's all so full there's no room left in the world for mystery anymore...

...No, that wasn't the moment of silence I mentioned earlier. I had a phone call, something I had to take care of. Ordinarily, of course, I'd have been playing music while I talked, some Bessie Smith, maybe the Mound City Blue Blowers. But tonight's different.

Some of *you* may be trying to call, too. So I need to save you the trouble, tell you the phone's not working anymore. Lot of things stop working after a while.

I'm standing at the window now looking out, with the headset on, so you can still hear me. Nothing but darkness out there. I'm standing in darkness, too. Desks and the circle of light back there like a campfire, or a city, I've walked away from. Stars overhead. Tiny points of light all but lost in the sky, that people keep trying to make sense of.

Most things, you *can't* make sense of, it's that simple.

Back when we first got together, I spent hours playing sides for Martha, telling her about New Orleans, the Chicago sound, bebop, Bill Evans. I'd turn down the volume on Mozart arias to hum themes before they emerged. If the human voice isn't in it somewhere, I told her, it's not music...

...Now here we all are, on the night watch again. Walking the deck at midnight. You know what I sometimes think? That the only reason we're here is to keep watch while others sleep, make sure the world doesn't change too much on them.

I'm not sure what just happened. The lights went off. Black as the inside of a black box in here. Power failure of some kind, I assume—though I still see streetlights burning outside, half a mile or so away up the hill, where the houses start.

I can't see enough to tell, but probably the emergency generator's already kicked in. If it hasn't, then it will any minute now. So I'll just keep talking. Some of you could be in darkness too. Maybe my voice is all you have to hold on to. And if we can't help one another at times like this, what good's any of the rest of it?

But I've thought some more about it, and I'm going to have to go back on what I told you earlier. There *will* be music tonight after all, while we wait for them to get the power back on, wait for whatever broke to get fixed.

I've cued it up already, working by touch in the darkness.

I'm going to play Mozart's *Requiem* for you. Because it's great music, sure. Some of the finest ever written. But also because it's what I played for Martha after dinner tonight, before I came to the studio.

She loved it.

# *Others*

*T*HE BEST PART was when he got a new letter, walking back from the mailbox with it, reading it over and over, the possibilities that crowded in on him then. A few were so very powerful, so redolent of potential, that he never answered them. Sometimes he would put a letter, unopened, on his desk and force himself to wait an hour, even two, before reading it. Then he would read each line many times before going to the next. All during the day he'd be pulling out one or another of them, savoring their individual flavors, trying (though never successfully) to capture those first magic moments.

This was all he used the desk for now. Ever since he could remember, he had wanted to be a writer. And with his wife's sudden death (a stroke at age 34, then pneumonia) he had quit his job and set himself up as a novelist, living off the insurance money. The first novel had been about her and was titled *Julia*, her name; it went unpublished. There came then a string of books: mysteries, science fiction, teen romances, pornography, each completed in precisely thirty days. A few were published, each by a different house, and his royalty statements showed him owing more than the money advanced him. He attended college for a time, taking mainly philosophy courses; made a stab at learning Spanish;

worked briefly in a bookstore catering to collectors.

He discovered *The Pen* two years after Julia died, about the time he was writing his last book, a serious novel about a man who moves into a new apartment and gradually discovers (or becomes convinced) that his predecessor was an agent of some sort, a man more of shadow than substance whose whole identity was assumed, manufactured—then abandoned for another again and again, endlessly.

*The Pen* was a biweekly "alternative" newspaper devoted chiefly to the arts and left-wing journalism. But each issue contained five or six pages of classified advertisements grouped under such headings as Women Seek Men, Men Seek Women, Gay, Miscellaneous. He became an instant convert; subscribed, but haunted newsstands for early copies; responded to every plausible ad with lengthy letters in perfect handwriting. Certain things led him to discount automatically any advertisement: undue emphasis on appearance or wealth, statistics (age, measurements, weight, salary, height), puns, any reference to a 10, the words "sensitive," "gentle" and "professional," use of song titles, undue length, poor grammar. There still remained, however, a large number, and he answered them all.

Each morning he sat down with his second cup of coffee and again read through recent arrivals.

Dear John,

Thank you for answering my ad. I'm "Farmer's Daughter," all alone out here. I was glad to hear about your childhood on the farm in Iowa, how much that's meant to you. If you'd like, maybe we could get together over a homecooked meal some night and I could show you the place.

Not too many more possibilities to explore there; it was pretty obvious. He put that one in the dead file.

Carl,
    Yes, it *is* a lonely world and we *should* do everything we can to help one another —*must*. I hope very much that when you return to "the States" from Central America, you will write me. As I told you in the last letter, I am overweight and not very pretty, I think, but under the right man's hand I could be anything he wished.

Often after the third or fourth letter he would call, not uncommonly talking two or three hours, but then, after that, would not write again. He changed his post-office box frequently. All we truly want, and can never have (he had decided some time ago), is to know another person, to bridge this awful solitude we're locked into. Power, influence, knowledge of every arcane, recondite sort, our impulses to art, sex—all were merely analogs, pale reflections of that simple basic, unfulfillable drive. Instinctively he knew that with his letters he approached as close as one really ever could to other people. And certainly he knew that the rest would be messy: awkward pauses, inferred obligations, misunderstandings, rejection.

David,
    It sounds as though a single dip in your lake might wash off all the dirt of previous relationships.

Carlos,
    I just want someone to hold me sometimes. I am a career woman with three degrees, own my own

business, play aggressive racquetball.

Hi Jonathan!
    I'm "41, Mensa member." Want to push some pawns?
QP—QP4!

Once he'd gone so far (she had a lovely voice, and her interests overlay his own exactly) as to arrange a meeting. From afar he had watched her arrive, look about, seat herself and order tea, read for a while and finally depart. He was terrified the whole time. She did not seem unduly surprised or upset. He watched men's eyes following her out the door.

Dear Elizabeth,
    I have read your ad with great interest, noting in particular your love of cats and Bach. As it happens, at the time I first came across your ad I was sitting on the patio, my own Siamese curled in my lap and the initial strains of the Air for G-string drifting out from the house into the gathering twilight—surely an omen, if one could believe such things.
    This is all so new to me, I don't know what to write, what you expect to hear. I am in my late 30's, a widower, not bad looking but no prize either. I suppose that my strong points are kindness, caring, concern. I can recite the whole of Chaucer in middle English and tell *Beowulf* from Grendel's point of view.

Debra,
    Since you ask, my favorite movie is the first *Robin Hood*, because it has that scene where someone (a

beautiful girl?) says, You speak treason! And Robin responds: Fluently.

Judith,
   I'm sorry, but I am not *allowed* to tell you about what I do for a living; I can only say that it is boring, repetitious, often difficult. Many days I feel that I no longer belong to the human race. Of course I am quite well paid.

Around noon he always broke off for a while, brewed another pot of coffee, had a light lunch of cheese and fruit or soup if some was left over from the previous evening. He would browse randomly among favorite books, stories and poems: "Heart of Darkness," Gerard Manley Hopkins, later Yeats, *Moby Dick*, most of Hawthorne, "Entropy," Robbe-Grillet. Frequently he thought of the fascination for masks in Greek tragedy, romantic and gothic fiction, Durrell's *Alexandria Quartet*.

Dear Sammi,
   Like you I am tired of games, tired of bodies that won't quit and minds that have to be jumpstarted.

June,
   It is evening. Frogs on the pond not far away do Hoagy Carmichael songs you've never heard. From my garden seat all I can see are trees, grass, sky. All about me there is a low whisper.

And others declaiming the nonimportance of money, Marxist theory, the supremacy of art, how hard it was to meet people and how hard they were once met. Only in these letters could he, did he, truly live.

One in particular, however, bothered him. It was so adaptive, so labile, like the letters he himself composed so carefully on the pegs of others' dreams. He thought of the famous Marx Brothers mirror routine, Harpo (or was it Chico?) suspecting that the doorway was not in truth a mirror but unable to prove it, the "reflection's" movements never deviating from, or lagging behind, his own. Perhaps this letter was from a female counterpart. Perhaps there were many like himself, living submerged in this system of correspondence like deepsea animals, never coming up for air.

At five or so he would put the letters aside and have dinner on the patio, generally soup and fruit or a simple stew followed with bread (which he baked himself) and cheese. But this time he had brought with him her latest letter.

Dear John,

I am so comfortable writing to you, as though we've been friends a long time. Truly, I wonder if you are not the one I've waited for all these lonely years. We have so very much in common—more than you realize. Please write again soon or call me. I am waiting.

He finished his meal and sat watching a squirrel leap from tree to tree. Wind ferried in a smell of dust and the sun rolled across moving clouds. He thought of the bouncing ball over song lyrics in "short subjects" that once accompanied all movies. Nothing like that now. Nothing but ads now, ads and future attractions. Sex, violence, power, war, wealth.

After a time he stood and walked to the edge of the patio, looking out into the thick growth of oak, ivy, kudzu, honeysuckle. He knew that he would write to her again. He knew that he would call then, and just how her voice would sound. He knew that he would talk and talk—talk for an hour, two, three if she would listen—trying to hold off the inevitable moment there was no more to say: the moment the phone fell back into its cradle, taking her away from him forever.

# Pure Reason

*T*HERE IS SUCH GENTLENESS, such ease, in death: with a long sigh the world slips away.

In one of his letters Chandler describes the perfect death scene. A man, dying, has fallen onto his desk and far across it sees a paperclip. He seizes upon this. His hand reaches for it. It is all he knows, all that remains for him of the world, this single object, and his reaching for it.

I am writing this where I live, in a bone-white room in Fort Worth, Texas. Half an hour ago, hiding herself away again in jean skirt and long green sweater, Linda departed, moving back into her widowhood, into the loneliness that defines her, and her house full of things.

It's a warm night, and for a time I stood on the narrow balcony with a pear gone perhaps a bit ripe at the corner of a kitchen cabinet, and with a small knife. The epicene white flesh of magnolias hung before me. I heard the couple next-door quarreling.

Linda is a teacher, a geologist. Our conversations, when once upon a time we had them, encompassed the far reach of earth's history: seas becoming desert, fish swimming into the heart of stone. Now when she comes we drink, listen to music, maybe ask one another how life goes, and go to bed. Once she was bewildered by my bare mattress, battered leather chair, stack of odd-sized boxes against one wall, all of it bought for forty dollars at Thrift Town; now she accepts all this. It hardly matters by what we are surrounded, only that we are. Linda knows that silence is the greatest lesson the ages have for us. And this is the rock I've swum into, where you will find me someday.

When this began, I lived in motels, sometimes for two days or a week, often for a month, for several. There was a certain coherence to life then, a constancy of line: the same furniture and TV, tiled bathroom, white towels, view. I could have been (and imagined myself) anywhere in the United States, in any major city. A businessman, perhaps, or a journalist courting discarded truths. A fugitive on the run. I ate in whatever restaurants or fast-food chains had attached themselves like pilot fish to the motel, carting orders back to the room where sacks and containers nightly overfilled plastic trashcans sleeved with white. I packed the sink with ice and cans of beer from 7-Elevens. And woke at two or three each morning with the TV on (acquiring a sudden, terrible presence) and traffic spinning by relentlessly outside.

I had grown certain that I was not human, you see. This knowledge came to me, suddenly and without overture as such knowledge often does, some ten months after my wife's departure, as I sat one morning listening to Robert Johnson's "Stones in My Passway" blend with birdsongs from the open windows. Those windows, the quality of light there, were the reason I'd taken the apartment. Previously I had lived in cavelike quarters in nearby Arlington with a single window in one room and, in the other, a slit like a ship's gunport near the top of a wall. When I'd come to look at the apartment on Taylor just off Camp Bowie, it had just been repainted; everything was white, every window uncovered, morning light everywhere. On the second floor and set among trees, there was much of the treehouse about it, and I took it at once.

My third attempt at intimacy had ended that night with neither of us certain, after hours of earnest talk, just which had severed the Baptist's head. Though I had come to care for the women involved—one of them, at least, a great deal—none of these attempts had endured more than a month or two. I recognized certain patterns in my courting of these women, of course. Who could embrace so violent a need yoked at the same time to such apartness? Monday's roses and wrenching, confessional letters were abridged by a week's silence as I failed to call or to acknowledge her calls, calls that I would listen to again and again on the machine's brief tape, not knowing what I wanted, or rather, wanting the two conflicting things at once, perhaps.

Light was just starting up outside, and I turned my head towards the window where plants lined the sill. I thought: *What sort of creature am I?*

With that thought, that realization, many things fell into place. My solitude and yearnings became clear to me. Of course I had to be alone; there was no other way. I understood so much. I *knew*, knew as only the true outsider can know. I had said goodbye to all that, to the pain and pettiness of it, to newspapers and dentists and daily appointments, and was exempt.

A little past ten the mailbox rattled at the bottom of the stairs and I went down them. The mailman folded himself back into his car. I had been listening to Messiaen's *Quartet for the End of Time*, the second movement, *pour l'Ange qui annonce la fin du temps*, an angel who must be much like

Rilke's angels, I think. I sat on the porch then in a still, bright morning watching paired runners, a group of young women in Spandex walking briskly together, heads swiveling one to another, an elderly black man sorting through trash at curbside, his lightweight aluminum cart propped alongside, this landscape in which I did not belong, to which I was alien, and knew what I must do.

Something about her, a certain guarded, vulnerable look about the eyes, through which she peered, the curve of her calf just as it vanished beneath her shorts, caught my attention, and I followed her to the laundromat. Not so much that I sought her out as that she was presented to me. So often life is like this. The idea of a yellow bicycle, a blue guitar, occurs to you one morning, and suddenly there are blue guitars and yellow bicycles everywhere.

At McDonald's she had a McDLT and fries. She ate in small, precise bites, a magazine folded back on the table's tiny plateau. I'd scarcely begun my coffee but when she stood to leave, left it there on the table by the window. At two in the afternoon we were the only ones there. Traffic swept by just outside, on its way to downtown Fort Worth, art galleries, the riverside park, Omni Theater.

Her clothes were in a faded pink pillowcase. I took a seat near a bank of chugging washers as though they were mine and opened a paperback I generally carried in a back pocket, some harmless mystery, probably British, long since read and forgotten: protective coloration. Two small children pushed plastic laundry baskets into one another, bouncing back and laughing gleefully when they collided. Their mother sat suspended in the murky pages of a paperback romance so shopworn that pages occasionally fell away as she finished, and turned, them. A young Latin in muscle shirt and white shorts stood by a window staring out blankly, pursuing, or pursued by, memories, demons, the usual limping dreams.

The clothes all seemed to be hers. Two bright summer dresses, a pair of fraying black jeans, dark T-shirts and an oversize chambray workshirt, unmatched pastel washcloths and towels. Only the underclothes stood out: two sets bedecked with gingerbread-like lace, one pale pink, one light green, the rest workaday cotton, bras white and nondescript (at least one with safety pin attached), pants mostly blue and thinned by many washings. She used Fresh Start and added a sheet of Bounce when dryer time came, smelling it briefly before dropping it in.

By then I'd contrived to start conversation with her, crossing her aisle again and again on mock errands and managing to become a little more visible each time in a time-lapse version of people meeting week after week in some public place and finally introducing themselves. On the last swing by, having called my answering machine and listened to its *Yes*, then silence, then a dial tone, I spoke.

"Hottest part of the day."

"What?" Her eyes met mine directly for the first time, though I knew she had been increasingly aware of my presence, touching her hair and tugging at clothes, glancing at me then quickly away when I passed. "Oh. I don't mind. Less crowded, anyway."

"There's that."

She pulled the underclothes toward her, unconsciously, I think, tucking them under a towel. Her eyes kept wandering away, to the windows, game and vending machines, other patrons, and back to my own. Yeats was right: the dancer *is* the dance, or becomes it. Her arm was bare, the gentle swell of her biceps and bare armpit pulling at something deep within me, something long undisturbed which surfaced now as an almost unbearable ache.

"You live around here?"

"Why?" She had begun stacking folded clothes back inside the pillowcase.

"Noticed you were walking, that's all. Hot day. Especially in here. Thought maybe a cool drink might help, if you'd like. My dime."

Her face told me she'd already decided.

"Okay, sounds good. There's a little restaurant a few streets over—"

"The Como Cafe."

"You know it?"

"Saw it on the way here."

"That be all right?"

"Great."

"Best coffee in town."

She took it iced, with milk floated on top, not stirred.

The cook and waitress sat at a table in back, sharing a beer and crossword puzzle. Sounds drifted in from the self-service car wash across the parking lot and narrow street. I leaned back in the booth and, with only minor prodding, providing the faintest vacuum, found out about Tracy Harrings.

Born in the late Sixties, she came of a family which had somehow detached itself from the Fifties and floated, for the most part undisturbed, into the present. She opened her mouth and cheerleaders fell out. Bobby sox, breakfast cereals, the daring of a double-date for a show and Coke. It was a kind of innocence you don't see anymore, deluged as we are by media, assaulted by information at every turn, with the weight of the world settling on every one of our shoulders.

She had to know these things, of course; but distracted by life, by simple pleasures and expectations, she failed to acknowledge them: they existed outside herself.

I told her about Nabokov getting the idea for *Lolita* from a news story about an ape who, given crayon and paper to communicate, drew over and over only the bars of its cage.

I don't understand, she said.

There was a brother in law school somewhere, a father dead of multiple strokes at age 49 after almost thirty years of selling aluminum doors, sports and police equipment, an endlessly grieving mother.

Tracy worked for an optometrist (I have to wear a lab coat and plain-glass glasses Dr. Vietch made for me, she said) and went to school part-time at the community college— just, you know, taking courses. She lived alone.

For fun? Well, she liked to swim a lot. And horror movies. Not the gory ones they put out these days, but old ones, where you hardly ever *saw* anything, really, where it was all atmosphere and suggestion, something always just out of sight, offscreen, about to happen.

Self-knowledge, I said.

What?

The real horror of life is not that people do terrible, evil things; it's our capacity to persuade ourselves, whatever we do, however terrible those things are, that we're right. That somehow we're actually doing good. In classic horror movies, that self-delusion collapses. It's evil he's doing, and can't help himself. He knows that he is becoming unhuman, becoming *other*. And he is powerless to help that, too.

I guess, she said.

She'd been kind of patting at the pillowcase of laundry on the seat beside her and now said: Guess I better be going.

I could go with you.

Her eyes met mine and held. In her face, as it opened to me, I saw something of my own, something of the face I once had, something pure and human. In that moment she was exquisitely beautiful.

I told her that just before I killed her, and again just after.

The cook and waitress sat still sharing a beer, maybe the same one. An older couple occupied a back booth; when their meal came, they held hands and prayed.

He was waiting for me, in the booth Tracy and I had sat in, just as I knew he would be, his clothing little more than rags, his brimless, battered hat on the seat beside him.

"*Dobroy den,*" he said. "I have taken the liberty of ordering tea for you. *Po-russkie,* of course."

Hot tea, steaming, in a glass. One stirs in marmalade, or holds a sugar cube in one's teeth as one drinks.

"*Spaceba.*"

After a moment I said: "He had plunged so far within himself, into so complete an isolation, that he feared meeting anyone at all."

"Yes."

"Yet something now suddenly begins to draw him to people. Something new is taking place within him, and with this goes a kind of craving for people. After such melancholy and gloomy excitement he is so weary that he wants to take breath in some other world, he must."

"Yes. You do understand. You take to yourself the victim's own terrible suffering."

"And feel a great common humanity swelling within me. Just as you thought."

"As *we* thought, yes."

We sat together drinking tea. I sensed love flowing in warm, easy currents between the man and woman now conversing quietly over a second cup of coffee; felt the mute, accustomed comradeship of cook and waitress at their table. Water from the car wash cleansed and began everything anew. The sun outside was a hand, a heart, opening.

"*Dasvedanya,*" I said when Raskolnikov stood to leave, then "*Au revoir,*" knowing we would meet again.

# Wolf

WE HAD THIS ARRANGEMENT. My wife lived six months of the year with her parents, the rest with me—I don't know why we didn't think of it earlier. The last I counted, she'd left me eighteen times. Another couple of times the folks came and (to use her word) removed her. They said I make her crazy, but *they* wanted to keep her a child. It's all really strange.

It was working out pretty well. I'm a freelance journalist, the kind others call a wolf, and in a bag by the door at all times I keep two suits, four shirts and ties, underwear, socks, toilet articles, notebook and pens; I can be on the trail of a story in minutes. But I could afford to turn down assignments when she was with me and double up when she wasn't. So we really had a lot more time together than most people do. It was great—movies every afternoon, hanging out by the pool when everybody else was at work, late-night strolls, breakfast at 3 A.M.

But slowly she began to hate me. I could see it deep inside her eyes as she lay across my chest in the mornings, a hard edge of self-interrogation. What would it be like without me; could she cope; how will she go about ridding herself of me—that sort of thing.

Then one day as we stood side by side in the kitchen preparing dinner (a corn soufflé, asparagus vinaigrette, pasta) she told me that she wasn't going back to her parents.

In a panic I tried calling her folks that night and got no answer. I tried again the next morning, that afternoon, and twice that night. Finally I phoned around and told everybody to get me some assignments, fast.

"Sounds like life or death," Harrison at the *Globe* said.

"For all I know, it may be."

"Even the best domestic arrangements can't last forever, friend, and you've been luckier than most."

I once knew a guy who had a big doormat that said GO AWAY. Nicest guy you'd want to meet, do anything for you, but he just didn't like unexpected guests. Suddenly that's the way it was with my editors. Delighted to hear from me, they'd chat along for an hour or more about things coming up, but for now all trees and cupboards stayed bare. I began to think horrible thoughts like city desk, food editor, *political analyst.* (Such was my despair and terror.)

It was about this time that I realized all the movies we were watching in those long summer afternoons were mysteries: a Hitchcock festival, Bogart films at the museum, Charlie Chan on TV. Books by Hammett and Chandler littered the apartment. Since bizarre crimes were a kind of specialty—I had a knack for somehow getting inside the criminal's mind and more or less writing from in there—in my leisure time, generally, I steered away from such preoccupation. But now I found myself scanning the dailies for just such accounts.

### COWED HUSBAND SERVES POODLE TO WIFE IN STEW

# MAN TIED TO CHAIR AND *FED* TO DEATH

## THE LAMP TOLD ME TO DO IT, MURDERER SAYS

That sort of thing.

Life between us, except for that knowledge like a drowned body deep within her eyes, except for almost imperceptible pauses before she replied (as though she were drifting towards worlds farther from the sun, and colder), continued much as before. In mid-July we attended a retrospective of horror films from the past forty years, in early August an "atrocity exhibition" (photographs from Auschwitz altered to show the prisoners with wide smiles and contemporary three-piece suits) at a local gallery.

In slow, plodding fashion I'd begun gaining weight from the food we spent hours in the kitchen preparing each day and from inactivity, from the sheer inertia of our days together. Talking it over, and reading two or three books on the subject, we took to running several times a day in the park nearby, circling again and again the park's pate-like copse of trees and skirting narrow trails littered with family picnickers, scavenging dogs and benches carved deep with old lovers' initials. My wife quite early exhibited an altogether unsuspected natural gift for it, heaving out far ahead—a yard, two yards, steadily farther and farther—as I fell, huffing and lame, behind. Many nights she would go back out alone, saying that she loved to run in moonlight. At first, pro forma, she asked me to go along, but rather soon that civility (for it was no more) ceased; and this became, in fact, my only time apart from her, except in sleep.

Need I say that sleep was troubled? In one dream a man I knew, but whose face I could not place, stood on the other side of a locked door smearing the bloody entrails of a turtle against the glass, slowly robbing me of light. In another a child's legs were gone from the thighs down; only the bones protruded, and tennis shoes were laced to the knobby ankle sockets.

There was, too, the eventual revelation that I had not worked in almost eight months. Flurries of calls from editors had tapered off, then subsided, as I refused assignment after assignment: I could not now remember how long it had been since the phone rang. I didn't know, but thought that I must surely be almost out of money. I tried to recall what writing was like: bent over notebooks in cabs or planes or the bathrooms of hotels; the world that came into your head as you blindly strung together word after word and then, *in* those words, ever growing, appeared there before you, part of the *other* world now, at least as real as yourself. It was unimaginable. And yet for so many years this was what I did, what I *was:* a channel, a voice, a mirror at once giving back less, and more, than what entered it.

And if that was what I had been, what was I now?

Somber September slipped in through cracks beneath the door. My wife's time away from me, her moonlight runs, lengthened even as the days contracted. Our fare grew plainer, and we began foraging (though perhaps this is only another dream) in the gardens and basements of neighbors. Pounds fell away from her; she grew lean and brown. We seldom spoke anymore. I lay alone shivering against the night, watching my own breath rise in the air above me like a ghostly, insubstantial penis.

And now it is November, strangely my birthday. In the kitchen my wife prepares to eat. I can hear her but a wall away, padding about on bare feet (for she has given up shoes and, largely, clothing) as she makes that keening, unforgettable hunger sound. I hear her at the door, dropping (or do I imagine this?) onto all fours. I only hope that I can finish this, my last story, before the story ends. That is all I ask of life now.

# Dogs in the Nighttime

$B$ OB AND MARGE live in the house behind us, across the alley. They are incredibly in love and have been for fifteen years. Twenty minutes ago I heard gunfire from their house, a single, cracking shot, perhaps a .38.

Alice's eyes briefly lifted—other times I might not have noticed, but we'd just quarreled again and I was, as usual following these quarrels, especially sensitive to her moods— then returned to her magazine, a *Redbook*, I think.

I sat staring at the word *missing* on page 84 of a Raymond Chandler novel for some time before I spoke.

"Did you hear something, Dear?"

"Hear something?" She watched me over the half-lens of her reading glasses.

"Yes. Just now."

"Such as?" Eyes moving back to the magazine. Its cover bore the legend "How to Tell If He Loves You: Five Questions You Can Ask."

"I don't know, really. A slammed door? Backfire? A gunshot, maybe."

Her eyes quickly took in the cover of my book, went back to her own reading.

"I heard nothing, John, at least that I can recall."

"The curious incident of the dog in the nighttime..."

"Pardon?"

"Nothing, Dear. Just something from the Holmes' stories."

Alice put her magazine on the endtable and asked if I'd like a nightcap.

"Perhaps you should get away from mysteries and detective stories for just a while," she said as I followed her into the kitchen. "They've become almost an obsession, you know. We could pick up some nice science fiction at the library. Historical novels, romances, biographies. Whatever."

"I guess so." She handed over a brandy and soda and I sipped at it. "But this is what I really like. I've tried to explain why, how the truth very gradually comes to light, piece by piece, through layers of misdirection and camouflage. Like a worm fighting its way to the surface after hard rain."

"Yes, John, I know." Hers was Irish coffee, and she blew once across it, glasses fogging. "But there comes a time one wonders." She folded the glasses and laid them on the counter by a spoonrest. Released from bondage, her eyes became astonishingly blue and reactive. She sipped at her coffee.

"Last Thursday, after we'd eaten at Scobbo's," she said. "A drunk had fallen asleep on the bus. You insisted that he'd been assassinated."

"Humor, Alice. I was feeling good, from the food, from the wine. It was our anniversary. I thought it would make you laugh."

"And all that talk about the teacher who disappeared at the high school. What do you think the kids make of all that? They have to repeat it, you know, all that talk about plots and conspiracies."

"I guess so, Dear. I understand, and I'll be careful what I say. Just don't make me read any romances—please."

We took our drinks back into the livingroom where I sat

looking at the word *clues* (page 85) and remembering times I'd come home recently and found Alice and Marge huddled together over coffee in the kitchen, remembering their low voices and sudden, guarded looks. Once I'd asked if Bob and Marge could be having problems. The usual misunderstandings and squabbles, I guess, Alice said; those are inevitable.

We have closed our book and magazine and are about to go up to bed when the second shot sounds, slicing into the night's silence. For some reason Shawna's face comes to me—thirteen and Bob's delight, a quiet, gentle girl. Neither of us moves. Clearing my throat at last, I stand.

"I wouldn't go over there just now," Alice says.

I sink back into my seat. Outside there is a silence like stone.

# Memory

*A*T TWO IN THE MORNING in the new house he lies
awake staring past windows at the moon's blank face.
Faintly he hears from across the hall, or imagines that he
hears, the girls' breathing. The air conditioner cycles briefly
on, as though routinely checking its own vital signs. Never
an overtly imaginative man, nevertheless he imagines this
pulse of air as a sudden vortex: envisions it spinning hun-
grily out into the world then abruptly recalled, gone, only
the hunger left behind, perhaps. Faith remains fast asleep
beside him following their nighttime litany of household
costs, shopping plans, new redecoration. And how long has
it been since they made love? He can't remember. Trying,
he sees only her face: head thrown back, the narrow band
of white that always shows at the bottom of closed eyes, her
mouth straining open.

The way she looked the night Wayne died.

It was early morning then too, two or three, and he'd
had to pound at the door for what seemed a terribly long
time before she came down. Lights from the interstate caught
in the picture window, slid across the front of the house,
dropped onto her face. At last she raised a hand into the
light as well, as though to push it away, saying, It's Wayne,
isn't it, and he had nodded. Only later could he talk, only

then was he able to tell her how the car had been found abandoned, Wayne's body a mile or so further into the woods. She hadn't said anything else, simply reached for him. Afterwards they drank dark chicory coffee out on the gallery and talked about Wayne's pension, funeral arrangements, what she would do, the girls, as the sun floated up out of the bayou like a huge bubble and cars began lining up on the highway for their long daily glides into the city.

Faith turns onto her left side, into moonlight, and the gown falls away from one large-nippled breast. His hand moves there, nests there, without thought, without volition, itself now entering moonlight. Soundly asleep, she backs into him and covers his hand with her own. How subtly, how imperceptibly, things change and are lost. He can remember nights of such tenderness that tears ballooned behind his eyes; recalls watching morning after morning break in the small sky of the window across her bare body, a riot of birdsong outside, the loamy, sharp smell of cypress and swamp mingling with their own there in that bed, that room.

No one had been too surprised when he and Faith took up together. They'd always been together a lot anyway, what with him and Wayne being so close, and it all just fell naturally into place. The mayor himself was best man. They'd used Wayne's insurance money to build the new house. The girls took to him quickly and within the year were calling him Daddy.

He hears a siren and wonders what Jimmie's up to out there, what might be going on. Maybe he should call in and check. Wayne used to do that. Kept a radio beside the bed. And slow nights when he couldn't sleep at all, sometimes he'd bring a bottle down to the station and sit sipping Jack Daniels till dawn, then have breakfast at Ti-Jean's and a quick shower and go on about his day's work, never the worse for wear, near as anyone could tell.

Wayne had been so happy when the girls were born. *My life finally means something*, he said. And spent his meager spare time making things for them—toychests, walnut rocking horses, stilts—or remodeling the house, till it was like an idea that kept changing. Late one Saturday over a case of beer he and Wayne had put in a picture window he'd been talking about for months. Faith had a big meal waiting for them when they finished, everything from pot roast to homemade pickles and Karo pecan pie. Then he and Wayne stayed up most of the night drinking and went out for squirrel that morning. By then, Wayne had decided he didn't like the window where it was.

Lately whenever he looks at the older girl, at Mandy, he sees Wayne. Something in her face, hard and soft at the same time, or in those gray eyes. The way she lifts a hand to wave, barely moving it. He knows that Faith sees it too; he catches her sometimes, watching.

Mandy's twelve and remembers her father, even talks about doing police work herself when she grows up. June thinks of *him* as her father. The two girls are as different as sisters, as two children, could be. But they are forever polite, deferential; there's about them both a gentleness he knows all too well. And even in June now he sometimes encounters Wayne suddenly peering out at him.

With Faith, their apartness, it wasn't so much a forfeiture as it was a slow, cumulative exempting: a kind of forgetting, really. Days and nights fell away unquestioned, untried, until finally even desire, the possibility of it, seemed impossibly distant, and he found himself lying here beside her night after night in the company of memories.

The past (or so he tried to console himself) is all a man ever really owns anyway.

But he still loved her, still felt for her what he'd always felt. He was sure of that. That was almost all he was sure of.

There were reasons why it happened, of course—reasons upon reasons. Everything was so complicated. Whatever you did or didn't do, started four other things going. And so finally it had just seemed easier this way, to go along, get used to it, despite the longing, despite the ache and the hollows.

Whenever life takes with one hand, it gives with the other: he'd heard that all his life. But what could ever take Wayne's place in his own life, in Faith's, in the girls's? What could possibly ever replace the love he and Faith once had? And what could even begin to fill the space left behind, the hollow, now that it was gone, if it was?

He hears the siren again and almost immediately the phone rings. He reaches for it, hoping not to wake Faith; it's Mayor Broussard, who hates to disturb him this time of night. But he's just had a call from daughter Lizette, now working the radio desk on deep nights (a hopeless attempt to keep her out of strange beds and too-familiar bars), and it seems that Jimmie's got himself drunk and is driving his squad all over town with the siren and lights and occasionally the P.A. going.

"Doesn't sound much like Jimmie," he tells the mayor.

"That's exactly why I'm calling you, Al. It's woman trouble, Lizette tells me. Went home this morning and found his girl'd packed it all up and left, dishes, catbox, fly rod and all. Didn't even trouble to leave him a note."

"Funny he didn't say anything to me."

"You're like that boy's father, Al; I know that. But we both know what that kind of trouble can do to a man. He's a good boy, he doesn't mean anything by it. But you'd best get on out there and pull him down before I start getting citizen complaints and have to do something."

"I will, A.C. It's taken care of—and thanks."

There's a pause.

"I've backed you from the first, Al, you know that. Everything going all right?"

"Yes sir, it is."

"How's Faith?"

"Fine as ever."

"That's real good to hear. And those girls?"

"Prettier and smarter every day, A.C."

"And more and more like Wayne, I'd be willing to bet. Listen, you all have to come out here for dinner some night soon. It's been way too long."

"We'd like that."

"Good. Good, it's settled then. You give us a call."

"Right. And thanks again, A.C."

He hangs up the phone and listens for Jimmie's siren but doesn't hear it. So he steps out the French doors onto the gallery.

He can hear the guttural call of frogs deep in the swamp. Something, a bat, a pelican, flies against the moon, already gone when he glances up. This swamp itself is a kind of memory, he thinks, looking out at the ageless, ancient stand of cypress draped in Spanish moss: a deeper one than we'll ever know.

Wakened by the phone or by conversation, Faith has been to the bathroom. She comes back now and lies on the bed in a long cotton gown green like old copper. After a moment he lies beside her. Without thinking, without intention, he turns to her and puts a hand on her breast.

"I'd like to, Al," she tells him. "For a long time I've wanted to. I was afraid."

He moves onto her then, and into the old, familiar rhythms. Out in the streets somewhere, in *that* world, he hears the siren swing by again, Jimmie's voice a blur on the bullhorn. The telephone begins to ring, unattended, as Faith's hips rise to meet his own.

"I killed him," he tells her, feeling the shudder tear at those hips, "for you," feeling the vortex open beneath him, feeling the hollows fill, *the hunger, oblivion*.

# The Leveller

*H*E CAME OUT OF THE CITY (out of the smell, out of the steel, out of the squatting suburbs), over a hill and fell into morning: It opened around him.

Bouncing on cement seams, the little red Fiat moved slowly along the two-lane highway. On the narrow shoulder, tiny pools of water from last night's rain glinted in the gravel like bits of metal; and water lay in gleaming bands at the bottom of ditches off either side of the road. Beyond these were fences, long fields of corn and grain, a cluster of red barns with houses and sheds, and occasional dirt roads marked only with letters and numbers.

Larry smiled and reached above him to pull back the leather sunroof. Light spilled into the car; he could smell the freshness of the air, its purity.

He slowed, braked gently, stopped. To his right lay the blacktop that passed through Center Junction and led back to the city. Belying the careful grid of all the other roads, it wandered and rolled through the countryside, swinging this way and that, making its own way—a much longer route than the way he'd come. He considered for a moment, letting the car idle, then turned. The Fiat bounced off the highway onto scattered gravel, came down onto the smooth blacktop, and settled into a chugging throb.

Around him now, corn ripened up the stalks wrapped in green corduroy. The farms were farther apart, their colonies of buildings set off from the fields by hills, small orchards, or fenced chicken runs with manure piles steaming in the back. Windmills rose out above the plain white houses and sheds and, in many of the fields, cows grazed together in slow-moving, slow-changing groups.

Larry slowed to pass a tractor which was pulled off to the side of the road. Its driver stood beside it, talking with a man who held a hammer. Behind them, a fence sagged. They looked up and waved as Larry drove by.

A bit farther along, he passed an open buggy with bags stacked crisscross in the back. The young Amish driver, wearing what looked to be a new beard, smiled and nodded. Larry eased around the Clydesdale, came back to the right, and started picking up speed again. Around the next curve, he passed a single lone house sitting back off the road. An elderly man, looking somewhat awkward in oversize overalls, was crouched down, clipping grass along the side of the walk. As the Fiat went by, he dropped onto one knee, shaded his eyes, looked up, and waved, his garden tool flashing as it crossed out of the shade of an elm into sunlight.

Larry pulled off to the side and sat for a moment with the engine idling. Three motorcycles passed by him, girls clinging to the cyclists' broad backs, and swept up over the hill ahead. Their sound faded slowly to the drone of hornets in a hollow tree and vanished. Larry shifted into first gear and pulled back onto the road. Ahead lay a dip, another long curve, a new hill.

*Bllaarrreee*—then the screech of tires.

Larry's eyes jumped to the mirror and he saw the huge

green Pontiac. Its driver, red hat pulled down to meet wrapa-round sunglasses, was leaning on his double horn and blaring away. The car had shot from a side road as though it had been waiting there for him. Larry could see the rolling dust, looking like huge brown feathers, where it had come sliding and skidding out of the dirt onto the blacktop. The driver had one arm in the window; the other laid casually across the top of the steering wheel. His teeth were sunk into a cigarette. Smoke rolled about him.

*Bllaarrreeee! Bllaarrreeee!*

Larry straightened from the curve, pushed down on the accelerator until he was doing the limit, and started up the hill; but he lost speed and had to drop back to third gear. Behind him, the Pontiac raged. An old Ford pickup with splash guards came down off the hill ahead of them. Its driver was waving his hands and shouting something out the window, but Larry couldn't hear him over the blaring horn.

*Bllaarrreeee!*

The Pontiac swerved into the space between the back of the pickup and the Fiat, fishtailing, kicking up dirt and rocks. The driver sped up and came around Larry just as a school bus appeared at the top of the hill, then cut back in abruptly, making Larry hit his brakes hard to avoid piling into him.

Through the rear window, Larry could see what looked like a salesman's portfolio and sample case on the sun ledge, as well as a half-filled bottle of bourbon, its amber liquid splashing inside as the car swerved again and shot forward. The driver threw his hand up and poked his middle finger at the Fiat's reflection, moving it up and down and grin-ning as if the Fiat, its driver, and the whole disobedient world were being triumphantly violated. The Pontiac disappeared over the hill, with the school bus still blatting its warning.

When Larry topped the hill, he saw that it had gone around another curve.

He leaned forward, reached under the dash, and pulled a small switch.

A low whine began deep in the car and climbed in pitch to a scream. Needles of sound pricked at his ears; shock waves passed through the chassis and shuddered along his spine, snapping his head to attention, clamping his hands hard on the wheel. All around him, auxiliary engines came to growling life. Larry brought his seat belt down over his shoulder, across his chest, and buckled it. Thin blue smoke rose inside the cab. The taste of metal was in his mouth, the smell of octane sharp as a razor. Under him, the car bucked and rumbled. Gently, he released the clutch.

The Fiat shot forward like a thrown stone, engines bellowing. Larry swung easily through curve after curve, topping the small hills. The sun ducked under clouds.

And there was the Pontiac ahead.

Larry cut sharply to the right, dived around a truck, and streaked across the shoulder, kicking up gravel. Back on the road, running smooth and lean, he rapidly closed the distance. He came up short behind the Pontiac, tailgating, and hit his horn.

*Bllaaarrrrat!*

It sounded—was made to sound—like a raspberry.

The Pontiac's driver looked up at his rearview mirror, out at the sideview, then jerked around and stared. He raised a trembling hand and threw down his cap. Then he turned back, hunched over his wheel, and swerved just in time to miss a bridge railing. The Pontiac increased its speed and opened road between itself and the Fiat; soon it was out of sight.

Larry drifted for a while, then caught the Pontiac again without difficulty. He came up behind it, hit his brakes, and leaned on the horn. Then he swung in front, pulled to the shoulder, fell in behind, came abreast, and repeated his maneuver. He could see the driver quaking with fury; he noticed that the Pontiac again and again swerved from the center of the road and had to be hauled back. The driver raised his fist and shook it violently. Then his mouth moved in the mirror, making ugly shapes. Larry hit the horn again.

Ahead was Center Junction. Five miles—then ten more to the city. Larry played cat-and-mouse for another two, then shifted to overdrive and pulled away. The Pontiac vanished into a dot behind him.

He slowed as he approached Center Junction and pulled into the gas station-grocery store. He got a Coke from the machine—one of those old-fashioned small bottles—and leaned against the Fiat, drinking it. Looking up, he saw the motorcyclists standing off a bit, watching him. Behind them, by the store, their girls sat on the big Harleys. Two of the cyclists were bending down, trying to see into the car; but the windows were now opaque. The others looked at Larry and grinned.

"Hey, you were really cuttin' out in that thing, man. Must of been doin' one-twenty, one-thirty easy."

Larry just hunched his shoulders. "Sometimes you need to."

"That some kind of custom sports job?"

"Yeah, I guess you could call it that."

"Thought so. Some buggy—and some righteous driving, too. You ever been on a bike? Looks to me like, you know, a guy like you—*Man!* What *was* that thing?"

The Pontiac had just come tearing down the street past

the store. Still leaning against the car, sipping the Coke, Larry had raised his hand and waved. "Friend of mine," he told the cyclist. "A real hot dog." He finished his Coke and handed the bottle to the cyclist. "Later," he said, climbing back into the Fiat and buckling the seat belt around him. The guy stared into the car, eyes wide, trying to take it all in.

"Yeah man, later," he finally said. "Hey, you want some help?"

"Thanks. But not this time." He swung the door shut and moved out of the parking lot. By the time he reached the highway connection he was already pushing a hundred.

Larry caught up not too far outside the city, where the flat mud was staked out for a new housing development. He shot in behind the Pontiac; then, on a sharp, climbing curve, he turned abruptly off into the fields alongside. To the Pontiac's driver, it must have appeared that the Fiat simply vanished; but, when he leveled off at the top of the curve, he could see the little car coming across the field, back toward the road ahead of him. He must have know he couldn't get there first, but he tried; at the last minute, Larry eased off and let him slip in ahead. Larry dogged him for a while, then hung in close on his bumper, hitting the horn from time to time. The other driver kept looking up in his mirror every few seconds, letting the Pontiac run off to one side or the other. He almost missed three curves in succession; gradually, by increments, he was slowing down.

At the next hill, Larry repeated his abrupt turn into the fields; but, this time, he pushed the Fiat almost to its maximum and then sat near the top, waiting, as the Pontiac came into view. The driver hit his brakes and the Pontiac skidded out onto the shoulder, into the fields. It went up on its right tires, balanced that way precariously for a moment, then slammed back down. The driver instantly floored it and cut back out onto the road, tearing huge ruts in the field, fish-tailing wildly.

Larry let him pull ahead, then closed the gap. He fell back again, gained, and hung on his tail. Then twice he passed him, slowed, and swung off to the shoulder to let him by. The Pontiac was down to about 50 now; they were on a straightaway and would soon be getting into traffic.

Larry braked and sat with the engine pounding, letting the Pontiac pull out far ahead. Then he slowly brought up the speed, popped the clutch, and shot away toward the bigger car. He drew abreast, looked over and waved, and fell behind. He braked again to repeat the maneuver; but, this time, he shot out around the Pontiac—running out yards ahead, gaining speed steadily—then abruptly hit the accelerator and brake simultaneously, in precise, measured touches.

The Fiat swung full circle and came round, heading directly toward the oncoming Pontiac. Panicked, its driver tried to cut into the other lane, but lost control. Larry threw the Fiat into reverse as the big car came skidding and sliding across the highway. It plowed down the embankment; stood for a long moment, improbably, on its nose; and tumbled into the sludge and moss of a deep ditch. It lay there upside down, buried to the door handles. The wheels spun and the horn was stuck, blaring dully, muffled in the mud.

Larry reached over and disengaged the toggle under the dash. With a series of coughs and shudders, the auxiliary engines cut out. Larry shifted into first and pulled away slowly. He passed a church, made a right, and was soon back on the side road, heading toward home.

He passed a farm with dozens of bronze-backed turkeys gobbling and waddling, a rare outside stack of hay, and a half-built barn with *Brenneman 1967* already painted above the place where the doors would be.

He slowed still more and looked around him, enjoying the landscape, the last of this quiet farmland. He began to whistle tunelessly. The sun was up there smiling now.

Just outside the city, the motorcyclists came up behind him and sat very straight and still in their seats, eyes forward, hands held to their caps in silent salute, as they slowly passed. Larry smiled and waved. The cycles throbbed and shot away.

Larry guided his way among intersections, traffic lights, school crossings, and driveways. Finally, he pulled into his own driveway, turned the Fiat off, and sat looking for several minutes at the closed garage door. He started the car again and pulled it over to one side, to the edge of the grass, out of his way.

*Tonight*, he thought fondly. Tonight he'd take the Morris Minor out, the one with all the switches on the dash. The one with all the lights on the front.

# *Joyride*

W E DUMP THE BODIES in a ravine outside town, have some drinks at a roadhouse, and buy sixpacks at a Circle K for the ride home. None of us knows the others' names.

We ride along silently for a while, sipping at beers and popping new ones, as dark comes down. There's country music, kind of loud, on the radio. Finally the driver reaches over and turns it down.

"When I was a kid, not more than nine or ten," he says, "there was this girl down the block I always played with. Donna was her name, Donna Sue. I don't remember who made it up, but we always played the same game. *Play-play*, we called it; *play-play number one.* She was a beautiful princess and I was her wicked uncle, and I had stolen her from her parents, kidnapped her. They'd never see her again, or she, them. And in the meantime she'd learn to love me instead."

He hands me an empty can and I trade him a full one for it.

"You think you can fall in love that young?" he says, then shrugs. "Oh who the fuck cares?" He takes a long swallow. "But I been most of my life trying to find again what I had that year, the excitement, the sense of controlling it all. Picking up women in bars or laundromats and pretending I'd kidnapped 'em. Even had a few I got to know real well who'd kinda go along with the gag. Never thought it would really happen, though." He holds up his can in a toast. A blade of light slashes through the car. "Best day of my life, gentlemen."

We come around a curve into a traffic jam, cars as far as you can see. He pulls us across three lanes, horns and brakes screaming close behind, up onto the shoulder, then down the embankment to a service road.

He pulls into a 7-Eleven. "Might as well stop for more beer, since we're here."

"What's all this?" he asks at the counter as we pay, nodding back towards the tie-up.

"Accident, they tell me. Say there's bodies all over the road up there a ways. Always say that, though. That'll be twelve ninety-three. Don't need no gas?"

"Not this time."

"Ain't sold no gas all day long. Just beer and cigarettes and a sandwich or two and them girlie magazines there. Here's your change, and I thank you. Drive careful, now."

Two teenage girls are hanging around the Coke machine outside.

"You girls need a ride?" the driver asks.

They shake their heads, looking at one another. Both wear tight shorts and men's shirts tied at the waist.

"Anything else you *do* need?" Driver says.

The girls giggle at one another.

We climb back in the car, run the service road a few blocks and eventually get back on the interstate. We pop new, cold beers and sit watching lights stream by. Almost no traffic up here above the jam. A few cars going the other way, away from town.

"We were dirt poor," one of the guys in the backseat says after a while. "Lived in one room, first I remember. A garage apartment, I think; I remember trees, stairs. Friday nights my old man—I think he was my old man, anyway—would come home late and drunk. I'd get put in the bathroom, in the bathtub with my pillow and blankets and all. And out there I'd hear the old lady hollerin' and beggin' for him not to hurt her. He'd rape her's what he'd do. Have her right there on the floor, on the kitchen table. Wherever. Never touch her otherwise. Then later on he'd come in to take a piss and she'd still be out there cryin'. Hey, you guys think about getting something to eat?"

"*I* could do with something."

"Yeah, let's chow down."

"Sounds good."

Driver edges over into the right lane, scouting the roadside.

"I was, I don't know, twelve or thirteen maybe, when he left," the guy in the backseat goes on. "I always *was* sorry I didn't have a chance to get to know him. The old lady run off not long afterward. Some guy she met at church or something."

"Burgers, or what?" Driver asks.

"Mexican?"

"Whatever."

"Lotsa help," Driver says.

We wind up at Denny's. Half a chicken; Mexican plate; soup and salad; coffee and pie. A cop at the counter is asking questions about the bearded young man and scantily clad girl at one corner booth. He drinks five cups of coffee, heavy cream, before his radio goes off. Possible homicide, Main and Tenth.

"Death," I tell them. "It always fascinated me. At age eleven I killed my first bird, and wept for hours. The next day I killed a squirrel, a week later a deer. I began reading poetry about the same time, Donne and all the others. Pavese: *Death will come, and will have your eyes.* I wanted no other lover."

I look about, at their unknown faces, and know they understand. Amazing, that we've found one another as we have. That we've been able to help birth one another's dreams. I pay, and we again mount the car. Hang on, Driver says. He tears past stopsigns onto the interstate. Red moon in the sky. Billboards advertising condominiums, topless clubs, social services, Jesus, abortion, groceries.

"There's a story we haven't heard still," I say.

The other guy in the backseat lifts his head. He has longish hair, a trim moustache, fair skin. Trusting eyes.

"Nothing like what *you* guys have, I'm afraid," he says. "No great obsession or the like. Just a premonition, a vision I've carried with me from earliest childhood. The reason all your faces were familiar when we first met."

The rest comes in a rush, like ants from a damaged hill.

"Four men in a car, two bodies left well behind. Three of the men have lived their dreams, fulfilled their lifelong fantasies, today. The other is about to."

He drains his can and rolls its coolness along his forehead.

"The car is coming into a sharp curve. A limousine pulls alongside, then suddenly in front. Control is lost. No one survives."

I feel Driver haul us hard to the right and look around, ahead, in time to see the car pull into our lane. It's a long limo, blue as the sky, our sudden horizon.

# Delta Flight 281

*A*S I LEAVE MY APARTMENT on the way to see you, I hear the sound of heavy artillery in the distance. Two short bursts, a barrage, then silence. Far away, an aura about the buildings on the farthest horizon of the city, I see the flames still burning. Where the day went down.

Madam: We regret to inform you that at 11:31 p.m. last Thursday, the 4th of February, while crossing St. Charles Avenue, your husband was struck in the head by a passing idea. As far as we can ascertain, this idea had flown out the window of a late-model Chevrolet just then turning into Fern Street. Death was instantaneous; we are certain that your husband experienced no pain whatsoever and passed peacefully and at peace from this world to a better; we trust this will be of some consolation. Meanwhile, please accept our most sincere sympathies. Bureau of Ideas, New Orleans, Louisiana (Orleans Parish).

Mid-flight, with only twelve blocks remaining, the stewardess announces there is no more crabmeat for the canapés. Citizens (first class cabin only) in uproar. Shouts and threats, a few knives, broken two-ounce bottles of bourbon, Scotch, gin. I calmly suggest that we draw lots: We will pass out pieces of paper, on one of them will be a black spot, whoever gets the black spot will be slaughtered to replenish the supplies. My suggestion meets with approval all around.

Looking down on rooftops as we descend, I have the vague notion to write a novel, something which has never before occurred to me. Halfway through my third canapé the stewardess comes down the aisle with a gun in one hand, a phone in the other, and plugs the phone into the console beside me:

"Hey there, Hector my boy. How's it going? Just wanted to let you know we just sold out the second printing. Great book, Hector baby, great! We're looking forward to the next one up here at Halvah House, let me tell you that! Well, be seeing you then, my boy."

As the No Smoking light goes on, the stewardess returns with a sheaf of telegrams: the reviews of my second book, which my new publisher has wired me.

At the airport I push my way through the women, reporters, literary hangers-on, decline offers to teach and look for a cab. I finally find one, reasonably priced—a '68 Ford, $750—on the second lot I try. Driving through roadblocks and toppling camera dollies, with flashing lights behind me in the mirror, I head straight for your apartment. Make a good deal for the cab with one of the guys hanging around the corner newsstand.

I climb the ladder to your apartment, breaking each rung behind me so they can't follow. Throw my clothes down to them as I ascend.

I knock on your door and quickly step aside. *C-C-C-Cow.* Four bullets smash through the wood, stuttering.

Don't shoot again.

It's me.

# More Light

*I* NOTICED HIM the minute he came out the door at Dillard's. Wearing jeans and a square-billed red cap, a sweatshirt with a torn neck over a high-necked T-shirt: there was that look about him. He paced unhurriedly down one of the broad alleys between cars, puffing into his hands to warm them. I looked a few yards ahead to the well-dressed woman walking briskly to her car, wind whipping at the tails of her long coat. I turned and looked down the parking lot and there it was, maybe twenty yards off: a dusty brown truck, Toyota or Honda, white smoke pluming from its exhaust.

I snapped the lid back on the coffee I was drinking to stay warm and started my own engine. The radio came on to a news update. I turned it off.

It was mid-afternoon and the mall, this end of it anyway, away from the video games and food stalls, wasn't busy. Cars, trucks and vans, the occasional walker, straggled in and out. One elderly man with thick glasses sat in his ten-year-old Lincoln reading a paper. In the lane behind me a mother who didn't look much over fourteen herself bent over in pink stretch pants to haul out of the trunk a baby carriage that unfolded and unfolded again till it was almost as large as the car it came out of. Next they'll be putting TVs on the things. Halogen lamps, sound systems, a tiny Jacuzzi.

He kept blowing into his hands, pacing closer as she turned into the lane of cars and pulled out keys. He never looked up or around; his concentration was perfectly on her.

A silver Volvo.

She leaned in slightly to unlock it—and he was suddenly there.

I heard a crash as he struck the side of the car to draw her attention away, heard her scream "You son of a bitch, I saw you, you son of a bitch," and watched the two of them break like rabbits, he falling back into the long, continuous curve that had borne him close and now swept him away, she taking out in pursuit on low heels, holding her own at first (driven by adrenaline and rage), then losing ground.

"You son of a bitch," she said again, stopping.

Down the way, the dusty brown Toyota or Honda peeled out of its place.

And he ran.

He almost made it, too. He was a good runner. But he ran into something.

That was me.

His face flattened against the windshield by me, then slid down it. There was quite a bit of blood where his nose had been. I thought of those stuffed cats everyone used to have in their cars, hanging on for dear life to the inside of all those windshields. His red cap blew out across the lot.

The Toyota (I could tell that now), which had begun braking for the pickup, thought better of it and, with only the briefest of pauses, the instant it took a foot to swivel from brake to accelerator, heaved itself out of the parking area towards the perimeter road, gathering speed all the while, tailpipe bucking with the effort.

I let the binoculars fall back around my neck and scribbled the license number on a pad taped to the dash. I'd see the intended victim got it. The cops would be dropping by to chat with that driver. There wasn't much they could do, really, but it would give him something to think about. You never know what effect your actions might have, even the smallest ones.

I opened my door out over his legs, picked up the purse and handed it to her along with the license number. She took both but stood looking down at him there at our feet without saying anything. Whenever he breathed, there was a dull, far-off gurgling sound, and little gobbets of blood would belly up over the rim of his nostril.

By ones and twos a crowd was beginning to gather. Security would be along soon; someone would have gone in to get them.

The woman looked at me.

"I'm okay," she said.

I nodded.

In the rearview mirror I saw her take a sketchy half-step towards me until her foot hit his leg and stopped there. Others briefly watched me pull away and looked back to her, talking among themselves, couples mostly. Wind picked at their scarves, skirts and coattails.

I drove around to the other side of the mall, parked and went in for more coffee: mine was cold. The food court was packed with young people in outlandish leisure clothes and mall workers on dinner break in various interpretations of business dress. A few families sat in the center, near the escalators and fountain, several couples farther out in the overgrowth of chairs and tables. Sometimes I can almost remember what that was like, having someone there beside you, thinking it would be like that, could be like that, forever.

The elderly man had moved in from his car. A gray cardboard tray of tacos, each diapered in paper translucent with grease, and a waxed cup the size of a child's hat sat before him on a buttonlike table lost somewhere between yellow and tan. He had his paper folded in quarters the way city people on buses do, and I could make out partial headlines over the tops of irregular blocks of print.

MAN KILLS FOUR

MILITARY ACTION INCREASES IN

HOMELESS MULTIPLY

I looked away.

Then my coffee came and I went back out and sat in the car, holding the cup with both hands, breathing in that rich, earthy steam as it fogged up my glasses in a breath, a sudden tide, from the bottom up. All breath's like that, sudden and warm and alive—then just as suddenly gone.

The sun fell into a narrow pass between clouds and horizon and bathed everything in cold light.

I sat there thinking for a moment about Karyn, all the things I'd wanted to tell her, how I had never imagined there might not be time for them all. Our daughter would have been almost five now.

Traffic around the mall was beginning to pick up. Two police cars swung in off the interstate and headed towards the other side, by Dillard's.

Back when I was getting started in the business, I did

layout for our Dillard's account. Then, when we found I had a knack for it, I shifted over to writing copy. I'll grant you there've been some problems in recent years, especially after Karyn. But you ask anyone in the business and he'll tell you: Charlie's a pro, he's *good*. I still remember how it was when I first realized I could take all these bits and pieces of things and move them around, take out a word here, open up space there, and suddenly it turned into something, it started making sense.

I guess that's what I'm still doing.

# And then the dark—

"GOOD EVENING, Mr. Davis."

He lifted his head to peer into the dimness outside the influence of his lamp. (*Two shapes, men in coats. Fog on the window. Lights outside.*) He put down the pen; moved his hand out across the desk, out across the leather-framed blotter.

"No. Don't move the lamp, Mr. Davis. And I'm afraid we'll have to ask you to keep your hands where they are. Visible."

One of the men shut the door and stood with his back to it, eyes on the window. The other walked across the room (*in window light: tall, thin, dark eyes, pale; heels soft in the carpet*) and slumped into the padded chair. Reaching under his coat he brought out a cigarette, matches—struck a match and held it near his face (*yellow, shadows, cavernous eyes*). He leaned out across the desk to drag the ashtray toward him (*it was full; ashes spilled around it*), then sat in the chair smoking quietly.

And Davis sat staring out over a slab of white light at two men and a window.

Three o'clock. And the leaves are afraid, they tremble on the trees.

He is sitting in a dark room, a room of orange and green, smoking. Outside the window the limbs of trees move ponderously, like the legs of huge dying insects. A forgotten radio blats late news from the white-tiled kitchen.

*(How to escape this sense of the darkness, filling?)*

He hears the sound of feet on the stairs, and the door from the staircase opens into the room. "Darling…" She is gray-eyed with sleep, holding a gown close against her breasts.

"I couldn't sleep."

"Again."

There is a sudden thrust of wind and one branch dips violently, scratching along the glass. He lights another cigarette and, hand shaking, reaches out toward his cup. Cold, gray coffee and grounds like tiny cinders run out across the table's mirror top.

("We'll have to put on a new shift: twenty-four hour production."

"I believe Goodrich has a breakdown on the new figures."

They all look down the table toward Goodrich, who now stands, shuffling papers, his meerschaum pipe smoking away like one of the plant's chimneys.)

She is bending down to the table. The loose skin at her stomach swings gently, showing in outline under the gown; her breasts, still enlarged, move against her arm. She stands, damp rag in one hand, cup in the other, and goes out to the kitchen; comes back with a drink.

"They've doubled the order," he tells her. Her hair is disarrayed, tangled down around her face. The gown falls just above her knees and her feet are bare, toes curled against the cold.

*(When thoughts turn sour and refuse to stick; the whole thing shatters across like struck glass.)*

"Darling..."

Upstairs the baby wakes crying, frightened by the wind.

Finally: "Working late aren't you, Mr. Davis?"

"End of the year. Lot of paperwork to clear up."

The man smiled, looking over the things on Davis' desk. "But you're not working on that, are you?" He nodded toward the blotter, where Davis' arm covered a much-corrected sheet of paper. "A statement, perhaps? For the press?"

Davis started to stand and the one at the door jerked his head around to watch him. "Please sit down, Mr. Davis," the thin one said.

"Who are you? How did you get in here?"

"Sit down."

He sank into the chair. The man at the door turned his head away again, stared back at the window.

"Now, it doesn't matter who we are, does it? You remember that—just someone working late, like you. Just a visit; we just came to have a little talk with you. That's all."

"If this is a robbery, I'm afraid your timing is off. The vault's sealed for the night. And the payroll doesn't come in until tomorrow. Afternoon."

The thin one snubbed his cigarette out, pushing more ashes over the edge onto the desk. "Really, Mr. Davis, I did expect better of you." He laid his hand on the leather arm. His fingers were long and thin; they trembled slightly. "Don't make our little talk difficult, any more difficult than it has to be. Please. No need to be coy." Now Davis could make out the features of the man at the window. It was a nondescript face: chinless, balding, ordinary. He was heavy, and stood solidly on his feet, eyes on the window with (Davis suddenly thought) the attitude of a retired sergeant who, still, comes automatically to attention. Davis imagined he might be wearing combat boots, polished to a deep black shine.

"As for how," the thin one went on, "shall we just say that certain of your employees came to you with quite outstanding records and…recommendations." He smiled again, and the skin tightened across his face. "There won't be any record of our little visit, of course."

"I see."

The man lit another cigarette and tossed the match into the ashtray. Ashes puffed up where it hit. When he raised the cigarette to his face, Davis noticed again the odd contrast, the slackness of the man's body and the nervousness of his hands.

"Good." Blue smoke spiraled toward the ceiling, drifted into the lamp's light, from the cigarette held motionless in front of his face. "Like to talk now, Mr. Davis?" From behind the cigarette.

Davis shook his head.

Silence. Smoke.

"No? And I'd heard you had so very much to say, things you wanted to say so very urgently."

The man settled lower in the chair, put out his legs and crossed his ankles. A daub of ash fell onto the front of his coat, sparking for a moment before the tiny fire went out. He sat very still. Only his arm moved now, carrying the cigarette up to his mouth, away from his mouth, up to his mouth…

Finally: "Sedition, Mr. Davis. Shall we talk about sedition?"

* * *

His wife moves about in the room above, comforting the child. He hears her footsteps, her soft voice, the child's subsiding cries. Sometimes he fears they are spoiling the child; it meant so very much to them—between them—was so hard to conceive. And he fears the fault was his, borne on the failure of his first marriage.

He hears the mobile start up as the baby is put back into her bed, and as the music winds down, he sits quietly thinking. He was seven. His mother went away and brought back the new child...

(The child was sleeping: this was the whole house.

He lay in bed, watching the motion of carlights on the ceiling, until his parents were in bed. Then, quietly, he crept down the hall into the nursery and stood before the cot, looking down at the fragile, strange little body, infuriated at its helplessness. He raised one hand and hit it, hit it again, again—until the baby's screams woke his mother and she came running across the house.

By the time she got there he had the child in his arms and was cradling it and crooning and crying softly.)

When his wife came back down into the living room, he was thinking of small bodies, dark like Indians. They were lying strangely on fields, their arms and legs at odd angles.

"She was just frightened," his wife told him.

"Jane," he said, "I can't do it. Not any longer. No more."

"Your calls, your...arrangements...were naturally relayed to us, you see. You understand: patriotism, duty. A going thing these days."

He looked down at the paper under Davis' arm.

"You're a practical man, Mr. Davis. You understand how things work, how things get done, otherwise you wouldn't be where you are now." The smile again, the tightening skin. "And you're an important man, a very important man." He came up straight in the chair, leaned forward. "But you know that, don't you? That's why you're here tonight, why you made those…arrangements…this afternoon. It works both ways. But the thing you have to ask yourself is: *how* important?"

He leaned farther forward, putting out one hand to the silver frame. He turned it around and looked at it closely for several moments. "Your wife." Then put it back on the desk, facing Davis. "A beautiful woman." When he put his hand up to his lips, Davis noticed that the cigarette, with its glowing conical end, looked like a bullet.

"Let's see, how old *is* your son now—Dave, isn't it? Nineteen? History at Yale, if I remember right…."

Davis nodded.

"You're quite fortunate that he hasn't got himself involved with the Secessionists, you know: it's a cancer that claims more and more of our best young minds. The government's tolerated them up till now, but we've begun picking up some of the ringleaders, you see…." He punched his cigarette into the ashes, pushing it forward as though he were closing a switch. "Domestic strife. That's bad for a country. Splits it up, makes it dissipate its efforts—like a neurotic—makes it look bad. Besides, we need the troops. First the Black Riots, the coalition monopolies; then the Student Alliance, and now the Student Secession. A silly protest—symbolic at best— but it demands attention the government could put to better use elsewhere."

He forked another cigarette out from under his coat, lit it, breathed smoke.

"I'm sure you'll understand that."

There were several moments of silence, in which Davis sat looking at the photograph the man had replaced square on the blotter. Light from the lamp glared on the glass, obscuring the faces of his wife and son, the shape of their house behind. Smoke rose, heaving softly, into the light.

"You might be interested to know there's a rumor going around to the effect that the Secession is being indirectly funded by your company. An outright lie of course. But I've heard that some of the student leaders are prepared to testify to it—one wonders what their motives might be. And—"

"Headlights, Carl," the man at the door interrupted.

"Watch them." Without moving his head. "And I'm afraid...well, let's just say certain people—and groups—they might be a little upset with you. If the story got out?"

"Gone. The watchman."

"Time?"

"Twelve."

"On schedule."

The yardlights went off as the watchman's car passed through the west gate. Lee would be sitting in the booth now, radio on against regulations, eating the sandwiches his wife packed up in polyethylene. Davis looked out the window, blinking.

There were clouds the color of ashes.

Evening climbs the towers, tanks, derricks. From the window he can see only the plant and a slab of gray sky that seems to him now pendulous, impending. He knows that the tiny shapes moving among the scaffolding far away across the concrete, and against that sky, are men.

Father —

A product (as you say) essential to the security of the nation....

"The chemical reaction melts the flesh, and the flesh runs down their faces onto their chests and it sits there and it grows there. These children can't turn their heads, they are so thick with flesh. And when gangrene sets in, they cut off their hands, their fingers, or feet." "Their eyes are gone, melted away, and their ears are lumps of raw flesh, fused shut; they resemble nothing so much as huge pink cauliflowers, rotting." "Twenty civilians for every soldier."—Some relics of our past.

Ad hominem! Yes, I know how quick you'll be to think that—but does it matter? The fact remains: we are committing a crime—a sin, to use a word that you possess—of silence. That at least, at the very least. And what can it matter, *how* you find the darkness, *how* you finally penetrate to the horrible canyons behind all the words?

One has to decide: how much does he owe to his society—how much can that society demand of him—and how much can he, must he, keep to himself. Which of the million strings, the cat's-cradles binding him to all the other people, seem to him most important? It's for every man, that single question. And I, *for* myself, have finally found the answer, finally know....

Which is, in turn, my answer to your letter. The letter you dictated to Betty.

Love,
David

\* \* \*

Gradually it grows dark outside, sinking from steel-gray to plum to black, and finally he is staring at a vague reflection of himself and the office in the glare of the overhead light.

He withdraws and crosses the room to shut off the light; sits at his desk and touches the intercom.

"Betty, before you leave, could you get my wife on the phone?"

"Yes sir."

"And then Jim Morrison at United Press."

"Yes sir."

Waiting, he turns on the desk lamp and sits in a small circle of light.

"Now, you take Santos at Allied, there's a good man—and I understand he's just been given a grant to expand operations. A small plant, but quite efficient. Something about a new thickening agent, better than polystyrene, some say. Worked his way up from a technician. Now he's got a fine home, a beautiful wife, three sons—all of them draft age, as it happens. About the same age as Dave, as a matter of fact." He smiled again. "Always someone next in line, right Mr. Davis?"

The man lit another cigarette and sat in the chair, smoking, watching. His arm went up to his mouth, away from his mouth. Up, down. It reminded Davis of blinking neons. He looked down at the papers under his arm; he'd spent hours on them and now it was as though he saw them for the first time, as though someone had forged his writing and left them here on the desk. They seemed so distant, so unreal....

The thin man was smiling at him. "Is it strong enough, Mr. Davis? Is it after all what you wanted so badly to say?" He reached out and took the papers from under Davis' arms.

Smiling, and squinting in the dim light, he read them. His cigarette burned down in the ashtray.

Finally, he looked up.

"Quite good, actually. That part about the babies—you'd have made a good journalist. Ad hominem, of course." He stubbed out the cigarette. "But what's a logical fallacy or two when you're on the side of The Good…" He looked back down at the papers. "You know, I never noticed before, but the word has an Oriental ring to it."

The man at the door put his hand on the knob: "Twelve-twenty, Carl."

"Then that's about all, Mr. Davis. I hope you'll remember our little talk tonight, should you get the urge again to…express yourself?" He put a hand on the desk and stood. The hand moved. Ashes spilled out onto the red carpet. "Oh, I *am* sorry, Mr. Davis." He rolled the statement up, stuffed it into his coat pocket. "We'll be in touch. It's been nice talking with you."

The other was already in the hall. The thin one walked slowly across the room and turned back for a moment at the door.

"The papers wouldn't have printed it anyway, you know: their duty. Patriotism. It's a going thing, these days."

And then they were gone, the door closed.

Davis sat listening to their footsteps fade away, loud and hollow in the hall. Then the clank and whirr of an elevator descending. Then silence. He noticed how the top sheet of the pad was covered with pressure marks.

*(For God's sake, Dave, don't give up. Don't let go.)*

He got up and walked to the window. He looked out on the towers, tanks, derricks erecting themselves against the sky; at the clouds that moved among them. His breath made circles of frost on the glass. He smelled the spilt ashes.

The two men came out of the building below him—walking slowly, talking, finished with their night's work—and got into their car. Seconds apart, the domelight went on-off, on-off, with the two doors; then there was only the thin one's cigarette moving in the darkness: up. And down.

Finally the headlights came on and lay out along the field of concrete like two Doric columns. Dimly, Davis could hear the engine. And now he spoke softly to the room that watched over his shoulder, something remembered from college, and now the circle of frost spread, the circle of frost deepened and tugged at the light....

> *"But that was his duty, he only did his duty—"*
> *Said Judy, said the Judy, said poor Judy to the string.*

Davis stood staring at his own breath, at his face in the circle of frost. The edge darkened and began to recede; circle by circle, it crept ever inward, vanishing finally into its own center.

When the pane cleared, the car was gone. And then the dark was absolute.

The darkness that surrounds us.

# D.C. *al* FINE

*I*T WAS A BAD DAY. A year full of them, in fact. Or three, if you got right down to it. And I did. *Way* down.

The corporation was going like wildfire, sure—we'd been getting so many government contracts, we kept expecting a grand jury to descend on us—but when I took the suit off at night there just wasn't anything there, nothing left inside. The whole thing was like a series of snapshots in which I saw my life fading off into the distance, skipping away from me. And even the, the snapshots were out of focus, blurred, indistinct. Snap: Mary and the kids were gone, moved back to Boston. Snap: I started drinking too much, couldn't get anything together with another woman, either. Snap: Long "discussions" with my partners, very long. Couldn't sleep at night, lay there terrified, put away handfuls of Librium, stayed away from mirrors. And then the money was gone. All of it. And I was in debt.

But this one was the worst yet. I'd stayed on late at the office—it had been dark outside for several hours now—trying to catch up on work I should have finished months ago. The figures kept blurring, and the contracts sounded like gibberish, and when I played back my day's letters on the Dictaphone they sounded like lecture notes for some course I didn't have a chance in hell of passing.

Finally I got up and walked across the carpet to the window. Looked at all the little lights crawling along down there, going somewhere. Or away from something.

I don't think I ever made the decision consciously. It's just that I was suddenly standing there with the window open and I was leaning out, looking down. I felt my belt buckle sliding slowly across the sill and I was thinking, of all things, about my swimming coach back at Yale. Keep the legs together, boy, and your whole body rigid, taut; and don't be too quick off the board; you'll go in without a splash. It would put an end to the snapshots at least.

"Don't do it," someone said.

I looked around and there was a guy sitting on the ledge about two feet away, smoking a cigarette. Twenty-eight stories up.

He flipped the cigarette out into the air and said, "You know your trouble, man? You want to be a goddamned statistic."

I watched the cigarette disappear into all the other little lights down there. "Well, since you brought it up, that *is* being *some*thing. And you have to admit, it's easier than all this."

"Yeah I know. Wheels within wheels: it'll drive you mad, just watching them." He swung a leg onto the ledge. "Mind if I come in?"

I got out of the way, a process similar to pulling a Chianti cork out of a broken bottle, and he came on in. "Got a drink? Oh, that's right, you're off the stuff. Sorry." He paused. "Look, I'm supposed to give you this big philosophical hype now—you know, how knocking yourself off is a cop-out, how it doesn't take guts; that it's sticking it out, staying with *this*, that takes the guts. But if you don't mind, we'll just skip that part of it." He glanced around the room.

"Frankly, it bores the hell out of me. Do the same to you."

He walked across the room and sat down in the chair he'd selected with that first glance.

"I'm from Suicide Control," he said after a moment or two.

"You're from what?"

"Suicide Control. No, you don't know anything about it and you aren't supposed to. And we're government, not police. I've been specially trained by some of America's top psychologists and PR men to deal with potential suicides, some like you, some quite different. Been at it for about eight years now and I've done all right. Might even flatter you to know that one of the best men on the force—that's me—was assigned to your case."

"My case."

"Yeah. We've been watching you for I guess four or five years. I *figured* I had the time pretty well pinpointed." He gestured towards the window. "And I guess I was right. Damned good timing."

He sat for a while watching me from across the room. I was still standing by the window.

"Look, man, the point's past and you won't do it now," he finally said. "So why don't you shut the window; it's getting cold in here. It was bad enough out on that damned ledge. You *sure* there's not something to drink around here?"

While I was getting the bottle and a couple of glasses out of the bottom drawer of the desk, he said kind of distractedly, "Anyhow, they're *all* gonna be doing it soon. Sleeping pills, guns, carving knives, aspirin. Hell, you wouldn't even have made a good statistic, with all that going on."

"Look, Mr...?" I said after we'd settled back with the drinks.

"We don't use names."

"I see. Well, anyhow, let me get this straight—if I can. You must admit that the entire disclosure is rather startling, particularly coming, as it did, in such a circumstance."

"Precisely why it's effective."

"Of course. But, Suicide Control: I take it by that you mean that you maintain surveillance of potential suicides and then, when they eventually make the attempt, restrain them from doing so?"

He finished off his drink and started chewing the ice.

"Well, that's not *quite* it, Mr. Davis. The word 'Control' is most carefully chosen."

He paused, looking casually around the office.

"As a matter of fact," he said, "we're trying to get them *to* do so. A meticulously programmed system of propaganda. Quite subtle, insidious, of course. And using every available media resource, it goes without saying. The program has been in full effect for ten years and the results have been quite satisfactory—well above our expectations, in fact."

He held up his glass and looked through it at the window, closing one eye. "Every one of us has his own ghetto, Mr. Davis. It's something inside you. Each of us is *enclosed* by something—his background, the color of his skin, a psychological kink, some hang-up or a rotten childhood—something that contains him. And he feels it. And, sooner or later, one way or another, he tries to break out of it. We're just playing on that."

"And showing him *how* to break out."

He paused a moment and nodded. Then he got up and walked to the bookshelves, idly looking over titles, souvenirs.

"There are, of course," he continued, "many people—

professional men in medicine and law, scientists, technicians, top-level administrators—who must be saved. Protected from the indoctrination propaganda or from themselves, or in most cases, from both."

"And just how do you accomplish that?"

He shrugged. "Several methods. Guide them away from the propaganda, keep the propaganda away from *them*, insofar as is possible. Shock tactics, of course—which is why I was out on that damned ledge. And there's a program of counter-propaganda, naturally. And, for a few…well, what Kenneth Burke would call 'a symbolic action.' To give you some small idea of the scope of our operations, my own training took over three years." Then, almost as an afterthought: "Oh, yes. You are, of course, one of the men under our protection."

"A washed-out alcoholic failure. Fine choice."

"There *are* other ways of breaking out of personal ghettos. We're equally conversant with those, and can use them. We deal only with the abstract. In your case, potential and a considerable genius, proved in the past, for organization and executive function. Whatever interferes can be eliminated, one way or another."

I glared at his back for several seconds.

"Genocide," I finally said. "Regulated, scientific genocide."

He turned towards me. "If you wish. But efficient. And necessary." He stared at my face, his own brows lowering. "Or would you perhaps, as a humanist, Mr Davis, prefer the alternatives? Famine, panic, the dissolution and eventual collapse of any order within the boundaries of *our* country, and then all the others. Not to mention cannibalism, plague, an uninhabitable landscape, retreat to underground shelters which couldn't sustain us for more than a few years at best. It's coming much sooner than you think, Mr. Davis—or it was. Our government has an impossible burden to carry, and a great responsibility to the world at large. It's the only way. It was necessary. Believe me."

My mind had stopped working. I poured another drink, drained it, felt a brief, weak stirring of mental activity, like a car turning over on a cold morning but you know it's never going to start.

"I've got just one question," I said. "Who decides? Who says which ones get a chance to go on living?"

"That's classified. Top Security. And besides, I don't know myself."

"Great idea," I said. "Population explosion. Implode it before it reaches critical mass. Forgive the bad grammar: 'implode' isn't a word."

"Grammar or not, that's it, exactly. We thought you'd understand."

"Yeah. Great idea. Terrific." I was standing by the window again.

"Come here."

He crossed the carpet and stood beside me.

"Look down there," I said. "What do you see? Those are people, every one of them, and their lives are just as important to them as ours to us—and *they're* just as important. As important as us, as important as *anybody*. Those are *people*. They have the same hopes and dreams, the same fears, the same problems, the same hopelessly absurd little lives we all have. And every day they get hurt, and *they* hurt, and they try to understand how it happened, and why, and they never can. Just like us. Maybe that's not much, but it's what they have, all *any* of us has, and you're going to take it away from them. And you're not even going to tell them you're doing it."

He stood for several moments looking down. Finally he spoke.

"I guess maybe that's the difference between us, Mr. Davis. I'm a lot younger than you; I grew up in a world you've only read about. You say you see people down there? I'm sorry: all *I* see are a lot of lights and some things moving around that look maybe like bugs." Then, just as suddenly as it came, it was gone: the little chink I'd opened up closed, the man vanished inside again, and what I got next was a quote. "Besides, what's one man—a thousand, a million—when there's an entire country, quite possibly a world, at stake?"

I walked back over to the desk and poured two drinks. "And just where do you stand?" I asked, about the time the ice hit the second glass.

"I'm not on the list, if that's what you mean." He took the drink and had a long draw at it. "I'm a highly trained specialist, true. And immune, or at least inured, to the propaganda, of course. But when the time comes that I'm no longer essential...well, I'll go the way of the rest. One way or another."

"With great efficiency and...subtlety? On their part."

He nodded.

I was standing there by the window looking down at all those people, or all those lights and bugs, whichever, and he was beside me with the drink raised to his lips. "Don't think about it, Mr. Davis," he said over the rim of his glass. "It's too late, and it worked, and it's going to go on working." He finished off the drink and lifted his glass in a toast: "*C'est accompli.*"

I don't think I made the decision consciously that time either: I just pushed, and he happened to be in the way.

Then I threw the glasses out after him. And after a while, the bottle, too.

Nothing ever came of it, naturally, and I've been all right ever since. I stay away from newspapers and radios; the thought of liquor never occurs to me. Business has picked up incredibly, and there's more work than I can do since my partners killed themselves (one slit his wrists in a cheap hotel down on the Strip, the other went out the window next door) and the firm fell into my hands. Government contract after government contract, they just keep coming in, and I may be taking on a new partner soon. It's been a good three years. Except sometimes late at night I remember that *other* night by the window and I start wondering if maybe the whole thing wasn't part of their plan all along— if, even while he was sitting out there on the ledge, he knew what was going to happen. I keep meaning to go down to the library and look up Kenneth Burke, too. But somehow I never get around to it.

# Blue Lab

SOME YEARS AGO I lived next to a madman about whom I knew only that he was involved in "basic research—behavior and learning." This research had to be done every day. A few minutes past seven each evening, a half-hour or so after the joggers limped back in, I would watch as he walked into view beneath the trees with two sixpacks of beer stacked into a brown bag under his arm, checked the rusty, scaling mailbox by the street, and started up the gravel drive to the cottage just behind my own.

They were of course not cottages, but garages. *Bungalow*, the advertisement said, his bungalow comprising the whole floorspace, one-half of my own (there was a thin wall) yet garage. I had made mine livable, covering the worst stains with throw-rugs, scouring all available surfaces three times, covering cracks in the walls (not so much cracks as chasms) with duct tape. I don't know what he had done with his.

It was in fact from him that I rented the place; he had shown it for the owner, and that was when I heard about the "basic research," shuffled in among a generous ten or twelve other words. Then he took my check, gave me the key, and I neither heard nor saw anything more of him for a month or more. Gradually, though, as I became convinced that my marriage was indeed over, I started settling back into regular work habits, and so each day (I never saw him at any other time) caught sight of him returning from work. The first and second times, I was at the typewriter. The third, I was stuffing newspapers into the yawning space between air-conditioner and window. I had a roll of duct tape around my wrist like a bracelet.

"Little windy for you?" he said.

"No, no, I like a good breeze. It's the sound—that unending whistle. *D* is so bright and depressing...."

He stood there a moment, and when he said no more, I got back to work.

"Girl lived there before never did anything. Don't even think she was ever there, or much."

Then he went on past, shouted hello to the dog next door, and vanished into his bungalow.

That night it was windy, and waking in the early morning without knowing why, I slowly became aware of a persistent, variable singing in the air around me. Cut off from its customary passage, the wind had found its way into the house's many other cracks and crannies, often under some pressure, giving forth a many-toned moan that rose and fell with the bank of the wind; as in Gregorian chants, the harmonies were ever shifting. I fell asleep again shortly before dawn, the memory of that late-night concert spilling imperceptibly into the cries of the birds which woke me.

It was several days before I again saw my neighbor. Occasionally, always late at night, I would hear his radio on full-volume for a time, then silence. During the day I listened to his phone ring. In truth I had ceased to pay much attention, for a new book had begun taking shape and as always, I was half in that world, half out of this one. I watched birds coming to the feeder I'd put outside my window with no more recognition of their separateness than I had for my own fingers on the typewriter; both were simply random patterns shimmering and shifting around the stone of my concentration.

When I am at work, walking is my great problem solver, and four weeks or so into the book, about halfway through the first draft, I was out most of an afternoon trying to find a way to make one of the characters do what I needed him to do. The story was nothing terribly original in scope—I'd often before ransomed my life by turning it to fiction—but this time, I suppose, I lacked the necessary distance, and the story kept hauling itself, against my will, back from the fictional characters and episodes I'd intended, to what actually went on between Judith and myself.

Suddenly rain exploded from the sky, and I took refuge in a nearby cafe. On one of the orange seats (the others were green and purple) my neighbor sat with what looked like a porkchop, bone and all, between two slices of bread.

"Mind if I join you?"

He nodded his head towards me slightly and continued eating his sandwich, biting, swallowing, biting, swallowing. By the time I'd got seated the sandwich was gone and he was starting at a huge glass of iced tea.

"This part of your routine?" I asked, and again he nodded.

"Ever' day for two years, never missed one." He threw back the tea like someone might a shotglass. "Good food."

I wondered how he knew.

I asked the waitress for a cup of coffee and when he got up to leave said, "Keep me company?"

He looked as if he thought that was a strange request but settled back onto the stool.

"Have anything?"

"Already ate."

"Tell me about your work at the university," I said after several moments' silence.

"Not work—research."

"Research, then. What's it all about?"

He looked at me for some time, then turned away and began speaking.

"You ever wonder if a man can change? I mean change completely, like you take a crazy man and make him a bank president. Or you take a murderer maybe, someone who's done terrible things in his life, and you turn him into someone who doesn't remember all those things."

"Sure. Everybody must wonder about that, especially with the news these days."

An elderly couple came in and sat at the table behind us. *Usual?* the waitress asked them. They held hands as they waited.

"You think that's possible?"

"I don't know," I told him. "There's been a lot of debate about that, from Aristotle and Plato, Buddha and Gandhi, on up to people like Skinner. But I wonder if a man's essential nature isn't formed at birth and in the years just after. I wonder if you can ever really do more than change it superficially."

He sat nodding. "Maybe," he said when I was done. "Maybe not."

Outside, the rain had ended as it began, suddenly, and the couple, my neighbor and I all lined up at the register to pay.

"Is that what your research is all about, then?" I said as we stepped out of the smell of stale grease into fresh air. A taxi slowed. I waved it on.

"Something like that. Just animals, rats and monkeys and so on so far, but it's almost time for a man now. Almost. In the blue lab."

He thanked me for buying his dinner and said the next time was on him, but there was no next time.

That night I had a dream, though it seemed no dream then, that someone was in the room with me muttering on and on about evil and redemption. Still I can close my eyes and see behind them a face become mask: rigid, horrible, unyielding. I rose the next morning and, with that image as springboard, completed the new book in a week-long orgy of naps and marathon sessions at the desk, afterwards dropping the manuscript into the post to my agent and myself into a case of gin and a month of sleeping and drinking broken only by random daily liaisons with women picked up at the laundromat, library or A&P. Dimly I registered daily accounts of some guy in downtown Dayton attacking couples, always couples, and his eventual apprehension. In my fatigued, still-firing brain these stories mixed inextricably with worsening situations in the Middle East and South America, with planes shot down over questionably alien airspace, with the CIA's latest *coup*.

Probably I'd remember none of this if I had not, some months later, again run across my one-time neighbor.

After that evening I had not seen him, and a few weeks later our landlord drove in from north Cleveland (for the first time in how long, I wondered) to check his apartment. About ten p.m. he knocked at my door and when I opened it stepped in, looking about.

"Wilson," he said. "I own this place."

"You want it back, or what?"

"No. No, of course not, Mr. —?"

"Booth."

"Mr. Booth. But I haven't heard from Jefferson for a long time and I was wondering if you had any idea where he might have gone, or what was going on."

"Jefferson?"

He hooked a thumb to the rear. "Back there. The other bungalow. Guy that rented it out to you."

"Oh." I told him I hadn't seen my neighbor since the night at the cafe.

"Right. Then I guess we can assume he's split, no? Hey. You mind showing the place for me?"

"You're not gonna clean it up or anything?"

"Hell, man, why bother?" He looked quickly about. "No offense."

"Right," I said. "You check with the university?"

"About what?"

"Jefferson."

"Why would I do that?"

"Well, you know. His research and all that."

"We're not talking about the same person."

I shrugged. A 23-year-old blonde from the liquor store around the corner was scheduled to show up soon, I hoped with samples; why encourage this joker?

"Sure," I said. "I'll show the place."

He handed me a key and a handful of papers. Later I looked at the papers. Rental agreement, references, lists of things the apartment supposedly had (62%, I figured, were actually there).

"Call me if there's a problem. Otherwise just send the check and this stuff on through."

"Right."

Some girl moved in a month or two later—an ecologist,

she said, though what an ecologist would be doing in Dayton I can't imagine. Anyhow she had a pretty voice, nice long hair and huge tits and she jogged. I started getting up early again and keeping the drapes open later at night. Eventually the book was published, not by my old publisher but by a new one, and it did okay. Not too long after, I'd moved back in with Judith, and that did okay too, for a while. Some nights we'd read passages from the book to one another, alternately howling with laughter and moved beyond all expectation or reason. Then one afternoon I was hurrying between stores in a shopping mall when a well-dressed young man stepped into my way.

"Excuse me," he said.

I reached out to help him back to his feet. He smiled and took my hand.

"It's you!"' I said, and he looked at me, not understanding. "The bungalows."

He wore a blue blazer and gray slacks, maroon wool tie. A paper badge sheathed in plastic was pinned to his lapel.

"Your research project must have paid off, I guess."

"Research? Project?" You could almost see the gears spinning, failing to catch.

"On changing human nature," I said.

"Human nature. Changing. Of course—you're Booth. How have you been? I'm sorry, I should have recognized you, but..." He waved a diffident hand. "How are the roaches?"

"Still quite healthy, the little buggers. Fruitful and multiplying."

"Good little Christians."

"Exactly. And you?"

"I can't complain."

I pointed at the nametag.

"What's this, you gave up psychology?"

"Gave up...?" He looked around as though someone might walk up and explain. When no one did, he looked back at me and said, "I'm afraid you misunderstood. I thought you knew: I was not one of the scientists, I was the experiment."

He said good-bye, that it was grand to see me again (yes: grand), and stepped off into the crowd. A yard or so away he suddenly turned and said, "Come see me at the store," tapping a finger against the nametag, his own name beneath that of one of the major department stores. Then he was gone.

Many years have passed. The book is something of a classic now, I guess, taught in many literature courses and continuously in print in numerous editions. I am alone again, having weathered the spring and sudden winter of yet another marriage, living in a remodeled carriage-house across the street from (of all things) a monastery. Here a stream of polite, neatly-dressed young men comes to my door asking for the former tenant, Teresa.

# Blue Devils

ALL THE WAY UP from El Paso, which is where you first start noticing how much *sky* there is, the image stays with me. I've managed to shut it away for a long time, but now, maybe because we're on the spoor, getting close, it comes back. I look up at a cloud the size of Idaho, and there it is. At a mountain rising from the ground like a fist polished smooth: there, too. And in cholla and scrub cactus at the side of the road.

"I could definitely use a beer about now. You could probably do with a break, too. Unless you feel the need to push on, that is."

I look over at him. What he's said is slow to register. The world comes to me these days in a kind of stutter, like the time delay on radio talk shows.

"Maybe we could grab something to go?" I'm dry myself, from looking out at this landscape as much as for any other reason.

He nods once, eyes straight ahead as always. Both hands are loosely on the wheel, left elbow a buttress in the window. At the next exit he swings off into a service plaza larger than many of the Southern towns I grew up in. My father was career military, outspoken enough at the incompetencies and inefficiencies involved that he was repeatedly transferred. I counted once: eleven high schools. Maybe that's why I myself have always had such respect for authority. But it could have gone either way.

He fills up, goes inside to pay, and comes out with a six-pack of Heineken and the Slice I asked for. Back on the road he pops one of the beers and sips at it for the next thirty miles. The rest are tucked away under his legs. The two of us, the Slice, and the beer bottles just about fill the little Miata.

Flies.

The sound of them was what I always remembered, always thought of. Then Sergeant Van Zandt's voice at last penetrating. How many times has he already asked?

*You okay, Mr. Gorman?*

I nodded, said could I see her.

*Well, generally...* He stopped. Motioned with one hand for attendants to uncover her. A plain, somewhat muscular woman herself not much older than Faith folded back a corner, watching me closely the whole time. I nodded, and she put the cover back in place.

*It's Faith, then. It's your daughter,* Van Zandt said.

Yes.

"You understand that we can't do anything here," Delany says. I lurch back up into the world as it is. "There's no outstanding warrant, which severely limits the scope of my actions."

I went to him because of his reputation as a bounty hunter.

"So here's what we do. We go in, have a look, poke through the ashes of the campfire. We find something, anything at all, then we ask the locals to step in. You okay with that?"

I nod. I see my daughter's face below me, shimmering in heat that rises off the asphalt. An eye is gone. Ear and scalp are torn away on that side.

Delany pulls out another beer, drops the empty bottle back in the pack.

We're coming into the Chiricahuas, mountains unlike any others I know, ghostly somehow, the whole range eroded by wind, water and time to skull-like stands of stone honeycombed with caves and unlikely passages where Cochise eluded all pursuers.

Farther on, past Tucson, reservation lands lie slumbering to every horizon, cluttered briefly by trailers or tarpaper shacks, rusting automobiles and appliances, propane tanks.

"Unless you want to cancel all that and just blow him away, of course," Delany says.

He was, I was told, the best in the state at finding people— the best, period. That information came almost a year after Faith's death, on my last visit to Van Zandt's cubicle tucked away on the fourth floor behind rows of filing cabinets that looked as though cars had been driven repeatedly into them.

"There's just not much else I can do for you, Mr. Gorman," Van Zandt said. "The case remains open, of course. We don't officially close homicides. And bulletins will stay in circulation—till they're crowded out by new ones, at least. You never know. Sometimes things fall into our lap when we least expect it. Meanwhile, you might want to consider giving this man a call. I'm not telling you this as a cop, of course. I have a daughter myself."

He slid a business card across the desk to me with two crooked fingers, tapped it once with the index, and let go.

"He's a detective. Specializes in finding people, and he's damned good at it. Lots, including some who do the same kind of work, say there's no one better."

I looked down at the card. Buff-colored, almost translu-

cent parchment. And engraved: not thermography. Just
SEAN DELANY and a phone number.

Brought up on cheap detective movies and hardboiled
novels, despite the card I'd half expected to find Delany in
some gin mill with a cigarette hanging out one side of his
mouth and a madeover blonde on the other arm, with eyes
like bad sunsets and a tie that doubled as napkin. Instead,
by way of his answering service and a secretary who called
back immediately, I found him at Geronimo's, a mid-city
health club. He was finishing up a set of handball, had a
thing or two to talk over with the investment counselor
who'd been his opponent, and would see me outside in five
minutes if that was all right.

We met at his car, a British-green Miata. He had traded
sweatshirt and shorts for a full-cut cotton suit like the ones
Haspel used to make down in New Orleans and wore a knit,
alligatorless shirt beneath. At a mall nearby he ordered felafel
from a Greek fast-food stall, and I had three coffees as we
talked.

What do you do, Mr. Gorman? he asked at one point.

I'm an architect. I build things.

We talked a while longer, and he agreed to help me.

From the first I've been won over by Delany's quiet-spo-
ken, self-assured, ever-so-civilized manner. But now as we
move ever farther from the city—into the scruffy hills and
scrubland of West Texas, through ancient, barren New
Mexico, and on into Arizona, growth like bright green veins
in runnels formed by water washing down mountainsides—
I can't help but notice how that's begun changing. Simple
things, at first: endings dropped from a word here or there,
rougher cadences. Then articles and conjugations drop out,

leaving behind a language all nouns, present-tense verbs, prepositions. The man with whom I get out of the car in Tucson seems not at all the one with whom I began the trip back in Fort Worth.

"It doesn't have anything to do with justice or finding the person responsible," Chris said to me a few nights before. We'd met for coffee at a carefully neutral restaurant. She came directly from work; I, now unemployed, from the one-room apartment I'd finally settled into after months of motel rooms. "Don't you see that? That's why I left, why I had to. It's the *world* you want to hurt now, Joe. You want to hear it scream, want to tear something away from it, want to hurt it as much as it's hurt you."

Hurt? No. What I feel is numb. What I feel is nothing. I look out at the world and don't recognize, don't register, what's there. Only with effort, in a kind of forced gulp, will my mind take it in.

"Welcome to Tucson," Delany says.

The city has come surreptitiously up around us and now seems to go on forever, sprawling across this treeless, light-struck landscape. Distinctive mountain ranges stand at each point of the compass. A map names them for me: Catalina, Santa Rita, Rincon, Tucson. We drive along something called the Speedway past The Bashful Bandit, Empress Theater and Book Store XXX, Weinerschnitzel. Past bars, fast-food emporiums, video shops, used-car lots, hardware and auto-parts stores.

"The Miracle Mile," Delany says. "But most people around here just call it the Armpit." Pickup trucks with bodies rusted wholly through in moldlike patches overtake us, leave us behind. "Place we're looking for's up ahead a little ways."

He pulls into the parking lot of a motel that looks as though it might have been built early in the Fifties when such things were novelties. It's set back off the road half a lot or so. The wooden sign is shaped like a palm tree, with the legend REFRIGERATED AIR and its name, NO-TEL MOTEL, painted on.

"Room fourteen," Delany tells me.

It's on the second tier. Inside, a TV plays loudly: sirens, brakes screaming, metal slamming into metal.

"We're in luck." He knocks.

"Yeah?"

"Maintenance. Sorry to bother you, but we've got a major water leak downstairs. Have to check it out. Take us a minute or two, tops."

"Hang on."

Nothing for a time—Delany and I exchange glances—then the door opens a couple of inches, and a slat of face shows in the crack. Sharp, finlike nose, small mouth, drooping eyelid. Day's growth of beard.

He takes in Delany's clothes.

"Hell, man, you ain't—"

But Delany ducks his shoulder into the door, hard, and keeps going.

The man inside staggers back out of the way as the door slams against the wall. He reaches for the rear pocket of his jeans. Delany is there. Stomps down on his instep and, when he bends forward over the pain, pivots behind him on one foot, grabbing his long hair in a fist. The man's eyes round as Delany's hand tightens.

"Be nice," Delany tells him. "Man needs to talk to you."

I step inside and shut the door.

Wary, expressionless eyes follow me.

Delany pulls a gun out of the man's back pocket and hands it to me.

"Your call," he says, stepping off to the side.

So I shoot him.

Delany lets go of the hair as the man goes down. When he tries to breathe, air whistles out of his chest. He puts a hand gently against himself as if to hold the air in, says *Shit* with an even louder whistle, and is still. I notice there's no difference in the eyes.

"Cops be here in six minutes tops," Delany says.

He's standing by the bedside table looking through things piled up there, magazines, a cheap plastic wallet, stray bills and change, a couple of envelopes.

"But we got us another problem," he tells me.

"Yeah?"

"Wrong bird."

I look at him.

"This wasn't your man." He holds up a folded paper from one of the envelopes. "Gentleman here's freshly laundered, just out of the joint. Been a guest of the state almost three years."

"But how…"

He shrugs. "Information's what you make of it. I thought we had a fit. Sometimes it doesn't work out right. Sometimes it does."

Delany takes the gun from me, wipes it with his handkerchief, and puts it in the dead man's hand. He presses the hand hard against the grip, feeds the forefinger into the trigger guard.

"Thing is," he says, "does it matter?"

And I realize that it doesn't. That it doesn't matter at all. Someone's paid. A life's been taken. That's what matters.

Maybe I understood all along, understood without knowing I understood, that this was the best I could hope for. Maybe Delany knew that, too.

We go down the back stairs, get in the Miata, and pull away, north on Oracle to West Miracle Mile, then due west till we jump I-10, hearing sirens build to a scream behind us. I watch the Catalina mountains, the Tucson mountains, all this sky. Everything bright and alive, sharply defined, in the noonday sun. I can go back to building things now.

Later I look up again at the Chiricahuas and think how little we've changed. We huddle together in the vertical caverns of our cities, around our megawatt campfires, and try to fill up the darkness with chants, songs, magic. We understand so little, we're always afraid, and sometimes still, the best we can do is offer up a sacrifice—hoping to drive out whatever blue devils overtake us.

# *Oblations*

*T*HE FIRST OF THE LESIONS (as he'd come to think of them) had appeared three weeks ago after he and Anne had quarreled over a dinner engagement. He had drawn back a fist to strike her and, astonished at what he was about to do, almost fainted. Showering that night, he had found it on his thigh, a red excrescence the size of a pinhead, itching slightly.

He'd thought it nothing, a pimple or infected follicle perhaps. Then, listening to a report on Salvador over National Public Radio a few days later on the way to work, he had pulled off to the side of the road to watch another form on the inside of his wrist. There was a pressure, a warmth— then the lesion's appearance, like a tiny volcano.

That day at work Samuelson, a onetime champion salesman now gone to booze and bosses' girls in motelrooms, was finally fired, and as he sat in the coffee shop across the street at 9:56, Morgan felt the twitch, the quick spasm, as another lesion sprang up, this one just above his ribcage where the shirt rubbed whenever he changed position.

For several days then, there were no more. Perhaps, he began to think, it was over. From the office he called and told Anne to get a sitter and be ready for dinner and a night of dancing. "On a Tuesday? At our age?" she'd asked, laughing.

Not long after, Morgan heard someone say "Busy?" and looked up to see McDowell in the doorway, ducking his head slightly to fit.

"Beaverish. How's the family?"

"I don't know." McDowell had sprawled into the so-called client's chair, and when Morgan glanced up sharply, added, "I'm alone now, Bill."

"You? That's hard to believe, Sean."

"Hard for you, harder for me."

"How long? What the hell happened?"

"Six months. I woke up one morning and everybody was gone. A week's supply of clean clothes was folded and laid out by the washer. Alice had left a note beside them, weighed down by the iron. Said she needed more space for herself, and time. She didn't mention it, but apparently she needed money as well: she cleaned out the checking account."

"How much do you need, Sean?"

"I wasn't meaning that." He shifted in the chair. No one had ever built a chair he was comfortable in, and he sat in all of them as though half-expecting them to collapse under his broad, 6'6" frame. "But thanks. Tell you what I do need, though, Bill. That house gets awful lonely, going back there every night, sitting just waiting until bedtime. What I was wondering was, if you'd maybe want to go out after work and have a few drinks. You know, just talk awhile, then grab a couple of steaks."

"Love to. But hey, it's gonna have to be tomorrow, okay? Already told Anne we were going out."

McDowell stood. "Sure, Bill. Great. See you tomorrow, then. Looking forward to it." Going out the door, he ducked his head and pulled his elbows in close to his sides. His suit was badly rumpled.

They had pasta and veal at Arthur's, a rare extravagance, with brandy and espresso afterwards. They were at the Blue Wave then until almost two, but found the band so outstanding they wound up listening more than dancing. And talking. After twelve years of marriage, Morgan still could not wait to see her at night and tell her everything that had happened during the day; he could not hear enough about her childhood or college years before he knew her, about books she loved, people she remembered.

It was near dawn when they fell asleep, spent, against one another, and not much more than an hour later the radio began playing, very softly, Mahler's Second. He slipped out of bed without waking her, showered in the kids' bath (they'd sleep through anything), shaved in the car on the way to work. At 10:23 Anne called to tell him good morning. McDowell did not come in. At 12:41 they found him hanging from the doorframe in the basement gameroom of his house, an overturned chair nearby. A carefully penned will lay on the pooltable beside him, leaving everything to Alice. The room had been built especially large, probably the only room he ever felt comfortable in.

Seated at the desk as the office manager, Raleigh, told him this, Morgan felt new lesions erupt on his chest: that now-familiar pressure, the dimpling, appearance.

Raleigh gone, Morgan walked out into the general office and poured coffee into a plastic cup. Then he went back into his own office and stood at the window looking down, holding the cup in one hand. So many people he would meet, love, struggle with; so much sadness and pain. And standing there he could feel them, feel them all, tiny points of pressure beneath the skin, waiting to be borne.

# Winner

WE'RE GOING IN at the same time and only one of us is going to come back out. Ten in the morning. No dinner tonight, no breakfast. It's all set. I've told him that but he won't believe it. He just lies there groaning every few minutes saying We're gonna make it Joe, we're both gonna make it. And then a fit of coughing hits him and the nurse comes running.

Three, four times a day Bill goes through the ward taking the bets. They've picked up a lot in the last week or so. More of them, and higher—the coughs and the special nurse, I guess. There's only one guy in the ward now who hasn't kicked in, and we finally figured out he was deaf. Every night just before lights-out Bill comes round to tell me how much is in the pot. When he brings the pills. It's up to $348.83 now. Not bad. I've done worse on the outside in my day, a lot worse.

Bill's a grad student at Columbia in Black Studies. He's on scholarship, maybe a grant or two, but he's working nights as an orderly to help finance his Panther block. He's got light skin and fine features and he could pass for white a lot of places I know. But he's not too happy about that. So he wears an Afro and comes on pretty strong. First day I was here, back about a month ago, he told me he was black maybe four or five times. Nothing direct. Just a word here and there, an aside, like that.

The guy next to me. He's a little guy. Pushes a hack, and he got torn up pretty bad by two young Negroes up near Harlem. They brought him in about a week ago and it looked like he wasn't going to make it for a while there, but they stuck some tubes in him and he had needles all in his arm the first two, three days and they had him under an oxygen tent. Bill used to go over and stick his head inside and breathe deep as he could, then he'd come back with a big grin on him. Anyhow, they had to wait this long for him to get his strength back, like with me. When he came to and saw the orderly was black they almost lost him again and assigned a special nurse to him. First thing he said that day, and he wasn't talking to anyone, was, I been shoving that damn cab for fifteen years now, I oughta know better. He doesn't talk much, I don't know if he can, but there's something about him I like. One thing is he's got guts, he's tough. You can see that when the pain hits him and he clenches his teeth, holding on. He's not the kind that gives up easy—it's a long way from the Bronx, but he'll never forget it. And I like that, I know how it is myself.

Right before lights-out tonight Sanders comes over. He makes sure to wait till Bill's gone first, though. They don't have much use for each other, I don't think they even talk. Sanders never got through high school. He had to come up the hard way. And then there's the whole black thing of course. Seems a couple of his buddies on the force got gunned down by the Panthers a year or so back and he can't forget that, not for a minute. But he's a good guy. He knows what's going on, all about the pot Bill's holding I mean, and he's not doing anything about it, won't let it get out.

He stands by the bed a while looking around the ward,

then asks how I'm doing tonight. I grunt and shove the cigarettes toward him. They won't let me smoke but I like to keep the cigarettes around anyhow, I like to know they're there. And I don't figure he needs an answer, he knows I'm slated for tomorrow morning. That means he'll either stick around or pull down another assignment, maybe go back on the beat. But I think he's got a promotion coming up now so who knows. It's sure to be a lot better than this.

I light the cigarette for him and he thanks me and stands there smoking. Finally he says, "You're looking pretty good."

"I'm okay."

He takes another drag and a little smoke comes back out.

"Sorry I had to shoot, Vic. Mayor told us we had to crack down on the rackets. You know what that means. It means the little guys like you, not where it's really at. Order comes down though, not much I can do about it, right?"

"Yeah, sure. Just aim better next time, okay?"

He smiles and looks around again. I don't know what he thinks he's looking for. He knows every crack in the wall by now. "You need anything? Anything I can get you?"

"Yeah, I could use a lung and maybe a kidney. If you've got a spare."

He looks at me while he's snubbing the cigarette out in the bedpan.

"I don't have anything against you, Vic. You're straight. You never gave us any trouble like a lot of the others did. You know that."

"Yeah. I know, Sanders."

"Look. When the trial comes up. I just want you to know I'm on your side. I'll be pulling for you all the way."

"Great. We can say it was a hunting accident. I forgot to wear my red cap. How's that?"

He's watching my face very closely. "I'll do what I can, Vic."

I just nod and he finally says, "Right." He can't think of anything else to say. So he starts away, but I stop him.

"Sanders..."

"Yes."

"Do me a favor?"

"Sure, Vic. Anything. You know that."

"Ask Bill to come back in here for a minute. I have to see him."

"Bill...? Yeah. Yeah, sure. Why not." He starts away again and stops, turns around. "Hey. Thanks for the smoke, Vic."

"Anytime. Thanks for the slug." But I'm grinning for him. He goes out through the door and he's gone for a few minutes. Then I see him coming back and he takes up his post just outside the door, in a folding chair out there. A minute or two later Bill comes in. God knows where Sanders might have found him this time of night.

I cut him off before he says anything: "Got something for you, Bill." I reach around under the pillow, take out the roll and hand it to him. The bandages get in the way and it takes a while. "That'll make it about five hundred." When he looks back up at me I shake my head. "No questions." What the hell, there's no one else to give it to.

Bill stares at the money for a moment, then at me. He takes out a little notebook and makes an entry. He knows how to do it right. I could have used a man like him. Then he puts the money in his pocket and leaves. He doesn't say anything to me but I notice he stops outside and talks to Sanders for a minute, maybe two. Sanders turns around in his chair and glances at me.

I think I was right about the promotion.

# Shutting Darkness Down

*I*T WAS OVER, finally over, and they sat, the two of them, as they had so many times before, in a huge low-ceilinged room with windows along one end that looked out over downtown, letting in now, this early morning, a gray, smoky light. Folding steel chairs and collapsible tables with brown plastic tops stood about the room at random, some pushed close together in huddles, others drifting free. Tabletops were littered with Styrofoam cups, ashtrays, fast-food wrappers, legal pads, file folders. Computer screens sat with cursors blinking, surrendering their own light to the growing light outside. No one else in the room.

All the others were off duty.

All the others had gone home.

Still pinned to the board, arranged chronologically in sequences painstakingly reconstructed by Jackson, Meredith and members of the task force they headed, hung photos of victims, crime scenes, family and friends, workplaces, roadways and buildings, habitual routes. These ran in discrete blocks horizontally (young woman with her belly slashed open to a smile, children at rest in spoonlike curves around beloved stuffed bears, dinosaurs, dolphins) and vertically (downtown laundromat where teenagers found the baby going round and round in the dryer, abandoned bloodied Chevrolet Nova, suburban apartment with kitchen and bathroom surprises).

Like a crossword, Meredith thought. Fill in the blanks.

Filling in the blanks was what they'd been doing, trying to do, for almost a year now. And finally it was over.

"Well, that's it, then," Meredith said. "Cut. Print."

Jackson nodded.

So for a while (days, months, a year) that face he knew so well would be absent from the world. While he and others like him marked time, waiting for it to come up again grinning. He'd spent much of his life looking into that face. The sprawl of photos on the board made him remember all the others: single women, couples, children, old folk. Who they were, where they'd lived, what they'd left behind. Days, months and years a blur. His own life a blur. These memories, this job his only sense of time, his only real hold on it.

"Guess so," Jackson said, hand working hard at the muscles of his neck. He tugged at his tie, the dark blue one Betty gave him last Christmas, already at half mast. His coat hung on the back of his chair. Each time he shifted weight the coat shrugged its shoulders.

"What'll you do?"

"Try to find my way home, I guess. See if Margaret's still there. Find out what gangs the kids have joined, see if *they* bother coming home at night. Sleep. In three or four days— who knows? — I might just get up and have me a cup of coffee out of a real cup."

"Something to look forward to, for sure."

Meredith stared down at a coffee stain on his shoe. Who was it said that God is in the details. Blue shirtsleeves rolled up haphazardly onto biceps, underarms stained with sweat.

While Jackson's white dress shirt, sleeves folded twice, still looked fresh from the laundry.

"Yeah. What *else* is life about?" Jackson's eyes swept the room. Now that it was all over, time had slowed. Stop-action, they used to call it. Slow motion. People lived in this drudge all their lives. Hard to see why or how. "Be a gym again by the time we get back."

"More likely the captain's private studio. Backdrop of the city, a map."

"For all those TV interviews."

"Hey—he's a hero."

"Sure he is. Caught Mr. Road Kill." Jackson looked around again. "Still reminds me of my old school cafeteria. Every day they'd fold down these tables, otherwise it was just a gym. Dropping hoops, you'd still smell sour milk and cabbage, the sickly reek of cheap hot dogs."

He'd paid childhood dues in such cafeterias. Not many blacks back in Phoenix those days. Kids sat down by him, spat in his tray, called him a nigger and told him what they were going to do to him out on the playground once he'd finished eating. It all took time, the way these things do, but he'd managed to dodge it all, the pettiness, the violence, even the fear, and finally fit in.

Meredith got up and walked to the windows. After a while Jackson came up behind him. They stood together looking down. Buses pushed through the streets like giant land-grazing beasts. Cars skittered in and out among them. Sun like a wound bleeding light into the sky.

*Pilot fish*, Meredith thought, watching the cars. He was twelve years younger than Jackson, just enough difference that they'd come up, lived, in separate worlds. Meredith turned twenty in Nam sending kids his own age, kids dredged from Iowa City drive-ins and Memphis burger joints, out on patrol. Gave him a certain perspective.

Down on the street Jimmie shoehorned his cart into its usual space between newsstand and bus stop. Routine's a good thing, something you can hold on to. Hot dogs would be steaming inside. Pretzels hung from hooks above. Smell of mustard and sauerkraut.

"Don't seem a bad kid," Meredith said, "not really."

"They never do."

"Yeah." When's the last time he had a hot dog? "But you have to wonder why things went the way they did."

"For him? Or for the others?"

"Both, I guess."

"My oldest son John? Working on his master's degree in philosophy up at Columbia. The world's the case, he keeps telling me. What is, is. Try making it different, all you do is make yourself crazy. Maybe he's right."

Down in the street Jimmie slapped a dog between halves of a bun, slathered on sauerkraut, mustard, ketchup.

"Any of it ever more than a toss of the dice?" Meredith said.

Jackson shrugged. Hell if he knew. Maybe. On the job almost twenty years, and all his certainties had eroded to one: you never know what a person will do. Any person.

"Seeing yourself."

Meredith's eyes met his in the window's reflection: "I guess." Could it have gone that way with him? "For a couple of years after the war I was really messed up."

"Sure you were. You earned it."

For a minute or so, neither of them said anything.

"Besides," Jackson went on, "you don't see yourself in all this, you're not likely to see much else."

"So it's always ourselves we're chasing."

"You're gonna tell me you ever doubted it?"

"I doubt everything. More and more of everything as time goes on."

"Good. Always *figured* you were gonna turn out all right." Jackson's hand worked at his neck, crawled around again to his tie. "Choke down one last cup with me?"

Meredith shrugged. "Wouldn't do it for anyone else, but what the hell."

Jackson walked to a table along the back wall. On the table were coffee makers, a tray of sandwiches and half-sandwiches in plastic wrap, bags of chips torn open along the seams, boxes whose bottoms were sludged with powdered sugar, icing, doughnut fragments.

One of the coffee makers had a carafe almost full. Jackson lifted it off the heat, sniffed at it. Poured a cup for both of them.

They sat at another of the tables. Jackson pushed file folders and papers aside to make room for their cups, but both held on to them. Something reassuring about their physicality, the warmth, what this signaled—something far past simple sharing.

"Worst has to be that family in Canton," Meredith said after a while. "No way I'll ever get those kids out of my mind. Laying there like that, all opened up. *Ecorché*, they call it up in Quebec." Where Meredith had lived when he got back from Nam. Just couldn't face the States again at first. Lot of hunters in Quebec. See these deer dressed out, staked on boards outside houses. "You've been doing this a long time, B.J."

"All your life."

It was an old joke between them.

"You tell me how anyone ever thinks he's able to understand something like that?"

"No one does. Not really."

"Except Hargrove."

Their department expert. Guy grew up in Highland Park
driving a convertible, had a house in his own name there
by the time he was sixteen. Parents bought it for him—for
his future. Then he sailed through SMU and Galveston med
school, barely touching down the whole time, and elbowed
his way through a residency at Parkland like someone
caught in rush hour on the New York subway. *Sure* he knew
how someone like Billy Daniel lived, what was in his head.

Meredith picked up one of the file folders, scanned it
quickly and put it down, took another.

> In Billy's mind there is no connection between
> what he does—what he *has* done, more prop-
> erly—and the results. For him, the causal link
> simply does not exist. This is a difficult concept,
> I know. Let me put it this way: a metaphor, noth-
> ing more, but it may help you to understand.
> All the time, every moment of his life, Billy is
> passing through doors. He goes out a door and
> comes back in to where he was before —but
> there's a body there now. Or it's quiet again. Or
> someone is trying to kill him. Whatever he has
> done, he leaves there, behind the door. And he
> goes through the next door without a history—
> innocent, as it were. The causal connection's
> simply not there for him, never made.

Meredith closed the file folder, put it down.

"Innocent."

"Right." Jackson held up his cup. "Stuff tastes like mud from the Mississippi's bottom, catfish and all."

"Want some more?"

"Sure."

They sat quietly for a while then, two men dragged out so thin they scarcely existed anymore, yet reluctant to let go of whatever it was they had here, intimacy, purpose. Some tiny intimation, perhaps, of doing good, bringing things back to balance.

Around them the building stirred to life. Footsteps resounded in corridors and on steel stairs outside. A door at the far end of the room opened, someone looked in briefly then withdrew. Cars and pedestrians filled the street below.

"We're catfish ourselves," Meredith said. "All this muck we live in, day after day. Managing somehow to get sustenance from it."

He looked down the room towards where the door had closed moments ago. That door seemed to him now very, very far away, the room a kind of gauntlet. Some obscure test he'd sooner or later have to pass.

"You think it changes us? All this?"

"Don't see how it could help but. One way or the other."

"Yeah." Meredith tilted his cup and found it empty. How had that happened? No memory of drinking. "Sometimes at night I wake up and look around and nothing—the bedroom, the curtain on the window that's been there for twelve years, Betty asleep beside me—none of it seems real to me anymore. That ever happen to you?"

Jackson shrugged. "You ought to've married her, Ben, long before this."

"I know."

"There's never enough for us to hold on to, any of us."

"Guess not." He glanced at his partner's tie. Remembered the paper Betty had wrapped it in, gray with blue and green triangles. "So. We out of here?"

"We are for sure."

They went along the floor, down the stairs, out the door. Parting on the street by Jimmie's cart.

Jackson said call him in a couple of days, they'd have a beer—on him. I oughta be awake again by then, he said.

Meredith stood watching his partner walk away, stood still and alone in the milling crowd with blades of sunlight sliding through chinks in the buildings.

He was thinking what the boy, Billy, had said, what he'd said again and again, to arresting officers, to interrogators from the task force, to Hargrove and his night squad of psychologists, social workers and assorted evaluators, rolling it off like a catechism, his answer to almost every question:

"We went for a ride, and some people died."

# Dear Floods of Her Hair

MURIEL LEFT ME, left us, I should say, on Monday. The tap in the kitchen sink sprang a leak, spewing a mist of cold water onto sheets I spread on the floor, and a hummingbird, furious that she'd forgotten to refill its feeder just outside, beat at the window again and again. By the time friends, family and mourners began arriving, Thursday around noon, preparations were almost complete.

First thing I did was draw up a schedule. Muriel would have been proud of me, I thought as I sat at the kitchen table with pen and a pad of her notepaper, water from the spewing tap slowly soaking into the corduroy slippers she'd given me last Christmas. Here I'd always been the improviser, treading water, swimming reflexively for whatever shore showed itself, while Muriel weighed out options like an assayer, made lists and kept files, saw that laundry got done *before* the last sock fell, shoehorned order into our lives. And now it was all up to me.

Somewhere between 16 and 20 on my list, the hummingbird gave up its strafing runs and simply hovered an inch from the glass, glaring in at me. They could be remarkably aggressive. Seventeen species of them where we lived. Anna's hummers, Costa's and black-chinned around all year, Rufous, calliope and the rest migrating in from Mexico or various mountain ranges. In that way birds have, males are the colorful ones, mating rituals often spectacular. Some will dive 90 feet straight up, making sure sunlight strikes them in such a way that their metallic colors flare dramatically for females watching from below. These females are dull so as to be inconspicuous on nests the size of walnuts.

Muriel loved this place of cactus and endless sky, mountains looming like the world's own jagged edge, loved the cholla, prickly pear, palo verde, geckos with feet spurred into the back of our windowscreens at night.

Most of all, though, she loved hummingbirds. Even drew a tiny, stylized hummer for stationery, envelopes and cards and had it silkscreened onto the sweatshirts she often wore as she sat in front of the computer, daily attending to details of the business (cottage industries, they used to call them) that kept us comfortable here.

That same hummer hovered silently in the upper left corner of the notepad as I inscribed 24.

I gave it a pointed beard and round glasses.

Favorite bird. Hummingbird. Favorite music. *Wozzeck*, Arvo Pärt's *Litany*. Favorite color. Emerald green. Favorite poem. One by Dylan Thomas.

> The tombstone told when she died.
> Her two surnames stopped me still.
> A virgin married at rest.

Memories of my father were also in mind, of course. The one who taught me. I was ten years old when it began, sitting on the floor in a safe corner with knees drawn up reading H.G. Wells, a favorite still. Suddenly I felt *watched*, and when I glanced up, Father's eyes were on me. Good book? he asked. At that point I couldn't imagine a bad one. Just that some were better than others. I lit the next one off the smoldering butt of the last. They all are, I told him. No, he said. A lot of them just make up things.

Mrs. Abneg spoke then. Charles: he's too young, she said. Father looked at her. No. He's ready. Earlier than most, I agree, but this is *our* son. He's not like the rest. Mrs. Abneg ducked her head. The female must be dull so as to be inconspicuous on the nest.

And so I was allowed for the first time into my father's basement workshop. I could barely see over the tops of the sinks, benches, the tilted stainless-steel table with its runnels and drains. Shelves filled with magical jars and pegboards hung with marvelous tools loomed above like promises I would someday keep.

That first session went on for perhaps an hour. I understood little of what my father said then, though whenever he asked was something or another clear I always nodded dutifully yes. Knowledge is a kind of osmosis. And soon enough, of course, our time together in the basement workroom fulfilled itself. Others found themselves shut out. For a time I wondered what Mrs. Abneg or my younger brother might be doing there up above, but not for long. Procedures and practicums, the rigors of my apprenticeship, soon occupied my full attention and all free time. I had far too much to do to squander myself on idle thoughts.

Just as now, I thought.

I set to work.

As I worked, I sang *Wozzeck*.

Drudgery goes best when attention's directed elsewhere—not that pain and loss don't nibble away at us then. Stopping only to feed or rest myself when I could go on no longer, shedding gloves like old skin, I performed as my father taught me. Handsaws, augers and tongs, tools for which there were no names, came into use. I tipped fluids from bright-colored decanters, changed gloves, went on.

> She cried her white-dressed limbs were bare
> And her red lips were kissed black

*Wozzeck* was the piece Muriel and I had decided on; with tutorials twice a week and daily practice, I'd got it down as well as might be expected. Not a professional job, certainly, but competent. I sang the parts in rotation, altering pitch and range as required, hearing my own transformed voice roll back from the cellar's recesses.

I'd never really understood painting, poetry, old music, things like that—opera least of all. Whatever I couldn't weigh, quantify, plot on a chart, I had to wonder if it existed at all. I knew how important all this was to Muriel, of course. I'd sit beside her through that aria she loved from *Turandot*, "Nessun dorma," or the second movement of Mozart's Clarinet Quintet watching tears course down her face. I'd see her put down a book and for a moment there'd be this blank look, this stillness, as though she were lost between worlds: deciding.

Often Muriel and I would discuss how we'd come together, the chance and circumspectness of it, other times the many ways in which, jigsawlike, our curves and turnings had become a whole. Then, teasing relentlessly, she would argue that, as an anthropologist, I was not truly a scientist. But I was. And who more alert to the place of ritual in lives?

I died before bedtime came
But my womb was bellowing
And I felt with my bare fall
A blazing red harsh head tear up
And the dear floods of his hair.

My father trained me well. I had not expected ever to
bring my skills into practice so soon, of course. How could
we have known? Officers had one day appeared at the door
just past noon. One was young, perhaps twenty, under-
growth of beard, single discrete earring, the other
middle-aged, hair folded over to cover balding scalp. I was
twelve. Answered the door wearing shorts and a T-shirt that
read *Stress? What Stress?!* Mr. Abneg? the officers addressed
me— so I knew. The older one confirmed it: Father was gone,
he'd stepped unaware into one of the city's many sinkholes.
And so Mrs. Abneg became my responsibility. I had taken
care of her, just as Father taught me. Fine workmanship. He
would have been proud.

The skull must be boiled (Father taught, all those years
ago) until it becomes smooth as stone, then reattached.

This I accomplished with a battery-driven drill and eighteen silver pins from the cloisonnéd box my father passed
on to me, his father's before him. Singing Berg the whole
while. I'd learned *all* my lessons well.

Legs must fall just so on the chair.

One arm at rest. The other upraised. Each finger arranged
according to intricate plan.

Exacting, demanding work.

Fine music, though.

By Thursday Muriel looked more beautiful than ever before— I know this is hard to believe. That afternoon I lifted

the wig from its case and placed it on her. Draped the blue veil across the preserved flesh of her chest.

(I, too, can be practical, my dear, see? I can make plans, follow through, take charge. Do what needs be done. And finally have become an artist of sorts in my own right, I suppose.)

The doorbell rang.

Thank you all for coming.

Glasses clink. Steaming cups are raised. There is enough food here to feed the city's teeming poor. I circulate among our guests, Uncle Van, Mrs. Abneg's sister, cousins and nephews, close friends. Some, I can no longer speak to, of course. To others I present small boxes wrapped in bright paper: a toenail or fingernail perhaps, sliver of bone, divot of pickled flesh.

Yes. She looks beautiful, doesn't she?

Outside, whispering, night arrives. No whispers in here, as family, friends and mourners move from lit space to lit space. They manipulate Muriel's limbs into various symbolic patterns. Group about her. Pictures are taken.

It's time, Muriel's brother says, stepping beside me.

And *I* say, Please—as instantly the room falls quiet.

I want to tell you all how much I love her.

I want to tell you we'll be happy now. Everything is in place.

I want to tell you how much we will miss you all.

Listen....

One day you'll walk out, a day like any other, to fetch laundry, pick up coffee at the store, drop off mail. You'll take the same route you always do, turn corners as familiar to you as the back of your hand, thinking of nothing in particular. And that's when it will happen. The beauty of this world will fall upon you, push the very words and breath from your lungs. Suddenly, irrevocably, the beauty of this world will break your heart; and lifting hand to face, you will find tears there.

Those tears will be the same as mine, now.

# Moments of Personal Adventure

PROPELLORMAN does not want to marry Lucy.
But just now, plying his trade, he faces an expanse of dark glass and the light-studded world beyond.

"You have to understand," his host says, turning briefly to the window against which the city throws its bright self silently again and again. In soft light his hair gleams with health. His motions are graceful, almost athletic. "At age nineteen I had an idea, a single idea; it came to me as I rode the escalator to work one afternoon. Within three months that idea had become this company, myself its president and principal shareholder."

He holds his brandy up to the light. "You're certain you don't care for some?"

Propellorman shakes his head deferentially, smiles.

"The rest is largely silence, Mr. Porter. That single day, that one idea, has been my life. And the years since, only a waiting."

"For what, Mr. Mills?"

A smile as finely turned as French curves. "What do we *all* wait for, my friend? Salvation. An end to our pain and confusion, to our hungers. Some explanation for all this."

He places the snifter squarely on the blotter before him and leans, one inch, perhaps two, closer.

"I hope you'll not be too harsh with me in your article, Mr. Porter. I am not, generally, so melancholic an individual. My wife has just been admitted, for the sixth time in as many months, to a psychiatric hospital. I seem quite unable to help her in any real way, for all my resources. And should one be of an analytical turn of mind—a curse I indeed carry, though a quality of which my wife seems wholly innocent— then after a time one comes to reexamine values, to wonder if everything one has believed and lived might not in fact be false, fleeting, futile."

"I understand."

"Somehow I believe that you do. And I thank you once again for coming."

Propellorman leaves him there in that dark room and rides the elevator steadily down. It is brightly lit and smells of cigar smoke.

Near the entrance he comes across a bar and goes in. Eight or ten real wood tables, Doré prints on papered walls, Vivaldi. All his.

He never takes notes during an interview but afterwards scrambles for the nearest shelter to write down, as quickly as he can and often virtually verbatim, all that was said. It's a habit begun, like many others, in college, where he'd sit in the student union following American Positivism or Anthropology 402 and fill page after page of his notebooks (always, even then, yellow) with Pierce, Dewey, Australopithecus, Sapir-Whorf.

Sitting at the bar (the bartender doesn't even get off his stool behind it), he orders a beer and begins writing, two lines of precise script between each blue-ruled line. Orders a martini and writes more, some of it just as it will appear in the final piece, some only an associative word or phrase, rag-ends of description, brackets with nothing inside them.

Once he thought he might restore the world to readers with his language; now he knows that often he will only further obscure it. They will come to his words expecting him to say only what they already know, and even if he does not say it, that is nevertheless what they will hear, until finally the words will not bear even their own weight. But once, in an essay on living alone, he wrote one sentence of absolute truth, and it has haunted him since.

He is a man who has been much loved by women, and now, after many years of living apart from and alongside them, he loves two. Lucy is bright and childlike and cannot do enough for him, with him. In Valerie there is something fatally damaged, a wound deep at her center that sometimes surfaces in her eyes. With Lucy he knows the world is good; with Valerie he understands the tremendous, silent struggles that make it so.

Gradually he becomes aware of the woman sitting beside him, knows she has been there for some time.

"Welcome back," she says. "To the world."

"That obvious."

"Yes."

"Well." Propellorman looks around. There is danger everywhere, his archenemy a master of disguise. Nothing is what it seems. "Another drink?"

She nods, hair tumbling over the distal shoulder. "If you'll let me buy *you* one."

"Done."

Something, then, of Alphonse and Gaston, neither willing to accept the final drink till at last, mutually befuddled, they lose count of rounds and agree to call it even.

Her apartment is on the second floor above a florist's, a

single, rectangular room long enough that light coming in the windows at the far end tires halfway across the floor. Low screens, makeshift bookshelves and a scatter of bright rugs divide the room into ragged continents. Everything — walls, screens, shelves, floor—is painted white. There are no chairs. They sit on stacked mattresses by the windows drinking coffee, words rushing in to fill the space between them.

Poets console us, Apollinaire said, for the loose words that pile up on earth and unleash catastrophes. And so as the night deepens, they move closer, bailing words out onto the floor, hoping to stay afloat.

There is more coffee, then scrambled eggs, then a long-reserved bottle of wine.

"I have to tell you," she says beside him. "There was…an accident. Please."

He opens her shirt and follows the web of scars across her breasts (nipple torn from one) and down along her body onto her legs. In this lurid windowlight the scars seem to have a life, a luminous existence, of their own, and he finds himself responding as he had never known possible, with an urgency he could never have imagined, almost as though propelled by something outside himself, some terrible, irre-sistible force.

"Who did this to you?" he asks long afterwards through the darkness.

"I did," she tells him. And later: "Will I see you again?"

But he doesn't know, doesn't know anything now, and so he doesn't answer, letting the silence carry whatever message it will.

Later, back at his own apartment, he'll wake at three with a terrible thirst. For a long time he'll lie listening to feet on stairs outside, to the sweep of traffic. Finally then he'll rise and walk uptown to Horse's studio with its smell of sour wax and manifold mirrors. Horse, the sculptor, there among his ravaged steel bodies, will know what to say, will surely explain it all to him.

# Good Men

THIS ONE WORE gray-cotton slacks, a chambray shirt, and a corduroy sportcoat with the sleeves pushed up almost to the elbow. He propped himself against the door-jamb and smiled. He had a kindly, gentle way about him.

"This is Louis," Mom told me. She was leaning toward him the way she does, not really touching, but she put a hand lightly on his arm as she spoke.

"Hi, Danny," he said. "Homework?"

I looked up from my notebook. "Sort of."

"Like school?"

I nodded.

"What's your favorite?" he asked me.

"History, probably."

"That's unusual for someone your age." He came over and sat down on the bed beside me as Mom went for drinks. "I teach," he said. "Humanities, at the university. History, philosophy, art, literature. Your mom says you're a great reader. I can see that." He looked at the stacks of books and journals, the crates of file folders.

"Yes, sir."

"Louis. Not sir. Do you have any favorite writers?"

"Dickens and Twain, I guess. Victor Hugo."

"Wells?"

"The *Outline of History,* yes, sir—Louis. But I don't have much taste for fantasy."

Mom came back with drinks—wine for her, Scotch for Louis, hot chocolate for me—and told me ten minutes to bedtime. I drank the chocolate from the tin mug I've had all my life, went into the bathroom to rinse out the mug and brush my teeth, and then to the living room to tell them goodnight.

Afterward I lay listening to the rumble of their voices, like far-off trains. They spoke of the university for a time—their mutual acquaintances there, their routines, how they met—then of themselves. Four years ago (for the first time, at age thirty-two), Louis had married a woman with, as they shortly discovered, cancer of the bone. He took a year's leave, borrowed money from his family and friends, and spent that year wholly with Julie. After she died, he went back to work. Several months ago he'd finally paid everyone back. Now he was buying furniture for the two-room apartment he leased at a discount from the school, a piece at a time, his latest acquisition (the "latest possession to possess me," as he put it) a white-pine futon frame. Slowly the voices grew softer, then withdrew to the bedroom, out of hearing.

Early next morning I heard the front door open and close, then my mother moving about the kitchen.

"Hi, honey, want oatmeal?" she said when I wandered out to the kitchen. She was drinking coffee, rare for her in the morning, and listening to classical music with the volume turned low.

"Louis would like to take you to a movie," she said when the oatmeal was ready. "Just the two of you. At the university film club." She poured another cup of coffee.

"Did he say what film?"

"*Empire of the Sun.* He thinks you'd like it. Would you?
Want to go, I mean?"

"When is it?"

"Tonight, I think."

"Sure."

"Then I'll call and tell him it's on."

Glenn Gould worked his way through the Goldberg Vari-
ations as Mr. Clark's delivery truck coughed itself into life
for another day. I was eleven that year.

JOHN LUNDE. Born 1950, small town in South, perhaps Tennessee. Attended Tulane University, to which
he returned for a degree following a tour in Vietnam
as a medic. Married at age 23, one daughter, divorced
after six years. Freelance journalist, stringer for major
Eastern papers. Loved Janet Draper. Died 1982.

"She never says much about your father."

We were seated at a TCBY eating vanilla yogurt piled with
pecans. We'd been out together without Mom at least once
every week, mostly to movies, but one time to the Museum
of Natural History, another to tour a helicopter factory.

"I get the idea there's not that much to say," I told Louis.

"You remember him?"

"Sometimes, a little—just glimpses. His voice, mostly. All
we have left of him is a hat he hung over the back of a chair in
Mom's room the day he walked out. She's never moved it."

"She took it pretty hard, then."

"Glad to have him gone, is what she always said. I think
she hated him."

"She didn't go out much for a while, she says."

"Not at first. She never really has, a lot."

"If you don't want anything else, there's still time to catch some ice skating before we meet her."

We did that, then picked Mom up at Tate Hall, where she had piano lessons late on Tuesdays, and went shopping. Louis was looking at desks. We wandered through forests of lacquer, melamine and bamboo at Bright Ideas, Pier 1, Storehouse, Made in Denmark. Everyone's favorite was a small red-lacquered one, bright as a cherry and solid as stone, curving gently at every joint and corner. Louis paid for it and arranged delivery for Wednesday, his day off.

One of Mom's students last week, as they paused between movements of a Brahms sonata, had suddenly begun speaking to her of problems at home, and this became the topic for discussion during dinner at Bella Italia on the mall.

"He's a musician too," Mom said. "A violinist. And he used to make good money doing the restaurant thing, playing in places like this. But in the past few months he's gotten heavily into drugs—cocaine, mostly. He's been missing gigs. Bills are a problem. Collectors come to the door, even to the library where Gail works."

"It's a familiar story," Louis said.

Mom nodded. "What concerns Gail is that she watched as Robert lost all interest, first in her, and then in his music. She says it's almost as though he'd read an article on cocaine addiction and set about trying to match the profile perfectly."

"Addiction does that, I guess—a kind of progressive stripping-down, reduction to the lowest common denominator. Nothing matters any more except that high, that relief. The personality itself is obliterated, finally. The need is all that's left."

"Well," Mom said. "Enough of that. How was school?"

Louis and I looked at one another. "You first," I said.

"I did okay today," he told her. Then, biting his lower lip: "I may need some help in math."

"You don't teach math," I said.

"But if I did, I'd definitely need help."

"Very funny, guys," Mom said. She pushed her plate away. "You probably did dessert already, too."

"Yet are too much the gentlemen," Louis said, "to allow you to go without."

"We'll join you," I said.

"All heart."

Over cheesecake he told her about the student whose essay was written on the back of ten oversize pizza menus. He'd done it at work and the title was "Why I Hate Pizza."

"Write about what you know," Mom said.

"Exactly."

I tried to look into Mom's eyes without her knowing, wondering if the old restlessness was starting up in there. Maybe I only imagined it. She was looking at Louis, but it was as though he was far away, as though she watched him through thick glass, the way you watch a plane take off.

I excused myself, found the bathroom, and, coming back, overheard the end of their conversation.

"Sometimes he seems more your son than mine," Mom said.

"Janet—"

"I don't want company tonight."

"Jan, I love you."

"I don't want to talk about it now. I'll call when I can."

\* \* \*

ERIC KEEL (final entry). Like the others, Eric, suddenly, was gone. I began to understand why, and started this notebook. Over the following three weeks there were sporadic phone messages (I'd listen to them when I got home from school, then rewind the tape) and one final, tearful goodbye.

I remember something in Cocteau, from the journals, I think—that sexual need, sexual vice, is the most intriguing form of aesthetics. That selections are not made, sequences not followed, by the dictates of tastes or choice, but only after exhaustive research and obscure preparation, according to a template of needs that leaves no choice, "a masquerade where his senses desperately construct an equivalent, more baroque, but in fact hardly less individual than any other, for beauty."

I longed to tell him goodbye. To tell him something of what he had meant to me, and that he would not be forgotten, not entirely. That here, in this notebook, like the others he would live on.

Louis called four times the following day. By the fourth call, from anger, tears, or some blend of the two, his voice quavered on the machine. There were no calls the day after—then, midmorning of the next, a letter, weighty in its manila envelope. She would wait until the calls and letters dwindled to nothing, then call them.

I don't know how aware she is of this sequence. Once it begins, apparently, she is not in control.

She doesn't suspect, of course, that I know what happens to them. But perhaps it wouldn't matter if she did.

\* \* \*

Louis was waiting outside my school a few days later. "I've
missed you," he said.

I nodded.

"How's your mom doing?"

"Depressed, I guess. She sleeps a lot. Comes home, goes
to bed—and stays there some days."

"She won't answer my calls."

"I know."

He was wearing a cloth cap, which he took off and stuffed
in a coat pocket. "It's hard to get a handle on this. I know
she loves me."

"She does."

"So how can she just *go away* like this? Just suddenly not
be there? All the things we feel for one another, all our
plans—"

We walked on for a block or two silently.

"I have to get back to the college," he said.

"Louis?"

He looked at me.

I almost said: She's going to kill you. Because she loves
you, she's going to kill you. But I couldn't. I said, "Could I
have your cap? I've always wanted one like that."

He took it out and handed it to me. "To remember me
by?" he said.

"To wear till I see you again."

"Soon, I hope."

The lies we tell ourselves, or the lies we tell others—which
are worse?

Two days later, a Friday, Mom was happy again.

"I thought we'd eat out and catch a movie tonight if that's
okay with you," she said at breakfast. She was drinking or-

ange juice from either a very small goldfish bowl or a very large brandy snifter. She held it up and moved it, washing pulp from side to side. Liszt, softly, on the radio.

"By ourselves?"

Was there a brief pause, a catch?

"Just you and me, kiddo. Louis and I...well, he won't be around anymore."

"I loved him, Mom. You did too."

"Yes," she said. "Yes, I did."

She was wearing her navy-blue suit with a new red blouse—silk, I think—and had her hair pinned back loosely. Without her glasses, her eyes had a soft, blurred look.

"I've got a student coming in before class, so I have to leave," she said. She went to the sink and rinsed out her glass. "I'll be home early, about the same time as you, and we'll take off right away. Make a night of it. Remember to lock up when you leave."

"Sure, Mom."

After she was gone, I got up and turned off the radio. I stood looking at the bowl of apples, the brass colander catching the morning sunlight against the wall where it hung—all these ordinary things.

I went to get my books and sweater and looked for a moment at Louis's cap on the back of my chair. Then I put his notebook on the shelf with the rest and went on to school.